THE READERS OF BROKEN WHEEL RECOMMEND

The Readers of Broken Wheel Recommend

Katarina Bivald

Translated from the Swedish
by Alice Menzies

BOND
STREET
BOOKS
DOUBLEDAY
CANADA

Library and Archives Canada Cataloguing in Publication

Bivald, Katarina, 1983-
[Läsarna i Broken Wheel rekommenderar. English]
The readers of Broken Wheel recommend / Katarina
Bivald ; translated from Swedish by Alice Menzies.

Translation of: Läsarna i Broken Wheel rekommenderar.
Issued in print and electronic formats.
ISBN 978-0-385-68359-3 (pbk.). ISBN 978-0-385-68360-9 (epub)

I. Menzies, Alice, translator II. Title. III. Title: Läsarna i
Broken Wheel rekommenderar. English.

PT9877.12.I93L3713 2015   839.73'8   C2015-903576-7
                                                    C2015-903577-5

Printed and bound in the USA

Published in Canada by Bond Street Books,
A division of Random House of Canada Limited,
A Penguin Random House Company

www.penguinrandomhouse.ca

10 9 8 7 6 5 4 3 2 1

THE
READERS
OF BROKEN WHEEL
RECOMMEND

Broken Wheel, Iowa
April 15, 2009

Sara Lindqvist
Kornvägen 7, 1 tr
136 38 Haninge
Sweden

Dear Sara,

I hope you enjoy Louisa May Alcott's *An Old-Fashioned Girl*. It's a charming story, though perhaps a touch more overtly moralizing than *Little Women*.

In terms of payment, please don't worry about it; I've collected several copies over the years. It's just nice that it's found a new home now, and that it'll be going all the way to Europe! I've never been to Sweden myself, but I'm sure it must be a very beautiful country.

Isn't it funny that my books will have travelled farther than I have? I honestly don't know whether that's comforting or worrying.

With kind regards,

Amy Harris

Books 1: Life 0

The strange woman standing on Hope's main street was so ordinary it was almost scandalous. A thin, plain figure dressed in an autumn coat much too grey and warm for the time of year, a rucksack lying on the ground by her feet, an enormous suitcase resting against one of her legs. Those who happened to witness her arrival couldn't help feeling it was inconsiderate for someone to care so little about their appearance. As though this woman was not the slightest bit interested in making a good impression on them.

Her hair was a nondescript shade of brown, held back with a carelessly placed hair clip which didn't stop it flowing down over her shoulders in a tangle of curls. Where her face should have been, there was a copy of Louisa May Alcott's *An Old-Fashioned Girl*.

She didn't seem to care at all that she was in Hope. It was as if she had just landed there, book and luggage and uncombed hair in tow, and might just as well have been in any other town in the world. She was standing on one of the most beautiful streets in Cedar County, maybe even the prettiest in the whole of southern Iowa, but the only thing she had eyes for was her book.

But then again, she couldn't be entirely uninterested. Every now and again a pair of big grey eyes peeped up over the edge of the book, like a prairie dog sticking its head up to check whether the coast was clear. She would lower the book further and look sharply to the left, then swing her gaze as far to the right as she could without moving her head. Then she would raise the book and sink back into the story again.

In actual fact, Sara had taken in almost every detail of the street. She would have been able to describe how the last of the afternoon sun was gleaming on the polished SUVs, how even the treetops seemed neat and well organised, and how the hair salon fifty metres away had a sign made from laminated plastic in patriotic red, white and blue stripes. The scent of freshly baked apple pie filled the air. It was coming from the cafe behind her, where a couple of middle-aged women were sitting outside and watching her with clear distaste. That was how it looked to Sara, at least. Every time she glanced up from her book, they frowned and shook their heads slightly, as though she was breaking some unwritten rule of etiquette by reading on the street.

She took out her phone and redialled. It rang nine times before she hung up.

So Amy Harris was a bit late. Surely there would be a perfectly reasonable explanation. A flat tyre maybe. Out of petrol. It was easy to be – she checked her phone again – two hours and thirty-seven minutes late.

She wasn't worried, not yet. Amy Harris wrote proper letters, on real, old-fashioned writing paper; thick and creamy. There wasn't a chance in the world that someone who wrote on proper, cream-coloured writing paper would abandon a friend in a strange town or turn out to be a psychopathic serial killer with sadomasochistic tendencies, regardless of what Sara's mother said.

'Excuse me, honey.'

A woman had stopped beside her. She gave Sara an artificially patient look.

'Can I help you with anything?' the woman asked. A brown paper bag full of food was resting on her hip, a can of Campbell's tomato soup teetering perilously close to the edge.

'No, thank you,' said Sara. 'I'm waiting for someone.'

'Sure.' The woman's tone was amused and indulgent. The women sitting outside the cafe were following the whole conversation with interest. 'First time in Hope?'

'I'm on my way to Broken Wheel.'

Maybe it was just Sara's imagination, but the woman didn't seem at all satisfied with that answer.

The can of soup wobbled dangerously. After a moment, the woman said: 'It's not much of a town, I'm afraid, Broken Wheel. Do you know someone there?'

'I'm going to stay with Amy Harris.'

Silence.

'I'm sure she's on her way,' said Sara.

'Seems like you've been abandoned here, honey.' The woman looked expectantly at Sara. 'Go on, call her.'

Sara reluctantly pulled her phone out again. When the strange woman pressed up against Sara's ear to listen to the ringing tone, she had to stop herself from shrinking back.

'Doesn't seem to me like she's going to answer.' Sara put the phone back in her pocket and the woman moved away a little. 'What're you planning on doing there?'

'Have a holiday. I'm going to rent a room.'

'And now you've been abandoned here. That's a good start. I hope you didn't pay in advance.' The woman shifted the paper bag over to her other arm and clicked her fingers in the direction of the seats outside the cafe. 'Hank,' she said loudly to the only man sitting there, 'give this girl here a ride to Broken Wheel, OK?'

'I haven't finished my coffee.'

'So take it with you, then.'

The man grunted, but got obediently to his feet and disappeared into the cafe.

'If I were you,' the woman continued, 'I wouldn't hand over any money right away. I'd pay just before I went home. And I'd keep it well hidden until then.' She nodded so violently that the can of tomato soup teetered worryingly again. 'I'm not saying everyone in Broken Wheel is a thief,' she added for safety's sake, 'but they're *not* like us.'

Hank came back with his coffee in a paper cup, and Sara's suitcase and rucksack were thrown onto the back seat of his car. Sara herself was guided carefully but firmly to the front seat.

'Go on, give her a ride over, Hank,' said the woman, hitting the roof of the car twice with her free hand. She leaned towards the open window. 'You can always come back here if you change your mind.'

'So, Broken Wheel,' Hank said disinterestedly.

Sara clasped her hands on top of her book and tried to look relaxed. The car smelled of cheap aftershave and coffee.

'What're you going to do there?'

'Read.'

He shook his head.

'As a holiday,' she explained.

'We'll see, I guess,' Hank said ominously.

She watched the scenery outside the car window change. Lawns became fields, the glittering cars disappeared and the neat little houses were replaced by an enormous wall of corn looming up on either side of the road, which stretched straight out ahead for kilometres. Every now and then it was intersected by other roads, also perfectly straight, as though someone had, at some point, looked out over the enormous fields and drawn the roads in with a ruler. As good a method as any, Sara thought to herself. But as they drove on, the other roads became fewer and fewer until it felt as though the only thing around them was mile after mile of corn.

'Can't be much of a town left,' said Hank. 'A friend of mine grew up there. Sells insurance in Des Moines now.'

She didn't know what she was meant to say to that. 'That's nice,' she tried.

'He likes it,' the man agreed. 'Much better than trying to run the family farm in Broken Wheel, that's for sure.'

And that was that.

Sara craned to look out of the car window, searching for the town of Amy's letters. She had heard so much about Broken Wheel she was almost expecting Miss Annie to come speeding past on her cargo moped at any moment, or Robert to be standing at the side of the road waving the latest edition of his magazine in the air. For a moment, she could practically see them before her, but then they grew faint and whirled away into the dust behind the car. Instead, a battered-looking barn appeared, only to be immediately hidden from view once more by the corn, as though it had never been there in the first place. It was the only building she had seen in the last fifteen minutes.

Would the town look the way she had imagined it? Now that she was finally about to see it with her own eyes, Sara had even forgotten her anxiety about Amy not answering the phone.

But when they eventually arrived, she might have missed it entirely if Hank hadn't pulled over. The main street was nothing more than a few buildings on either side of the road. Most of them seemed to be empty, grey and depressing. A few of the shops had boarded-up windows, but a diner still appeared to be open.

'So what d'you want to do?' Hank asked. 'You want a ride back?'

She glanced around. The diner was definitely open. The word *Diner* was glowing faintly in red neon letters, and a lone man was sitting at the table closest to the window. She shook her head.

'Whatever you want,' he said in a tone that said 'you'll only have yourself to blame'.

She climbed out of the car and pulled her luggage out from the back seat, her paperback shoved under her arm. Hank drove off the moment she closed the door. He made a sharp U-turn at the only traffic light in town.

It was hanging from a cable in the middle of the street, and it was shining red.

Sara stood in front of the diner with the suitcase at her feet, her rucksack slung over one shoulder, firmly clutching her book.

It's all going to be fine, she said to herself. Everything will work out. This is not a catastrophe . . . She backtracked: so long as she had books and money, nothing could be a catastrophe. She had enough money to check into a hostel if she needed to. Though she was fairly sure there wouldn't be a hostel in Broken Wheel.

She pushed open the doors – only to be confronted by a set of real saloon doors, how ridiculous – and went in. Other than the man by the window and a woman behind the counter, the diner was empty. The man was thin and wiry, his body practically begging forgiveness for his very existence. He didn't even look up when she came in, just continued turning his coffee cup in his hands, slowly round and round.

The woman, on the other hand, immediately directed all her attention towards the door. She weighed at least 150 kilos, and her huge arms were resting on the high counter in front of her. It was made from dark wood and wouldn't have looked out of place in a bar, but instead of beer mats, there were stainless-steel napkin holders and laminated menus with pictures of the various rubbery-looking types of food they served.

The woman lit a cigarette in one fluid movement.

'You must be the tourist,' she said. The smoke from her cigarette hit Sara in the face. It had been years since Sara had seen anyone in Sweden smoking in a restaurant. Clearly they did things differently here.

'I'm Sara.'

'You picked one hell of a day to come here.'

'Do you know where Amy Harris lives?'

The woman nodded. 'One hell of a day.' A lump of ash dropped from her cigarette and landed on the counter. 'I'm Grace,' she said. 'Or truth be told, my name's Madeleine. But there's no point calling me that.'

Sara hadn't been planning on calling her anything at all.

'And now you're here.'

Sara had a definite feeling that Grace-who-wasn't-really-called-Grace was enjoying the moment, drawing it out. Grace nodded three times to herself, took a deep drag of her cigarette and let the smoke curl slowly upwards from one corner of her mouth. She leaned over the counter.

'Amy's dead,' she said.

In Sara's mind, Amy's death would forever be associated with the glow of fluorescent strip lighting, cigarette smoke and the smell of fried food. It was surreal. Here she was, standing in a diner in a small American town, being told that a woman she had never met had died. The whole situation was much too dreamlike to be scary, much too odd to be a nightmare.

'Dead?' she repeated. An extraordinarily stupid question, even for her. She slumped onto a bar stool. She had no idea what to do now. Her thoughts drifted back to the woman in Hope and she wondered whether she should have gone back with Hank after all.

Amy can't be dead, Sara thought. She was my friend. She liked *books*, for God's sake.

It wasn't quite grief that Sara was feeling, but she was struck by how fleeting life was, and the odd feeling grew. She had come to Iowa from Sweden to take a break from life – to get away from it, even – but not to meet death.

How had Amy died? One part of her wanted to ask, another didn't want to know.

Grace continued before she had time to make up her mind: 'The funeral's probably in full swing. Not particularly festive things nowadays, funerals. Too much religious crap if you ask me. It was different when my grandma died.' She glanced at the clock. 'You should probably head over there now, though. I'm sure someone who knew her better'll know what to do with you. I try to avoid getting drawn into this town's problems, and you're definitely one of them.'

She stubbed out her cigarette. 'George, will you give Sara here a ride to Amy's house?'

The man by the window looked up. For a moment, he looked as paralysed as Sara felt. Then he got to his feet and half carried, half dragged her bags to the car.

Grace grabbed Sara's elbow as she started off after him. 'That's Poor George,' she said, nodding towards his back.

Amy Harris's house was a little way out of town. It was big enough that the kitchen and living room seemed fairly spacious, but small enough that the little group which had congregated there after the funeral made it seem full. The table and kitchen worktops were covered with baking dishes full of food, and someone had prepared bowls of salad and bread, laid out cutlery and arranged napkins in drinking glasses.

Sara was given a paper plate of food and then left more or

less to herself. George was still by her side and she was touched by that unexpected display of loyalty. He didn't seem to be a particularly brave person at all, not even compared to her, but he had followed her in and now he was walking around just as hesitantly as she was.

In the dim hallway there was a dark chest of drawers on which someone had arranged a framed photograph of a woman she assumed must be Amy, and two worn-looking flags, the American and the Iowa state. *Our liberties we prize and our rights we will maintain*, the latter proclaimed in embroidered white letters, but the flag was faded and one of the edges was frayed.

The woman in the photograph was perhaps twenty years old, with her hair pulled into two thin plaits and a standard-issue, stiff camera smile. She was a complete stranger. There might have been something in her eyes, a glimmer of laughter which showed she knew it was all a joke, that Sara could recognise from her letters. But that was all.

She wanted to reach out and touch the photograph but doing that felt much too forward. Instead, she stayed where she was in the dark hallway, carefully balancing her paper plate, her book still under her arm. Her bags had disappeared somewhere, but she didn't have the energy to worry about it.

Three weeks earlier, she had felt so close to Amy that she had been prepared to stay with her for two months, but now it was as though every trace of their friendship had died along with her. She had never been someone who believed you needed to have met in person to be friends – many of her most rewarding relationships had been with people who didn't even exist – but suddenly it all felt so false, disrespectful even, to cling to the idea that they had, in some way, meant something to one another.

All around her, people were moving slowly and cautiously through the rooms, as though they were wondering what on earth they were doing there, which was almost exactly what Sara was thinking too. Still, they didn't seem shocked. They didn't seem surprised. No one was crying.

Most of them were looking at Sara with curiosity, but

something, perhaps respect for the significance of the event, was stopping them from approaching her. They circled around her instead, smiling whenever she accidentally caught their eye.

Suddenly, a woman materialised out of the crowd and cornered Sara, halfway between the living room and the kitchen.

'Caroline Rohde.'

Her posture and handshake were military but she was much more beautiful than Sara had imagined. She had deep, almond-shaped eyes, and features as pronounced as a statue's. In the glow of the ceiling lamp, her skin was an almost shimmering white across her high cheekbones. Her hair was thick and streaked with grey strands. Around her neck, she wore a black scarf made from thin, cool silk which would have looked out of place on anyone else, even at a funeral, but on her it looked timeless – almost glamorous.

Her age was hard to guess but she had the air of someone who had never really been young. Sara had a strong sense that Caroline Rohde didn't have much time for youth.

When Caroline started talking, everyone around her fell silent. Her voice matched her presence: determined, resolute, straight to the point. There was, perhaps, a hint of a welcoming smile in her voice, but it never made as far as her mouth.

'Amy said you'd be coming,' she said. 'I won't claim I thought it was a good idea, but it wasn't my place to say anything.' Then she added, almost as an afterthought: 'You've got to agree that this isn't the most . . . practical situation.'

'Practical,' Sara echoed. Though how Amy was meant to know she was going to die, she wasn't sure.

Others gathered around Caroline in a loose half-circle, facing Sara as though she were a travelling circus making a brief stop in town.

'We didn't know how to contact you when Amy . . . passed away. And now you're here,' Caroline concluded. 'Oh well, we'll just have to see what we can do with you.'

'I'm going to need somewhere to stay,' said Sara. Everyone leaned forward to hear.

'Stay?' said Caroline. 'You'll stay here, of course! I mean, the house is empty, isn't it?'

'But . . .'

A man in a minister's collar smiled warmly at Sara, adding: 'Amy specifically told us to let you know that nothing would change in that regard.'

Nothing would change? She didn't know who was madder – the minister or Amy or the whole of Broken Wheel.

'There's a guest room, of course,' said Caroline. 'Sleep there tonight, and then we'll work out what we're going to do with you.'

The minister nodded and somehow it was decided: she would stay, alone, in dead Amy Harris's empty house.

She was bustled upstairs. Caroline went first, like a commander at war, followed closely by Sara and then George, a supportive, silent shadow. Behind them, most of the other guests followed. Someone was carrying her bags, she didn't know who, but when she reached the little guest room her rucksack and suitcase miraculously appeared.

'We'll make sure you've got everything you need,' Caroline said from the doorway, not at all unkindly. Then she shooed the others away, giving Sara a brief wave before pulling the door closed behind her.

Sara sank onto the bed, suddenly alone again, the paper plate still in her hand and a lonely book lying abandoned on the bedspread next to her.

Oh hell, she thought.

Broken Wheel, Iowa
June 3, 2009

Sara Lindqvist
Kornvägen 7, 1 tr
136 38 Haninge
Sweden

Dear Sara,

Thank you so much for your kind gift! It's a book I probably wouldn't have bought myself, so it was all the more welcome. What an awful tale. I had no idea such things took place in Sweden, though I don't know why they shouldn't. If you ask me, there's much more violence, sex and scandal in small towns than in the big cities, and if that's true of towns then I suppose it might also be true of small countries? I presume it's because people get closer to one another there. We've certainly had our fair share of scandal here in Broken Wheel.

But a Lisbeth Salander? That we definitely do not have. A remarkable woman. As I understand it, there are two more books in the series. Would you do me the honor of sending the second and third books? I won't be able to sleep before I find out what happens to her. And that overwrought young man Mr Blomkvist as well, of course.

I'll pay you for them, naturally. Speaking of small towns, murder and sex, I'm sending you Harper Lee's *To Kill a Mockingbird* as a first installment.

With kind regards,

Amy Harris

The Broken Wheel Newsletter

You have four new messages. Received today at zero five thirteen hours.

'Darling! It's Mum . . . What? . . . Yes, yes, Dad too, of course. We're just back from Anders and Gunnel's. Remember them? Our old neighbours who moved to that lovely villa in Tyresö. How is everything? Have you arrived yet? What's it like out in the sticks? Is Amy a complete nutcase? Did you manage to find the right bus? I don't understand why you had to go to . . .'

Received today at zero five fifteen hours. Her mother continued as though she had never been interrupted:

'To the countryside . . . Wait, I'm not finished . . . Fine, here's your dad, who absolutely has to say a few words, even though I'm not done.'

Short pause, serious throat clearing.

'Sara! I hope you're not just staying inside and reading. You've got to get out and talk to people. It's a fantastic opportunity, travelling. I remember when your mother and I . . .'

Received today at zero five eighteen hours.

'What is it with these answerphones? Why don't they let me finish? Well, bye for now then . . . Wait. Your mother wants to say something again.'

'You know if you change your mind, you can always go to New York instead. Or Los Angeles.'

The message was cut off again, and the next hadn't been recorded until three hours later. It was her mother again:

'Sara! Why aren't you picking up? Is Amy a serial killer? I know what America's like. If you're lying in pieces somewhere, I'll never forgive you. Unless you call us back right now, I'm ringing the CIA . . .' Her father mumbled something in the background. 'FBI. *Whatever.*'

When Sara finally managed to get through to her mother, she was no calmer.

'I don't like this small-town thing, not one bit,' she started. It was a discussion they had had several times before.

Sara rubbed her forehead and lay back down on the bed. The room she was in was small, maybe three by five metres. Apart from the bed, there was an armchair directly beneath the window, a bedside table and a little chest of drawers. That was all. The wallpaper was brightly floral and looked like at least a couple of decades old. The curtains were made from an entirely different floral pattern and were much too short for the window.

'Small towns are so . . . boring. You could've gone wherever you wanted.'

It was ironic. Sara's mother was always nagging her to travel, but now that she had finally gone and done it, her mother still wasn't happy.

'And exposed. Who knows what kind of madmen are hiding there.'

It wasn't clear which was worse, the tediousness or the risk of bumping into one of the many serial killers hiding in every nook and cranny. Her mother's words triggered something in Sara's memory.

'It's because people get closer to one another there,' she said.

'Honestly, though, what do you know about people? If you didn't have your nose in a book all the time . . .'

This was another discussion they had had many times before.

Perhaps it wasn't so strange that her mother saw her elder daughter as a challenge. Her little sister Josefin worked as a trainee lawyer for the district court in Södertälje. Eventually, she would be a solicitor, a socially viable profession carried out in suitably expensive suits. Sara, on the other hand . . . A *bookshop*. In a suburban shopping centre. That was only marginally better than being an unemployed former bookshop assistant like she was now. And now that she had finally gone abroad? She had chosen to go to a little backwater in the American countryside, to stay with an elderly lady.

Sara didn't normally care that her mother so clearly thought she was boring. After all, her mother had a point. Sara had never done a single thing that was even the slightest bit adventurous. But the constant jabs at Amy had started to get on Sara's nerves even before she had left, and now, with the tragedy of the funeral still fresh in her mind, her patience was wearing thin.

Her mother seemed to sense that she had gone too far, because she quickly added: 'Oh well, at least you haven't been chopped into pieces.' Her tone was so openly pessimistic that she didn't even need to add a *yet*. 'What's Amy like then? Is she being good to you?'

'Amy is . . .' Sara stopped. 'She's nice.'

She was. It was just that she was also dead.

Sara crept out of her room and down the dark hallway like a jumpy burglar. Outside her door was a narrow corridor which led first to the bathroom and then to Amy's bedroom, as Caroline had pointed out when she had first shown Sara to the guest room. She walked quickly past, trying to avoid looking at the grimly closed door. She wondered whether anyone would ever open it again. She, for one, had no intention of doing so.

When she reached the stairs, she stopped for a moment to listen, before making her way slowly down.

At each new room, she hesitated and glanced cautiously inside. She didn't really know what she was expecting. A couple of townspeople hiding behind the sofa? Angry relatives in the hallway, accusing her of staying in the house without paying? Amy's ghost in the kitchen? But the house was deserted.

She walked around Amy's home, in and out of the rooms in which she had lived, touching the surfaces Amy had touched. The stillness of the house scared her. Small reminders of routine, of everyday life, surprised her when she was least expecting it.

Someone had left a jar of Nescafé and a gallon of milk for her in the kitchen. There was bread from the day before, and when she opened the fridge she discovered food in abundance, carefully wrapped in plastic and marked with the dish's name and the previous day's date.

She ate the bread plain before creeping up to the bathroom to wash. The shower was ancient, hanging above a little oval-shaped tub. She undressed, folding her night clothes into a neat pile and placing them on the worn old stool opposite the toilet. She hoped they would stay dry there, but neither the drain nor the shower curtain looked particularly trustworthy.

A whining, moaning sound came from the pipes and the water never got any hotter than lukewarm.

This really wasn't how it was meant to be, Sara thought. Her hair was twisted up in a hand towel and she had just unpacked her bags before retreating to the kitchen. So far, she hadn't spent more than twenty minutes anywhere except the guest room in which she had slept. For some reason, it felt safer to keep moving.

Unpacking had taken all of thirteen minutes; it was now half past ten and she had nothing at all to do. Outside, the air was already growing oppressive. The smell of dry earth and stifling greenery was coming in through the screen door. It was competing with the smells inside the house, of stuffiness and wood and old carpets.

She sat down on a kitchen chair, looking for some signs of Amy's life, but all she could see were battered cupboard doors and dead potted plants in the window.

This was meant to have been her adventure. She and Amy would have sat there, maybe on these very same chairs, talking about books and the town and the people that Amy had known, and it would have been nice.

'Amy,' she said, 'what the hell have you gone and done?'

By the kitchen door, which led out onto the porch, there were two pairs of different-sized rubber boots. The grass was long and yellow from the summer sun, and the vegetable garden had gone wild long ago. There was presumably a whole trove of treasures out there, hidden in the grass, but Sara could only make out two crooked apple trees, a little patch of herbs which had gone to seed, and a couple of enormous tomato plants.

She went inside again and spent an hour spreading her books around the house in an attempt to make it more cosy. But thirteen books wasn't nearly enough to cover all the rooms.

At home, she had almost two thousand books. And three friends if you could count her former colleagues from the bookshop as friends.

She had started working there when she was seventeen, initially only at Christmas, during the annual Swedish national book sale and in the summer holidays, but then she had gone full-time. And that was where she had stayed. Half an hour from where she was born. Her life hadn't been any more exciting than that.

One of the girls from the shop had once claimed that all stories started with someone coming or someone going. No one had ever come to Josephssons Bokhandel for Sara, and absolutely no one had ever come to her little apartment in Haninge either. The only thing that had come were the letters, beautifully handwritten letters. For a while, Sara could have sworn that they brought a piece of Iowa with them, a faint but unmistakable reminder of another, more timeless life, full of adventure and opportunity.

But now that she was finally there, all she could smell was musty wood and old carpets.

'Pull yourself together, Sara,' she said. Hearing a human voice calmed her down, even if it was her own. The only other sounds she could hear were overgrown branches scratching against a window upstairs, and water pipes which occasionally rattled for no reason.

How could it be possible to have travelled thousands of miles and still be the same person when you arrived? Sara couldn't understand it.

Aside from the fact that she now had thirteen books and zero friends, of course.

'Pull yourself together,' she said again, but it didn't quite work this time.

* * *

Sara assumed that the majority of people who ever thought about her believed she used books to hide away from life.

And maybe it was true. As early as high school, she had realised that few people paid attention to you if you were hidden behind a book. Now and then, she needed to glance up to duck a flying ruler or other object, but they hadn't usually been thrown at her in particular, and she didn't often lose her place in the book. While her classmates had bullied or been bullied, carved meaningless symbols into desks or scrawled on one another's lockers, she had experienced irrepressible passion, death, laughter, foreign lands, days gone by. Others might have found themselves stuck in a tired old high school in Haninge, but she had been a geisha in Japan, walked alongside China's last empress through the claustrophobic, closed-off rooms of the Forbidden City, grown up with Anne and the others in Green Gables, gone through her fair share of murder, and loved and lost over and over again.

Books had been a defensive wall, yes, though that wasn't all. They had protected Sara from the world around her, but they had also turned it into a fuzzy backdrop for the real adventures in her life.

You might have thought that ten years in a bookshop would take some of the magic of books away, but for Sara the opposite was true. Nowadays, she had two memories for every book: the memory of having sold it and the memory of having read it. She had sold countless copies of Terry Pratchett before, only a few years ago, she had given in and read one of them, making the acquaintance of one of the most fantastic, and definitely most reliable, authors living today. She remembered the summer when it felt as though almost all she had sold was Ulla-Carin Lindqvist's memoir *Rowing without Oars*, about her struggle with an incurable disease, and the night three years later when she had finally read it. She remembered that the cover featured a dark silhouette and earthy, muted colours, like a hot evening just after the sun has gone down; that the book was small and short and that everyone who bought it simply had to talk about it. 'It's her, the news anchor'; 'the newsreader who died'; 'she was so good on TV'; talking as though it had somehow broken their hearts that someone from TV could die. Sara knew it was one of those books which moved people even before they started reading it.

She had carried more piles of Dan Brown novels from the storeroom than she could bear to think about, sold the Harry Potter series in at least three different paperback editions, and seen the remarkable Swedish crime wave emerge, grow and continue for evermore. She hadn't really noticed Camilla Läckberg's arrival, but she had discovered her in paperback. That was how it often was with Sara.

She must have sold tens of thousands, maybe even hundreds of thousands of books, but it was pointless trying to keep count. If she had ever considered her future during those years, she would probably have assumed that she would grow old in the bookshop, that she would gradually become greyer and dustier than the unsold books in the little storeroom, calmly selling paper and ballpoint refills for all eternity, before retiring on a pension consisting mostly of the books which she had, over the years, bought with her staff discount.

But Josephssons Bokhandel had closed, she had found herself unemployed, and now here she was, all alone in the USA.

When a car pulled into the driveway, she was almost grateful for the distraction. The minister from the funeral climbed out, and as he walked towards the house, she tried out three different smiles in the mirror in the hallway.

'Just be normal, Sara,' she said to her reflection, but the woman staring wide-eyed back at her looked, tragically, like a petrified mouse wearing a turban. She had been walking around the house for over an hour and completely forgotten to take the towel off her hair. She threw it into a cupboard, tried to comb her hair with her fingers and went out onto the porch to greet the minister.

Your smile, Sara, she reminded herself.

The minister looked as nervous as she felt. His white clerical collar should have been enough to give him a certain dignity, but it was ruined by his thin hair, which refused to lie flat, and his cheap orange quilted jacket which looked like it had been bought on sale in the eighties.

'Amy's death has been a real blow to the town,' he said. He stood in front of the porch with one foot on the first step, as though he couldn't decide whether he was going to come up or leave again. 'A real hard blow.'

'Yes,' she said. 'How . . . how did she die?'

Perhaps it was inappropriate of her to ask, but she realised she really did want to know. The minister mumbled something about 'illness'. Not an accident, then. But it still must have been sudden, her death. As little as three weeks ago, Sara had sent Amy all the details of her trip and hadn't heard anything other than the plan that she would be met in Hope.

She wondered whether she should offer him a coffee. What exactly were the rules of hospitality when you were a non-paying guest in a dead woman's house?

'I don't really know where I should be going,' she said.

'Going?' The minister looked, if possible, even more nervous. He took his foot from the step. 'But you're staying here, aren't you?' When that had no effect on her, he added: 'Everyone loved Amy, you know. It's nice for us to see that her house isn't standing empty and abandoned. Do you need anything, by the way? You've got food?'

'Enough for several weeks, probably.' She told herself this didn't mean she had agreed to stay, it was just that at that precise moment she wasn't sure what other choice she had. She doubted that the minister would agree to drive her somewhere else, and besides, she had no idea where that might be.

'Good, good. And anything else? You'll probably need a car?'

'I don't have a driver's licence.'

He gave a start. 'Ah, OK. Hmm, yes . . . I'll have to talk to Caroline about that.' He seemed relieved to have made a decision, and said goodbye before Sara had the chance to decide whether she should have asked him if he wanted a coffee.

She still hadn't solved the coffee question when her next visitor arrived. This time, it didn't matter.

Mrs Jennifer – 'Call me Jen' – Hobson was an American

housewife worthy of the vice president's office. She had perfectly styled dark hair which seemed almost to be an entity in itself, and the slightly manic smile of someone who spends too much time with small children. She marched straight into the kitchen, and put the coffeemaker on.

'I'm in charge of the Broken Wheel newsletter,' she said over the clattering of cups and spoons.

She opened one of the bottom cupboards and found the sugar. Her hair swung around her as she bent down. 'We write about all the big events here. Just a couple of years ago, a guy from New Jersey stopped by. Some kind of freelancer. He wanted to *find himself* but he moved to Hope after just two weeks and refused to give any interviews.'

It wasn't clear to Sara whether Jen was more put out by the moving to Hope or his refusal to give an interview.

'One of my friends in Spencer does genealogy,' Jen continued over her shoulder. 'I'm from Spencer. Moved here when I got married.' A resolute expression passed over her face. 'Anyway, she did some research. Found relatives from Sweden. She was really pleased about that. Much better than relatives from Ireland or Germany, I told her. Everyone has relatives from there. Sweden is much more exotic.'

She glanced at Sara and quickly shook her head, presumably in despair at Sara herself being so ordinary.

'What's your surname? Maybe you're related. Stranger things have happened, and there aren't so many people in Sweden, are there?'

'Nine million.'

'Do you have oaks?'

'Oaks?'

'Iowa's state tree. We've got fantastic oaks here.'

'Yeah, we . . . we've got oaks.'

'Do you have a few words you'd like to share?'

Sara didn't.

'Nothing? Not even a little greeting? A first impression of our town, maybe?'

'I've only been to the diner.'

'I guess I'll just have to put something together,' Jen said. 'I'm sure you'll come to love the town once you've got to know it.' Then added: 'Don't worry, you'll express yourself nicely in the article. As soon as I've worked out what you're going to say.'

Broken Wheel, Iowa
August 23, 2009

Sara Lindqvist
Kornvägen 7, 1 tr
136 38 Haninge
Sweden

Dear Sara,

I'm pleased you liked Harper Lee. I don't have any real opinions on the Swedish title, but perhaps calling it 'Mortal Sin' does make it sound more like a cheap thriller. You'd know better than me.

Since you liked *To Kill a Mockingbird*, I'm sending you Kathryn Stockett's *The Help* too. They've got racism in common, at least. I know there are those who doubt that racism is still such a big problem, but if you ask me it's only middle-aged people who think that, those who think the world has automatically become better simply because they're old enough to shape it now, but without any of them having made the slightest contribution to improving it. This is one of the few things which still gets me riled up. Too riled up, according to my good friend John. He's black and well past middle age, and he says that everything *is* much better. In Broken Wheel, in any case. John isn't much one for sweeping generalizations. I've no intention of claiming his view says anything about the world really, it's just because people around here are used to him. He's the only black person in town and he also runs the only shop which still sells milk, so how anyone could dislike him, I don't know. I think it's impossible not to like him, of course, but he doesn't agree with that either.

With kind regards,

Amy Harris

It is a truth universally acknowledged that a Swedish tourist in Iowa must be in want of a man

There was an old cinema in Broken Wheel, across the street from Grace's diner. Its classic fifties architecture lent a certain dignity to that side of Main Street, but the cinema itself had long since stopped showing the latest releases. Then it had stopped showing films altogether. The projector had broken. These days the building was used only for town council meetings.

Calling the group of people who met there the town council was a bit like calling the cinema a cinema; it said more about what they had once been than what they were now. In the past, there had been elections and a certain prestige in being a member. There had been money to spend and battles to be fought over what it should be spent on: new benches outside one of the churches; new street lights; the colour of the benches; the type of street lights. Whether the cinema was the pride of the town or the ruin of its children.

Nowadays, only a handful of the town's 637 residents were still interested in being involved in what went on in the town, and there was no longer any money to be spent.

Still, they continued to meet on Thursdays every other week, gathering along the front row of cinema seats.

With an air of faint dejection, Caroline Rohde watched as Jen gestured energetically up on the little stage in front of what had once been the screen.

'A tourist!' Jen was saying, and Caroline resisted the urge to massage her temples.

The town's latest tourist wave was the sole item on the agenda, and Caroline was already deeply tired of it.

She missed Amy Harris. Caroline knew that people thought she was much too hard-hearted, much too particular about every-thing relating to God and Jesus, and, ultimately, that she was boring. But she also knew that towns needed someone to keep an eye on them and someone to help them out; someone who knew what was right and someone who knew what was good. Caroline was one of those people, and Amy had been another. Things had always worked well while Amy was alive, but now Caroline felt alone and insufficient.

She had never been able to help people like Amy could. Amy always seemed to know precisely what people wanted to hear. Caroline knew only what they *should* hear, and the two were very rarely the same thing.

But both of them were needed, and now Caroline was the only one left and she would have to take care of this tourist who started shaking the moment you spoke to her.

Amy had a lot to answer for there. May she rest in peace, of course.

Which would be easy for her, since Caroline was the one stuck down here with all the hard work to do. She certainly wouldn't get any help from the rest of the town council.

There were three of them left. Caroline presumed that Jen Hobson took part because she dreamed of turning Broken Wheel into the same kind of middle-class commuter paradise as Hope, perfect for folks working in Cedar Rapids. Jen was born in what she called 'nice, pleasant' Spencer, in the north-west of Iowa, and Caroline couldn't help but think that it would have been no great loss to the town if she had just stayed there. But Jen's husband was from Broken Wheel and was, by all accounts, as nice as you could expect a Hobson to be. They had never exactly been known for their intelligence, but Caroline didn't care for judging people on things they had no control over. There were enough conscious sins to focus on. However, she couldn't escape the suspicion that Jen saw the move to Broken Wheel as some kind of personal failing and that annoyed her. She couldn't imagine Spencer having anything that Broken Wheel didn't. Plus, Jen had only been living here for ten years.

The town had its problems and its shortcomings, of course,

things which Caroline herself didn't hesitate to point out, but the idea that someone from *outside* could look down on the town and want to change things . . . she shook her head.

She wasn't afraid to contribute, though. Caroline had to admit that much. But if only Jen had as much sense as she did energy, she would have been able to accomplish so much more. She was in charge of Broken Wheel's newsletter, as well as its only journalist and its main source of news. She ran a *blog* about the town, too. Caroline had never cared to find out what, exactly, a blog was. No good could come from such a thing, of that much she was sure. As far as she knew, the only people who even read the newsletter were Jen's relatives, all of them living in Spencer. None of them had shown any interest in moving to Broken Wheel despite, or perhaps because of, the newsletter.

She didn't have much more time for the other member of the town council. Andy, the last member of the Walsh family still living in town. Caroline had truly disliked his father, Andrew Walsh Senior, and was prepared to forgive Andy a lot just because he wasn't him. But there were limits.

Andy ran the Square, the town's most popular bar, along with his much-too-close friend Carl; he had once lived as far away as Denver. Caroline didn't like gossip, but on the other hand there was no need to invite it either, coming home from Denver and taking over a bar with your . . . *good friend*.

Today, Andy was wearing vivid blue jeans, a checked shirt and a belt with a buckle that looked as though it weighed as much as his cowboy boots. He pulled it all off quite well, but his clothes were much too new-looking. In Caroline's eyes, he looked like a tourist, fresh from the east coast, despite his family having lived in Broken Wheel for generations.

'A tourist in Broken Wheel,' he said, standing up and joining Jen on the stage.

'It's strange,' she added, 'that we don't have more.'

'Not *that* strange,' Caroline said. She often spoke in italics. 'And a tourist without a driver's licence.'

She remained where she was, sitting in one of the comfortable cinema seats. It had been twelve years since the last movie had played, but the scent of popcorn and melted butter still lingered faintly. It didn't awaken any memories of dates Caroline had gone on long ago, but she was impressed that the chairs' fabric was still in such good condition.

'We've got to find things for her to do,' said Jen. 'She's got to be entertained!'

'With what?' asked Andy. 'That's the big question.'

'Trips, mainly,' Jen replied. 'All that beautiful nature. The oaks!'

'And the corn,' Caroline added drily. She was actually just as fond of oaks as the others, she was even chair of the Association for the Preservation of Oaks, but they were far from being a tourist trap.

'Not just corn,' said Andy. 'Soybeans too.'

'Maybe Tom can drive her,' Jen said, as though the thought had just struck her. 'When he's not working, I mean.'

Caroline closed her eyes. The innocent tone wasn't fooling her. My goodness, she thought. The woman had barely been in town two days and Jen had already started offering up its young men to her altar. Though, to be fair, it might just as well have been the woman being sacrificed. Like the oaks, the town's bachelors weren't exactly a tourist attraction.

For once, Andy and Jen didn't seem to be on the same wavelength. 'Tom?' he asked dumbly, though anyone could have guessed where Jen was heading.

She hesitated. 'Yeah, Tom . . .' she said. 'I was wondering whether they might not . . . get on well?' Her gaze was fixed somewhere above Caroline's head. 'Don't you think a holiday romance would be just the thing to get her to enjoy her time here?'

Andy laughed. 'Yeah, why not? Tom's never been much good at picking up women. And this Sara, she seems like she'd need a push too. I'll talk to Tom and warn him about his duties.'

Jen didn't seem to want to go that far. 'I wonder if it's not better to just let things happen a bit more naturally . . .'

'It would be better not to let it happen at all,' said Caroline. If she knew Jen, she wouldn't be satisfied with a simple holiday romance – which would have been bad enough. She was probably already dreaming about a wedding and then yet another person to add to the population statistics, maybe even several, with special editions of the newsletter on weddings, births and christenings following one after another.

'We can ask Tom to drive her in any case,' said Jen.

'George can drive her,' said Caroline. 'We can pay him for it. Symbolically anyway. We can start a collection.'

Anything worth doing was worth doing with a collection.

She caught the quick glance Andy and Jen exchanged but she didn't care. All towns needed a woman who kept an eye on what was what. She knew that they laughed at her behind her back, but at least she got things done. And no one dared laugh when she was within earshot.

'But is poor George . . .' Jen seemed to be searching for a euphemism but eventually gave up. '. . . sober enough?'

'He hasn't had a drink in a month,' Caroline said. 'His hands hardly even shake any more. He needs something useful to do, rather than just sitting at That Woman's drinking coffee all day.'

'A good man,' Jen mumbled.

'George is driving her,' said Caroline, and with that it was decided.

Sara Lindqvist
Kornvägen 7, 1 tr
136 38 Haninge
Sweden

Dear Sara,

Broken Wheel isn't actually much of a town. There's very little about it that's interesting. There's actually very little of it in general. But I like it. I was born and raised here, and that makes all the difference.

There's one big street called, quite simply, Main Street, and then there are three others crossing it. They're called Second Street, Third Street and Jimmie Coogan Street. The last one might need some explanation. Until '87 it was called Fourth Street (we're a prosaic, literal bunch without any predilection for flourishes or big words). But now it's named after a real joker. I'm glad. It gives the town a certain dignity to have had one.

With kind regards,

Amy Harris

Asphalt and Concrete

Reading books isn't a bad way to live your life, but lately Sara had begun to wonder what kind of life it was, exactly. She had first been struck by this thought when she found out that Josephssons would be closing. It was as though ten years of her life had disappeared along with the bookshop; as though everything she had ever been had only existed on the greyish-white bookshelves of that dusty shop, among the people who bought four-for-three paperbacks in the summer, and anything-at-all-that-was-shiny-and-wrapped-up at Christmas.

Of course, she could probably get another job in a different bookshop, but there and then, during those endless summer days in the suburban shopping centre, with the countdown to closure relentlessly ticking, she had asked herself whether this life was really enough. And that had scared her, because what else was there other than books and work?

There really wasn't much else, except for Amy and her small town in Iowa, one which seemed to have come straight out of a Fannie Flagg or Annie Proulx novel. Sara had bought a book from Amy through an online second-hand bookshop, where private individuals could also sell books. When Amy had declined to take any payment for her book, Sara had plucked up the courage to send a book back in thanks, and things had continued from there. Amy wrote wonderful letters about books and about the people in her little town, and that summer, they were all Sara had to cling on to. The only lifeline in an existence which had otherwise started to seem overwhelmingly pointless.

So when Sara reached Broken Wheel, she naturally turned to books to help her. It was what she had always done.

That morning, Sara took *Bridget Jones* out onto the porch, together with her third cup of almost undrinkable instant coffee.

She moved quickly down the hallway, keeping her eyes fixed on the front door. She was trying to avoid having to look at the little altar. She wished someone would at least take the flags away, but didn't think it was her place to do so.

It felt better outside. The rocking chairs were comfortable and the overgrown garden looked more charming than neglected. When she rocked back and forth, the chair creaked pleasingly beneath her.

As the sun inched slowly up above the treetops, she tried to imagine that everything was as it should be, as it should have been.

Maybe Amy wasn't dead? Maybe she was just busy with her flowers in the kitchen? Maybe she was upstairs somewhere, book in hand? It might have been true.

Sara sighed. It was like trying to change an unhappy ending in a book. However much you tried to convince yourself that things could end differently if only you could get rid of the sadistic bungler of an author, it was all still there in the back of your mind. Rhett Butler had dumped Scarlett just when she had started to deserve him. Against all sense, against his own personality, the nature of love and his word, against all rhyme and reason. Not even Charlotte Brontë's awful father had been able to prevent M. Paul from dying in *Villette*, however much Charlotte had tried to fool him by writing such an apparently ambiguous ending.

Incomprehensible.

That was just how things were. You simply had to try not to think about it. Margaret Mitchell was stupid and Charlotte Brontë was determined and Amy Harris was dead.

She picked *Bridget Jones* up from her lap and forced herself to keep reading. There was something so comforting in the fact that the book was just the same as it had been in Sweden. Bridget failed to keep her new year's resolutions in exactly the same way as she had before, Mr Darcy wore the same mad, festive sweater. By the time Daniel Cleaver finally appeared on the scene, Sara had disappeared into the safe haven of the book and would have stayed there if she hadn't been distracted by a car turning off towards Amy's house.

George was wearing the same checked shirt as on Saturday and it was just as crumpled. His hands were shaking more than before. She remembered how he had followed her into the wake after the funeral and smiled at him over the top of her book.

'I came to tell you I'm your chauffeur.'

She lowered the book slowly.

'I'll drive you,' he explained. 'Wherever you want. Just give me a call.' He reeled off his telephone number. 'If I'm not at home I'll be at Grace's.' He gave her that number too, without waiting for her to write either of them down.

'But I can walk,' she said.

'They told me I should drive you.'

'They?'

'Jen and Andy. Caroline too.'

That was presumably that.

'So?' he said. 'Can I give you a ride anywhere?'

'There's not so much to see any more,' he said as they drove into town.

The only thing there seemed to be an abundance of was corn. At that time of year, the end of August, it towered up around them in enormous fields. The bright sunlight transformed these fields into a swirling sea of gold and green which dazzled Sara, blazing in her eyes until Broken Wheel appeared almost as a relief. As they reached the town, the corn gave way to a row of grey concrete houses and a trailer park.

'That's where I live,' said George. She hoped he meant the row of houses, because the trailer park looked completely abandoned. They drove past a broken fence and a parking lot and a few solitary trees on a strip of useless land. The only thing between where George lived and the heart of Broken Wheel was a disused gas station consisting of a white corrugated-iron shed, beside which someone had dumped a couple of tractor tyres and a broken pram.

The road grew wider and more buildings appeared. 'There used to be more shops,' George said apologetically, as though the town was his fault, 'but most of them closed sometime after the crisis. Not enough people for them to break even.'

At least she would get to see Jimmie Coogan Street, she reminded herself. That was something. Still, she was struggling to work up any enthusiasm. Now that she was rested and showered and seeing the town properly, it looked, if possible, even more depressing than when she had arrived.

The flat, expansive landscape of the Great Plains had inspired its own architecture, with low, sweeping houses that blended into the surrounding prairie and town centres lined with pretty wooden covered walkways, a kind of hybrid of porch and promenade for wandering up and down while looking in the shop windows. In many towns it had worked, and created a calm, cosy mood.

Broken Wheel, however, was a complete waste of brick, asphalt and concrete. The buildings were certainly low, but that was because there had never been any need for more than two storeys. Nowadays, there wasn't even the need for one. Instead of wind-swept prairie, the crude brick buildings blended into an unnecessarily wide road. It was hardly used any more, since it had long ago been made redundant by the nearby interstate.

Once George had dropped her off and disappeared into Grace's, Sara walked at random. Before long, she stopped, as though she had been overpowered by the atmosphere. There was something sad about the town, as though generations of problems and disappointments had rubbed off onto its bricks and its roads. A group of men were standing on a street corner. They must have been over fifty, maybe even sixty, it was hard to tell from their worn-out T-shirts and tired-looking faces, but they were radiating the same kind of restless idleness as the teenagers had in the shopping centre where she had worked. Like the days no longer had anything to offer them and the future would never arrive.

Could this really be Amy's Broken Wheel? The same town in which her brother had run a newspaper called the *Bent Farmer* and where one of the schoolteachers had started an improvised mobile library using a cargo moped?

She continued down the street anyway, mostly to get away from the looks the men were giving her. Not hostile, exactly, just very focused on her, perhaps because there was nothing else to look at. If she could just find Jimmie Coogan Street, she thought, then Amy's town might magically reveal itself, complete with wooden facades and women in skirts and the kind of timeless Amish-esque existence she had imagined when she read Amy's letters.

The midday sun was bearing down mercilessly on one empty shop after another. Many of them did actually have beautiful old wooden fronts, suggesting the town had, once, been charming and lively. But this impression was ruined by the shops themselves. Some of them had badly covered windows, others had broken windows no one had bothered fixing or boarding up.

Slender trees which didn't seem to have ever taken root properly had, at some point, been planted outside some of the shops, and there was something which looked like an attempt at a park at the end of one of the crossroads. The town didn't get any more charming than that.

It took her twenty minutes to walk the length of Broken Wheel, and she hadn't even caught a glimpse of a Jimmie Coogan Street.

On the other side of the road there was an advert for a pesticide: *Control corn root worm!* it shouted to the world, two by three metres in size and at least twenty years old. *With Dyfonate 20-G Intersectitude. Ideal for the big corn grower!*

Underneath it was a smaller sign announcing that this was Broken Wheel. That was all. They hadn't even bothered to add the 'Heart of Iowa' or 'Garden of Iowa' or any other attempt at civic pride. The sign was so small that it seemed to Sara almost to be apologising for intruding.

It took two trips back and forth before she finally found Jimmie Coogan Street, and then only by a process of elimination. There was no sign and the street itself was nothing more than a dark alley with high brick walls on each side.

After that, she felt completely deflated. She stopped in front of the diner. Above the door, she could make out faint gold lettering on the washed-out red background. *Amazing Grace.* When Grace herself waved her in, she was almost thankful to let someone else decide what she should do.

Grace poured her a cup of coffee without waiting for her to order and slapped a lump of pink minced meat on to the griddle behind her.

The diner was practically empty. Only three cars were parked outside: two dusty, faded blue pickups, and a white van used to repair the roads. Three men wearing yellow reflective jackets were sitting around a table eating eggs and bacon and drinking coffee, an early dinner rather than a late lunch or very late breakfast. George was sitting in the far corner at a table on his own.

'Not much town to explore, right?' said Grace, her enormous arms resting on the counter again.

'A pretty town,' Sara said, without quite believing it herself.

'A damn hole, that's what it is. If I were you, I wouldn't stay.' She paused for effect. 'Run while you can, that's all I'm saying. I've never understood why Grandma chose to stay.' She lit a cigarette and continued in almost the same breath: 'So George is your driver? I'm not one to gossip, but he's had a rough time of it. Might need a little support. Wife left him. It was after that he started drinking. Not constantly, you know. Periodically. Managed to keep his job at the slaughterhouse for a few years.'

Grace hadn't bothered to lower her voice, but George showed no sign of having heard what she said. Perhaps selective hearing was a talent he had been forced to develop.

'Good thing he got the boot, really. Not exactly the best job for a man who doesn't have the steadiest of hands.' She winked at Sara. 'Could so easily end up with him having none.' She quickly added: 'But he's sober now. Been on the wagon for over a month. A good man.'

Sara forced herself to take a sip of coffee. It was much too weak and had the faintly burnt taste of coffee that has been standing on a hot plate for too long.

'Why do you call yourself Grace?'

'My mom's name was Grace. Her mother's name was Grace. Her mother's mother's name was Grace.' Sara was worried that this would continue for some time. 'But me? Madeleine. That's a name for proper, old-fashioned ladies. The kind of women who faint if you touch them. Women who get married and embroider handkerchiefs with their initials on them. Their married initials, that is. It's hardly a name for a woman who flips burgers or keeps drunk labourers at a distance with a sawn-off shotgun.'

'Maybe she was thinking of a different line of work for you?' Sara suggested. She glanced nervously at Grace over her coffee cup to check whether she had gone too far.

Grace looked happy enough.

'It's not a line of work. It's a family tradition,' she said. 'The women in my family have always been tough, they've always served liquor, they've always been called Grace.'

She slapped the hamburger onto the bun with such force that Sara thought it was going to jump right off again. Then she scooped a serving of French fries onto the plate and pushed the whole lot across the counter. It rattled, but made it safely over to Sara.

'My mom fell in love with a man with a little farm just outside of town,' Grace continued. 'And what do you think the stupid woman did?'

Sara didn't care to guess, but Grace continued immediately.

'She got married. I was born a good two years into the relationship. A Grace who wasn't illegitimate. That set the rumour mill on fire, I can tell you. Grandma was still living then, taking care of the bar, so my mother and her husband were never really accepted. Just as well, if you ask me.'

Grace lit a cigarette. Sara carefully took a bite of her hamburger.

'Mom, she tried to get them to accept her. Have you ever tried that?'

Sara thought for a moment before she answered. 'I don't know,' she said, though she assumed that everyone had faced that problem at some stage.

'It's pointless,' said Grace. 'If you play by their rules, they'll beat you every time. It's like the saying, don't ever argue with an idiot. They'll drag you down to their level and then beat you with their experience. The same applies to the way you should live your life.' She tapped the ash from her cigarette into the already overflowing ashtray. 'Never live your life according to the idiots' rules. Because they'll drag you down to their level, they'll win, and you'll have a damned awful time in the process.'

She looked closely at Sara. 'Just look at Caroline. She's even more boring than her mother, and that says a whole lot. Old Mrs Rohde was damned dull, but at least she had some attitude. Cockiness. Caroline's been bowing to other people's expectations her entire life and now she spends her time trying to force her own onto everyone else.'

Sara said nothing. She hadn't thought of Caroline as being someone who would ever bow to anyone else's expectations. Aside, perhaps, from the expectations she had of herself.

Sara Lindqvist
Kornvägen 7, 1 tr
136 38 Haninge
Sweden

Dear Sara,

A bookstore! That must be a very nice place to work. We've never had a bookstore in Broken Wheel, but we did once have a mobile library on a cargo moped. Miss Annie, our schoolteacher, decided to start a school library and take it out to the community every Saturday. There were never many books, and those we did have got in a complete mess on the moped Miss Annie drove. But what adventures! I borrowed *Little Women* from there, I suppose the good Louisa's slightly sanctimonious tone was a good fit, and *Uncle Tom's Cabin* too, which I think must have been a mistake on their part. A lot of people in Broken Wheel had abolitionists in their family, but I don't think they realized just how liberal the values I picked up from Harriet Beecher Stowe were. For some people, there's a hair's breadth between Christianity, Liberalism and Communism. There was a copy of the Bible too, naturally, but I'd already read those stories by that point.

Book lending in town survived until the school itself closed. But the school library hadn't been the same toward the end in any case, when we were given a government grant for buying in prescribed books. There's something uninspiring about school libraries, I think. Class editions of twenty copies of the same book, as though everyone should be reading the same thing, and that special scent of obligation that goes along with it. We've never been a town of readers.

We're too practical, I guess. You've got to be something of a dreamer to enjoy books, at least to begin with. But I suppose it's different in slightly bigger towns. There was a library in Hope, but never a bookstore. There's something strange about a town which has three stores selling home furnishings but no bookstore, don't you think? Hope, that is. We don't have a single home furnishing store here, not since Molly's Corner closed, but she only sold porcelain figurines anyway.

A good friend of mine, Caroline Rohde, was just here. She's very nice, but very active in the church. She tells me that we've got a kind of bookstore there, since the Bible Society (Caroline is chair of their division in Broken Wheel) has a room in the parish house. They've got twenty Bibles that you can buy for five dollars each, or take for free if you can prove you don't have one at home.

Excuse my long-windedness. I'm under orders to stay in bed at the moment and I've got much too much time to feel the need to express myself concisely.

There's not so much to say about my own life, but it's kind of you to ask. When I was younger, I was convinced that all old folks had a dramatic life story of their own. I think it's because I grew up in the countryside. All the families around here seem to have their dark secrets, unexplained pregnancies, near-misses with tractors and combine harvesters, or natural disasters. Often of biblical proportions, sometimes literally, like in 1934 and 1935 when we were hit by swarms of grasshoppers. But nowadays, our lives seem so ordinary. I'm much more interested in our youngsters' lives – now *there's* some drama.

There aren't so many young people left in town nowadays, of course, and those that I see as 'mine' are all grown up by now. My youngsters are those who were young when I was already an adult. Claire, Andy and Tom are all over thirty now. Tom is my nephew, my brother Robert's son. Claire has a daughter who is seventeen, one of those unexplained pregnancies. I don't think it was Tom, I've never believed that, but I've wondered whether it might've been Andy. Though he moved to Denver at around the same time (there were some people who thought that was a bit suspect – sometimes I think his father spread that rumor deliberately, not that it helped him in the long run). Andy came back with a very good friend called Carl, who is very nice despite the fact that he's almost unbearably handsome. There aren't many people I'd forgive for that kind of appearance, but Carl is one of them.

Caroline was wondering whether you had a Bible. I took the liberty of saying I thought you did.

With kind regards,

Amy Harris

A *Tourist in Their Town*

If Sara had known just how much talk she was causing in the town, she would have been surprised. She wasn't interesting. She wasn't exotic. She definitely wasn't pretty.

She would have been the first to admit she was unremarkable. As young as seven, she had been forced to accept that her hair was mousy. There was no escaping it. Not even with the best will in the world could you call it *strawberry blonde* or *chestnut brown* or any of those other colours used to describe the hair of heroines in the books she read. Besides which, she had never had even the slightest sense of style. The nicest thing her mother had ever said about it was that she was, at least, clean and tidy.

In reality, her eyes were her greatest asset. They were big and expressive, when they weren't wide with fear or hidden behind a book.

But Broken Wheel had never had a real tourist before.

The day after Sara's visit to Amazing Grace, she was the main topic of conversation between two of the town's elderly inhabitants. They had gone to the diner for a quick cup of coffee purely so they could find out the latest gossip about the newest addition to town.

'She definitely came at the right moment,' one of them said. From a distance, it was hard to make her out, sitting there at one end of the counter – partly because her slight frame had shrunk with age and partly because she seemed to be surrounded by a constant cloud of smoke. Despite appearances, smoking in public spaces had been prohibited for years, but while Grace made an exception for herself, Gertrude refrained as a courtesy to Grace. But even when Gertrude wasn't smoking, it never really left her. Gertrude drank, too. Neither that nor her cooking (she was fond of additives and fat, ideally a combination of both) had managed to kill her yet, to the despair of her two husbands. Until the food and the passive smoking had put a stop to them. She had been widowed twice.

'A funeral,' Gertrude continued. 'A town's always at its best at a funeral. Always nice when something happens.'

Her friend, May, waved her hand to break up the smoke.

'And so neat,' she said. 'Everyone in smart, black clothes. And so much food.'

'I took my corn casserole,' Gertrude said. 'With extra bacon, of course.'

Both women looked expectantly at Grace.

Grace leaned forward against the counter. 'Nice woman,' she said. 'She came by yesterday, stayed at least an hour. I met her when she'd just arrived, too.'

'Oh?' said Gertrude, which was about as much encouragement as Grace needed to tell a story.

'Nice, but probably a bit weird. She was clutching a book when she came in. Hugging it like it was her only defence in the world. I saw her first, so I should know. What in hell is a book meant to be able to protect you from? A good shotgun, on the other hand . . .' She let her voice trail off knowingly, but both Gertrude and May knew better than to provoke yet another of her anecdotes. 'Well, I'll say nothing about that,' Grace continued when no response came. 'Us Graces have had our own obsessions. One of the first Graces was even obsessed with a sheriff. Didn't end well, that one, but anyone could've worked that out. She ended up being chased out of town.'

May made no comment. Instead, she said: 'But is she going to stay?'

'Why wouldn't she?' Gertrude asked in an irritated tone, since she herself hadn't thought of any other eventuality.

May had thin white hair, fastened up in a loose bun. She looked like a sweet old grandmother and had done for the past fifty years. She wasn't married – one of nature's cruel whims. It was all fine and well looking like a grandmother if you actually had grandchildren, but it was hardly the right look if you still wanted to go about *getting* some. Ironically enough, May had always been more interested in the men than the children. Children were so unromantic.

'I think she's going to meet someone,' she said.

'Meet someone?' Gertrude sounded alarmed.

'They always do, you know,' May said defensively.

'They?'

'Single people arriving in a new town. In stories, I mean. Even the men.'

'Men,' said Grace. It didn't seem as though she thought the men were worthy of further comment. 'If she's got even an ounce of sense, she'll be off like a shot. This town isn't worth staying in.'

'Which town is?' asked Gertrude. 'We're better than *Europe*, in any case.'

Books and People

A gas stove. How, exactly, do you turn on a gas stove? And what happens if you do it wrong?

Sara had never come across a gas stove before. She had lived at home with her parents, where they had a perfectly normal but clearly expensive cooker, a gleaming marvel of black and chrome. And then she had lived alone in her flat in Haninge, which also had a perfectly normal but much older cooker with old-style electric cooking rings and which had, at one point, been white.

She had hovered around the gas stove in Amy's kitchen for a few days now without daring to turn it on. She had a vague notion that doing so would involve matches, and in a fit of bravado she had even managed to find a box of them in a drawer in the kitchen. Then her courage had deserted her.

Sometimes it felt as though the house itself was working against her. Perhaps it was just her guilty conscience over not having paid any rent colouring everything, but she couldn't escape the feeling that most of the rooms had been unhappy long before Amy died. There weren't even any books in the living room, just a black leather sofa which could never have made anyone happy.

She had almost come to the conclusion that it would be best to eat dinner cold again when the phone rang. She froze.

Think, Sara.

It continued to ring, shrill and insistent.

Whatever she decided to do, it would be painful. A lot of people knew she was staying there, but there must also be others who had no idea. If it was someone who didn't know, it would be fairly awkward if she suddenly answered the phone. And if it was someone who didn't even know that Amy was dead, that would be unbearable.

The ringing stopped.

She regretted not having answered. She was almost entirely certain now that she should have done. Then the phone started ringing again, and she was thrown back into indecision. Eventually, she answered with a 'Sara', just to avoid having to think about it any more.

A warm, cheerful voice greeted her at the other end. 'Sara, it's Andy here. We met at the funeral.'

'Andy!' she said, immediately fearing that she had probably sounded a bit too familiar. She didn't remember him from the funeral, but she knew who he was from Amy's letters.

'D'you fancy swinging by the Square tonight? Have a drink or two with a few of the guys here in Broken Wheel. Really laid-back. Cold beer, good people.'

She looked at the gas stove. It didn't give her any answers. She ummed and ahhed instead.

New people were terrifying, of course. Though in a way, it was a bit like she already knew them. Plus it would mean getting out of the house.

'Thanks,' she replied. 'I'd love to.'

'Great. We'll pick you up at six. No, no, it's no problem at all,' he added before she had even considered that it might have been.

By five, she was as ready as she would ever be. She had completely forgotten about dinner and spent the time going through her things instead, looking for something which was nice but not too nice, pretty but not too pretty. She was quite pleased with the result. Her grey trousers were sharply creased, making her look almost elegant. Her black V-necked sweater was nipped in slightly at the waist, and showed off her slender build, her clavicle and a hint of cleavage. She had even put on a little mascara and some eyeshadow.

Now she was sitting in the kitchen, straight-backed, trying to keep as still as she could so that she didn't crumple her trousers or smudge the mascara. But underneath she was beside herself at the prospect of meeting Amy's youngsters. Part of her excitement and her racing pulse might actually have been down to nerves, but if that was the case then it was different to the fear she normally felt about meeting people. This time, she suddenly felt as though anything could happen, as though Amy had, in some way, returned through her youngsters. Sara knew them in the same way she knew Lizzy Bennet, Jack Reacher and Euthanasia Bondeson. None of them had ever let her down, and she was convinced that Andy and the others wouldn't either. Her disappointment over Jimmie Coogan Street had vanished into thin air.

When a red pickup pulled up outside, she got quickly to her feet and told herself not to act like an idiot. They don't know you, she reminded herself. To them, you're just a stranger who knows nothing about them, about Amy or the town. The thought made her smile.

The man who stepped out of the car wasn't Andy, she was certain of that. There was something tense and reluctant in his movements which didn't tally at all with the warm voice on the phone, or with the descriptions in Amy's letters.

'Tom,' he said.

'Sara,' she replied automatically, blinking at him in confusion. There was a web of fine laughter lines around his eyes, but he wasn't smiling. His eyes were the same deep greyish-green colour as the sea in November, and they were radiating about as much warmth. His body language exuded distance and irritation. She didn't know what she could have done to make him dislike her already, but there was no doubt about it. Dislike her he did.

For a moment, her world was thrown off-kilter, just like it had been with Jimmie Coogan Street. Only by a few degrees – enough to make everything seem distorted and unreliable, but not enough that she could put her finger on exactly what had changed.

He was dressed in a pair of jeans and a T-shirt, which made her grey trousers seem ridiculously inappropriate. She was no longer under any illusion that her trousers made her legs look in any way elegant. They were back to their usual, scrawny selves, and she was back to being utterly plain.

This has happened before, Sara, she told herself. If you were stupid enough to think that things would change just because Amy's youngsters were involved then it's your own fault. Mascara! You idiot.

She found a certain consolation in that, or she was used to it, at least.

'Andy asked me to give you a ride,' Tom said, as though it was, in some way, her fault.

'I could've walked.'

'Sure.'

She thought about turning around and heading back inside. She didn't think she would be able to cope if Andy turned out to be this unfriendly too. But Tom had already opened the car door, and now he gave her arm a gentle boost to help her up into the seat.

'So you're Sara,' he eventually said. He sounded tired, but apparently he still believed in trying to make polite conversation.

Small talk was not something Sara excelled at. She couldn't think of anything to say, so she stayed silent. Without realising it, she was clutching her jacket pocket, where she had shoved a paperback just to be on the safe side. She didn't think she could really take it out, even though it was entirely obvious that Tom had no desire to talk to her. People were strange like that. They could be completely uninterested in you, but the moment you picked up a book, *you* were the one being rude.

As soon as they turned out of the little lane which led to Amy's house, the cornfields appeared again. She couldn't decide whether they were protective or threatening.

'Sara who likes reading.'

For a second, she wondered if he could read her mind.

'You've got a book hidden in your pocket.' He was sounding more and more dismissive.

'People are better in books,' she muttered. She said it so quietly she didn't think he could have heard her, but when she stole a glance at him, she thought she could see one of his eyebrows twitch. 'Don't you agree?' she asked defensively.

'No,' he said.

She knew that most people would disagree with her too. 'But they're so much more fun and interesting and . . .' Friendly, she thought.

'Safer?'

'That, too.' She actually laughed.

But then he seemed to lose interest again, both in the conversation and her. 'But they're not real,' he said, as though that would put an end to the discussion.

Real. What was so great about reality? Amy was dead, Sara was stuck here in a car with a man who clearly disliked her. With books, she could be whoever she wanted, wherever she wanted. She could be tough, beautiful, charming; she could come up with the perfect line at the perfect moment, and she could . . . *experience* things. Real things. Things which happened to real people.

In books, people were charming and friendly and life followed certain set patterns. If a person dreamt of doing something then you could be almost certain that, by the end of the book, they would be doing that very thing. And that they would find someone to do it with. In the real world, you could be almost certain that person would end up doing absolutely anything other than what they had dreamt of.

'They're meant to be better than reality,' she said. 'Bigger, funnier, more beautiful, more tragic, more romantic.'

'So in other words, not realistic at all,' said Tom. He made it sound as though she had been talking about some romantic schoolgirl fantasy about heroes and heroines and true love.

'When they're realistic, they're more realistic than life. If it's a story about a meaningless, grey, normal day, then it'll be much more meaningless and grey than our own grey, meaningless days.'

Sara thought he seemed to be struggling not to laugh. But then his smile vanished as suddenly as it had appeared.

'The books you got Amy to order arrived two days before her funeral,' he said, and with that, the conversation was definitely over.

Just at the same moment, Sara was feeling selfish enough to

think: so where are they, then? Her thirteen books wouldn't last long at all. Especially if she continued getting through them at the rate she had been.

The Square was a large, bulky building surrounded by empty parking spaces. It rose in lonely majesty above the asphalt. Tom stopped the car and looked around as though he too was seeing the bar for the first time. Then he shook his head and opened the door for her. 'Maybe I should warn you about Andy and Carl,' he said. 'They're . . . well, they're together. Everyone's very understanding. We don't talk about it.'

'I know,' she said. Tom raised an eyebrow, but didn't comment.

There were only two other customers in the entire bar; one looked as though he was sleeping, the other was eating non-stop from a bowl of peanuts. Sara hadn't realised that people in the USA actually wore cowboy hats, but when she turned round to comment enthusiastically, Tom looked so unimpressed she decided that now wasn't the right time.

He gestured for her to keep going and followed her over to the bar. She climbed carefully up onto one of the bar stools and he pulled out the one next to her and sat down in one single relaxed movement.

When he caught sight of Andy, he smiled the first real, genuine smile she had seen from him. It made him look younger.

Andy didn't look at all like she had imagined from Amy's letters. The only similarity was the boyish glint in his eye, which somehow suggested he still expected life to be full of adventure.

He grinned at her as though he was sure they would get on well, a grin which was impossible to resist. Then he looked back and forth between Tom and Sara in a way which made her cheeks burn and Tom straighten his stool so he ended up further away from her.

'Welcome to the Square,' said Andy. 'A piece of history, a constant source of alcohol, a gathering point in Broken Wheel long before I was here.' He gestured around him.

Sara blinked.

'I only took over . . .' He looked questioningly at Tom. 'Seven years ago? Can it really have been that long? When Abe departed this life. By then, he'd become worryingly obsessed with female country musicians.'

Sara felt increasingly relaxed the more obvious it became that she wasn't expected to take part in the conversation. Andy seemed to be doing fine on his own.

He leaned forward across the bar. 'His wife left him. And it wasn't Cash or Williams or Nelson he turned to for comfort but Dolly, Emmylou, Patsy, Loretta and Tammy. For five years, their lovesick, miserable voices put a downer on things here in the Square, right until the Dixie Chicks put a stop to all that.'

'Oh, for God's sake, Andy.' Tom had clearly heard this story one too many times.

'He was one of the first to burn their records, in protest over those things they said about Bush and Iraq, in a green trash can out in the yard. It's still there. I kept it. History, you know? He died a week later. No one thought there was any real link, but you can't help but wonder, can you? So that's when I brought Carl back from Denver with me and we set up here.'

'And the country music started blaring from the speakers again,' Tom said quietly to her.

It certainly had, but Sara had no idea who or what she was listening to.

'And we've been here ever since.'

Tom ordered two beers which Sara, unsuccessfully, tried to pay for. Tom simply held out his own money, certain that Andy wouldn't take hers. He was right.

She wished Tom had let her pay. There was something tragic about being bought a beer by someone who didn't even like you. He sat there, silent and unmoving, looking as though he would rather be anywhere other than here, beside her in the bar. She took a cautious sip of her beer and regretted that she had ever left the kitchen.

'Carl,' said Andy, 'come say hi to Amy's tourist.'

As Carl made his way from the other end of the bar, Sara looked expectantly towards him and then she froze, her beer half raised to her mouth. He really was indecently handsome. He looked like he belonged on the cover of a Harlequin novel. Though he was wearing a white T-shirt instead of a purple silk shirt, of course. Not that it made much of a difference.

She tried not to let any of this show as she held her hand out to him, before realising that you probably weren't expected to look quite so blank when you met new people for the first time.

She tried a relaxed smile instead.

Carl shook her hand quickly before retreating back to the wall, as though he was afraid she would throw herself at him. Even though he had an entire bar in front of him for protection. She could understand why. Looking like that, it was probably best to be on the safe side.

'Just like a Harlequin novel,' she said quietly. Tom snorted into his beer.

'Read a lot of those, do you?' he asked.

'Every woman has read one,' she said. 'Harlequin have sold six billion books. They publish over a hundred new titles a month. They've sold one and a half million books in Sweden alone, and there are barely nine million of us. Believe me, even if you include the fanatics with drawers full of them, it's a statistical fact that every woman has come across at least one.' She looked at Tom. 'The majority of men too, probably.'

'Ah'. He seemed slightly taken aback.

She shrugged. 'I worked in a bookshop.'

'And you sold a lot of Harlequin books there?'

'No, actually. Jilly Cooper and Judith Krantz were about as close as we got.'

Andy pushed another beer over towards each of them and shook his head at her money.

'So, Sara,' he said. Their book talk was clearly over. 'What is it you're doing here?'

'I'm on holiday,' she said decisively. 'And I need to talk to someone about Amy's house. I haven't paid a thing to stay there. It doesn't feel right.'

'Paid,' said Andy. 'Who were you planning on paying? Tom?'

Tom looked as though he found the whole topic distasteful. But it wasn't *right*, staying there completely free.

'Amy wanted you to stay there,' said Andy.

'There must be someone I can pay.'

'She wouldn't have let you pay,' said Andy.

'But we'd agreed on it. She *promised* I'd be able to pay my way. It was completely impossible for me to bring enough books to pay her that way, you see. Not when SAS only gives you twenty-three kilos of baggage.'

'There was no chance she'd have let you pay, not once you'd got here,' said Andy. 'What does it matter, anyway? She wanted you to stay. And she'd been ill for so long that if she invited you over for two whole months, she must've known there was a risk she'd die during your trip. Sorry, Tom, but that's how it was.'

'She knew she was going to die?' Sara asked idiotically.

Amy knew she was going to die? Her grip on the beer tightened.

'She's always been ill,' Andy said, sounding troubled. 'Several years. But only bed-bound more recently. It didn't come as a surprise to anyone. You, on the other hand, did.'

Why had Amy invited her here if she had known she might die during her stay? Who invited someone to their *deathbed*? Sara felt strangely betrayed. She had never found meeting new people easy. The thought of staying with someone for two whole months had terrified her, but there had been something in Amy's letters, in the knowledge that she also loved books, which made her feel brave, made her want to take that chance.

'Maybe you should go to Hope instead,' said Tom. 'There's a perfectly decent motel there. It might be more comfortable for you.'

'Hope!' Andy blurted out. 'Why would she do that when she's got a free house here?'

He pushed a small glass of liquor over to her. She sipped

cautiously from it and pulled a face. Whiskey. Maybe it would help. She knocked it back, coughed, and nodded thanks as Andy refilled it.

Behind the bar was the refrigerator, covered with advertisements for Coors and Bud, a string of coloured lights hanging above it. They twinkled before her eyes and reflected prettily in the mirror. It all seemed annoyingly festive.

'There's really no reason for you to stay here,' said Tom. His voice sounded distant. How could someone invite a complete stranger to visit when she knew she might die during the stay? It was incomprehensible. Sara took another gulp of whiskey.

'But, Tom, you're the one who's always defended Broken Wheel. Even when we were young, you never thought about leaving. I wanted to get away, go to the gay bars, and Claire wanted to do something big, but you . . . you always planned on staying here, helping your dad –'

'Yes, but now he's dead,' said Tom.

Sara looked up. 'I'm sorry,' she mumbled to no one in particular. Everything around her was spinning.

'– with the farm.'

'Yes, but now it's been sold.'

'Helping Mike with the business. Always loyal, always here.'

'Yes, but where has any of that got me?' Tom had clearly grown tired of the conversation. 'Why did you want to come here anyway?' he tried asking Sara, but she didn't know how to reply.

Maybe she should just drink herself silly, she thought. She took a few deep gulps of her beer. She had never been drunk, so she had no idea if it would actually help solve her problems. Others seemed to get drunk a lot, so maybe it did help a bit. Though if her colleagues were anything to go by, it seemed mostly to create new problems instead.

'Sara?' Tom said. She looked up. 'Another beer?'

She nodded. How many new problems could it create?

'So, why did you end up here of all places?' It was Andy's turn to try.

Because of Amy. 'Why not?'

'Did you even know Iowa existed?'

'Of course.'

'What did you know about us?' Tom asked.

She thought about saying that she knew his father had run his own newspaper but decided at the last minute that it wouldn't be a good idea. 'I knew there was a cat,' she said instead.

It didn't quite have the effect she had been hoping for.

'A library cat,' she added. 'Dewey Readmore Books. You must know the one?'

'God,' said Andy. 'Spencer's cat. How the hell did you know that?'

'Amy had –' Sara began, but stopped short.

'A book about it, I bet,' Tom finished dismissively.

She drank more whiskey. Maybe it would help.

By the end of the evening, Tom was forced to give her a supporting hand as she clambered down from the bar stool. She was drunk, that much she knew, but not so drunk that any of her problems had been solved. She felt disappointed. Why did people drink if it didn't make them feel better? Maybe she just hadn't drunk enough.

Tom had to help her fasten her seat belt, too. She looked at him. She didn't quite know what to make of him. She pulled a face.

He raised an eyebrow at her scrutinising gaze and turned the ignition key.

'So you *can* be nice?' she said, as much a statement as a question.

He smiled. 'It has been known,' he said.

She nodded. 'That's good to know.'

She leaned her head against the cool car window and closed her eyes.

He took her right up to the door. 'Can you manage?' he asked.

'Sure,' she said confidently, adding 'Goodnight' to emphasise her point. She did actually feel braver now that she was drunk, and that was a fantastic feeling. Even though it had more to do with Amy's betrayal than the whiskey. If she had been lured over to America by a woman who knew she was going to die, then at least she didn't have to feel bad about staying there. Or at least that was what she told herself as she trudged into the house as though it was her own.

She would go to bed, and in the morning she would decide what to do. But as she passed Amy's bedroom, she stopped.

She hesitated. She was drunk enough that she could think of nothing at all for a few moments, and then, suddenly, she had an idea.

Books!

There had to be books somewhere in the house. The stack of books she had brought with her was all she had been able to fit in her luggage, even after she had taken out some of her clothes and her second pair of shoes. And besides, she had already read some of them, bringing them along more as familiar old friends than exciting new acquaintances. Amy must have more for her to read.

She stood still a moment longer. Swaying. Laughing to herself as she swayed, she slowly opened the door.

She sank down onto the bed and glanced around in amazement.

Amy's room was like her dream library. A large bed in the middle where Amy must have spent her days, slowly dying of her 'silly little complaint'. Along each of the walls: bookcases. The bedside table was a pile of books. On top was a collection of aerial pictures of Iowa, covered in water rings from a glass.

Someone had taken the glass away, made the bed and vacuumed, and there was a closed-in feeling to the room which couldn't have been there while Amy was still alive.

On one side there was a curtainless window, the only section of wall not covered by books. From where Sara was sitting, she could see a treetop swaying in the breeze. And she could see hundreds, maybe even thousands of books flickering in front of her as the room started spinning before her eyes.

The books were a rainbow of colours; they were thin books, thick books, books with luxurious text and illustrations; cheap paperbacks, classic editions, old leather-bound volumes, incompatible genres. Sometimes sorted in alphabetical order, sometimes by genre, sometimes without any obvious system.

She stayed where she was on the bed, looking on in astonishment as books and colours and life and stories soared up around her.

Jane Austen was there, all of her works, as well as a biography and a book of collected letters. The three Brontë sisters were there too, but she seemed to have had a particular fondness for Charlotte: there were three different editions of *Jane Eyre*, a copy of *Villette* and a biography too. There were biographies of American presidents, even Republicans, and weighty tomes on the civil rights movement – a healthy balance of power and resistance.

Paul Auster, Harriet Beecher Stowe, plenty of Joyce Carol Oates and a couple of Toni Morrisons. A copy of Oscar Wilde's collected plays, a few Dickens, no Shakespeare. All the Harry Potters, hardback. On the next shelf, Annie Proulx, all the ones Sara had read – Proulx was one of her absolute favourites. There were hard and paperback copies of *The Shipping News*, the others were all well-thumbed paperbacks.

A few Philip Roths, F. Scott Fitzgerald's *Tender is the Night*, and a whole host of thrillers: Dan Brown, John Grisham and Lee Child, a discovery which pleased Sara almost as much as the Proulx.

There was also some Christopher Paolini: *Eragon*, *Eldest* and *Brisingr*, and Sara was forced to pause there, slumping back down on the bed.

Amy might not have had the most exciting life over the past few years, up here in her room, but she must have been fighting death to the very end. Sara could understand why she had been in denial for so long. It must have been a frightening realisation:

so many books she would never get to pick up, so many stories which would happen without her, so many authors she would never get to discover.

That night, Sara sat in Amy's library for hours, thinking about how tragic it was that the written word was immortal while people were not, and grieving for her, the woman she had never met.

Broken Wheel, Iowa
February 26, 2010

Sara Lindqvist
Kornvägen 7, 1 tr
136 38 Haninge
Sweden

Dear Sara,

I completely agree with what you say about the Bible: with so many interesting stories, it's a shame no one edited it better. I do understand that it must've become tedious by the third and fourth gospels. By that point, you know fine well how it's all going to end. I've always thought that the very best stories are in the Old Testament. What a God they had in those days. If my father had been willing to sacrifice me, I wouldn't have taken it as a sign of religious integrity. Not that my father would have done. He was just like my brother Robert. Much too kind for his own good. Sometimes I think that Tom might have managed to escape that particular family trait. Don't get me wrong, he is very kind – much too kind to me, that's for sure – but he keeps himself to himself. Which my father and Robert never did. They also died young, the both of them.

I hope you'll forgive me if I tell Caroline that you have a Bible and that you've read it. I don't think she's someone who appreciates taking a literary view of it. She leads our poor minister William Christopher by the nose and she would take control of God too, if He came down and set foot in Broken Wheel. Though, of course, when it comes to God perhaps someone should. I hope that this conversation can stay between the two of us, if ever you happen to meet Caroline?

With kind regards,

Amy Harris

Comfort in Bridget Jones

'There are plenty of nice places to visit around here.'

Jen's voice struck Sara's ears like a cheerful hammer.

'We've got a river, for example. A nice late-summer picnic maybe? I'll tell Tom to bring some typical Iowan food with him so you can have a nice time together while you get to experience the best of Iowa's food and nature.'

'No.'

Sara covered her face with one hand. She had a headache, she was hung-over, and she had already made a fool of herself in front of Tom once.

She had woken up cold and stiff on Amy's bed, with the sharp edges of the book of photographs digging into her back and four Lee Childs as a pillow. She rubbed her cheek. She should probably have checked to make sure none of the embossed lettering from the *Gone Tomorrow* cover was imprinted on her face.

'He can take you to a forest fire.' Jen was dressed in a salmon-pink, Jackie Kennedy-style dress, and looked shamelessly fresh. 'I know the Association for the Preservation of Oaks was planning on organising one.'

'Wh . . . A forest fire?'

'It has something to do with the undergrowth,' said Jen. 'Controlled, of course. But it must be exciting to see. Tom can give you a ride.'

'No,' she said again. Then she froze. She raised her eyes from her cup of coffee and took in Jen's eager face, her early visit, her countless suggestions – all of which seemed to revolve around Tom.

She sat up straight with the shock. She had read enough books to suspect that Jen was trying to pair her off with Tom. *Her.*

'Walk in the woods?' Jen asked hopefully.

Sara laughed. 'No,' she said.

What were they thinking? She was ordinary and Tom . . . well, Tom wasn't. She always tried to be a fair person, so she made an effort not to judge him for it. But the fact remained, she was instinctively suspicious of a fit body. So often, they seemed to be entirely incompatible with other qualities, like intelligence or kindness or even basic politeness.

But then again, she was also well aware that an ordinary appearance by no means guaranteed charm either.

She stopped smiling. Oh God, imagine if they had suggested it to *him*? Was that why he had picked her up yesterday, forced against his will, part of some crazy plan cooked up by Jen and, presumably, Andy? Andy did seem like the kind of person who would come up with something like that. No wonder Tom had been so stand-offish. She really wished she hadn't called him nice now.

There was only one thing to do. Change the subject.

'Have you found anyone I can pay the rent to?' she asked, which immediately made Jen look unhappy.

George had started stopping by the house every morning, to see whether Sara needed to go into town or run any errands. He was taking his role as chauffeur very seriously.

Today when he arrived, she was sitting on the porch, reading. She lowered the book and looked up at him as he sat down next to her.

'What're you reading?' he asked.

She held up the book. '*Bridget Jones's Diary.*'

He nodded as though the name sounded familiar.

'Coffee?' she asked. 'With milk and sugar? Though I don't actually know if I've got any milk.'

'Doesn't matter,' he said quickly. 'I can have it black too. It's no problem.'

'But you normally have it with milk and sugar?'

'Sometimes I do.'

'I'm going to guess you like both,' she said.

'Yeah . . . It's probably not so much the milk, though I must admit I usually go for cream, or the sugar as having to choose, if that makes sense?'

She knew all too well what he meant.

'Sometimes I just think there are too many choices in life,' he continued. 'It gets tough.' He turned towards her, and said: 'Sometimes I almost wish I could get sick just so I could lie in bed all day. Not have to do a thing. No decisions for days.'

'That's what books are for,' she said, smiling at him. 'The perfect excuse to do nothing. Make no decisions.'

'Really?'

'Sure. Do you want to borrow one?'

Sara had meant it more as a joke, but he answered her seriously and slightly hesitantly. 'A book?'

'Yeah, a book.' It wasn't actually such a bad idea, Sara thought.

'The one you're reading, is it good? Could I borrow it?' he asked, adding quickly: 'Not 'til you've finished it yourself, I mean.'

'I've already read it a few times.' A few times more than she wanted to admit. She must be up into double figures by now.

'A few times? It must be good then.'

She held it out to him with conflicting feelings. She hoped it wouldn't put him off reading for good. She would just have to suggest something tougher next time. A hard-boiled thriller, maybe. Michael Connelly, nothing but dark manliness and violence and alcoholic policemen. Or maybe not Connelly, then. But when she thought about it, it would be hard to find a manly thriller which didn't involve alcohol problems.

She glanced at him. He was hardly a Jack Reacher. Still, Reacher never drank more than a beer now and then, which might be OK. She would just have to keep thinking about it.

George touched the book doubtfully. On the cover, Bridget was curled up on a windowsill, smoking. One of the early paperback editions, before the films were made.

'Keep it,' she said.

He placed it uncertainly in his lap. 'Do you need a ride anywhere?' he asked, as though one favour immediately demanded another, which was illogical since he had already been driving her around without asking for anything in return.

'George,' she said slowly. 'There's one thing you could do for me. The gas stove.'

He looked at her uneasily. 'Is there something wrong with it?'

'I don't know how it works.'

He seemed relieved. 'I do,' he said, and went ahead of her into the house.

After having revealed the mysteries of the gas stove, George drove Sara into town to buy food to cook on it. He dropped her off by the hardware store along from Amazing Grace and strolled off for his third coffee of the day.

The Hardware Store had earned its name because it had, at one point in time, sold the kind of tools and machines that every self-respecting man and farmer needed, and every self-respecting boy wanted. Now it was more like a supermarket which also sold hammers.

A little bell jingled when she opened the door and the man behind the till looked up. She hesitated for a moment in the doorway – as though she was waiting for some sign from Amy, a vision of some kind that would show her what to say or do. Then she nodded nervously at him and entered the shop.

The place was nice, in its own way. Aside from various tools, nails, screws and old fishing rods, there were refrigerators stocked with dairy products and a bit of meat, a few shelves of bread and cakes, a shelf of canned goods and a sparse selection of ice cream and candy. She walked slowly around, taking the things she needed from the shelves: more bread, some mincemeat, a can of chopped tomatoes and a few eggs being sold individually from a box at the front.

At the counter, she paused again while she looked at the man sitting there. Since she hadn't taken one of the rickety baskets at the entrance, she was forced to stand perfectly still to avoid dropping any of the things she was clutching. He had to be Amy's John.

He had grey hair and a hint of a beard peppered with grey,

but perhaps it was sorrow which made the rest of him seem to blend into the dusty items behind him. He was wearing a thick wool suit and his body was lost in its big, padded shoulders.

When she eventually started handing over her shopping, he put her items through the register without saying a word.

His movements were completely automatic, something she recognised from her own time behind a till. It reminded her of the Christmas rush, when you were so exhausted that the only thing saving you was the fact you had done it all so many times before. *Is there anything else? Would you like it wrapped? Do you need a bag? Thanks very much.* When the Christmas rush was at its worst, she could go to a cafe to buy a cup of coffee and find herself saying 'Thanks, was there anything else, would you like a bag?' to whoever was serving her.

John had that same empty, slightly desperate look. She hesitated but eventually held out her hand to him.

'Sara,' she said.

'Amy's guest.' His voice sounded like he was clearing his throat. He didn't bother taking her hand. She lowered it again.

'You must be John,' she said.

'Yes.'

'Amy often wrote about you.' It was a silly thing to say, but it was the only thing she could come up with.

She wondered whether he had even heard her. It was only when she held out the same crumpled dollar bills she had been trying to pay with all week that his gaze changed and he actually focused on her.

'No, no,' he said. 'This one's on me.'

'You can't give someone their shopping for free,' she protested. A cup of coffee was one thing. Beer at a pinch. But chopped tomatoes? No, if she was going to be staying in town for a while, then they were going to have to let her pay.

But John waved her money away again. 'Your letters made Amy really happy,' he said. 'They meant a lot to her. Especially towards the end.'

* * *

In between the hardware store and Grace's was an abandoned shop. While Sara waited for George to finish his coffee, she stood outside it, clutching her thoroughly authentic American brown grocery bag.

Something about it had caught her attention but she couldn't work out what. It was far from being the only empty shop on the street; over half of them were standing vacant. That was one of the reasons Broken Wheel felt so abandoned – the town had so clearly been built for *more*. The roads had been laid for more cars, the houses built for more children, Main Street for more shops, and the shops – those which were left – for more customers.

Maybe it was just because its windowpanes were still intact or because it didn't seem to have been treated quite as badly as the others. It was dirty, but only with two, maybe three years' worth of dust.

'When did this shop close?' she asked George as soon as he came out.

She leaned in towards the window and rubbed a circle to look through. There was a counter in the middle of the space, and a couple of shelves against the walls. Two chairs had been left behind, and both seemed to be in one piece. The lighting consisted of a lone naked bulb, and though the sun was managing to make it through the dirt on the windows, it was hard to tell what colour the walls and few furnishings were.

'Amy's?' he asked.

'This is Amy's shop?' Was, she thought, but he didn't seem to notice that she'd used the wrong tense.

'Yeah,' he said as he fiddled with his car keys. He looked around as though he was worried someone might hear them. 'Her husband bought it. It was never much of a success while he was alive, but I guess it kept him away from her for a couple of hours a day at least.' The expression on his face was uncharacteristically grim. 'She closed it as soon as he died. Not a day too soon.'

It wasn't clear whether he meant the shop closing or Amy's husband dying.

'When was that?'

'Almost fifteen years ago, but she kept on cleaning it. I don't

really know why, I don't think she thought she'd be renting it
out. She stopped, of course, when . . . when she got worse.'

Sara could just picture Amy cleaning her dead husband's shop
year after year. Neat and tidy.

'What kind of shop was it, when it was open?'

George looked even more disapproving. 'A hardware store.'
Then he said nothing more about it. He drove her home in silence.

That evening, Sara sat in the kitchen enjoying the first warm
meal she had made for herself since arriving. She had one of
Amy's books wedged beneath the edge of her plate so that she
could eat and read at the same time.

The warm food gave Sara renewed courage. She didn't even
bother to go round and switch on all the lights before it got dark.
The light in the kitchen was the only one she needed. She was
starting to feel like she might manage, like she might get her
reading holiday, her stories and her adventure, after all.

She had told people at home she was going to Broken Wheel
to get away for a while, to have a real holiday, to read and to
meet Amy, but that hadn't been the whole truth. She had wanted
to experience something . . . big. To be able to say to people,
though she didn't quite know who, that she had once spent two
whole months in a small town in America.

'Amy,' she said, 'did you know that over 300,000 new books
are published in the US every year? And now here I am.'

Regardless of how it all turned out, she would have *done* something for once.

Two hours later, she had spread Amy's books out on every
available surface and was sitting contentedly in one of the rocking
chairs on the porch, a forgotten cup of tea by her side.

She had three books on her lap but wasn't reading any of
them. She was listening to the sounds of the evening breeze
playing in the old house. Somehow, her discovery of Amy's books
had changed the atmosphere of the place. It was as though it
had become Amy's once again, and Sara her guest. The constant
noises had made her nervous those first few days, but now they

were a comforting addition to her evening. The branches rapping at the window upstairs made her feel less alone, like the tree and the window were keeping her company. The rattling pipes, the constantly creaking wood; it was as though something was still present in the house, as though it would never be completely empty, even once she had gone back home.

By nine o'clock, it had grown cool outside, but not so cold that a blanket and one of the work jackets she'd found in a wardrobe wouldn't keep her warm.

She saw the headlights first. They swept like searchlights over the overgrown garden before swinging up onto her and eventually going out completely. Only then did she realise it was Tom's car.

He got out of the car but didn't come over to her. He leaned against the driver's door instead, and crossed his arms.

'I just thought I'd check you were OK,' he said.

'I didn't drink *that* much,' she said. She hadn't been that drunk, had she? Or did he think she was part of Jen's crazy plan, and want to make sure she knew he wasn't interested? She was just about to reassure him that she would never have chosen to be paired up with him when he continued.

'With Amy and everything. Staying here by yourself. It must have been a bit of a shock for you when you arrived.'

She waved the book self-consciously. 'I found Amy's book stash,' she said. 'And met John.' Those two things seemed to go together somehow. He nodded but didn't say anything. Still, he didn't seem to be in a hurry to leave. She pulled the blanket and the jacket tightly around herself.

It still wasn't comfortable, the silence. He was standing there, right in front of her, only faintly illuminated by the light from the kitchen window, not exactly looking relaxed. But despite that, Sara thought that there was a kind of calm between them which hadn't been there the night before. Maybe it was being at the house, maybe he had simply accepted that she was staying there. Maybe, but Sara herself was convinced it had something to do with Amy's spirit. It could be felt more strongly in the house now.

'Tom,' she said, 'George told me about the empty shop next to the hardware store. Amy's.'

He nodded.

'He said it had been her husband's?' Tom still said nothing, so she continued. 'George said it had been a hardware store?'

'George seems to have said a whole lot.'

'But, Tom, *John* has a hardware store.'

'Yeah.'

'So they were . . . competitors?'

'Amy's husband –' Tom broke off as though he was thinking. He shifted position. His eyes were fixed on the patch of gravel in front of the car. 'Amy's husband wasn't a happy man. He was confused. And angry. He had problems with a lot of things, but especially with John, because he was black and because he was . . . accepted.'

It sounded as though he was thinking about saying something else, but she didn't dare ask what, for fear that he would lose his thread.

He moved his hand absent-mindedly over the car. 'Amy's husband thought he could drive him out of business. Which was crazy, because people here liked John and weren't especially keen on Amy's husband. When he bought the shop, everyone had already been shopping at John's for years. It was the shop you went to, simple as that. In the end, it was just another of her husband's bad business ideas. He kept trying for a while but then he gave up.'

Sara willed him to go on.

'He wasn't a popular person. Amy was much better off without him. I don't think many people grieved for him when he died. Maybe not even Amy, and she was a really kind person.'

He smiled briefly. So briefly that she wasn't quite sure she had seen it. 'I definitely didn't,' he said. It was clear from his tone that he didn't want to say anything more on the matter.

So she changed tack. 'How do the shops around here break even?'

'Most of them don't.'

'But they're still open?'

'Some of them.'

'Not Molly's Corner though,' said Sara, wondering whether it was stupid to bring it up. She still hadn't worked out how open she should be about the fact she knew so much about the town from Amy's letters.

But Tom simply laughed. 'How the hell do you know about Molly's?' As luck would have it, he didn't wait for her to answer. 'It must be twenty years since it closed. I was just a kid when she was selling her porcelain chickens and whatever else. Boys weren't allowed through the door. Not that we wanted to go in anyway.'

He shook his head as if to get rid of the memory. When he straightened up and took a half-step forward, she didn't know whether it was because he had managed to escape the feeling or because he had given up trying. He came slowly towards the porch and sat down beside her. She shifted in her chair so that she could look at him, but he kept staring straight ahead.

'Do you know when I realised that everything was changing?'

He didn't have to add that the changes weren't for the better. Sara had already worked out that they never were around here.

'It was when my old school closed. When I was a kid, that school was more certain and more unavoidable than death. It had tormented my dad before me, it would do the same to me for eternity.'

'Why did it close?'

'There just weren't enough kids. When the family farms disappeared, most people moved to bigger towns. Broken Wheel used to be surrounded by smaller towns, and they sent their kids here. Nowadays, our kids get sent to Hope. There aren't enough farmers here for there to be a school. Next time you go into town, just look at the cornfields and count how many farms you see. When Molly's closed, it didn't bother me at all,' he continued. 'There was a shop selling fridges and freezers too, but it closed after Wal-Mart opened on the other side of Hope, and most people were already used to shopping in the bigger chain stores. But the school was different. I was still young enough to be surprised that things which had been there in my childhood wouldn't be there forever. It's funny, really. Dad was dead by that point. I should've already learned that lesson.'

He smiled at her, but it wasn't a happy kind of smile.

'Welcome to Broken Wheel,' he said. 'There's nothing left to see.'

'John's still here,' she said. 'And Grace. Andy and Carl.'

He shrugged.

'Not Amy,' she admitted quietly.

'No,' he said, 'not Amy.'

And with that, he stood up, nodded to her and went back to the car. One hand on the door handle, he said: 'I haven't been back to the school in over ten years. Of course,' he added, a hint of a smile in his voice, 'that probably has something to do with the meth lab they started up there.'

She had no idea whether he was joking or not.

'I just don't want you to have any illusions about this place. You can't say I didn't warn you.'

She still didn't know whether or not he was joking.

'Oh, Amy,' she said to herself as she gathered up the things she had left outside once he'd gone. 'Meth labs. So much for the small-town idyll.'

Broken Wheel, Iowa
April 8, 2010

Sara Lindqvist
Kornvägen 7, 1 tr
136 38 Haninge
Sweden

Dear Sara,

In answer to your question: I think I've led a happy life. I know I've been lucky. I've had good friends and kind people around me. No children of my own, unfortunately, but I actually think that's just as well. I haven't regretted it in any real way since I finally accepted it, anyway. I've had so much to do with other people's children that I haven't had time to think about it. Take Andy, for example. His own father left a great deal to be desired, but since I had plenty of time and space to spare, I didn't have any problem giving him a bed for the night that time, and a couple of hundred dollars for his first few weeks in Denver.

I've had my sorrows, of course, but nothing more than I could cope with. Sometimes I think that it's not the degree of sorrow which matters, but how much of a hold it can get. Maybe some people are just more susceptible, or maybe everyone is more susceptible at certain times, but I've seen people survive terrible things, even losing a child (my own mother lost two children between myself and Robert, but things were different in those days). I've also seen people completely caught up in their problems; they practically creep in beneath their skin and eat them up from within, until it seems as though their reaction to the problem is worse than the problem itself ever was. They grow cruel and bitter, too, so it's difficult to remember to feel sorry for them.

I'm not an instinctively kind person, and I think this has spared me many sorrows in this life. I guess I should try to be a better person, but it would probably be difficult. I fear it's too late to teach this old dog any new tricks.

Anyway. I think that life and sorrow go together like farmers and rain: without a little, nothing will grow. But the right amount? I don't think it's really ever possible to get that. And people can talk about it as much as they like, but it won't make the slightest bit of difference.

Warmly,

Amy Harris

Favours and Return Favours

Ever since Sara had arrived in Broken Wheel, she had been feeling that she was, somehow, in debt to the town. It wasn't just the rent, even though that still bothered her. It was the coffee and the beer and the hamburgers and John's chopped tomatoes.

Neither micro nor macroeconomics had ever been Sara's strong point, so she hadn't noticed the fine, complex and occasionally – when it came to some of the items in John's shop – slightly dusty web of economic transactions and mutual dependence which bound the inhabitants of Broken Wheel together.

In reality, the town survived by performing a delicate balancing act. A lot of its cash came from outsiders. Because her greasy food was the cheapest for miles, a few customers from out of town still came to Grace's, and others continued to make the trip to the Square because watering holes always have regulars, even in the most underpopulated places. Some of the inhabitants of Broken Wheel did have jobs and money, of course. Those who didn't have money were treated by others, who were paid back in return favours whenever there was something that needed to be fixed.

Many of the shops had completely adapted to these conditions. John, for example, didn't sell much. Not many people could afford to buy new fishing gear or allow themselves the luxury of constantly buying new screwdrivers. But that also meant the shop didn't need to buy much in. By not selling his fishing nets, John was actually saving money. Before Amy became seriously ill, he had occasionally put up advertisements for new items he had been sent by his suppliers, creating an illusion of prosperity and growth, even though no one ever ordered anything.

Madame Higgins owned the only clothing store in town. She almost certainly hadn't bought in any new products since the sixties. Ugly, unflattering ball gowns never really went out of fashion. Sooner or later, all women needed a meringue dress, though they didn't tend to need them more than once in their life. And when the dresses were no longer needed . . . well, Madame Higgins was there for that, too.

The problem was that Sara had no experience of this kind of economic system and, what was worse, she had nothing to offer. Each time someone refused to let her pay for her beer or coffee, and each time she tried, she thought about how she needed something to repay them with. And each time, without really realising it, that left her a little more entangled.

George was the straw that eventually broke the camel's back. He tried to pay for her lunch.

George, *George*, who was unemployed, barely sober and who also spent all his time driving her wherever she wanted.

Right there, in Grace's, she was filled with a powerful new feeling of purposefulness. She was a grown woman, she had *the right* to pay her way, she *would* pay for the both of them.

'B-but . . .' George stammered.

Sara stood her ground. 'I'm paying,' she said.

She was just pulling out her money – crisp dollar bills this time – when Grace came past their table.

'Oh,' said Grace, 'this one's on me.'

When she needed to be, Sara was a woman with a good deal of resolve and an active imagination.

At first, she did nothing.

She let Grace pay for her lunch, she let George drive her home, and she spent the evening pacing back and forth across the kitchen, muttering to herself. She had spoken to everyone she could think of about paying rent. She had tried to pay her own way when it came to what she ate or drank. All without success. The yellow Forex wallet and the crisp new banknotes inside it were lying untouched in a drawer.

Still, she didn't despair.

The next day, she was back on Main Street.

If she couldn't pay in cash, then return favours would have to do. She would offer to help out in all the shops still trading. She had time and she had experience. Apart from her job in the book-shop, she had worked in a school dining hall and had once had a summer job in a graveyard. She had more than ten years' experi-ence behind a till. She had seven days a week and as many evenings as they needed. Just a couple of days and her debts would be paid.

She would start with the hardware store. If that didn't work then she would move on to the Square. After that, Amazing Grace.

She was sure John could do with a little time off.

'Hi, John.'

'Sara.' Perhaps it was just her, but she thought he was already looking a little nervous. Maybe he suspected she was after some-thing he wouldn't like; maybe he didn't want her to talk about Amy. She felt as though he was almost recoiling from her.

She asked anyway. 'Can I help out with anything?'

'Help out?'

She shrugged in an attempt to seem self-confident and noncha-lant. 'With anything. Putting things out, helping behind the till. I've worked in a shop before.'

'But I don't need any help.'

'Don't you want some time off? If you just show me what to do, you can leave me in charge here. You can have as much time off as you want. I've switched alarms on and off before, and I've been on my own behind a till.'

'I don't have an alarm.'

'Well, OK.'

'I can't afford to take anyone on, but if you need money then . . .' he trailed off, confused. Eventually, sounding desperate, he added: 'Have you talked to Caroline about this?'

'No, no,' Sara said quickly. 'I don't need money. I'm not allowed to work on my visa anyway. I just thought you might need some . . . help.'

'No, no,' John replied just as quickly. 'I don't need any help. No help at all. But thanks a lot, Sara. If I need any more staff . . . I'll come to you.'

She backed out of the shop, anxiously assuring him that she didn't need a job. God, it was hard work being independent.

She wondered whether she dared try Grace, but decided to put it off.

She would probably have more luck with Andy. George drove her to the bar but didn't come in. 'Just to be on the safe side.'

'Help out?' asked Andy. 'But we don't need any help.'

She looked around the bar. It was almost empty. There was one customer but he didn't need any help. He was half asleep, clutching a full glass of beer.

In the cold light of day, she noticed new details: the pale, worn, wooden floor; the scratches on the table; the scent of stale beer and sweat; the Iowa Cubs shirt on the wall, right next to the police notice about how to recognise meth users.

'So there's nothing I can do? Cleaning? Washing dishes?'

'If you need –?'

She cut him off. 'I don't need money, I need something to do.'

'Can't help you there, I'm afraid.'

Ever the host, he offered her a beer. She sighed and tried to pay for it, but before she had time to get out the damn money, he quickly said: 'This one's on me.'

She sighed again, more deeply this time.

'Whiskey?' he asked hopefully. 'Dinner?'

'George is on his way back to pick me up,' she said, adding quietly to herself: 'This isn't normal.'

Andy looked as though he was inclined to agree.

'I've heard Sara's short of money,' May said.

'Short of money?' Gertrude asked. 'Interesting.'

They were back at Grace's, where both of them had sat through the entire lunch rush with a small cup of coffee in front of them. It was an art they had long since perfected. Gertrude's trick was to let the coffee go so cold that she wasn't tempted to take a sip too soon. May's was to look especially friendly and grandmotherly and rely on the free refills.

'Dear me,' said May. It was a clichéd thing for an elderly woman to say, and it earned her a sharp look from Gertrude.

'I'm saying nothing,' said Gertrude. 'Anyone can have problems with dough from time to time.'

At that very moment, Grace left the counter and leaned out of the doorway. 'Sara!' she shouted. 'Are you hungry? Can I treat you to lunch?'

Both Gertrude and May craned round, squinting towards the window. They looked as though they hoped Sara would jump at the offer so they could study her in peace and quiet and close up. So far, neither of them had managed that. If their luck didn't change they would be forced to do something drastic, like cornering her on the street and actually talking to her. But Sara simply looked guilty, mumbled a 'no, thanks' and moved swiftly on.

Gertrude shook her head. 'Says no to a free meal? I never heard of such a thing.'

Tom hadn't seen Sara since the evening he'd stopped by. When he caught sight of her in town, he parked his car and clambered out.

He didn't even know what he thought of her and her constant reading. There was something almost insulting about a woman who so clearly preferred books to people. There was also something he needed to ask her.

At that moment, she wasn't reading. She was leaning forward strangely in front of Amy's old shop, her face pressed against the dirty windowpane.

'Is it true you're short of money?' he asked.

'Short of money? I mean . . . of course I'm not. I just got here.'

'It did seem idiotic that you'd have come here if you couldn't afford it.'

'Of course I can afford it. But no one will let me pay for a single thing.'

She straightened up and turned towards him.

'My God,' she said, 'is that why no one will let me pay for anything? For the food from John's or the coffee from Grace's, or the beers at Andy's? Why do they think I don't have any money?'

There was something charming in the way she opened her

grey eyes wide, like she thought he somehow knew all the answers.

'I'd guess they're not letting you pay because they see you as Amy's guest. Or our shared guest now.'

'But that's ridiculous. I've got money. How are they ever meant to survive when they go around treating everyone to everything?'

'Good question. But I'd hardly call that ridiculous. It's friendly.'

A furrow appeared between her eyes. 'So when I asked if I could help out, they thought . . . Then why would they offer things but not let me help out in return?'

'Help out?'

'Yeah, I could help John put things out on the shelves or behind the till or help Andy with the dishes –'

'You offered to do the dishes?' he asked, just to be sure he had understood her. My God, he thought, he would have liked to have seen Andy's face when she'd asked that.

But Sara answered as though it was the most natural thing in the world. 'Yes, I'm good at it. Not just the dishes, I mean,' she added, 'but working the till or putting things out on shelves. I've definitely done enough of it before. Strictly speaking, I've never worked in a bar, but I did once work in a dining hall in a school, so I know how to do the dishes. And I've been behind the till in the bookstore for years.'

'I'm sure,' he said. 'But it's not really the same thing, offering a beer or a cup of tea to a guest, and that guest offering to do the dishes in return.'

He could see that she was struggling to come up with an objection.

'Maybe not,' she said eventually. 'But they would have been doing me a favour. I need something to do. I've got to be able to pay my way at some point.'

'Are you bored here already?'

'It feels like I've had nothing to do for so long. How am I going to cope with two months of not doing anything other than reading and being bought coffees?'

Tom glanced at his watch. He was late for work. 'But you knew what kind of town Broken Wheel was before you came, didn't you?'

'Yeah . . .' she said hesitantly. Her expression revealed that she hadn't. 'But it's not the town so much as not working. I've never really had a long holiday before.'

She turned away from him and leaned against the shop window. He glanced at his watch again. He really should get going soon.

Sara had almost forgotten that Tom was standing there next to her. It seemed stupid that the shop should be standing empty, she thought, even though she wasn't quite sure why this particular shop should be any different to the others, or why it deserved its fate any less. She tried to picture a shop selling computer games or something similarly modern. Not computer games, she thought decisively. A bakery would work. Everyone likes fresh bread. Though maybe there wasn't enough of a customer base in Broken Wheel to support an entire shop.

For a while, she amused herself by imagining it as a Starbucks. She could just see the stressed-out teenagers in green aprons behind the dirty grey counter while George tried to work out what a decaf non-fat mocha latte extra-shot espresso was, and whether he wanted one. She glanced at Tom. For some reason, she didn't think he would be particularly impressed by a Starbucks. He looked back at her with an amused wry half-smile. Sara wasn't sure if he was laughing at her or at some private joke he had no intention of sharing.

And it was there, outside Amy's empty shop, that the shadow of an idea started to form. Still much too vague to tell anyone about it, or barely even admit to herself, but it was an idea, definitely an idea.

'Tom,' she said, 'could you drive me home?'

Broken Wheel, Iowa
May 11, 2010

Sara Lindqvist
Kornvägen 7, 1 tr
136 38 Haninge
Sweden

My dear Sara,

I really can't say which of the American classics you should read. In actual fact, I think about as much of the notion of 'classic' as you do, but at least the literary critics who compile those lists have a good sense of humor. How else can you explain them adding Mark Twain's wonderful books to their lists, given his view that 'a classic is something everybody wants to have read, but no one wants to read'? Unless it's some kind of disguised jibe, but they surely can't be that petty?

Though I don't think that justice is the main argument against classics lists. Or rather, in a way it's clearly a question of justice, but not against those who don't make it. No, the books I feel sorry for are the ones they add to these lists. Take Mark Twain again. Once, when Tom was young, he came to me complaining that he had to read *Huckleberry Finn* for junior high. *Huckleberry Finn*! Our critics and educators have got a lot to answer for when they manage to make young boys see stories about rebellion and adventure and ballsiness as a chore. Do you understand what I mean? The real crime of these lists isn't that they leave deserving books off them, but that they make people see fantastic literary adventures as obligations.

You can have the names of some of my American favorites in any case, so long as you promise you won't feel obliged to read them.

Paul Auster. I prefer *The Brooklyn Follies* to his *New York Trilogy*, even if it's blasphemy to say so.

I reread *The Great Gatsby* by F. Scott Fitzgerald this summer. I read it as a 'classic' when I was young and I never appreciated it to the extent it deserves until now. I'm afraid that my real favorites are reserved for the women though. Maybe I'm just biased.

I don't think any book has moved me as deeply as Toni Morrison's *Beloved* did, and there's no author I admire more than Joyce Carol Oates. I think the only reason she hasn't won the Nobel Prize (what are you lot playing at over there? can't you have a word with them?) is that she writes too much. Productivity like hers just overwhelms the male critics' sense of self – she writes more quickly than they can critique her. How are you supposed to be able to review a new work if you can't manage to read fifty other books by her first?

Best,

Amy

A Bookshop in their Midst

'Your father and I have talked about this, and we think that it's time for you to come home.'

'Home?' Sara said. She couldn't go back now. She'd just learned how to use the gas stove, for God's sake.

'We feel it's for the best.'

Her parents used 'we' when they wanted to present a united front at the same time as emphasising that they outnumbered her.

'Why?' Sara said.

'You've been there quite long enough. We understand that you wanted to meet that Amy woman, and now you have.'

Sara sighed. She would have to tell them. 'About that –' she began, but her mother interrupted her.

'We're not even sure it's *polite* to stay any longer. I'm sure she says it's all right, but really, what kind of person lets a perfect stranger stay with them for weeks? When Per and Gunilla –'

'Who?' Sara asked, not that she cared particularly. Her mother's conversations were always full of people Sara didn't know.

Her mother happily ignored her. 'When Per and Gunilla had American relatives coming for a visit they only stayed for two days. And they stayed in a hotel! And they were related. Well, distantly at least. I'm sure Amy never dreamed that you would stay for so long.'

'Amy is dead,' said Sara.

For the first time in her life, she left her mother speechless. The silence stretched out between them for so long that Sara eventually said: 'Hello?' in case her mother had actually hung up on her.

'Dead?' said her mother. Sara heard her passing this crucial information on to her dad, despite the fact that he must have already heard as he was suddenly talking animatedly in the background. Her father was seldom bothered about what Sara did, but when he did care, he made his opinions known. Her mother could be relentless and persistent, no matter how small the issue; her father could be loud, but only on special occasions. This was one obviously.

'But where are you staying?' her mother asked.

'In Amy's house.'

More silence. More discussions in the background. 'That settles it, then,' Sara heard her father saying, but her mother still seemed to be focusing on the practical side of things.

'But how can you be staying there? Who gave you permission?'

'It was a . . . collective decision.'

Her father had apparently managed to take control of the phone, because his voice suddenly boomed in Sara's ear. 'This is ridiculous! Is it even legal?'

'Wait a minute,' her mother said. 'When did she die? And, well, *how?*'

'This is not something you should be involved in,' her father said, as if the police might knock on the door any minute now. Sara couldn't help but notice that neither of them had expressed any kind of sympathy about Amy's death.

'She was my friend,' she said. 'And . . . and I've got other friends here now. I can't just leave.'

'Of course you can,' said her mother, at the exact same time as her father said: 'Just change your ticket and come home.'

'You can always stop for a few days in New York,' said her mother.

'No. I can't come back yet. In any case, my ticket is non-refundable.' Sara wasn't sure that it was but it was the first thing that popped into her head. 'And I like it here. People here have been . . . they've been nice to me.' She thought about the kindness they'd shown her since she arrived. 'I owe them a lot.'

'You're *in debt?*' said her father. His voice had increased in both volume and shrillness. 'You're involved in some crazy woman's death, you've spent all your money, you've –'

'She was my friend!' said Sara. 'And it's not that kind of debt.' She took a deep breath and forced herself to calm down. 'This is something I have to do,' she said. 'And I don't see why I shouldn't stay for as long as I'd planned. I'm sorry if you don't like it, but there it is.'

Sara suddenly felt much clearer about staying than she had at the start of their conversation. Her parents had unwittingly reminded her of just how little she had to get back for. And in a flash that shadowy idea came to life. She knew exactly how to repay everyone, how she could help.

The more her parents tried to convince her to go back to Sweden, the more determined she became not only to stay but to make something of her time in Broken Wheel.

'Well, if you're staying, you're on your own,' said her father. 'Don't come running to us when something happens.'

When, not if. Sara didn't care. She was going to do this.

This town was in desperate need of a bookshop.

'A bookstore?' Jen asked.

She might not have sounded openly hostile, but she was clearly sceptical. Andy looked strangely at Sara, and Caroline simply sat there with an inscrutable expression on her face.

Sara was standing on the stage in front of them. She wished she hadn't had to do that. Wished she could have sat up in the projection room instead. She was wearing her most businesslike clothes: a pair of black trousers which, with a little imagination, looked like part of a suit, and a white three-quarter-sleeved shirt which almost looked like it had been ironed. It didn't help.

'I'd like to . . .' She swallowed and began telling them about the rest of her idea in one single breath, before she had time to change her mind: 'I'd like to open a bookstore in Amy's old place. Using her books. As a tribute, to her.'

She had rehearsed that last part at Amy's house, but it didn't sound quite so good now.

'You want to sell Amy Harris's books?' Andy asked.

'Not for myself, for the town. It wouldn't be *my* bookstore. I'm not allowed to work on my visa.'

The American embassy had emphasised that she was not, under any circumstances, permitted to work; a fate worse than death would await her if she tried. It had actually been surprisingly difficult even to get hold of a proper tourist visa. She had been encouraged to use the visa waiver programme instead, giving her an automatic ninety days in the US.

Her reasoning had been that she wanted a longer visa just to be on the safe side, to have the possibility of extending her stay if her money stretched further than she thought, and for the simple freedom of it, but that had only made them more anxious. The American embassy, she discovered, weren't keen on words like extension or freedom. Choosing to visit a small American town and wanting to stay longer than originally planned were deeply suspicious, much too similar to simply deciding to stay. They would probably have preferred it if she hadn't wanted to come to the US at all.

'It would be more like . . . *our* bookstore,' she said. 'I would just be helping out.'

'*Our* bookstore,' said Andy.

'A bookstore.' Sara could hear the head-shake in Jen's voice.

'The place is going to need cleaning,' she said. 'And redecoraring, probably. I can do it myself, though. I'll pay and everything.'

'It's not a bad idea,' Caroline mused. 'It could do with a clean. It's not like you would be registering the store or anything.'

'But –' Sara protested. She was extremely law-abiding.

That spurred Andy on. 'Of course you wouldn't,' he said. 'Just think of the taxes.'

'No real point,' said Caroline. 'I doubt you'll make any profit, so it's not exactly as though we'd be cheating the IRS out of any money.'

The way she said this implied she was someone who didn't think it was even possible to cheat the tax authorities out of money. They had considerably more experience of the noble art of evasion.

Sara always followed the rules. Especially when it came to tax. Not once in her life had she made any claims for expenses, for fear of being accused of fiddling them. But at that moment, she wasn't thinking of the tax authorities or about visa rules, or any of the thousands of other reasons there must have been for not opening a bookshop in an unfamiliar town.

She was thinking about being able to give something back to the town. Whether they knew it or not, they needed books. That much was clear. And she was thinking about Amy's books, about how they would be read and appreciated once more, like they should be. She could order more, as well, to fill in any gaps. Used books, not so expensive, personally selected – and paid for – by her. People could donate their own books too. They would start on a small-scale, of course, but it could work. She had the money and she had the time. She could *do* something.

Andy and Jen looked at one another.

'Are you sure you want to open a bookstore?' Andy wondered.

'I think you should just let us organise a nice picnic instead,' said Jen. 'Or maybe a trip into the woods?'

'I'm going to open a bookstore,' Sara told George.

The words came out the moment George opened the car door. George simply nodded.

'I mean, I wouldn't own it,' she added quickly. She was worried that people would think she was just trying to make money from Amy's books. 'Just help out. While I'm here. I worked in a bookstore in Sweden, so I know how it works.'

That wasn't entirely true. She had never been in charge of the shop. And she had definitely never opened one of her own.

'I think it sounds like a good idea,' George said.

Though he was the only one.

After the meeting at the cinema, Sara was well aware that no one in Broken Wheel had much time for her temporary insanity, as Andy called the project. Still, they had all agreed to meet her in the shop the next day. Now they were grimly inspecting the dust and the dirt. The bare bulb hanging from the ceiling cast a stark, merciless glow across the abandoned room, but at least it showed that the shop was still connected to the mains.

'I want it to be yellow,' said Sara. She was picturing the shop before her bathed in light and in colour, a cosy meeting place for books and other stories, with big armchairs you could sink down into and plenty of time for long conversations. Books, too. Thousands of books, in every colour and shape imaginable.

'You'll need to need to buy the paint,' Caroline said disapprovingly. 'Unless anyone has a couple of cans left over, that is.'

'Cheerful yellow,' said Sara.

'Cheerful, yellow paint,' Caroline said doggedly. 'I guess John can help you with that,' she added reluctantly.

'And I'll be in charge of the cleaning,' said George. The others stared at him for so long he blushed from the attention. 'I know how to clean,' he said, though a hesitant note had entered his voice.

Andy, Jen and Caroline had clearly heard enough, because they disappeared, one after another, leaving Sara and George alone in the shop.

Suddenly, the whole idea seemed crazy again. She didn't know if it was because she no longer needed to act all confident in front of the others or because she was seeing the dirt more clearly now the shop was empty. She had been so caught up in her dream of a colourful, cosy bookshop she had managed to forget that the walls were brownish yellow and the floor grey.

She and George against years of dust and rubbish. Where would they even begin?

George, on the other hand, didn't seem to be nursing such doubts. 'We'll start with the windows,' he said as soon as the others had gone. 'That way, we can see how the rest looks when there's a bit more light.'

He wouldn't let Sara near the windows, even during the first wash. 'It'll go streaky if it's not done properly,' he explained kindly. But she was allowed to change the water, at least.

He was tireless. Twice, he even cracked a joke, and later, he said: 'You know, *Bridget Jones?*' He fell silent while he dealt with a tricky part of the window, and then continued. 'Not a bad book, really. But do women really talk about men like that?'

Sara had no idea, now that she thought about it. 'Maybe in London,' she suggested.

He nodded. 'Yeah, maybe in London.'

When they paused for lunch, Sara's muscles were aching and George had become more soldierly in his instructions. He allowed her a lunch break only because Caroline had come by and suggested it. Faced with Caroline, his new-found authority became weak again, and when Andy and Jen arrived soon after her, he became Poor George once more.

They ate lunch outside the shop. The sun was still warm, when it actually decided to shine, and Sara was much too hot from the cleaning to care about the cool autumn breeze which had crept into the air.

Grace came over with hamburgers and loitered at the edge of the group.

'You'll never be able to open a bookstore here,' she said. 'It's madness.'

No one bothered to reply.

'A bookstore,' said Grace, in the alarming narrative tone which usually meant there was yet another family anecdote on the way. Andy and Jen glanced nervously at her. Caroline froze. Sure enough, Grace carried on. 'Have I told you about the time the Bible salesmen visited my grandmother?'

Everyone looked at Caroline. It was an exceptionally bad story to choose. Caroline had strong feelings about Bible salesmen.

'What a lot you've got done,' said Jen, the first to recover. It was a pointless comment, but she had, at least, managed to change the subject.

'A whole lot,' Andy added quickly. 'And a whole lot left to do. Might as well get back to it.'

He and Jen bustled Caroline away, and George got Sara back to the cleaning.

Gradually, the dust inside the shop was replaced by the strong smell of cleaning products and artificial lemon.

The following evening, Sara caught a brief glimpse of the floor as it had once been – dark and stylish – before it was covered over again with paper and cans of paint.

As she walked back and forth, the floor creaked beneath her feet. It was past eight and George was still there, and eventually they both sat down in comfortable silence outside the shop, each clasping a coffee from Grace's and daydreaming about books and defeated dirt. It was still almost warm.

Sara smiled. The town felt more alive in the evening. It regained some of its dignity.

She could make out kilometre after kilometre of straight, dark road stretching out in both directions. During the day, the town was dominated by the road – threatened by it, too – but in the evening, the facades of the buildings stood out more in the shadowy light and became part of something bigger. During the day, you could drive right through the town in a minute, virtually missing it if you blinked; at night, it came creeping up to you and demanded your attention.

'Do you like stars?' George asked, in the same tone he would have used to ask whether she liked spaghetti bolognese.

'I think so,' said Sara, looking up at the night sky.

She didn't know any of the constellations. It felt liberating. It was tragic that people were so obsessed with patterns that they even tried to force the stars into them. Like the Great Bear – when she was younger, she had thought it sounded magical, like a fearsome, ferocious creature from a fairy tale, but when she finally learned to recognise it, it looked more like a saucepan. Seven stars, millions of miles apart, forced into the shape of a saucepan by people down on Earth. Or maybe it was more like a shopping trolley.

'I don't really know what I think about them,' George admitted. 'Sometimes they make me feel so small.' He smiled at her. 'And I hardly need any help feeling insignificant. I like that sometimes, though. That we're so small that two people can be standing in two different towns, looking up at the very same sky.'

'Are you thinking about anyone in particular?' Sara tentatively asked.

He surprised her by saying 'yes' as though it was obvious. 'Sophie,' he said.

'Your wife?' Sara ventured.

'God, no,' he said, laughing. 'So you've heard about *her*, then. No, Sophie was my daughter. Did they tell you about her too?'

'No.'

'No? She wasn't *my* daughter, of course. That's what they would've told you, if they'd said anything.' He had been gazing up at the stars the whole time they had been talking, but now he looked at her. 'Damn them,' he said. 'She was mine.'

When he spoke again, his tone was completely different. 'I like to think that sometime she'll look up at the stars at the exact same moment as me. If I look at them often enough, that is.' He grimaced. 'Idiotic, right?'

She smiled at him. 'It's a nice thought,' she said.

'Yeah, it's almost like looking at them together,' he replied. 'In any case,' he continued after a moment. 'I started drinking after Sophie disappeared. They told you about that, I guess.'

'Yeah.'

'No sense pretending it didn't happen.'

'They said you've been sober a while,' she said.

'A month and a half now. Some days are still tough.'

George's Theory about the Economic Crisis

George didn't mention anything when he gave Sara a ride home, but he was determined to do a good job of the cleaning and prove himself worthy of her trust.

He was, in his own way, neither more nor less strange than anyone else who had stayed in Broken Wheel and survived. Like most of the others, the town's history had left an impression on him, though it was also true that he had been badly affected by life's small catastrophes and become Poor George – a good man, 'all things considered' – relatively early on.

The American countryside had, at one point in time, been tamed by brave, tenacious, resilient pioneers; farmers searching for fertile earth, prepared to weather the trials and tribulations involved in cultivating it. And in reaching it in the first place.

Those who had attempted to tame the area around the Great Plains were, according to legend, particularly crazy. Mad enough to choose a place right in the middle of nowhere to settle down. And crazy enough to manage to live there.

Surviving became a kind of warped Darwinian test in many areas of the Midwest, with only the maddest surviving. That which didn't kill them made them stranger.

Just over 150 years ago, groups of courageous settlers travelled in convoy, achieving an early (and less materialistic) version of the American dream.

In one of these convoys, a wheel had broken: the town of Broken Wheel was founded as a result of, and named after, a mistake, and it seemed as though the town had been doing its best to live up to its name ever since.

Nothing was ever simple in Broken Wheel. Even during the good years when farming was booming in Iowa, when the family farms were still going strong, when there was enough corn and money and apple pie to go around, the inhabitants of the town had been forced to fight. The odds were always ever so slightly against them, they were always trailing slightly – still playing the game but always a few points behind. They had to keep chasing.

Those were the years people remembered as the town's golden era. But George had been Poor George even then. Though he was the eldest, his siblings had taken over the family farm. His father hadn't trusted him with it, said you had to be aggressive to succeed with a family farm nowadays. Pushy. And George wasn't, even George knew that. Then for quite some time, he remained single in a place where no one even used the word. That hadn't helped either.

Then the wheels of Iowa's family-centric agricultural economy really did come off, and everything started to go downhill.

George could remember that time and he had his own explanation for the crisis. He knew that everything had started when he lost Sophie.

That was also when he had started drinking.

When his wife married him, he hadn't really understood why. Then it became all too obvious: after seven months of marriage, she gave birth to a baby girl. George knew that Sophie wasn't his; he had been a virgin on his wedding night.

But it hadn't mattered. He had a wife and a wonderful daughter, and people looked at him with respect. All of a sudden, he was no longer Poor George. He was a husband and a father, a grown man.

His daughter was the first person he had really been good with. Others noticed it too: 'What a great father you are, George,' they said, as he carried the baby girl around with him. There was no mention of his not having taken over the farm despite being the eldest, or about his having worked in the slaughterhouse for ten years without ever supervising a shift, not even during the period when there had been jobs available and only Mexicans wanting to do them.

Now that he was Poor George again, he sometimes struggled to remember how it had been back then, when he had almost been respected. He could still remember Sophie though. It didn't matter that Michelle had left him, but she had taken Sophie with her. His Sophie. He could still remember each expression on her little face, and how soft her skin had felt against his. Like velvet on sandpaper, he had once thought to himself, though he wasn't normally particularly poetic. And her laugh. The way she smelled when she slept, and how gentle he had been when he – carefully, so Michelle didn't see and mock him for it – buried his nose in her hair. He couldn't remember what Michelle had smelled like.

Regardless, the whole wretched state of affairs had begun when Sophie disappeared. Others said that the crisis was the result of oil prices and interest rates and overenthusiastic bankers lending too much money and politicians in Washington making decisions over things they had no idea about, and God knows what else. But George knew that those things weren't the real cause.

Sophie disappeared, and after that single, impossible, inexplicable event, nothing made sense. The town was left defenceless and suddenly anything at all could happen. The price of goods had nothing to do with the cost of machines or loans, interest rates didn't indicate anything, and the banks, which had previously been more like friends to them, showering George and all the others with money, now behaved as though they had never seen him before, even though the man at the bank was from the area.

Their houses were levelled to make room for more corn. All that damn corn, he thought. The familiar old crop became greedy and unpredictable.

Before his wife left him, she had told everyone that he wasn't Sophie's father. He became Poor George again immediately. He started drinking.

Then, when more and more people were being forced to sell their farms and no one could fill the role of good husband or father any longer, more and more of them became Poor Someone, keeping him company in his drinking.

The others never quite believed him when he explained that the darkness had started with Sophie. Maybe everyone had their own source of darkness, he thought now that he had been sober for a while.

And sober he was; he hadn't had anything to drink for a month and a half. It was true that there had been periods during the fifteen years which had passed since Sophie had gone, when he hadn't drunk very much, but there was a difference between not drinking and being sober, and now George was sober.

He would find something useful to do. He would help Sara, and he would manage.

'I'm taking it a day at a time,' he often said to Sophie. He didn't promise he would never drink again, he had no intention of making promises that he might not be able to keep. Not to Sophie.

'A good woman, Sara,' he said to Sophie instead, as he drove home, his head full of thoughts of cleaning.

Caroline Organises a Collection. Again.

It was half past one in the afternoon and Caroline had visited five houses so far. She had taken it upon herself to find the furniture Sara said she would need. She couldn't help but wonder what kind of bookstore needed armchairs, standard lamps and old-fashioned table lamps, but this was Sara's project. What she wanted, she would get. Unusual decoration was a small price to pay for a newly cleaned shop in town.

Caroline rarely had trouble getting people to donate things. The trick was to keep moving. Go and see everyone. Talk to everyone. Keep it short but sweet and make sure they all understood what was expected of them. But for some reason, she felt tired today, as though she was suddenly finding it exhausting to put pressure on those around her.

Though with Henry and Susan, whose house she had just come to, there wouldn't be any problems. Henry and Susan always seemed to have more things than they knew what to do with. Occasionally, she suspected that they saw life as some kind of reverse garage sale, where the idea was to collect as much rubbish as possible.

She sighed and stepped carefully over a broken tennis racket. She knocked firmly and determinedly on the door, as though she was trying to convince herself just as much as Henry and Susan.

Susan answered. A nice, nervous woman in her mid-sixties, who always seemed excessively grateful and surprised at the smallest kindness, though she herself never had any intention of being unkind.

'Susan,' said Caroline, 'we're having a collection.'

Susan lit up. Her entire face creased into a smile. 'How nice!' she said, meaning it.

'Armchairs and tables, mainly.'

That had given others pause for thought. People had plenty

of things they wanted to get rid of, but it was usually easier when they themselves were allowed to choose what to donate.

'I'm sure we can manage that,' she said, shouting through to the living room: 'Henry! A collection!' She turned back to Caroline. 'Coffee?'

She had been given coffee in each house she had visited, but it went with the territory, so she nodded and followed Susan into the kitchen. She was handed a cup of coffee and a plate of cookies.

'We're going to . . . um . . . open a bookstore,' Caroline said. She wasn't quite comfortable with that part of the story. It seemed so . . . overoptimistic. 'With Amy Harris's books,' she added.

'So sad, that,' Henry muttered. 'About Amy.'

Susan wore a sad look on her round face for thirty seconds or so, until Caroline remembered to ask about the grandchildren – then the smile came back.

Susan and Henry had three children, all of whom had moved away from town, as well as four grandchildren who had never visited them and who had, as yet, failed to remember a single birthday. Despite that, their house was full of pictures of the children, and they loved to talk about them.

After that, Henry and Susan disappeared to go through their stash. Caroline stayed where she was, wondering why people even bothered getting married, never mind having children.

She herself had done neither.

Sometimes she thought that married women looked at her as if they felt they were more Christian than her, having started a nuclear family of their own. Or else they didn't look at her at all, as if you didn't really exist if you hadn't managed to find yourself an idiotic man. She had lost count of all of the weddings and christenings she had been to where people had seemed so determined *not* to look in any meaningful way at her that she felt she was invisible. As though an unmarried woman blended seamlessly into the wallpaper, something people's eyes drifted over before they landed, relieved, on all the married couples with children.

Though not nowadays, of course, she thought to herself, taking a sip of coffee and trying not to grimace. Very few got married in Broken Wheel now.

And you're older now anyway, she told herself. Once she had hit forty, no one had expected anything of her any more. Apparently forty was some kind of magical age limit.

Caroline normally steered clear of those who thought they were better because they had managed to get married. She didn't have much time for the nuclear family. It was better than many of the alternatives, that was true, but that was hardly grounds for being so smug and condescending. What was Jesus if not some kind of early, long-haired hippie who left his parents to drift around in a big, collective family?

Not that she had much time for hippies, either. They were extremely condescending too.

Henry interrupted her thoughts by peeping into the kitchen to say, with a certain hopefulness in his voice: 'Lawn furniture not of any interest to you, is it?'

She shook her head apologetically. 'Indoor furniture, I'm afraid,' she replied, adding in the name of diplomacy: 'This time.'

Anything was possible. Sooner or later, she would be organising another collection for the church. Then, they would take anything people wanted to donate and they would be thankful for it. And, of course, she would be the one going around convincing people to donate their broken old lawn furniture; she would be the one organising the sale; she would be writing the thank-you cards. Again.

Sometimes it felt like she was the glue holding the church together, and with it the entire town and its history. When she was young, the work had been almost magical, a glimpse into an exciting, adult world where Things happened and Conversations took place. The work had been done by women of all ages, each with different experiences, lives and opinions, who had also helped one another out. And argued, of course.

She could still remember that good-for-nothing Samuel Goodwin who had once beaten his wife just a tiny bit more than people were prepared to look the other way over. Caroline had been twelve then, maybe thirteen, adult enough for the serious, whispered discussions not to automatically stop whenever she was nearby, and old enough to understand some of what they were saying. She remembered how they had all, in some way, been there – even those who had never cared for his silent and subdued wife. Mrs Goodwin had lost a child late on in a pregnancy, and that seemed to have been the opening salvo. Women had suddenly materialised out of nowhere, visiting her and cooking food and providing almost imperceptible help with the cleaning and the child-minding. Things had simply been done. No thanks necessary.

People had taken care of one another back then. There had been a kind of neatness and order to the chaos of life. People had also been expected to put up with their lot and suffer in silence, of course, but whenever things got too much, everyone had understood that they weren't expected to go through it alone.

Caroline sometimes wondered whether those women were the reason she had never married. Because she had seen her mother helping out with all those problems and developed a kind of distaste for relationships, or for men. That wasn't to say that all the world's problems were related to men, but there was almost always a man involved somewhere, in her view.

Susan and Henry were still busy in the cellar and, outside, the wind had picked up. Through the kitchen window, she could see the trees bending and she was in no rush to leave the warm kitchen and head out again. She took another sip of coffee and tried to stop herself from sighing.

She didn't regret that she had never married. Not really. It was just that she sometimes wondered when, exactly, she had become so old.

Perhaps it had happened when her mother died. Some kind of generational shift – the mantle being passed from Mrs Rohde to Miss. Her mother had died, and women were still being hit, or getting divorced, or breaking down over much too early, unexpected pregnancies. Or over pregnancies which never materialised, even when the nursery had been standing ready for years, the baby clothes long-since sewn. Amy had taken care of the day-to-day support of many of the women, but when catastrophe struck, Caroline was the one who had stepped up to get the others to pull their weight like good Christians. Time and time and time again. Then, before she knew it, she had turned forty. And then forty-four.

But when, exactly, had she decided that she wanted to be alone for the rest of her life?

From the cellar, she heard Susan's merry voice, slightly distorted by the stairs: 'We've got *four* armchairs!'

She assumed they would need to gather everything at the church, and she would then have to find somewhere to store them.

She sighed.

Don't be ridiculous, Caroline, she scolded.

Then she had an idea.

'Thanks so much,' she said. 'I know just where we can store them.'

A Different Kind of Shop

'Sure. You want to open a bookstore. Why not? But have you really thought about what you want it to be like?'

Jen's tone of voice seemed friendly, but there she was, standing with her arms spread out right across the width of the hallway, forcing Sara to stay in the doorway. Behind her, she could see a wide staircase, with piles of sports clothes, gym shoes and toys on each step. That was the only sign that there were children in the house. Downstairs, everything was varying shades of coffee: cappuccino and latte walls; living-room furniture of dark, espresso-coloured leather.

Jen's place was twice the size of a typical Swedish house. Space clearly wasn't an issue in Broken Wheel; the next house was at least twenty metres away. The strip of land between the two wasn't exactly a no-man's-land, more . . . nothing at all. Just superfluous space which no one seemed to care about.

'Have you found any furniture at all?' Sara asked. When Jen had phoned her, she had assumed it was because she had managed to find everything they needed, but now she wasn't so sure.

'There's furniture and furniture . . .'

'I want it to be cosy,' said Sara. 'Armchairs and things like that.' Caroline had promised it wouldn't be a problem. A collection would solve it, she had told Sara with absolute certainty.

'We can get you some armchairs, but wouldn't you rather have . . . I don't know, something more stylish?'

'No.'

'Not even a little glass table? A pair of matching leather armchairs maybe? It'd be fake leather, of course, but they'd still look so nice.'

'I want them mismatched, and fabric. Proper reading chairs, the kind you can really sink into.'

Jen sighed and reluctantly welcomed Sara in. 'Come on, then,' she muttered as she wandered to the living room. She shuddered noticeably as she entered the room, her expression one of untold suffering. Sara paused in the doorway, a smile creeping slowly over her face.

Spread out among the espresso-coloured armchairs (genuine leather, Sara presumed), a glass table and a display cabinet made from dark, polished wood, was an assortment of armchairs and tables. Winged armchairs; footstools; slender pieces; mammoth things which looked like they could swallow you whole; small wooden tables; round ones with metal tops; red tables; blue tables; all the varieties of wood Sara knew of, plus a few she didn't.

'Caroline's been going round asking people to help out,' Jen said unhappily. 'I guess they thought it was for the parish. And she told them to leave everything *here*. They've been dumping stuff all day.' She glanced around desperately. 'What am I going to do with all this?'

Sara laughed. 'Give it to the church,' she said. 'I just need two armchairs and one table.'

She also needed bookcases, but she wasn't so worried about that. Of course, they were the very foundation of a bookshop, but they would also be covered by the books, so whatever they looked like, they would blend in. You would barely notice them. In the bookshop in Sweden, the shelves had been greyish metal which had once been painted white. Anything would be better than that.

Tom had been given that responsibility. He turned up at Amy's house the next day to take her to see them. She didn't really think she needed to see the bookcases – how bad could they be, after all? – but she was curious about Tom's house.

If she had been expecting it to reveal anything about him, she was about to be disappointed. They didn't even go inside.

A poorly maintained gravel driveway led up to the house, with a line of larches stretching almost right to the front door. The front of the house seemed to be in constant shade, with small, nondescript windows which couldn't have let much light in.

Tom took her straight into the backyard. The house had clearly been designed with the back as the most important part. The moment they rounded the corner, the garden opened up before her eyes. The house had been built on a hillock and the trees had been cut down so that you could look out over the cornfields, all the way to the gathering of rooftops which made up Broken Wheel.

The whole of that side of the house was made up of large, panoramic windows which seemed out of place here in the countryside.

A porch stretched the length of the house, morphing into a workspace so seamlessly that it was hard to say exactly where one stopped and the other began. There was an outbuilding at the far end. The door was open, and through it Sara could make out sturdy-looking workbenches and tools, shelves of neatly marked bottles and cans, and two old car seats covered in cream-coloured leather.

Outside the shed there was another long workbench by the side of the porch. There was also a paint-flecked tap and a sink.

And out in the garden itself – which was nothing but dry, trampled earth – there were three rickety bookcases, painted an awful reddish brown and so unsteady-looking that Sara doubted they would hold even a children's book.

'Don't worry,' Tom said. 'I'm going to repaint them.'

'But there are only *three* of them.' She couldn't hide the dejection in her voice. In her old – and tiny – bookshop, there must have been over fifty bookcases. There would virtually be more armchairs than bookcases, for God's sake.

'Too many?'

'*Too many?* They'll barely cover half a wall.'

A gust of wind made the bookcases shudder. They seemed to be practically huddling up in fear of the elements. They looked so wretched that Sara was suddenly struck with sympathy for them. 'I'm sure they'll be really nice,' she said. 'But I need more. At least six more.'

Tom looked at her in surprise. 'How many books do you have?'

* * *

Amy's book collection didn't contain anything unusual or valuable, but she had managed to create a room of pure, unadulterated reading joy. There was something for everyone, even those who 'never read books' or 'preferred films'. Sara was utterly determined to make her – their – bookshop just as much of a temple.

She tried sorting the books into different piles to see what gaps there were and to work out what she still needed to order online, but it was impossible not to get lost among them all.

She spread them out around her as she worked, opening them at random, laughing, talking to Amy, getting caught up in the best parts of her favourite authors and finding countless new gems.

When a sudden rain shower started lashing at the windows, she barely noticed, surrounded as she was by the voices of hundreds of stories waiting to be discovered by the readers-to-be of Broken Wheel.

It was love at first sight. The first time Yossarian saw the chaplain he fell madly in love with him.

I may be sitting here at the Rose Terrace Nursing Home, but in my mind I'm over at the Whistle Stop Cafe having a plate of fried green tomatoes.

Dear Sidney, Susan Scott is a wonder.

We are in camp five miles behind the line. Yesterday our relief arrived; now our bellies are full of bully beef and beans, we've had enough to eat and we're well satisfied.

At the stroke of eleven on a cool April night, a woman named Joey Perrone went overboard from a luxury deck of the cruise liner M.V. Sun Duchess. Plunging toward the dark Atlantic, Joey was too dumbfounded to panic. I married an asshole, she thought, knifing headfirst into the waves.

Mr and Mrs Dursley, of number four, Privet Drive, were proud to say that they were perfectly normal, thank you very much.

Sara tried to save a pile of books that she herself wanted to read, but there were too many of them, and she realised that she would just have to go through them, one by one, once they were in place.

That evening, she reluctantly went to bed in her own room. She slept uneasily a couple of metres away from the books.

When she woke the next morning, she was full of expectation. She made a brief stop in the kitchen for coffee before returning to Amy's room, ready to get back to work.

She stopped in the doorway. Somehow, she had expected to see Amy's room as it had been – the pretty, muted colours of the thick patchwork quilt spread across the bed, the calm serenity of the books awaiting her. But now the room had an air of chaos to it, a chaos that she herself had created the day before.

The bedspread lay crumpled beneath a collapsed pile of books. Several of the shelves were completely bare; dusty marks the only clue that books which had stood there for years had been taken away. At that moment, of course, the majority had made it no further than the floor, where they lay spread out in a fan shape, a clear space in the middle where Sara had been sitting. The empty boxes Sara had left leaning against the bed had fallen down during the night.

It was only a feeling, and one she cast off almost immediately, but standing there, in front of the ravaged bookcases, she couldn't help but wonder whether this really was what Amy would have wanted. Each time Sara had entered this room, it had been as though she was somehow stepping into Amy's world, a kind of timeless, parallel story where everything was still as it should be.

Just then, though, it felt like Amy's presence was waning, as though her spirit was being disturbed along with the dust, whenever Sara moved her books.

She'll be coming with them to the bookshop, she told herself, but she couldn't shake the niggling feeling of doubt.

When Tom came by later that afternoon, full boxes were stacked along one of the walls, and the bedspread had been smoothed out. Sara had also dusted the shelves, though that had been a mistake. It felt like she had been trying to wipe away Amy herself. She had been forced to put a couple of books back after that.

Tom said nothing about the empty bookcases or about Sara

sitting in the middle of the floor, surrounded by books and with an uncertain, almost teary look in her eye. He leaned against the door frame and watched her in silence.

She wanted to ask whether he thought Amy could see them now, or whether she was, in some way, helping them in their project, and what he thought she would make of the madness if she was, but she didn't dare.

Eventually, he gestured towards the boxes, and raised a questioning eyebrow.

She nodded. He bent down and picked up two boxes, but didn't carry them away immediately. He stood there looking at her instead, as though he was about to say something. The heavy boxes made the muscles in his tanned arms seem even more prominent, which made Sara think of something other than books for the first time in two days.

'Tom,' she said hesitantly, making him pause once again. 'Nothing,' she said. 'Be careful carrying them. Books are heavy.'

She could have sworn that she saw a flicker of amusement on his lips as he disappeared down the stairs.

Men, she thought.

Her years in the bookshop had taught her that moving books was more a marathon than a sprint, and that it was always the men who exhausted themselves first. Not that any of the men who had worked in the bookshop had ever listened to her.

Or any other men, for that matter.

The night before the shop was due to open, Sara stayed on alone.

'So, Amy,' she said. She was standing by the window, through which the yellowish light from one of the town's remaining street lamps was casting a ghostly glow over the entire shop. From where she was standing, she could almost see Jimmie Coogan Street. The thought made her smile to herself.

It had taken three days to paint the walls, bring in the furniture and the bookcases, fetch the books and put them out on the shelves. Tom had managed to collect just enough bookcases to satisfy Sara, but when there had been no more room on the shelves, she had put the remainder of the boxes in the little cubbyhole for future use. She was probably the only person in town who thought there ever would be a future, but she would show them.

The deep sunshine-yellow counter was the first thing you saw when you entered the shop. Sara thought that it made it seem like you were stepping into some kind of magical shop; what, she asked herself, wasn't possible with a yellow counter?

Aside from the bookshelves, which Tom had painted white, nothing matched. The walls were a rich shade of yellow which seemed to catch the daylight and spread it throughout the room. They didn't match the counter, but that didn't matter. It was a happy colour, and most of the walls were covered by the bookcases anyway. In the window, there were two mismatched winged armchairs, one of them in a faded green pattern and the other dark blue. Between them she had placed a small, round, cedar-wood table which clashed with the floor. The entire thing looked more like a family home, one where everything had been collected down the generations, or else a young couple's home, where they hadn't had the money to buy new things. She liked the idea of both.

George, Caroline and the others had stopped by earlier to inspect the results, but now she was finally alone. There was nothing left for her to do, but she didn't want to leave.

So she spun slowly round in the middle of the floor. She smiled. Her bookshop was ready. Perfect in its own way.

'Do you think we'll be happy here?' she asked Amy.

Amy didn't answer. Perhaps she hadn't quite found her bearings yet.

'Don't worry,' said Sara. 'We'll spread books and stories in Broken Wheel together.'

A Town Dying

John was making coffee in the kitchen. Tom was standing by the window in the living room, looking down onto Main Street, but he could hear the methodical sound of cups and saucers being placed onto a tray with precision.

Strictly speaking, kitchen was an exaggeration. It was more like a cupboard, with a tiny counter and two hotplates. The fridge was outside, in the living room.

It was funny to see how little had changed in his apartment. The living room had the same brown-striped wallpaper as the first time Tom had visited with his father, when John had only just taken over the hardware store and the living space above it. It still smelled strongly of old age. The scent of old furniture and clothing must already have been there when John moved in.

But what really struck him was how little it had changed over the past few weeks. The entire town had been affected by Amy's death, but these walls, this ceiling, they looked just as they always had. Maybe that was the reason John so rarely left home these days.

Recently, Tom tried to come over a few times a week, as though his presence might prevent John from tumbling over the precipice he seemed to be standing at the edge of. He had the feeling that the only reason John hadn't jumped was that he hadn't quite managed to work up the necessary energy yet.

Maybe the reason the apartment hadn't been affected by Amy's death was that it had never been anything to do with her. Tom hadn't been inside for years, maybe even decades before Amy's death. He had always seen John at her house.

That evening, the lights in Amy's shop were spilling out onto the street below him. Sara must still be there, even though the shop was as ready as it would ever be.

'Do you have anything against all of this?' he asked, loudly enough for John to be able to hear him in the kitchen. 'Sara living in Amy's house. This whole bookstore thing.'

'A bookstore,' John said somewhere behind him. It sounded like a question.

'Yeah.'

'With Amy's books?'

'Yeah.'

The clink of sugar lumps could be heard from the kitchen, as John filled up the sugar bowl. Neither Tom nor John took sugar in their coffee, but it was part of the ritual.

'I like her,' John eventually said. He came out from the kitchen carrying the tray with the cups of coffee and a plate of biscuits neither of them wanted. 'She seems happy.'

He placed the tray on the little side table, but Tom stayed where he was.

'Happy?'

'But she's not going to stay.'

Obviously she wasn't going to stay. 'Do you know why she came here? Did she tell . . . did Amy tell you?'

'I don't think it's right to try to keep her here.'

'God, no,' he said, with more feeling than he had intended. But then he turned to John, asking. 'Why isn't it right?'

John handed him a cup of coffee rather than answering. Something in his movements suggested he had no intention of doing so. Tom's eyes wandered down Broken Wheel's empty main street while John continued talking behind him.

'There's not enough of a future here,' said John. His voice was insistent, as though it was absolutely imperative that he make Tom understand. It was the first time since Amy had died that Tom had seen him engaged with anything.

Of course. Tom understood, but he didn't agree. He wondered whether there was really any future anywhere, whether people were happier in the bigger cities where they were constantly on the hunt for that new job, that new house, that new wife. From what he had seen of the world so far, he didn't see that people in Broken Wheel were any less happy than you could expect to be anywhere else.

'If there aren't any jobs then the young people and the families won't stay, and if the families don't stay then there aren't any new young people, and there's no town without young people. Old people die. Eventually, there'll just be people like me left.'

'Not a bad basis for a town,' said Tom. 'Plus, we've got young people.'

'Not many,' said John. 'And they're growing up. Lacey and Steven might be our last.'

'Jen's kids are going to get older.'

'They'll move.'

Tom was silent. John looked down at the empty street as though it was proof. Sara came out of the shop. She just stood there, perfectly peaceful, as if she had no reason in the world to hurry.

John walked over to the window. 'The fact is,' he said, 'Broken Wheel is dying.'

Broken Wheel, Iowa
July 2, 2010

Sara Lindqvist
Kornvägen 7, 1 tr
136 38 Haninge
Sweden

Dear Sara,

John came here from Birmingham, Alabama, at the end of the sixties. He came with his mother and his siblings. I don't know if his father stayed behind in Alabama or whether he'd cleared off long before. He might already have been dead by that point. John hasn't ever talked about his father. He actually talks very rarely about Alabama at all. Only once did I manage to get him to talk about it, but I was forced to get him drunk first.

Back then, Birmingham had the dubious honor of being an almost international symbol for racial segregation and state-sanctioned racial violence. When the desegregation of schools was put into effect after the Supreme Court's ruling in Brown v. Board of Education of Topeka, pictures of children in school uniforms being sprayed with water cannons – by the police – spread all over the world. Buses were set on fire, churches were bombed, people were lynched and burned to death. People called the town Bombingham for a while because of the white population's terrorism against the blacks. And Martin Luther King wrote his famous Letter from Birmingham City Jail.

It's funny, the way we talk about terrorism nowadays as though it's only Muslims and Arabs threatening our society. I'm afraid my understanding of terrorism was shaped long before September 11. It was the fear, the arbitrariness, the violence that affected people indiscriminately – even those who said they didn't want to get involved or had no intention of fighting against segregation. For me, terrorism is still the image of white men, people active in society, standing over the charcoaled, lynched body of a black man, looking pleased with their work.

John says I think about historic injustices too much. Maybe he's right, but it's just that it doesn't *feel* historic to me. We never seem to be able to accept responsibility for them. First, we say that's just how things are, then we shrug our shoulders and say that's just how things were, that things are different now. No thanks to us, I want to reply, but no one ever seems to want to hear that.

We never really had that kind of problem in Broken Wheel. It's probably just because we didn't have any black people. John was the first to stay. I think he belongs here. That day I got him drunk, he said it was the first place he hadn't felt afraid.

Do you understand now? How can something like that be forgiven?

Best,

Amy

Fox & Sons

On the first morning, George gave Sara a ride to the bookshop. She had decided, for no good reason at all, that ten would be the perfect time for her shop to open, but today, she was already there at half past nine. George seemed to understand the gravity of the moment, because he hovered slightly behind her as she unlocked the door, letting her go in alone, the very first time she had properly entered her own bookshop.

She stopped in the middle of the floor, George still hesitating in the doorway behind her.

'It scrubbed up well,' he said, and Sara smiled though she knew he couldn't see her.

She walked slowly around, switching on the standard lamp by the armchairs and the little table lamp on the counter next to the till, patting the armchairs. She ran her hand along her magical, bright yellow counter before going round and standing behind it. She was, in some way, taking possession of the shop.

She glanced around.

'Well, then,' said George, 'I think . . . I'll go for a cup of coffee.'

Sara nodded.

She had taken a dusty grey shop and transformed it into a charming, cosy little bookshop, and if that didn't mean she had achieved something with her life, she didn't know what did.

It was as though she could breathe more easily behind her counter, as though the bookshelves and the counter and the display window were keeping her anchored, making her sharper around the edges, making her stronger.

The majority of the books were paperbacks, so the shelves looked bright and colourful. She could see the cheerful, scrolled lettering and soft pastel colours of the chick lit; the tougher-looking black covers and cool, metallic titles of the thrillers; and the beige, grey and white of the more sober novels. Here and there, a hardback rose like a mountain among the paperbacks, and several of the non-fiction and photography books were sticking out over the edge of the shelves, or lying down if they were too big.

It was, in many ways, her dream bookshop. Not least because all the books had already been read.

Books which had already been read were the best.

She hadn't always thought that. When she first started working at Josephssons, she had longed for a pristine, shiny bookshop. One of the big chain shops, with enormous piles of new titles, a paperback section where there were ten copies of each title – covers facing out, with books from the charts displayed on special shelves (which weren't greyish white), with proper plastic labels instead of sloppily written signs made from yellow paper, hastily laminated in the little office behind the shop. Thrillers. Novels. Paperback Chart. New Titles. That's what it would say on the shelves.

If she was honest, she had never been able to watch *You've Got Mail* without secretly thinking that Fox & Sons' latte and book emporium was more attractive than Meg Ryan's claustrophobic little shop. Akademibokhandeln on Mäster Samuelsgatan in Stockholm was probably about as close to an emporium as you got in Sweden. The smell of lattes drifting over from Wayne's Coffee, dark leather armchairs which Jen would have liked, people with piles of shiny new books beside them, and entire sections devoted to specialist non-fiction, in case you ever felt the urge to impulse buy a book about particle physics.

But that kind of thing only worked on a large scale. Could you see Fox & Sons in a small shopping centre in the suburbs? Hardly. A local shopping centre needed a bookshop which also sold rolls of fax paper and refills for ballpoint pens. They needed a fax machine which still sent faxes abroad, and a stand full of useless objects you could buy as ugly little gifts for your children. White plastic boxes full of damaged and dusty paperbacks, in which you could find half-price treasures from the nineties. *That* kind of bookshop.

She had always loved paperbacks. One of her favourite stories was about Penguin Books. Its founder, Allen Lane, had the brainwave of producing quality paperbacks one day when he was travelling and had nothing to read. The only thing you could buy from kiosks at that time were newspapers and cheap romance or crime novels. Allen Lane dreamt of good literature in simple, cheap editions; books which cost no more than a packet of cigarettes and could be bought everywhere you could buy cigarettes. Sara had always thought that was such a great principle, and it was a shame that in Sweden today, even with the tax on tobacco included, books were more expensive than cigarettes.

The first Penguin paperbacks had arrived in the summer of 1935, and consisted of works by Ernest Hemingway, André Maurois and Agatha Christie, among others. They had been colour-coded, with orange representing novels, blue biographies, and green crime. They had cost sixpence. The same price as a packet of cigarettes.

Then – and this was why Sara was thinking about the story of Penguin – they had started the 'Armed Forces Book Club' to spread a little joy and entertainment among the soldiers, far from home, from their families and their friends. Best of all was the fact that the smaller paperback format fitted easily in their uniform pockets. 'It was especially prized in prison camps,' Penguin's official history claimed. Which Sara had always thought was a particularly sad sentence.

But still, it said something about the power of books. Not that they could somehow lessen the pain of war when someone beloved had died, or create world peace or anything like that. But Sara couldn't help thinking that in war, like in life, boredom was one of the greatest problems, a slow, relentless, wearing-down. Nothing dramatic, just a gradual erosion of a person's energy and lust for life.

So what could be better than a book? And a book which you could fit into your jacket pocket at that?

She was convinced that as soon as they started reading, the inhabitants of Broken Wheel would be much the better for it.

She wasn't nearly done yet, just because her bookshop was ready. On the contrary, she was just getting started. She didn't for a moment doubt that she would get the people of Broken Wheel to read, regardless of what they thought.

To read or not to read, that is the question

Work on the bookshop had changed the mood in town. It was tempting to think that there was a new determination in the air, but truth be told, that had been there long before. Caroline and Jen were living proof of that. Maybe it was simply that this determination had found a new outlet, maybe it was because people had something to gather around for a change. In any case, the fact was that for a few days, Broken Wheel felt almost like a town.

Once the bookshop was ready, though, no one really seemed to know what they were meant to do with it. What did they need a bookshop *for*? No one had any intention of buying the books. Not for themselves, anyway.

'John might like one?' Jen said to Andy, for example. They were standing outside, looking hesitantly at the shop. Sara was behind the counter, waving awkwardly to them. Jen waved back. 'Now that Amy –' she broke off. 'I mean, he might need something to do.'

'Sure,' said Andy. 'And George has plenty of time for reading.'

'That's exactly what I was thinking.'

'Don't really have time myself . . .'

'Absolutely not. The kids . . .'

'The bar . . .'

They parted company soon after, having mumbled 'John' and 'George' to themselves once again.

'Come on,' said Grace. She was sitting wide-legged in one of the armchairs, looking around her as though she found the fact that she was in a bookshop absolutely fascinating. 'You'll never break even. No one buys books here.'

Sara wasn't the least bit worried. It wasn't about breaking even. All towns needed a bookshop.

'Believe me, this isn't a town worth staying for. No town is.

They drag you into their problems, and then they want to take charge of you, and then they spit you out. Though not always in that order, of course.'

Sara didn't bother to say anything. Instead, she just arranged a pile of books on the counter that didn't particularly need rearranging.

'And now you're stuck here. Maybe I shouldn't have sent you to Caroline that day.' She shrugged. 'Not that you're my problem.'

Sara averted her eyes. 'Obviously I'm not going to stay. I'm just . . . repaying everyone. And thinking. A bookstore is a good place for thinking,' she added defensively.

'Especially an empty bookstore,' Grace remarked laconically.

Gertrude was even more merciless. She and May were at her place, chewing over the latest developments. They lived less than five minutes apart, in remarkably similar apartments. There were differences when it came to the detail, of course. May preferred embroidered tapestries with messages on them, messages of the sort that Gertrude called 'idiotically cheerful'. Gertrude liked paintings, in oils or acrylics. What they depicted wasn't important, so long as you got plenty of frame and painting for your money.

May liked delicate, light furniture; Gertrude had always chosen the sturdy and reliable. Otherwise, they were confusingly similar. Both apartments were small and dark, mainly because the windows were swamped by curtains and an assortment of plants, and both were filled with far too much furniture, a consequence of down-sizing when they had become too old to get used either to new furniture or to throwing things away.

They spent a considerable amount of their time together, almost always at Gertrude's. Her ceiling and walls were used to the cigarette smoke. On the rare occasion they did actually go to May's, she would subtly try to air the apartment, which meant that Gertrude mistakenly believed that May's apartment was horribly draughty, and that she should do something about the windows.

'A collection's all well and good,' said Gertrude, lighting a new cigarette. She smoked as though every cigarette might be her last.

She had donated an armchair which had found itself in quarantine because of the stench of cigarette smoke. Oh well, it was the thought that counted. 'But if she thinks anyone from round here is actually going to buy her books, she's crazy.'

'Maybe a love story . . . ?' May said. She looked out of the window as she said it, wondering whether the weather was nice enough for a walk. She could walk along Main Street and just happen to pass the new bookstore. Not even Gertrude could say anything about that.

'Bah!' Gertrude snorted. 'Immoral.'

May fiddled with her blouse. 'A nice love story, I meant,' she said quickly. 'Nothing . . . indecent.'

There was a certain longing in her voice.

'That's exactly what I meant,' said Gertrude. 'They've been leading girls astray for years. Prince Charming and all that. Frogs, too. Nothing but lies.'

George split his time between Grace's and the bookshop, and could often be seen sitting in one of the armchairs with *Bridget Jones: The Edge of Reason* in his hand. It was just as incomprehensible as the first one, and every now and then he laughed with delight at her latest bout of madness, before reading on, fascinated.

Andy wasn't quite so easily impressed. He came by, of course, glancing around critically before sitting down next to George and looking at the books with deliberate disinterest.

Sara stood up straight behind the counter.

'Have you sold any yet?' Andy asked.

George heard the challenge in Andy's voice, closed his book and mumbled something about 'lunch'. It wasn't even eleven yet. He was gone before Sara even had time to decide whether to answer truthfully or not.

While she tried to come up with an answer, she put two books out on the shelves, more so that she had something to do than because she really needed to. It still felt like she was just playing shop. Not that she would ever let on to Andy.

'I'm sure I will,' she said.

He laughed.

Andy, she thought, would be taking some books away with him even if she had to hide them in his bag.

He looked around the shop again. 'You should get a little gay erotica,' he said. 'Then even I might buy a few books.'

She clenched her fists in frustration. 'Why did you help out with all of this if you don't even believe in it?'

'Ah, it doesn't do any harm.' He winked at her. 'Plus, Caroline was in favour of the whole thing. You've got to pick your battles where she's concerned.'

'She seems . . . tough?'

'Caroline's an unemployed former teacher. She practically ran the school before they shut it down.' He hesitated, glanced around and whispered: 'She was a damn good teacher.' Sara looked uncomprehendingly at him. 'She took care of the kids.' He lowered his voice further and leaned forward in his chair, as though he was afraid that Caroline might come marching through the doorway at any moment, scolding him for praising her qualities as a teacher. 'One-third mother, one-third social worker, one-third –'

'Teacher?'

'Prison guard. You laugh, but now she's completely wrapped up in taking care of Broken Wheel full-time. Same philosophy.'

'She's always been nice to me,' said Sara.

'If you don't watch out, she'll take control of your entire life.'

She smiled faintly. Perhaps someone should.

'What is it with her and Grace?'

'History. Their history is nothing compared to their relatives'. Caroline's mother couldn't stand Grace's grandmother. They used to drive one another crazy.'

'One second,' she said, squeezing between the boxes of books to get to the cubbyhole. She came back a couple of minutes later with two mugs of coffee. She handed one of them to Andy and sat down in the armchair next to him.

'Mrs Rohde – Caroline's mom – was even scarier than she is. Rumour is that her husband once lost their house in a poker game. Only he never dared tell Mrs Rohde. The man who'd won didn't either. Caroline's still living in that house. But Grace's grandmother, she loved to provoke her. She was probably the only one who dared to contradict her toward the end. She was never really the same once Mrs Rohde died.'

Sara choked on her coffee. Andy had to hit her on the back.

'Exactly,' he said. 'It was just after the town council moved. We were just meant to get a temporary representative. No one thought they'd have any influence, so as some kind of protest vote, people voted for Grace. She didn't take part in a single meeting. Honestly, I don't know who was angrier, Caroline or Grace. Though I wonder how much they really care about that old feud.' He thought for a moment. 'They do share common ground. Both of them probably think the town could do with a few traditions.

'So,' he said. 'How's it going with you and Tom?'

He was forced to hit her on the back again.

Sara Lindqvist
Kornvägen 7, 1 tr
136 38 Haninge
Sweden

Dear Sara,

When I said that Iowa isn't a state of great stories, that isn't altogether true. Stories abound here. We just don't seem to get around to actually writing them down. Before the railroad, it was impossible to travel in wintertime: the roads were too bad for the wagons, and the river froze so that the steamboats couldn't get through either. It is my belief that people who are stuck during cold, idle months will find their own ways of traveling in their minds to make time pass.

My brother Robert was a great storyteller. We all thought he'd grow up to be a journalist. That was about as far as it went for us, as far as dreams go. A novelist would have been far too impractical as a job, but a newspaper man was all right. At that time, the *Wallace Farmer* and the *Prairie Farmer* were a big part of our lives. Dad had a whole box of newspapers in the attic, and Robert would never let us use any of them for lighting fires. 'Respect the words!' he cried every time we threatened to use them, and I think we did, in our own way. Just as we respected money and disapproved of people who wasted it.

When he was at high school he started his own paper, the *Bent Creek Farmer*, named after the only river in Broken Wheel. It quickly became known as the *Bent Farmer*, which was a more appropriate name, really. It was full of blood-dripping mysteries, dramatic love stories and false agricultural advice. He wrote all the articles himself, but he allowed other people to be the inspiration for them. Not the love stories. I'd like to think he made those up completely, but it was them that got him into trouble. A few stories were a little bit too close to home as it turned out, even though I'm sure he would never consciously have used real people. Perhaps he just couldn't imagine that reality could be found in his imagination.

Best,

Amy

On Romance
(Books 2: Life 0)

Tom had other things to worry about. He wasn't interested in Sara, and he had absolutely no desire to ask her out as part of some absurd plan cooked up by Andy and Jen. He knew they were trying to pair them off with each other, of course. You'd have to be an idiot not to. Subtlety had never been one of Jen's or Andy's strengths. He tried simply to ignore the whole thing, but for some strange reason, he couldn't stop thinking about her.

Every time he passed Main Street he would see her, either reading or just standing behind the counter with a smile on her face, as though she thought customers might start flooding through the door at any moment.

Why the hell would anyone want to open a bookstore in Broken Wheel?

He knew he should be more polite to her. She was Amy's guest, a stubborn voice in his head kept telling him. But Amy was dead. It was funny how much that realisation still hurt. She had been the last link to his father and a world in which the adults knew exactly what was going on. A last piece of his safe, comfortable childhood.

Pull yourself together, Tom, he thought, though he could feel Amy's loss like a physical pain in his chest, similar to the time he had cracked a rib playing football.

Amy is dead, he repeated to himself, more resolutely this time, and if her guest was selling her books in an attempt to pay back an imaginary debt, it wasn't his problem.

Oh hell.

'Sorry?' His boss gave him a strange look.

Great. He was turning into a basket case. He really ought to stop thinking about her and start focusing on Mike, the office and a conversation he could really do without.

Mike continued: 'They're mainly after our trucks and client list.'

'Bullshit,' said Tom. 'They've got newer cabs and hardly care about our unimportant little clients. What they want is to be the only freight company in the area.'

His boss shrugged.

Mike was a short, stout man; barely forty, but already thin-haired. The job of trying to keep the family business afloat had given him a sad, stooped posture. He resembled a nice old dog, afraid of being beaten, which made Tom feel all the more irritated at that moment.

'Maybe they want to build up the livestock side,' said Mike.

They were sitting opposite one another at a cluttered desk. All around them were clear signs of a family business on its way out. The files full of information about the clients and their orders were few and far between, and those they had were old. The two computers were from the late nineties, already antiques when they were bought second-hand from the old local government offices.

'I'm assuming the computers won't be going too,' Tom said with a faint smile.

Mike looked at him in confusion. 'The computers? Why the heck do you care about the computers? You want them?'

Big grey monstrosities. The screens were practically half a metre thick. 'No thanks,' Tom replied.

'They're willing to offer anyone with qualifications a job.'

'What about you? Are they willing to hire you, too?'

'I'm moving to my sister's. Her husband needs help with his business. Home electronics. Not quite as exciting as freight, but their kids are nice and there's a room for me.'

There were yellowed news clippings hanging on the walls. They had been framed several years earlier in an attempt to make the office slightly more appealing to new customers. *Broken Wheel Truck and Transportation sponsor baseball team (1997). BTT voted*

Business of the Year for their involvement with the *Broken Wheel Baptist Church.* And the most ominous: *BTT moves local government to new offices,* with a picture of smiling politicians on their way to Hope, surrounded by desks and office chairs and filing cabinets, standing alongside a less-smiley Mike.

'Are the others going to Hope as well?' Tom asked. He didn't actually care. It was hard to care about much nowadays.

'Who knows. They're both young guys, they'll be all right.'

There was a silent 'but' in there somewhere.

Mike continued, sounding more troubled: 'They're offering you a driver's job. You don't have the qualifications for management and they've already got all the admin staff they need. You know how it is. Maybe if you'd kept studying –'

'I needed this job, Mike, you know that.'

'Maybe you should've taken that job in Iowa City.'

'It was too late by then, I needed to stay –'

'I'm sorry, Tom. It was the best I could do.'

'Sure, sure. You did your best. Not your fault.' He stood up. 'Back on the road, then.' He smiled. 'I guess they don't have your approach to weekends and long-haul shifts?'

Mike said nothing.

'No worries. I get it. I'll be the new guy. It's not like I've got much keeping me here.'

'Hell, I'm sorry about your aunt Amy, Tom. Nice lady.'

'Yeah.' He paused by the door. 'How long do I have to think about it?'

'They need your answer within two weeks. It was –'

'Yeah, I know. The best you could do.'

He walked out into the hallway and closed the door softly behind him. The hallway was quiet and so he allowed himself a few moments just standing there. He was thinking about his father and about Amy, about the years working two jobs, on the farm and for Mike, and how everything seemed to be disappearing. Seventeen years.

What the hell would he do now?

* * *

After a quick trip to John's, he was just on his way back to the car when the other two drivers from Mike's appeared on either side of him.

They positioned themselves demonstratively between him and his car. Both looked angry, and terribly young. As though they still expected life to be fair.

'You going to Hope?' one of them asked. Local boys, the next generation.

'I just don't get how Mike can sell up like that,' the other said. 'The business has been in his family for generations.'

'Only two generations,' said Tom. 'His dad started it.'

'Still. Just giving up like that.'

'And selling it to Hope. When the school moved, none of us got to play.'

Tom didn't really know what baseball had to do with Mike selling his business, but to them, everything was probably still linked to baseball.

'It would've been better to just close down.'

'Better for who?' Tom asked wearily.

They were blocking the way to his car. Furious, they expected him to feel the same way.

He spotted Jen heading over to him with determined steps, a backdrop of empty shops and road behind her. Elsewhere, more asphalt was being laid at high speed as towns and suburbs grew, even though there was already so much of it going spare in Broken Wheel.

'I'm going to say yes to the job,' he said. 'It's a decent offer.'

'Decent?'

'Don't be such damn idiots.' He pushed between them and had almost reached the safety of his car when Jen caught up with him.

'How's it going with Sara?' she asked. She sounded out of breath.

Tom didn't bother answering. One of the boys did it for him: 'He's gonna move to Hope.'

'I'm going to *work* in Hope,' he corrected, though when he

thought about it maybe he would just move. Where was the sense in living in Broken Wheel if he was working in Hope?

'Hope!' Jen stared at him.

He shrugged and wished they would all just leave him in peace.

Ironically, Sara seemed to be the only one doing that. She was standing behind the counter in her bookstore, staring stubbornly outwards. At least *she* wouldn't care if he moved to Hope.

'I know you're upset about Amy and . . . everything, but you can't grieve forever,' Jen said loudly.

'Or at all,' he said. 'And what the hell does that have to do with it?'

'You wouldn't be moving away if Amy were still alive.'

That was probably true, though he would still have taken the job. He was an adult.

He walked around his car and opened the door.

'Ask her out to dinner!' Jen shouted after him.

Tom had no intention of asking Sara out for dinner, or doing anything else which might encourage Jen's scheme. Despite that, when he passed the bookstore a few days later, something made him pause in front of it.

Sara was sitting alone in one of the armchairs, her big eyes wide and tears flowing silently down her cheeks. She was gazing solemnly down, her eyes fixed on her lap, and she didn't seem to care that the whole world could see her crying.

Jesus Christ, he thought. He hesitated outside the door, wondering what he should do. Go in? Leave? Pretend nothing had happened? For some reason he felt like he should say something comforting, something friendly, but who sat crying out in the open in the middle of the day?

He cautiously opened the door.

'Hi,' he eventually said.

She looked up, and as she did so her eyes seemed to fill with tears again. He towered above her like a mute shadow rather than a supportive friend. 'Is everything OK?' he asked stupidly.

'What?' Then she suddenly seemed to notice the tears still

glistening on her cheeks, and wiped them away self-consciously. 'Sad book,' she said, sniffing.

'Am I intruding?' He was definitely out of his depth now, but for some reason he couldn't explain, he sat down in the armchair next to her.

She placed the book on the table between them. '*Jane Eyre*,' she explained. 'I'd forgotten how intense it was. The first time I read it, I sat up half the night, curled up on the floor.'

He glanced at the cover, at the picture of an old-fashioned, ordinary-looking woman in profile. Grey and boring.

'Stupid, really, crying when you know it's going to end happily. But it's so sad, when she finds out he's already married, that his wife is locked in the attic, and she has to force herself to get away from him, and then her idiot of a cousin tries to convince her to marry *him* instead, even though he doesn't love her and even though he knows she's not strong enough for missionary work. And his hypocritical Christian argument, even though it's pure *ambition* making him want to take her to India or wherever the hell it is he wants to convert people.'

'As long as it ends happily,' said Tom, casting around for safe ground.

'Yeah,' Sara said gravely. 'Or, happily for her. He goes blind and loses a hand.'

Tom shifted in the armchair.

'But happy,' she reassured him quickly. 'He got his Jane.'

'Jesus,' Tom said involuntarily.

Sara Lindqvist
Kornvägen 7, 1 tr
136 38 Haninge
Sweden

Dear Sara,

What a shame about your job. Maybe things will still work out? After all, it's not certain that they'll open a clothes store or a cafe in your old store. Right? Perhaps it'll be a new bookstore, and if they don't hire you on the spot then they must be mad.

Many of my 'youngsters' still live in town. Claire's still here, and she's never told anyone who Lacey's father is. Claire's surname is Henderson, but she's Caroline's niece. Caroline's sister married Bob Henderson, so Claire's half Henderson and half Rohde, and that, let me tell you, is quite a combination. It's because both of the families have red hair, I think. You can't have flame-red hair and let someone else lead you by the nose, or be content just being a part of the flock. The Hendersons have always been a bit wild, the men and the women, and even if no one ever says it, the same is true of the Rohde men. It's just that the Rohde women have always overcompensated for them. At first glance Caroline certainly seems to go against the theory of having red hair. Hers isn't quite as vibrant nowadays, but she had Claire's hair when she was younger, and of all the words you could use to describe her, wild wouldn't be one. Though I actually think that there's more than a touch of the red hair in her struggle for decency. She's tried to be part of the flock her entire life, but it always ends up with her shepherding the flock.

Claire is a typical Henderson, but I think she got her strength from Caroline's side of the family. It's not exactly a perfect combination, being wild, self-sufficient and strong. I see her, Tom and Andy as 'my' youngsters, but as Claire grew up, she was much too proud to accept any help, even from me. The only time she really accepted any was when she was just seven, and it was related to jelly. That girl loved sweet things. This was the time when mass-produced jelly full of artificial sweeteners and very few actual berries began to appear in Broken Wheel (we've always been a little late to the party, and as far as jelly is concerned, we resisted for as long as we could). Proper, home-made jelly suddenly wasn't the same. It never had the same bright, clear colour, or the same artificially sweet taste; it had real fruit in it, and berries. I used to buy jelly just for her, even though we never managed to eat all the jars I'd made myself. But when she was older, she was much too proud to take any of my help, and once she got pregnant, she stopped coming over at all.

Andy always found it much easier to both give and receive help. He never took things especially seriously, and I think that's probably what saved him.

Best,

Amy

The Commitment of Trees

Some of Broken Wheel's inhabitants were already starting to get used to the new bookstore and to the odd Swedish tourist who spent her days there. Those who knew Sara now visited it only to talk to her. But the vast majority of people in Broken Wheel and the surrounding area felt confused. How had it – the shop, the tourist – suddenly appeared among them? Of all the shops they might have needed, why would someone choose to open a bookstore? And why would they travel all the way from Sweden to do it?

Most simply shook their heads as they passed, but without really knowing it, they had started to get accustomed to the sight of a new display window on their street, and to the strange, idle woman standing behind its counter. Some even found themselves confusedly nodding at her. She always smiled back in her odd, beaming manner.

But that afternoon, she was sitting in one of the armchairs, and her reading caused two of the town's children to pause outside the window. They were on their way home from the school bus and were in no hurry at all to start their homework.

From the street, Sara looked like part of the window display. The name of the bookshop was painted on the window, and she was sitting directly beneath the welcoming yellow letters which spelled out the words *Oak Tree Bookstore* in a broad arc.

Her hair fell like a curtain around her face as she sat curled up with a book in her lap, an enormous pile of books on the table next to her. Her long, slender fingers were turning the pages so quickly that the two boys wondered how she had time to read them.

It made them stay standing there. At first, they had stopped only in the hope that she would nod to them or shoo them away, but now an hour had passed and she hadn't even noticed that they were there. When George appeared, the younger of them amused himself by pulling a face at her, his nose pressed against the window.

Even that didn't lead to any obscenities or weary request for them to clear off, either. Strange.

'What're you up to?' George asked. He was slightly overprotective when it came to Sara.

'We're seeing how long she can read in one go,' said the elder.

'She hasn't even noticed us,' said the younger.

George leaned forward and peered in through the window, curious despite his better nature. 'How long have you been standing here?'

'An hour.'

'And she hasn't looked up once?'

'Nope.'

The younger joined in. 'Even though I've been pulling faces.' George frowned at him and moved back from the window, in case Sara looked up at that moment and thought he was part of the whole thing.

'We're gonna stand here till she looks up,' the younger said confidently. 'We're gonna time her. Right, Steven?'

His big brother nodded. 'I'm going to anyway. Go home if you want.' He said it in that nonchalant kind of tone big brothers resort to when they know their younger siblings are going to copy them anyway.

If they had known that Sara had just settled down with Douglas Coupland's *All Families Are Psychotic*, they might have chosen a different day for their experiment. A day when she was reading a weighty biography, for example, or something else which made breaks seem more necessary. As things stood, she just carried on reading. Every now and then she laughed or smiled to herself.

Their group grew steadily as the afternoon wore on. By the time Jen and her husband came by, there were ten people standing there. Her husband had decided to go with her to visit the tourist his wife was always talking about, and she had graciously taken him along to do so. She wasn't the slightest bit amused to find a crowd blocking her way into the shop. Once the children had told her everything, she threatened to ruin the entire thing by going inside and telling Sara.

'It's not good manners,' she said. Whether she meant standing outside, watching Sara like she was a circus animal, or preventing her from going into the shop was unclear.

George agreed, but he couldn't help suspecting that Jen's disappointment stemmed partly from the fact that she hadn't come up with the idea herself. Her husband announced that he intended to stand there and watch, too.

Jen, on the other hand, still seemed prepared to march in and alert Sara. She loved her husband, of course, but that wasn't the same as letting him decide what she should do. She put a hand on the door.

'Wouldn't this be something to put in the newsletter?' her husband asked.

Jen paused. She stood for a few indecisive seconds before turning round to go and fetch her camera from the house. 'Wait here,' she said. 'Don't go anywhere. If Sara looks up while I'm gone, stand here till I get back. I mean, just let me get my camera and we can always take a posed picture.'

But when she got back, everyone was still there, and Sara was still reading.

Jen immediately took a photo of Sara sitting in the window with her book.

'Who the hell wants to watch someone reading?' Grace asked from the doorway of her diner. She had lit a cigarette, but it was more an excuse to see what everyone was up to.

'What else is there to do?' asked Steven.

'That's true, I suppose,' she admitted after a moment. 'You're gonna need food,' she said. 'Help me carry the grill out from the backyard and I'll cook you all hamburgers.'

While she was getting everything she needed ready, she realised that while food was good, it would be even better with beer. She made a quick call to Andy, who came straight over with Carl, some crates of beer and their regular customers.

* * *

Tom saw the crowd of people before he saw the bookstore, since the group which had gathered in front of it had, by that point, completely hidden it from view.

He had been on the way home from work when he saw everyone, and for a moment he was determined to drive straight past them, but he suddenly found himself stopping and parking his car, without really having made a conscious decision to do so. He could feel the tension from work lessening with each step he took towards the shop, and that bothered him.

For some reason, he seemed to relax when he was around Sara. He had felt it the first time they were in the car together, when she had demonstrated so clearly that she wasn't expecting anything of him. It had actually seemed more like she wanted him to just leave her alone. And later, when they had been sitting outside Amy's house, he had felt an almost physical sensation of peace. He hadn't been thinking about work or about John or about anything else that should have been on his mind. Which was what made Sara's company so unsettling.

He swore he wouldn't make the same mistake again this evening. He would just go over and see what was going on. Nothing more. Five minutes, tops.

There was something subdued about the scene. Everyone seemed to be straining to whisper. Andy sought him out as he reached the edge of the group, giving him a beer and taking him to the front.

It was already dark, but the light from Amy's shop was spilling out onto the street. Sara was curled up in an armchair holding a book, her eyes fixed on it. She turned the page. At one point, she pushed a strand of hair from her eyes.

It felt strangely private, seeing her read. Like watching her when she slept, he thought. She was so obviously unaware of their presence. At least there were no tears this time. Thankfully.

Beside him, Andy was whispering loudly. Tom caught fragments of it, but he wasn't really listening. 'Reading . . .', 'Been waiting here since this afternoon . . .', 'Changed the book but didn't look up . . .', 'Got a sandwich with the book still in her hand . . .'

Sara smiled.

Her expression was so comical that he found he was intrigued despite himself. Her face was open and expressive when she thought no one was watching, warm and friendly and disturbing to his peace of mind.

She had never smiled at him like that. Maybe you needed a book to coax that kind of smile out of her, he thought, even though he had never bothered trying to make her smile. Maybe he would actually try it sometime, he found himself thinking.

He forced himself to look away. Next to him, Andy was still talking. 'Shouldn't you be at the Square?' Tom asked him.

Andy laughed. 'No point. It's all happening here tonight. Grace called us, so we packed a couple crates of beer, closed up and came over. Everyone's here tonight.'

'Why . . . ?'

'To watch Sara read, obviously.' He explained the backstory. 'Incredible, right? She started a new book two hours ago but she's barely looked up. Like a relay, you know?'

Tom shook his head.

Sara continued to read.

Until she didn't.

She read the last line, smiled as though at an old friend, and closed the book. She unfurled her legs and stretched. When she finally saw the crowd outside, she stood up suddenly and went confusedly out to them.

'My friends!' Steven shouted when she stepped through the door. 'That was exactly five hours and thirty-seven minutes.'

Sparse applause broke out. The smell of charcoal, grilled meat and beer filled the air, and empty beer bottles littered the floor. There was a spontaneous party atmosphere to the whole thing, and people began talking more loudly now that they no longer had to worry about Sara hearing them.

Sara blushed and blinked at them. She had never been good at being the centre of attention.

* * *

It happens occasionally. Certain groups seem to exist only to make one person, the one we are meant to see, appear more clearly. It rarely happens like it does in films, where rooms filled with people unconsciously part to give the heroine a glimpse of the hero, or the other way round. And yet for some people, there are similar moments of insight, when they turn to a group of people and instead see only one.

For Sara, it was when she stepped out of the bookshop that evening and found herself faced with betting and crowds and beer and hamburgers; it was that evening when, for several confused moments, all she saw was Tom.

Someone had thrust a beer into her hand and she drank it gratefully while Grace and Jen talked away next to her.

'For God's sake, woman, haven't you got anything better to do with your time than read?' Grace asked.

'What were you reading? Can I have some book tips for the newsletter?' Jen asked. Her camera flashed before Sara had a chance to reply.

It was as though all previous thoughts of avoiding Tom had vanished; she was acutely aware of exactly where he was the entire time. As though a quietly murmuring radar, placed high in her chest, was keeping track of where he was standing and who he was with. She wanted both to avoid and for him to come over to her. Every time she saw him talking to someone else – and he seemed to be determined to talk to everyone except her – she found herself thinking that he should be talking to her instead, standing next to her, smiling at her.

Caroline was hesitating at the edge of the improvised street party. She kept herself close to the other side of the street, doing her best to blend into the shadows.

No one looked in her direction. They seemed too busy drinking themselves silly and becoming even more idiotic than normal, which said a lot about the damaging effects of alcohol.

Caroline had been on her way over to Sara to say a few nice words about the name she had chosen for the shop when something – she wasn't quite sure what – had forced her back into the safety of the edge of the group.

Maybe it was the laughter, the way that everyone, even the usually nervous Sara, seemed so relaxed and self-assured, but Caroline had suddenly felt as though she was seventeen again: wearing her best dress, even a little make-up, she'd been forced to sneak out so that her mother wouldn't see, on her way to make a fool of herself, and tragically expectant at the thought of it. Expectant and vulnerable.

Charcoal.

It was the smell of beer and fire which had taken her back to that evening, she realised as a gust of wind blew the smell over to her side of the street again. The force of the memories struck her like a slap in the face. Completely unexpected, and more humiliating than painful.

Pull yourself together, Caroline, she thought, but even her inner voice sounded shaky.

It's just a party, she thought.

But that was the problem. She didn't belong at parties. She wasn't someone who let her hair down at them. She was the one who fixed the problems they created. None of her friends had ever come to her for advice when they were happy. They had married off left, right and centre without taking the slightest bit of notice of what she thought, and it was only once they ran into trouble that they came to her. An endless stream of women with husbands who had lost their jobs, who drank or cheated, husbands who hit them or their mistresses, or both.

But that didn't mean she couldn't go over and join the group right now. Make small talk with Sara, that was all. Ten minutes. Just because she was passing by.

What are you so afraid of, Caroline? she demanded of herself before straightening her back, swallowing and heading straight towards the group with as much dignity and self-confidence as she could muster.

Sara saw Caroline coming over to her, but all she could really think about was Tom. He was talking to a woman who had just turned up. The woman looked tired and had dark circles beneath her eyes, and she was dressed in an unflattering uniform. Despite that, she was pretty in the kind of tough, fiery way that only reminded Sara how dull and colourless she was. The woman was slightly overweight but radiating a kind of confident, calm sensuality which, even from a distance, overwhelmed Sara and made her feel like moving further away, so that the difference between them wasn't so obvious.

Part of her was relieved when Caroline interrupted her thoughts. Maybe it was the glow from the street lights, but it struck Sara that she looked more human. Her posture was still poker-straight and military, but her gaze was softer, and something in her seemed to relax when she reached Sara. She was wearing jeans and a black coat, and Sara could see a hint of a soft, cream-coloured sweater beneath.

'I'm chair of the Association for the Preservation of Oaks,' Caroline said, without bothering with the usual greetings. 'I wanted to thank you in person for supporting our cause by naming the place Oak Tree Bookstore.'

Perhaps she should have told Caroline that it hadn't been entirely for Iowa's sake that she had chosen the name, but she wasn't sure she could dare to. It was part of an acknowledgement in an obscure book about machine learning in computer science. The authors, Forsyth and Rada, wrote that many people, not just the author, contribute to the making of a book, from the person who had the bright idea of alphabetic writing through the inventor of movable type to the lumberjacks who felled the trees that were pulped for its printing. It wasn't customary to acknowledge the trees themselves, they went on, even though their commitment was total.

'Ah,' said Sara. 'Actually, it's –'

'It'll get people to pay more attention to our work.' Caroline smiled. 'It's nice that someone who isn't from Iowa can see the importance of the oaks to our state. Do you have any books about oaks?'

Tom laughed at something the red-haired woman said, and Sara was forced to look away. She cursed herself for it. She couldn't fall for someone like him. She knew what she was, and she knew her limits. She might be able to cope with opening a bookshop, but she would never survive falling in love with someone like Tom.

If she even was falling for him. It felt more like falling ill.

'I can order some,' Sara answered.

Eventually, Caroline was replaced by the woman Tom had been talking to.

'So,' she said, 'you're the one they've been trying to pair Tom up with, are you?' She placed a slight emphasis on *trying to*. 'Claire,' she said, smiling with amusement. 'Yep, '*That* Claire. Teenage pregnancy.'

'That . . . I mean, that's not what I was thinking.'

Claire nodded towards Tom. 'You should,' she said coolly. 'He was great when Lacey was a kid,' she continued. 'Lacey, my daughter. More than a few people thought he was the father.'

Amy had never thought that. Still, Sara couldn't help but ask: 'Is he?'

Claire laughed. She walked away without answering, and Sara remained where she was at the edge of a group which, somehow, she had managed to gather. It was a strange feeling. People were smiling at her and raising their beers in improvised toasts, patting her on the shoulder as they passed, but she wasn't really there. Country music was playing somewhere in the background. She couldn't hear the words, but the tunes brought a feeling of memory and history; not quite nostalgia, but firmly rooted in the past.

For a moment, she was convinced that she could sense Amy in the cool evening air, in the smell of hamburgers and cold beers. But it wasn't Amy, not really. Maybe she was out there somewhere, but it wasn't just her. It was as though the town itself was present, a kind of collective deposit of the lives and memories of various generations. The facades of the buildings which, just a few days ago, had seemed like dull backdrops, were now playful spirits. Between Andy and Carl and Tom – who was talking to

Claire again – she could almost see Miss Annie speeding past on her cargo moped, and there was a quiet murmur of long-forgotten stories hanging over the entire scene.

When Tom finally came over to her, she was much too distracted to be able to say anything. They stood next to one another in silence, shoulder to shoulder, so close that she could feel the warmth of his body and the slight pressure of his arm. She couldn't help but steal a glance at him, and the comforting presence of the past was replaced by a racing pulse and a cold sweat.

'So how does it feel?' he asked.

For a few seconds, Sara worried that he really had read her thoughts this time, and she stared at him in confusion. 'F-feel?' she stammered.

'The bookstore.' He made a sweeping gesture over the illuminated window, strangely empty and deserted despite all the life around it.

'No one's bought anything yet,' she said.

He laughed. 'D'you think they will?'

'Of course. Why would I have opened it otherwise?' Tom shrugged, and she involuntarily took hold of his arm. 'They *have to* buy books,' she said. She couldn't have gone through it all, practically laid waste to Amy's room, for the inhabitants of Broken Wheel to refuse to start reading. What would be the point if she didn't even manage to spread stories among Amy's friends?

Tom was spared answering by Andy, who waved for the man nearest the radio to turn it off. 'A toast,' he said, looking insistently at Sara.

'To Miss Annie's cargo moped,' she said.

She smiled, half sorrowful, half laughing, at her own private joke.

'To Miss Annie's cargo moped,' they echoed.

She didn't think anyone knew what she was talking about, and that felt strangely liberating. She might not quite be a part of the town, but she had become a part of its history.

And she swore to herself that she would force books on them before she was done here.

'You know,' said Tom, who had seen the determination in her eyes, 'if you're going to get this lot to read, you're going to need to be more cunning.'

Sara Lindqvist
Kornvägen 7, 1 tr
136 38 Haninge
Sweden

Dear Sara,

Books or people, you ask. It's a difficult choice, I've got to say.
I don't know whether people mean more than books – they're
definitely not nicer, or funnier, or more comforting . . . but
still, however much I twist and turn the question, I've got
to opt for people in the long run. I hope you don't lose all
confidence in me now that I've admitted that.

I can't for the life of me explain why I've got the bad sense
to prefer people. If you went purely by numbers, then books
would win hands down – I've loved maybe a handful of
people in my entire life, compared with tens or maybe even
hundreds of books (and here, I'm counting only those books
I've *really* loved, the kind that make you happy just to look
at them, which make you smile regardless of what else is
happening in your life, which you always turn back to like
an old friend and can remember exactly where you first
'met' them – I'm sure you know just what I'm talking about).
But that handful of people you love . . . they're surely worth
just as much as all of those books.

Your question got me to start rereading *Walden*. Sometimes,
I still long to be in a little cabin in the woods, together with
some books, and free from all the strange demands we humans
place on one another and ourselves. Maybe we would all
benefit from a break from 'civilization' for a year or two every
now and then (that said, there are so few people here in
Broken Wheel that we might be more like the village

Thoreau fled to, rather than the big city he left. I've never thought that his depiction of the farmers was his strongest suit – he's better when he's aiming higher, but who isn't?).

Walden is one of those books you simply have to quote from. I haven't even made it through the first fifty pages yet, but John is already bored with it. Maybe that proves I was right about books and people: books are fantastic and probably come into their own in a cabin in the woods, but how fun is it to read a fantastic book if you can't tell others about it, talk about it, quote from it constantly?

'The greater part of what my neighbors call good I believe in my soul to be bad, and if I repent of anything, it is very likely to be my good behavior. What demon possessed me that I behaved so well?' Isn't that a wonderful quote? I especially like the idea of good behavior being caused by demons. I'm afraid I was stupid enough to quote the lines above to Caroline. She simply raised her eyebrows – Caroline is someone who can raise an eyebrow without needing to actually say anything – and said: 'Good behavior?' in a slightly questioning tone. As though she wanted to remind me that that particular demon hasn't affected me especially often but was too polite to say it straight out.

Thoreau also said: 'Public opinion is a weak tyrant compared with our own private opinion,' but I think that's more depressing. I prefer the idea of a wild demon causing us to toe the line over the thought of us doing it ourselves, worrying what others will think even though they're much too concerned with themselves to even give us the slightest thought.

Best,

Amy

What's in a name?

The newsletter was a big hit when it came out. It was dominated by a picture of Sara reading in the display window, seen through reflections in the windowpane, directly beneath the big yellow letters. Below that was a smaller picture of her in front of the shop, smiling hesitantly and squinting at the camera flash.

The article itself described a party celebrating the two latest additions to Broken Wheel – Sara and Sara's. Though the bookstore was called officially Oak Tree Bookstore (a name to make Iowans proud!), everyone called it Sara's. It was there for anyone who liked to read. No order was too big or too small, and that was lucky, Jen wrote in a barely concealed stab at the neighbouring town, since it was the only bookstore for miles around. The newsletter didn't hesitate to recommend a visit soon!!! (Just to be on the safe side, Jen ended her article with multiple exclamation marks.)

For the first time, the people of Broken Wheel actually read their newsletter. The article was also printed out and pinned up in various places around town.

For the first time, it was also pinned up in Hope.

In Broken Wheel, there were many who said that Hope existed purely to be unkind to them, that it thrived on annoying them. In Hope, the inhabitants weren't quite sure whether Broken Wheel still existed.

Whenever talk of the neighbouring town came up there, it wasn't unusual to hear something along the lines of 'Didn't that place die out during the nineties?', or something equally smug and condescending.

Hope was a town so modern that it had a butcher, a greengrocer and a bakery, as though supermarkets had never been invented.

It was the kind of small town used in political campaign films, whenever politicians wanted to emphasise traditional, decent, American family values. Iowa's last two governors had done it, and both had won – clearly, according to those who lived there, thanks to those films. The town also straddled party boundaries. It didn't matter whether it was the Democrat Chet Culver or the Republican Terry Branstad, so long as their banners could be seen in public places. Hope was the kind of town where neat, well-ironed American flags could be seen fluttering in the afternoon sun long after the elections were over, even when the country was at peace.

No politicians ever visited Broken Wheel. It didn't find itself being courted by the men and women who governed it even towards the end of tightly fought elections in which, they claimed, 'every vote counts'. Whether that was because the politicians didn't think the inhabitants voted, or because they didn't even know the town existed, was unclear.

For Sara, the improvised party was followed by days of firm determination.

She was convinced that the inhabitants of Broken Wheel would buy books. They *would* do it, and not all of them would need to be tricked into it, regardless of what Tom had said. Though perhaps she would have to rethink the way she displayed the books.

She stared at the bookshelves in front of her. As things stood, the books were divided into three categories: thrillers, fiction and non-fiction. They were satisfactory categories as far as she was concerned, but maybe they weren't enough to entice the uninitiated into reading.

She had been to the hardware store to buy some thick, bright white card. It was now spread out in a fan shape in front of her. Fifteen sheets. She doubted she would need that many signs, but she might need a sheet or two to practise on. Next to them was a fat black marker pen, waiting for inspiration to strike.

What did people want to read about?

Classics, maybe? She shook her head. Even she didn't buy

books from the Classics shelves, despite the fact that she loved all the old British and American stalwarts.

Think, Sara, think. What would convince someone to buy a book? What convinced people to watch films? How hard could it be?

She laughed, picked up the pen and wrote, in big, clear letters: 'SEX, VIOLENCE AND WEAPONS', and pinned the piece of card up above the thrillers.

After that, it was much easier. The book of photographs depicting natural Iowa was the lone volume on the IOWA shelf. She thought about making one for Sweden too, but the only Swedish authors she had were Jens Lapidus and Stieg Larsson, both of whom clearly belonged among the sex, violence and weapons.

It was actually quite disheartening. Broken Wheel's only image of Sweden comprised sadomasochistic conspiracies and organised crime, with a touch of Serbian mafia thrown in to confuse things.

Amy's Lonely Planet guide to Stockholm was there too. Sara found it surprisingly moving, but also unfamiliar, as though Sara was seeing her capital through Amy's eyes. The historic buildings, the sun glittering on the water, the orderliness the entire guide promised; it was all a far cry from Sara and Broken Wheel.

She wondered whether Amy would have liked to see Sweden before she died, but she couldn't really imagine her or any of the others from Broken Wheel so far from their home town. They belonged here, as certain and constant as the buildings and roads. In the end, she decided against a Sweden shelf. She didn't really want to be reminded of home.

SMALL-TOWN LIFE felt like a given, when she thought about it. People wanted to read about themselves. The only problem was that the category involved a lot of sex, violence and weaponry too, but no categorisation system would be perfect.

She paused at Steinbeck's *The Grapes of Wrath* and *Of Mice and Men*. Clearly small-town life, but also with such loathsome endings that she wondered whether it was morally defensible to sell them. Eventually, she put them out anyway, but used one of the pieces of cardboard to cut out a smaller sign which she stuck up next to them. 'Warning: unhappy ending!' she wrote.

If more bookshop owners had taken the responsibility to hang warning signs, her life would have been much easier. Cigarette packets came with warnings, so why not tragic books? There was wording on bottles of beer warning you not to drink and drive, but not a single word about the consequences of reading books without tissues to hand.

There were, of course, some fantastic unhappy endings. Sometimes, you just needed an excuse to let the tears flow freely. On Sara's list of books which were irresistible despite being sad were: all of Erich Maria Remarque's books, Lauren Oliver's *Before I Fell* (a kind of depressed version of *Groundhog Day*), Louis de Bernières' *Captain Corelli's Mandolin* (despite what others said, Sara was adamant it was an unhappy book; the ending was a real disappointment – why would Captain Corelli suddenly turn into an idiot?). Jodi Picoult – Sara had shed floods of tears over *My Sister's Keeper*. Maybe Nicholas Sparks belonged there too, mainly because if you ever felt like crying a little about love, he always delivered.

Next, she placed Fannie Flagg's *Fried Green Tomatoes at the Whistlestop Cafe* under SMALL-TOWN LIFE, a book which also contained its fair share of unhappiness. People often thought that feel-good novels were happy, banal stories, but a real feel-good tale wasn't worth the name unless it involved a couple of murders, accidents, catastrophes or deaths. In the case of *Fried Green Tomatoes*, there were illnesses and deaths (at least two of them tragic), murder and cannibalism. The point was that it didn't end unhappily. They were books you could put down with a smile on your face, books which made you think the world was a little crazier, stranger and more beautiful when you looked up from them. Sara wondered whether she should make signs saying 'Happy ending guaranteed!', but maybe that would be revealing too much.

For Christmas, she would buy in copies of Fannie Flagg's less ambitious *A Redbird Christmas*, possibly the ultimate Christmas present. A story so charming that it could even be given away and enjoyed at midsummer. She resolutely pushed away the thought that she wouldn't be here by Christmas.

The last category was for those who really didn't read. She called it 'SHORT BUT SWEET' and placed all the books she could find under two hundred pages in length beneath it, as well as all of Hemingway. According to a popular and diehard legend, he had once made a wager that he could write a story in under ten words.

He won the bet: *For sale. Baby shoes. Never worn.*

Before long, her work organising Oak Tree Bookstore seemed to be constantly interrupted by customers from Hope who had somehow found their way to the shop. They were easy to spot. Firstly, they always drove cars, newish models, rather than the pickups and vans Sara had grown used to. Secondly, they always stopped at the red light. They started off looking surprised that a town like Broken Wheel had a traffic light, then irritated that it was red, then even more annoyed when they realised it was *always* red. When they finally arrived at the bookshop, they were ready to regain their lost composure.

On that particular morning, she was interrupted by a customer who looked around in confusion the moment he stepped into the shop, as though he still couldn't believe that Broken Wheel had a bookshop – this despite the fact that he had seen the shop window with his very own eyes and was now standing in the middle of the shop itself.

He nodded when he saw the yellow counter and the armchairs. If Broken Wheel was going to have a bookshop, he seemed to be thinking, at least it came as no surprise to find that it wasn't a normal one. He smiled when he saw the shop was empty and Sara could read his mind: 'They might well have a bookshop, but do they have anyone who can read?'

She wasn't amused.

Still, she should have been grateful. Most of the customers

from Hope actually bought books. She had sold her first few a couple of days earlier and for once had been able to use the cash register she counted up so carefully every morning and evening. Exactly fifty dollars in small change.

At the same time, there was no point pretending she wasn't bothered by the glances the Hope residents gave to one another when they saw that the shop was empty; as though they wanted to say that it was one thing opening a bookshop in Broken Wheel but something entirely different to keep it afloat.

This particular customer quickly left the bookshop with a Michael Connelly in hand, straight from the SEX, VIOLENCE AND WEAPONS shelf.

The Hope customers weren't Sara's only problem, though. A stubborn voice had taken up residence in her head and was refusing to leave her in peace. The voice constantly asked what she thought Tom was doing that very moment, or when she thought Tom might stop by the bookshop next, and wasn't it time to look out of the window to see whether . . . a certain someone was passing by?

She had no intention of giving in to it.

Instead, she carefully cut a sign from her white cardboard and wrote 'GAY EROTICA' on it, in the same big, clear letters as the other signs. She hung it above a special shelf and started filling it with books.

All the while not thinking of Tom.

The next day, she was interrupted by Jen, who opened the door and marched determinedly over to her. She was wearing a light pink sweater and an even lighter, almost white skirt. The overall impression was one of pale neatness, in marked contrast to her dogged expression.

'Can I help you with anything?' Sara asked.

'Men!' said Jen. She fixed her eyes on Sara. 'Have you heard anything from Tom?'

'From Tom?'

'Because I told him to ask you out to dinner.'

'Oh God,' said Sara.

Jen nodded. 'Exactly. You can't trust them. Maybe you should talk to him yourself. Sometimes they need a push.'

Jen stayed where she was, as though she expected Sara to say something.

'I can't ask him out,' she protested.

'Why not?'

'Honestly, I think he thinks I'm . . .'

'Yeah? Pretty? Mysterious? Interesting?' Jen said hopefully.

'Strange.'

If she had been on the hunt for books for herself, Sara would have appreciated a shelf clearly marked 'Chick lit to curl up with', preferably with a star confirming its quality was guaranteed. There was nothing worse than bad chick lit.

The good included: all of Helen Fielding (the *Bridget Joneses* plus *Cause Celeb*) aside from *Olivia Joules and the Overactive Imagination*. Elizabeth Young (the author behind *Wedding Date*. Gigolos always cheered romance up). Marian Keyes. Jane Austen.

Bad chick lit included: most of the titles which had appeared in the wake of *Bridget Jones*, seemingly in the belief that all you needed was a heroine who worried about her weight and had a gay best friend. They never seemed to realise that you needed a heroine with a voice of her own; a funny voice, self-mocking, but with a whole load of inner ballsiness too. And a proper ending. The only problem with a chick-lit shelf was that, so far, George was the only one who would have been interested in the books on it, so it felt like a misleading name.

What she really wanted was all those books you could sit back and read like a magazine, with a glass of wine or a Coca-Cola with ice and lemon on a Friday evening; or with a bowl of crisps on a lazy Sunday. The book equivalent of a Meg Ryan film. Enjoyable, easy-going stories with happy endings so certain that you didn't even need to think about them. Books where the heroine was always funny and the hero always handsome, or the opposite if the book had been written by a man, doubtless made into a film with John Cusack in the lead role.

Eventually, she simply wrote 'FOR FRIDAY NIGHTS AND LAZY SUNDAYS'.

After hesitating for a moment, she also placed Terry Pratchett there, with a smaller card beneath on which she wrote: 'Reliable author guaranteed!'

One of the most difficult things when you were trying to navigate the world of books was dealing with all the unreliable authors. They were so unbelievably tricky to keep track of. An author might write a brilliant book, only to follow it up with something utterly mediocre. Or, and this was almost worse, one might have written a brilliant book but then turn out to be dead. Then there were those authors who started a series but never finished it.

Sara's list of unreliable authors included: John Grisham. How someone could write books like A *Time to Kill* and *The Rainmaker* and then come out with completely flat, idiotic stories the rest of the time was a mystery. Maybe he simply pushed out all those other books just so the publisher would pay him his millions, but if that was the case then Sara wouldn't have hesitated to try to raise enough cash so that he could relax and take it easy, in exchange for only writing good books.

Reliable authors: Dick Francis, Agatha Christie, Georgette Heyer. Strictly speaking, Dan Brown also belonged here, she thought. He was so reliable that you got the exact same story every time. A kind, older mentor! Surely he won't turn out to be the villain?

Terry Pratchett, on the other hand, was reliability in a class of its own. It wasn't enough that he was producing books at a tremendous pace, he also took on an admirable amount of responsibility when he created new characters. He always alternated fairly between wizards, witches, Death and the rest, so all his readers got books about their favourites.

When he revealed that he was suffering from Alzheimer's, he comforted his readers by assuring them that he would have time for a few more books. His readers were loyal to him, too. When he donated a million pounds to Alzheimer's research, his fans started an online campaign called 'Match it for Pratchett', to raise an additional million. Sara thought that said a great deal both about humanity and books.

It was just as she was putting Pratchett's books on the shelf, organised chronologically by publication date, that she realised someone was watching her. The bookshop was empty but when she looked up, she saw John standing outside.

They simply stood there for a moment, Sara clutching four paperbacks and John with an expressionless, empty gaze which made her feel strangely nervous.

She smiled uncertainly at him, but it didn't seem as though he had even seen her. His eyes panned over the shop and the books, but it wasn't clear whether he was seeing any of it. He didn't seem disapproving, exactly, but there was something in his reserved posture and in the fact that he hadn't bothered to come in before which made her feel uneasy. She wanted to do something for him but she didn't know what. She wanted to ask him whether he thought Amy would have been against the bookshop, but didn't dare.

Then, a customer from Hope came in and John shuddered as though he had suddenly realised he was standing there. Sara turned reluctantly to the customer. The man looked at the sign she had just hung, and then back to her, and she met his eyes, challenging him to say something about it.

'The people from Hope don't think the bookstore's going to succeed,' said Sara. She was sitting at the bar in the Square with Andy and Tom. 'They don't think anyone here's interested in buying books.'

'We're not,' said Tom.

He had turned up at the Square after her, so she had convinced herself that she hadn't stood a chance of avoiding him. When he arrived, he had nodded, sat down next to her and absent-mindedly listened to the conversation she and Andy were having.

The voice in her head hadn't stopped. Now, it was nagging her to touch him, trying to convince her that it was completely normal to touch his arm simply as part of the conversation, or to touch his back in order to draw his attention to something, or his hand, which was worryingly close to hers.

He wouldn't even think it was strange, the voice was saying, people are always touching one another. She wrapped both of her hands around her beer glass to resist temptation.

'Of course you are,' she said, adding for the sake of honesty: 'Or you will be.'

'And that's not the point,' said Andy. 'The point is that they think they're so superior.'

'Aren't they, though?'

'What's Hope got that we don't?' Andy asked.

'Jobs,' said Tom.

'Apart from that.'

'Shops.'

'Ha!' said Andy. 'Have they got a bookstore, though?'

'Exactly,' said Sara.

Without really knowing it, her words had planted a seed of resistance. Or at least as far as Andy was concerned. But that didn't take much.

He was an enthusiast through and through – the type of person who embraced every new project that came his way. He was the first to welcome anyone new who turned up, and for him, every stranger was a friend he simply hadn't told his stories to yet.

Broken Wheel was his main interest, and it had been ever since he had moved back from Denver and bought the Square with Carl. Small-town life was the only real life, no one appreciated it as much as Andy, and homophobia in the countryside was nothing more than a myth and a big-city conspiracy these days. Carl endured Andy's convictions patiently, even though most people suspected that he hadn't been quite so keen on the idea of moving to Broken Wheel. Which was probably a good thing for the health of their unregistered partnership, since a relationship between two enthusiasts like Andy would have been too much for anyone. And their friends.

The seed which Sara's words had planted would soon blossom into full-blown madness. Andy phoned Grace, and together they came up with a simple, idiot-proof plan for defending Broken Wheel's honour and messing with all the condescending Hope residents who kept visiting their bookstore. Grace abandoned her principle of not getting involved in the town's business; any chance to mess with Hope was worth it.

The plan was genius in its simplicity: whenever a Hope customer appeared, Grace would be making sure that any Broken Wheel inhabitant who happened to be in the vicinity was sent over to the bookstore to calmly stroll between its shelves, buy books, ask about book orders, and generally act like someone who loved their bookshop and subscribed to the *New York Review of Books*.

Andy asked Carl about well-known authors that literary, educated people might read. Carl mentioned Proust, which would turn out to be an unfortunate suggestion.

'A Frenchman, too,' Andy nodded approvingly. 'Very good. Literary, educated people read obscure books.' He passed the name on to Grace.

The day the plan was going to be put into action, George made the mistake of visiting Grace's. He was only stopping by for a cup of coffee, but he was forced against his will into taking part. Andy had gone through everything one last time on the phone, and Grace had been standing in the doorway all morning, on the lookout for the first customer from Hope.

It was time.

Since the customer was still waiting at the traffic light, she spent a few minutes briefing George. With each word, he grew more nervous.

'Can't someone else –?' he asked, but she interrupted him.

'Just look educated. How hard can it be? Off you go.'

It was easier to agree than to stay and protest. He hesitated outside the bookstore, and glanced at Grace, who was gesticulating for him to go in. He snuck in nervously just ahead of the Hope customer.

He tried to hide himself in the far corner of the shop, looking literary. He didn't exactly know what that entailed, but he tried furrowing his brow and staring knowledgeably at the spines of the books. Unfortunately, he had happened to stop in front of Sophie Kinsella's *Shopaholic* series. At that moment, he was looking at *Shopaholic Ties the Knot* in a literary, educated way.

Sara looked questioningly at him before she was forced to attend to the customer from Hope.

He was in his fifties, and fat in the kind of way that comes from having an office job and long lunch breaks. He was also excessively tanned, the kind of tan that comes either from an addiction to barbecuing shirtless, or from a sunbed.

'Ha ha,' he said, rather than laughing. 'You must be Sara.'

She admitted that she was.

'Ha ha,' he said again. 'Only a European would come up with the idea of opening a bookstore in Broken Wheel.'

Somehow, he had managed to insult both the entire European continent and the whole of Broken Wheel in one fell swoop.

Two more people entered the shop. They were both wearing well-ironed, new-looking checked shirts, with gleaming buckles on their too-tight belts. It was obvious that the three of them had come to town together and that Suntan hadn't bothered to wait for the others. Impolite, Sara thought with satisfaction.

'From Sweden, aren't you?' asked Suntan.

Sara nodded. She was distracted by George, who had furrowed his brow even more and was now almost glowering at poor Kinsella's books. That in itself did actually seem quite literary.

'Not so many folks here,' Shirt Number One said to Suntan. Both Shirt Number Two and Suntan nodded.

Sara wished she was one of those people who could come up with a sharp retort on the spur of the moment.

'Can I help you with anything, George?'

He stared at her like a drowning man who has just had a life ring thrown at his head, and is still about to drown, but now with a headache. His hands were shaking more than usual, and tiny beads of sweat glistened on his forehead.

But the Hope customers' barely concealed criticism of Sara had given him enough courage to say, in as formal a tone as he could manage: 'I'm looking for books by Proos.'

He looked meaningfully at the customers. They didn't appear to care.

Sara mimed '-T' at him, like a prompter in the theatre.

That just confused him more. 'Proot?'

'Yeah,' said Sara. 'Proust. Of course. We don't have his *In Search of Lost Time*, unfortunately, but I can order them for you.'

'S . . . sure,' George stammered. 'Order it for me.'

'Them,' said Sara.

'It's more than one book?' asked George. He didn't quite manage to mask the panic in his voice.

'Seven,' said Sara.

The customers from Hope laughed. Outside the window, Grace had snuck over and was trying to look as though she was just standing there, smoking nonchalantly.

'European,' Suntan said to the Shirts.

'I actually voted no to EU membership,' Sara said to no one in particular, mostly because she felt as though she should say something.

'Did you know that I changed the name from French fries to freedom fries in all my restaurants a couple of years ago?' Suntan asked.

The Shirts laughed.

'Did you know that you got the Statue of Liberty from France?' Sara asked. 'So strictly speaking, your name change owes a nod of thanks to the French?'

A mean look appeared around Suntan's mouth, but he didn't say anything. The men left the shop without even buying a book.

She turned to George the moment the door closed behind them.

'OK, George,' she said, 'what was that whole Proust thing about? Do you really want me to order the books for you?'

'God, no,' he said. 'It was Grace's idea. Or Andy's.' He explained the whole fiasco.

She laughed. 'I can't believe you let yourself get drawn into it.' Then she remembered Suntan. 'But it wasn't a bad idea,' she added thoughtfully.

'Are you planning on doing it again?' George asked uneasily. He looked at the clock. 'Because I've got to . . . go now.'

'From a purely practical point of view, I think we'll have to develop the idea a bit. Maybe it would be best if I chose the book titles and authors in the future.'

Grace was trying to catch their attention to find out how it had gone. She gestured so wildly that the ash from her cigarette fluttered through the air.

'Not a bad idea at all . . .' Sara said to herself. A worryingly set look had appeared in her eyes.

Andy and Grace's idea had actually been alright, she thought. It was just that it had been on too small a scale. To really catch Hope off guard, they would need to mobilise the entire town.

Over the next few days, Sara called Andy, talked to Grace and visited Jen.

When she finally explained the plan to Jen over a cup of coffee, it was easy to convince her as soon as she mentioned the newsletter. Her boys were out playing, thankfully. Jen kept an eye on them through the kitchen window, while she nodded at the reworked version of Andy and Grace's idea. 'A book sale,' she said. 'Why not?'

Which, of course, would need to be advertised in the newsletter. The book sale was, of course, nothing but a pretence, but it was as good a reason as any to get customers from Hope to come. Once there, the inhabitants of Broken Wheel could dazzle them with their literary tastes and their unusually keen interest in books.

'Don't forget to put the newsletter up in Hope too,' she said.

'Book?' said Sara.

She was standing outside the shop, handing out books to anyone unlucky enough to walk past.

The elderly lady in front of her gripped her cigarette more firmly in her mouth and looked sceptically at her.

'A book, huh?' she said. 'Indeed.' She held out her hand. 'Gertrude.' Her handshake was hard and when she brought her hand back, she took the book Sara had held out to her with it.

'Sara,' she replied politely, though she suspected that the majority of the town already knew her name. She looked unhappily down at *The General's Daughter* by DeMille, which Gertrude was clutching.

Maybe she should be thinking more carefully about which books she was giving out. However good *Word of Honor* had been, *The General's Daughter* was little more than a foray into bondage, scantily clad as a thriller. Not quite as bad as *Spencerville*, but hardly the right kind of book for the woman in front of her. She made an attempt to swap it, but Gertrude was clutching the book so tightly that her knuckles were white. It had turned into a question of status.

'Read it on Saturday!' said Sara, though she hoped that Gertrude would never even open it. 'On Main Street, somewhere near the bookstore.'

No one was safe.

The minister from Amy's funeral also happened to pass by the bookshop at the wrong moment.

'Father!' said Sara.

He paused obediently. 'William,' he corrected her.

Sara was holding a new book. This time, she had chosen it with care, but now that he was standing in front of her, she was less certain. She had wanted to give something to the nervous minister and didn't think that anyone could fail to be charmed by Giovannino Guareschi's portrait of the Catholic minister Don Camillo Valota and post-war Italy. She hoped the minister would be taken with Don Camillo's conversation with Jesus, and his squabbles with the local communist leader, but religious people were sometimes a bit sensitive when it came to their prophets. Entirely understandable, Sara thought. She didn't enjoy it when people joked patronisingly about books.

But she didn't pause for long. 'Here you go,' she said, holding out the book.

'*The Little World of Don Camillo?*' he read aloud.

'I hope you'll enjoy it,' she said.

He made a movement towards his pocket and his wallet. She waved it away. 'No, no,' she said. 'It's on us.'

'Why?' He sounded confused.

'What's the point of having a bookstore if you can't share books with people who deserve them?' she said innocently. 'Read it. You're going to like it.'

She ruined the innocent impression by adding: 'And if you see anyone from Hope, you can always take it out and look as though you're captivated by it. On Saturday, ideally. Round here.'

'Why?' he asked again.

'Because . . .' She hesitated. 'They're so condescending, Father!' she eventually exclaimed.

'William,' he corrected her automatically.

She told him about the customers from Hope, about Andy's idea and George's Proos, more enthusiastically than coherently.

'My God!' he blurted out, blushing immediately. Then he leaned towards Sara. 'How will I know if they're from Hope?'

'They drive cars, stop at the red light and have well-ironed shirts.'

He nodded. 'There's a lot of truth in what you're saying.'

'And Grace will give a sign.'

It wasn't actually so strange that the minister decided to take part in Sara's campaign. He knew what it meant to be a disappointment and to be subjected to condescending jokes and glances. He had been 'Poor Will Christopher' for a long time now. And he didn't even drink.

He came from a long line of ministers. His father had been a minister, and his father's father, and a whole host of uncles. His great-aunt had wanted to be a minister and had caused some kind of scandal with her involvement in the civil rights movement. She had even had a brief fling with a black man. A preacher, of course.

His father had been just as charismatic and successful as the other men in the family. He had always known he would become a minister, but that hadn't stopped him from specialising in the pastoral care of young women during his teenage years. 'Son of a Preacherman' had practically been his father's signature tune.

And he had taught many, many women, if the nostalgic looks which the town's older women gave William were anything to go by. They looked at him as though they were remembering wonderful moments from their youth, expecting him to live up to his genes and make a move on their daughters at any moment. They always seemed disappointed when he didn't. Apparently they wanted their daughters to have as good a youth as they'd had. Most of the daughters had left Broken Wheel for bigger towns when the economic crisis struck, but William had stayed put.

Now he was the only minister in Broken Wheel and was responsible for all the common religious denominations. Baptists, Methodists and Presbyterians all turned to him when they couldn't make it to one of the many other churches in the surrounding towns. As a rule, the Catholics went to Hope. A Jewish family lived somewhere on the edge of town, and he had once hosted a bar mitzvah – with mixed results. An elderly man had once insisted he was a Druid, and had forced William to lead him in the worship of a tree.

That man was resting in peace now, thank God.

William assumed that some people were simply born to lead (his father had clearly been one of them), others to follow on, every now and then irritating their leaders with suggestions and opinions. Others seemed doomed to be left behind: they trailed along from the very beginning and never quite caught up. Else they stumbled at a point in their lives and ended up at the back that way.

That was how it was in all towns. Some were leaders, others were led.

He had accepted all of that by now, but there was something in Sara's new-found charisma which had given him a jolt. When she had first arrived in Broken Wheel, Sara had been quiet and polite and lost, not entirely unlike himself. Now she looked like a woman on a mission.

Surely it couldn't hurt to join her in putting up a bit of resistance?

Sara's campaign stormed ahead. Grace refused to believe she would enjoy a single book, but agreed to have one on the counter. Sara gave her Dylan Thomas's *Collected Poems*, the 2000 edition.

'The legend goes that he died in his room at the Chelsea Hotel after drinking non-stop for days. His last words, uttered when he staggered in to his lover, were: "I've had eighteen straight whiskeys; I think that's the record. I love you."'

'I see,' said Grace, looking more closely at the book.

Sara didn't think she needed to add that the general belief nowadays was that none of this was true. He probably hadn't drunk half that many.

Andy came by the bookstore to lend his support. The Square was too far away for him to take part in person, but he would have loved to see the Hope customers' reaction.

'Someone has to sell the alcohol,' said Sara.

'That's true, I guess.' He looked around the shop, froze, and leaned towards one of the shelves. 'My God,' he said, straightening up and spinning over to Sara. 'You got some gay erotica in!'

She forced herself to look completely expressionless, but the corners of her mouth were twitching. 'You asked me to,' she said.

'But I didn't think you'd actually do it. Caroline's going to have a heart attack.' He went back to the shelf to look at the titles more closely. 'Even though these aren't the most explicit. You should see some of the stuff you can get hold of online.'

She blushed, though she knew he was saying it just to embarrass her. She answered him surprisingly calmly: 'They're not so bad. You should give them a chance.' She walked round the counter and took two from the shelf. 'Try these, they're the best, I think.'

'Have you read them?'

'How else would I know what sells? And I actually know a whole lot about what you can find on the Internet, too.'

Much, much too much, she thought.

Andy laughed the whole way out of the bookstore, but not before he had taken both books. She hadn't let him pay.

A first victory, she thought, allowing herself a couple of improvised dance steps in the shop. And tomorrow, Broken Wheel would show Hope exactly what a town which read looked like.

The Readers of Broken Wheel Recommend

Sara was ready to take Hope on. She had drilled her fellow soldiers and felt like everything was set for their revenge.

The signal had been chosen and disseminated: when the first car appeared, Grace would go out, light a cigarette, and blow three smoke rings. After that, everyone would pull out a book and stare fixedly down into it, as though they were captivated by some fantastical literary adventure, as though they were generally the kind of people who spent their Saturday mornings reading in public. Under no circumstances would anyone name a book or an author. If anyone was near the store and Sara offered them a particular book, they would say yes.

Even the weather was on their side. It was a warm, sunny Saturday. Though half of September had come and gone, the warmth of summer still lingered in the air. It was the perfect day for anyone out for a stroll to stop, lean against a wall and read a book.

The last thing Sara had done was get hold of a new shelf, on which she placed every unreadable book she could find, alongside every Pulitzer Prize-winner, Nobel Prize recipient and nominee for the Booker Prize.

Sara had read a few, but far from all of them. Her knowledge of books had never been particularly systematic. On a few occasions, she had tried to improve it, to give herself a general education. If you were someone who spent the vast majority of your time with books then you should, at the very least, have read the Nobel Prize-winners and the classics, as well as all those books people talked about but had never actually read, as Mark Twain would have put it. She had thrown herself into one ambitious reading project after the other, but things had rarely gone to plan. It was boring to think of books as something you should read just because others had, and besides, she was much too easily distracted. There were far too many books out there to stick to any kind of theme. When she was sixteen, she had tried to work her way through the classics. She had gone all the way to the Stockholm City Library and practically broke down when she saw how many books there were. Too many to read during her lifetime, even if she had shut herself in there full-time, even if she had been able to speak that many languages. So she had pulled herself together and carefully written a minimum reading list for each letter of the alphabet. She had already read both Austen and Dickens, so that was something. But she needed to read one Dostoevsky, preferably two. One Bulgakov.

She had stopped at G, after Goethe's *The Sorrows of Young Werther*, mostly because she got distracted by Gabriel García Márquez and embarked on an odyssey of Latin American authors instead. Then she had seen the film of *A Walk to Remember* which set her off searching for Mr Rothberg's list of the best American authors, but she hadn't managed to find any trace of Mr Rothberg or his list. She had been forced to create her own list and had taken on Fitzgerald, Auster and Twain (when she got distracted by *Pudd'nhead Wilson* and switched to books dealing with racism). When she should have been reading the Swedish working-class authors, she read four novels by Moa Martinson but not a single one by Harry. She had read the majority of Shakespeare's comedies but none of his tragedies, and she had read all of Oscar Wilde. She had read many of the Nobel Prize-winners, but never before they had actually won the prize.

Amy had owned copies of plenty of Sara's more literary favourites, as well as works by a great number of other authors she looked forward to reading. Once she had placed them all on a shelf, she labelled it 'THE READERS OF BROKEN WHEEL RECOMMEND'.

She gained a certain satisfaction from carefully placing *In Search of Lost Time* on the shelf. Two copies of each of the seven volumes. She removed five and hid them behind the counter, to show that someone in Broken Wheel was currently enjoying the series in an educated and literary way.

When the first well-polished SUV rolled into Broken Wheel that Saturday afternoon, stopping at the red light, the town was ready. A few of the regulars from the Square had been sent over by Andy. One was holding his book upside down, another seemed dangerously close to falling asleep. Otherwise, everything was going according to plan.

William Christopher was leaning against the wall of the cinema, laughing with genuine joy at Don Camillo's conversation with Jesus.

Grace had forced books onto each of her customers, and made them pause mid-meal to gloomily eye the books by their plates. One customer protested, he was in a hurry, but Grace simply glowered at him – nothing more was needed.

George was sitting in one of the armchairs in the bookshop, not reading Proos. Sara had given him one of the *Shopaholic* novels instead.

And Sara herself was also prepared. She was standing in the doorway of the bookshop, ready to flash a friendly smile at the Hope customers the moment they stepped out of their cars.

'What the hell?' one man said, confused as he took in the scene before him and headed purposefully for the bookshop. A woman smiled spontaneously at Grace, who glared back at her.

Sara gestured frantically to Grace, who swapped her dark expression for a wide, friendly smile which caused the woman to take a step back in alarm.

Sara took over. 'Can I help you with anything?' she asked.

Broken Wheel was well on its way to seeming like a sunny, well-meaning and almost normal town. Even the asphalt seemed warmer and more friendly with people walking around, book in hand.

'I'm not much of a one for books, but this seems really good,' Gertrude admitted reluctantly to May when she was halfway through *The General's Daughter*.

May looked at the book sceptically. 'Isn't it a bit . . . nasty?'

Gertrude snorted.

Her window looked out onto a small corner of Main Street, where both cars and people, their heads deep in books, seemed to be gathering. 'What on earth is going on today?' May asked.

Gertrude had no idea, but she would never have admitted it. She therefore refrained from answering the question.

'And she gave you that book?'

Gertrude nodded. She turned it over in her hands.

May sighed dreamily. 'Wouldn't a nice love story have been better?'

'Nonsense. Princes and –'

'Yes, I know. Frogs.'

An hour later, May was gazing longingly at the beautiful weather. She glanced at Gertrude, dozing in the armchair with a cigarette still smoking in the ashtray and the book open on her knee. Perhaps she should take a walk? The sun was shining. She could go for a stroll and just happen past the bookstore on her way.

No one could say a thing about it.

It was hot and chaotic inside the bookshop. The Hope visitors were ambling around between the bookshelves, taking in the curious arrangement of books. One customer was nervously fingering James Joyce's *Ulysses* and Gertrude Stein's *Geography and Plays*, while another seemed to be wondering who in Broken Wheel had recommended Iris Murdoch's *The Sea, The Sea*.

May chose that moment to slip in. She pushed her way over to the counter. The Hope residents stepped kindly to the side for the grandmotherly figure, which unfortunately meant that they were gathered around her, facing Sara, when she leaned forward and said, in that kind of whispered tone audible to everyone:

'Excuse me. I'd like a couple of . . . *romantic novels*.' She glanced about, leaned further forward, and said just as loudly: 'Nothing *smutty*, though. Do you have any Harlequin novels?' she added hopefully.

The readers from Hope whispered and sniggered among themselves. Sara thought she heard the words 'losers' and 'Barbara Cartland'.

And when the customers from Hope finally left, the minister was the only person still reading. The regulars from the Square had dozed off over their books. Grace's customers had finished their meals and gone. The strollers had headed off home.

There was only one thing to do.

Sara laughed at the entire thing. She managed to keep herself together until the last person from Hope had left the shop, but then she laughed for several minutes over the fiasco with the Harlequin novels and the sleeping book lovers. Even once she had managed to pull herself together, her eyes were glittering with tears of laughter. She tried to keep a straight face as Jen talked about their success with the newsletter and the book sale. George was still sitting in the armchair; Andy had already called for a debrief on how it had all gone. Sara hadn't said a thing about the regulars.

'It makes me think we really should have some kind of tourist information,' said Jen.

It was all a bit much for George. 'Are you sure that's such a good idea?' he asked hesitantly.

'Why not? Now that we've got the bookstore, we should exploit it. There are a few nice things to do in Broken Wheel. Like . . . well, I'm sure we could come up with something if we put in a little effort. Effort. That's what we've been missing in this town. What about starting with a tourist information newsletter,' she said again. 'It's worth a try.'

'But what would you give people information about?' asked George.

'The Square, maybe? People could buy books here and then have a drink there – maybe we could even have dance nights. They used to have them, I know that much. My husband told me about them.'

'You should include a photo of Carl in the newsletter in that case,' Sara said absent-mindedly 'Wouldn't that attract visitors?'

Sara Lindqvist
Kornvägen 7, 1 tr
136 38 Haninge
Sweden

Dear Sara,

It's funny that you're so interested in our little town. I've been thinking about laughter today, so it fits that I should write a bit more about Andy. I've been thinking about laughter because Andy visited me, along with Tom and Carl, Andy's very good friend. Andy has laughter in his blood. He's also got wild, curly hair. Sometimes I think the two go together.

I don't think it was easy growing up with curls like Andy's. The girls were jealous of them, I know that, and the boys mocked them. But Andy always just laughed. Once, I heard a boy poking fun at him, saying that Andy had stolen his mother's curlers. Tom was furious and wanted to fight with them all, of course. Claire looked like she would've been happy to help. Tom takes things much too seriously sometimes. Not himself, but other people, especially his friends. That day, I was just thinking about whether I should step in when the whole thing was suddenly over and Andy was laughing so hard he was bent double, holding his stomach. 'Sorry,' he panted, 'but the idea that I'd dare steal anything from your mom is crazy.' The boy's mother was known for being quick to lash out. 'Can't you just see me trying to r-run' (he was laughing so much that he was stammering) 'away from her with my p-pockets full of curlers? L-like stolen apples.' The thought of stolen curlers was enough to make them all laugh, even Tom. I've often thought that laughter is the best defense, though it didn't work for Andy against his own father. It's always been some comfort to me that I was the one Andy came to when he decided to leave Broken Wheel.

Best,

Amy

Encouraging Homosexuality

News of the gay erotica shelf seemed to have spread far outside of town, almost as though Jen had written about it in the newsletter.

A few days after the book sale, a new customer came into the shop. He didn't look much older than twenty-five, but he moved with a self-confidence which made him seem older. As though, at some point in time, he had simply decided not to be nervous any more. Despite that, he didn't seem too sure what he was doing in a bookstore. He came in with determined steps and then just stopped dead. He was standing there straight-backed and with an almost aggressive glint in his eye, but there was something in the way he looked at neither Sara nor the books which said that he wasn't quite as comfortable as he would have liked you to believe. His face gave nothing away, but Sara thought he must be having some kind of internal debate with himself.

Eventually, she said: 'Let me know if I can help with anything.'

That made him walk slowly back and forth along the shelves.

'Are you from around here?' Sara asked.

'Nope,' he said, 'I live in Hope.'

'Do you like it there?' she asked for want of anything better to say.

'Not really.'

'Are you looking for anything in particular?'

With that, he seemed to make a decision. A boyish glimmer appeared in his eyes. She had meant a particular book, of course, but when he replied, he said: 'A boyfriend?'

She laughed. 'The shelf a bit lower down, to the left.'

'My mom told me about you. She said you'd burn in hell because you were encouraging homosexuality.'

Sara felt a certain amount of indignation at this attack from a woman she didn't even know, but she had to admit that she also felt a certain amount of pride. She, Sara Lindqvist, encouraging homosexuality! Who would have thought it? Good-humouredly, she said: 'What can I say? You can't buy that kind of publicity.'

He hesitated. 'Are you . . . ?'

It seemed to mean so much to him that she thought about lying. She liked him. She compromised. 'Bisexual,' she said, though she hadn't ever even watched the Pride Parade in Stockholm, and she blushed slightly.

He smiled. 'Aren't we all?' he said. 'You're not from round here, are you?'

'From Sweden.'

He nodded, as though that explained something. 'Ah,' he said.

He went over to the gay erotica. She continued reading. After a while, he came over to the counter with two books.

Sara had ordered nice plastic covers with a picture of an oak tree and the name of the shop on the front. She placed the books into these covers without even asking. He paid but then lingered for a moment, standing between her and the door without really making any attempt to leave.

'Can I . . . ?' she eventually asked.

'I'd hoped . . .' he said, hesitating. 'I'd hoped I'd meet others here.'

'The Square,' she said. 'Talk to Andy and Carl.'

'Are they . . . ?'

'Together.'

He didn't seem to know whether he should be happy or disappointed.

'Maybe they know somewhere good to go,' she added. 'Tell them I say hi.' She held out her hand. 'I'm Sara, by the way.'

'Joshua,' he said. 'But everyone calls me Josh.'

Sara's comment about Carl and the tourist information newsletter had been nothing more than a joke, but she suspected that Jen had taken it seriously. When Andy called to ask her to stop by the Square, she was full of apprehension.

'You'll never guess who came by today,' Andy said when she was finally sitting at the bar with a glass of beer in front of her.

'Who?' she said carefully.

He raised an eyebrow. 'Josh,' he said.

'Oh, right,' she said, relieved. 'I hope that was OK.'

'Sure. Why shouldn't we be every LGBT's personal ad?'

Don't go red, she thought to herself. For some reason, it all felt embarrassing. The constant fear of being politically incorrect, she thought.

Carl leaned over the bar, as though he had decided that she would no longer throw herself at him. 'It was a nice thing to do,' he said.

'So, Sara,' said Andy. 'Bisexual, are we? Still waters run deep . . .'

To her great relief, she didn't hear any more about Jen's tourist information plans. She wished she hadn't said anything, even as a joke. The newsletter featuring the opening of the bookshop seemed to be reaching further and further outside Broken Wheel, however, and was continuing to attract visitors.

There was a surprising number of people in town that Saturday. An overwhelmingly large proportion of them were large women in ugly jeans, checked shirts and dusty boots.

She couldn't take her eyes off them, in the same way that it was impossible to look away from a car crash. She still wasn't used to the idea that women like that really existed. Still wearing cowboy hats. Unironically. Didn't they know what films and books and TV series had done for cowboy paraphernalia? Had they never seen *Dallas*?

They came to the shop in groups, with a few of them buying books, and lingered afterwards. They never said more than was necessary.

Grace came over just as the women were squeezing into the bookshop. She wove her way up to the counter where Sara was pretending to read, leaned against it and looked demonstratively around.

'Once upon a time,' she said, 'all these women would have come to me.' She didn't bother lowering her voice. 'All these women – real, strong women the lot of them, I can see that right off. The kind of women who built this country.' She shook her head. 'That they're finally back in town, but around books, not liquor . . . it's not natural.'

Sara closed her book and looked up at Grace. 'What's wrong with meeting in a bookstore?' she asked. She gestured widely, including all the books. 'What's wrong with all of these real, strong women wanting to read about other tough women?'

'Bull. No one's ever written a book about the real USA. Just about namby-pamby men and their namby-pamby thoughts. Real life is hard, raw, *genuine*. Books are sugary-sweet, complicated, and far too obsessed with what everyone's thinking and feeling the whole time. And with a load of men, too. What have they ever done for Iowa?'

'Just because they're wearing cowboy hats and are tough and loud doesn't mean they can't enjoy books' Sara muttered. 'Why should books be reserved for namby-pamby men? If anyone deserves books, surely it's these fantastic women . . . ?'

She made another sweeping gesture with the book in her hand. Sure, she might have been more judgemental a minute ago, but a woman can change her mind, can't she? They clearly were strong, tough women, all of them. And ever so slightly scary. She would have continued her passioned, albeit whispered, speech if one of the strong women hadn't just come over to her and asked:

'Sorry, but do you know how to get to that bar?'

Grace laughed. 'So, girls,' she said, 'what're you really doing here in the bookstore?'

'The newsletter said it was worth a visit,' the woman replied. She glanced around as though she wasn't entirely convinced. 'And besides, the bar doesn't open till five.'

Sara looked at the horde of cowboy women with a strong feeling that something was going horribly wrong.

'We heard there were a few good reasons to visit the Square,' the same woman said. 'Or one, in any case.'

Sara had an extremely bad feeling about all of this. 'Don't worry,' she said gloomily. 'There are two.'

Tom was waiting for her when she got home from the bookshop. The Hope campaign had almost put an end to her keeping an eye out for him. Now, suddenly, he was standing right in front of her.

'Hi,' she said hesitantly as she walked up to the porch.

She stopped right in front of him, desperately trying to come up with something to say, if only so she could stand close to him for a while longer. It was one of those moments in life where time seemed to be going both unbearably slowly and much too fast, as though every second was ticking away in her body. She knew she would need to say something or move away from him soon.

Before she had come up with anything, he cleared his throat and said: 'Carl sent me.'

She blinked.

'He needed your help, he said you owed him. He sounded really stressed. I offered to drive you.' But he was still standing there, right in front of her, much too close for her to care about Carl and whatever problems he might be having.

'Now?' she asked.

'It seemed urgent.' He took a few steps away from her and opened the car door. She tried to feel relieved at being able to breathe again.

The first thing to hit her was the sound. She could hear it from outside in the parking lot, the deep, pulsing sound of loud voices and lively conversation between people crammed into a too-small space. The second thing to hit her was the heat. It struck her as she opened the door. Stale air and the stench of sweat, beer and warm bodies. The third thing was the absurd number of big, stocky women in unflattering jeans and cowboy hats.

'Jesus,' she said. 'There must be at least fifty of them here.'

Tom looked shocked. He stood in the doorway behind her, as

though she were his shield. 'Where've they all come from?' he asked.

'The bookstore,' she said despondently. She didn't have time to explain; Carl was waving to her, and he didn't look amused.

They pushed their way over to the bar. There was a real sense of urgency behind it. Andy was pouring beers and drinks at high speed, taking money at the same time, and smiling and joking with all of the customers. He looked like a slightly foolish but still incredibly professional Tom Cruise. Sara was sure that he would have juggled the bottles of spirits if the crowd had been the least bit receptive, but they were drinking Bud and whiskey and didn't want anyone to throw anything.

Carl was pressed up against the shelves and the mirror on the back wall. He was pouring beer by leaning forward, the rest of his body still at a safe distance. His face was completely expressionless, but there was panic in his eyes. Sara wondered whether she should tell him that his posture only made his shoulder and chest muscles look even more impressive. She decided not to risk it.

He was demonstratively touching Andy the whole time, calling him 'honey'. More than one of the customers thought he was saying 'honey' to them and they smiled in delight. More than one of the customers also managed to touch his arm or stomach as they reached out for their drinks.

'Sara,' he said doggedly, 'you'll never guess who came by the other day.'

'Josh?' she said hopefully.

'Jen.'

A woman pushed forward and ordered a whiskey. Carl served her quickly without letting Sara out of his sight. The woman gave a generous tip, but Carl didn't allow himself to be distracted.

'Any idea what she wanted?' Carl asked.

The woman with the whiskey glanced from Tom to Sara, sussing them out, and he quickly put an arm round her.

'No,' said Sara. The music and the voices around them were loud, but unfortunately she didn't have any problem hearing what

Carl said. Because of the crowd, she was practically forced to press herself up against Tom, and could nearly feel the sheer terror in his body.

'She wanted to take a picture. For the tourist information newsletter.'

'That woman knows nothing about advertising,' Andy suddenly said. He had to shout to make himself heard from his end of the bar.

'A picture of the Square in the newsletter surely isn't a bad idea,' said Sara. With the lightest of touches, she slid an arm around Tom's waist. When he didn't protest, she leaned in towards him and was captivated by the feel of muscle and rough denim beneath her hand.

'Exactly what I said!' Andy agreed.

'Only, she didn't want a picture of the Square, did she?' Carl said accusingly. 'She thought a picture of me would be more "appealing".'

Sara could hear the quotation marks around the word. She noticed that Tom appeared to be finding her discomfit amusing and she glared at him, as though they were one of those couples who laughed and teased one another.

'I offered to be in it,' said Andy. 'But she didn't think it'd have the "desired effect".'

'She was surprisingly shy when it came to whose idea it was,' said Carl. 'She didn't want to take the credit. Said it was all yours.'

'How could a picture of me not have the desired effect?' Andy continued, opening a beer and pouring three glasses of whiskey simultaneously.

'I just thought it'd be good publicity for the bar,' Sara said.

'How would having me in the picture stop that?'

Carl slapped a crumpled, slightly damp piece of paper onto the bar. It was a copy of the newsletter. Underneath a large – ridiculously large – picture of Carl, it read: 'The friendliest bar in Iowa: We live to serve.'

Next came an absurdly short box of text about the Square

which explained that they (not unlike other bars, Sara couldn't help but think) served alcohol and food, and that they were also very friendly and very, very service-oriented.

Jen had outdone herself. Tom was laughing now.

'I'm holding you personally responsible for anything that happens here tonight,' said Carl.

'Do I get commission?'

'If you take my place then you can have half my kingdom and my firstborn son.'

'You're gay,' Sara reminded him.

'We can adopt.'

'I don't want kids.'

'My kingdom?'

She laughed. 'Sure. Call me Queen Sara.'

She made a reluctant attempt to move away from Tom. He protested by pulling her towards him.

'Don't leave me,' he said desperately. She knew that it was only because the women around them were more terrifying than she could ever be, but all the same, she couldn't help but lean in for a moment longer.

Carl looked pleadingly at her, and she forced herself to leave Tom and go behind the bar. A woman tried to squeeze in alongside her, but Carl blocked her way.

Sara was surprised by how different everything seemed from that side of the bar. The warm crowd was transformed into a faceless mass which washed over her in waves. She had more space, though, and she could see the expressions of those closest to the bar, read their thoughts and hopes, and eavesdrop on their conversations (which, at that moment, all seemed to revolve around Carl and herself. Most of them seemed to be envious of her new-found, elevated position). Tom was squashed up against the bar only a few metres away.

'What do I do?' she asked, looking at the bottles and the glasses and the chaos around her. Slices of lemon on a chopping board, a sink with empty glasses in it; bottles, glasses and refrigerators along the wall. OK, Sara, she thought. Let's go.

'Open the beers and pour the whiskey,' said Andy, showing her where the bottles were. 'Don't worry about other drinks. Most of them just want beer and whiskey. If they want anything else, send them our way.'

'And whatever you do, don't be stingy with the whiskey,' said Carl. 'They'll burn the place down.'

Sara laughed.

'Hey, lady,' said one of the women. 'Two beers, two whiskey. And snappy. I'm parched.'

It took her three times as long as Andy or Carl to pour the whiskey. Payment went more smoothly; she'd had plenty of practice at that, after all. She quickly worked out the change and gave it to the woman, who kept it. The woman being served by Carl, on the other hand, left a tip. Sara's presence would seriously reduce their takings.

Three hours later, she was tired, hot and sweaty, and Tom had left without her noticing.

'Thank God that's over,' Carl muttered. He switched on the overhead lights and watched, relieved, as people stood up and started heading out. In their wake, they left empty bottles, spilled drinks, scrunched-up napkins and half-empty bowls of peanuts.

Carl poured each of them a whiskey and Sara slumped exhausted onto one of the bar stools, resting her weary feet. 'Thanks for tonight,' he said, which was surprisingly generous of him.

'Sorry,' she said.

'D'you think they were serious about coming back?' Andy asked.

'Seemed that way,' Carl replied as he went once around the room, picking up half-full glasses and used napkins.

'Especially if you organise that dance they were nagging you about,' said Sara. At any moment, she would get down from the stool and help him tidy up, but for now she simply sipped her whiskey and subtly tried to massage her feet.

'I don't dance,' said Carl.

'I do,' said Andy. He seemed inexhaustible and added, even more enthusiastically: 'A dance!'

'We don't have enough staff.'

'Sara can help.'

'We can't afford to hire anyone.'

'What about Josh?' said Sara. 'I'm sure he'd help without wanting to be paid much.'

'A dance,' said Jen.

'A *dance?*' said Caroline.

They were gathered in the bookshop once again. Sara was behind the counter, trying to read, but it was impossible, given that Caroline was standing right in front of her. Jen was sitting comfortably in one of the armchairs.

'It'll only lead to drunkenness and loose morals,' said Caroline.

'I can write about it in the newsletter,' said Jen. Caroline glared at her. 'The dance, I mean,' she explained.

'Improper,' said Caroline, but she seemed to be lacking her usual severity. There was something different in her eyes. Sara made an effort to avoid looking at her.

'Maybe,' she said innocently, 'maybe we can combine it with a market? For the church. A day for the entire family. With an organised, well-behaved dance at the Square in the evening.' Sara was sure that organised and well behaved weren't what Andy had in mind, but she thought it was best to avoid going into that with Caroline.

'The church does need money,' Caroline admitted.

Josh stopped by the bookstore two days later. The only other customer was a woman, wrapped in an elegant black scarf and wearing big, dark sunglasses. Josh looked admiringly at her. A woman with style, he thought. He couldn't be sure, but it seemed almost as if she was hovering around the gay erotica shelf, like he had done that first visit. He was on the verge of asking her what she was looking for, but then Sara greeted him and he turned to her.

'They phoned me, from the Square,' he said. 'They asked if I wanted to work there, they said I'd get paid in kind.'

Sara choked on her coffee.

'OK, so I'd quite like to pay them in kind. What he said was that I'd get to keep the tips. Apparently it's mostly women who go there, but generous women.' He clasped and released his hands. 'I can charm women, too,' he said.

'Sure you can.'

He looked around. The woman with the sunglasses had vanished. 'Who was the woman that was just here?' he asked.

Sara looked away. 'Ah, that was . . . I never reveal the names of my customers.' I really need to learn how to lie, she thought.

'Do you know what she wanted?'

'I have no idea.'

Josh shrugged, turned to leave, and then hesitated in the doorway. 'Thanks, Sara,' he said.

Caroline 0: Books 3

Caroline had found out about the arrival of sin in their little town, of course. She hadn't believed it at first, but her short reconnaissance in the bookstore had proved it. There it was, a whole shelf dedicated to it, as open as you please, right there in front of her.

She had, of course, been rightfully upset. She had left the shop as quickly as possible. It was unthinkable that Broken Wheel was selling gay porn. The very word was unthinkable.

Broken Wheel might only have one church nowadays, and a minister who left a great deal to be desired, but as long as she, Caroline, was around, then such a clear attack on virtue and propriety wouldn't be permitted. At least not until she had done her very best to prevent it.

Besides, you need a challenge, Caroline, she said to herself. She was an honest woman. She had started to get too comfortable and it had been much too long since she had achieved anything. Too comfortable and too faint-hearted.

She couldn't imagine that Sara would put up much of a challenge. The woman shrunk back in an irritating manner whenever Caroline went near her. Nice, without a doubt, but obviously not Christian in the way that Iowans were.

European. It explained a whole lot, but *not* the importing of gay porn into their upstanding, beautiful town.

Caroline marched into the bookstore ready for a fight.

Sara shrank back behind the counter just like Caroline had known she would.

'Sara,' she said ominously.

'Caroline?'

'You're selling *porn*.' Caroline was a woman who got straight to it.

Caroline had been a teacher in Broken Wheel's school for almost fifteen years. There were very few people in town that she hadn't, at some point, told off.

'Not at all,' said Sara.

'*Not at all?*' Caroline echoed. Whenever she was annoyed, her tendency to speak in italics became even more pronounced. 'I *can see* the shelf from here. You've *marked it out.* And now you're *daring* to claim that you aren't? Whatever faults you might have' (she said this in such a way as to imply that Sara had many), 'I didn't think dishonesty was one of them.'

'It's erotica, not porn.'

'Don't quibble with me.'

Caroline stared at her.

Sara looked her in the eye.

For a few seconds, at least, before she looked away. 'It's erotica. Literature. Stories about love and friendship. Sure, there's sex in them, but unlike *porn*' (she was unconsciously making use of Caroline's emphasis here, which made Caroline gasp at such overt provocation), 'it's not the main point. Even heterosexual love stories have sex scenes in them.'

'Are you really claiming there's no difference?'

'Yes,' said Sara. 'Unlike you, I've actually read them.'

'You've *read* them?'

'Yes,' Sara said again. 'I've always thought it's wrong to judge books, or people, blindly.'

'Wrong?' Caroline was aware that her face had turned an unflattering and shameful shade of red. The conversation wasn't going as she had planned, and an unpleasant thought struck her. She couldn't quite catch hold of it; it was just there somewhere, at the back of her mind, without really making itself known.

'Yeah. Un-American. Almost . . . unchristian.'

'*Unchristian?*'

The unpleasant feeling grew stronger. Caroline realised what was bothering her. Sara might have a point. And somewhere in her words, there had been a clear challenge. Caroline didn't normally shrink from a challenge.

'I've got to think about this,' she said heatedly, storming out of the shop.

She was very, very angry.

The minister was interrupted in his gardening by the shadow of Caroline's upright figure obscuring the plant he was busy with.

'William Christopher,' she said with clear distaste. He shuddered. She had been his teacher. 'Shouldn't the only minister in Broken Wheel have more important things to do than pulling weeds? It's not dignified.'

William sighed (albeit quietly, to himself) and stood up from the flower bed. 'Yes,' he said, and Caroline nodded. 'What can I do for you?' He had no doubt she was the one planning to help him, doubtless with something he hadn't realised he needed help with yet.

But she surprised him by saying: 'I've got a question I've been wondering about . . .' Her voice trailed off as though she was expecting him to say something.

He waited.

She seemed to be trying to find the right words, because she stood there in silence for almost an entire minute, before confusedly continuing: 'If you heard about . . . something which should be wrong, but you yourself hadn't experienced it, but had heard it was from reliable sources, and all logic pointed to it being wrong, would it be acceptable to judge something without having investigated it yourself?'

William hadn't followed what she was saying at all, but admitted that, as he saw it, and it was, of course, only his personal opinion, you could never be careful enough when it came to judging something about which you yourself didn't have all the facts; or even when judging at all.

Caroline snorted. Not judging something was also a judgement, and not doing something was also an act. But he had given her an answer, and she admitted to herself that he may actually have been right.

The whole thing was deeply unpleasant.

She sighed. 'Thanks so much,' she said, and William winced. 'You're welcome,' he stuttered.

Having Caroline ask him for advice and then thanking him for it made him nervous.

She marched back to the bookstore.

'OK,' she said, after having made sure the shop was empty. 'Give me one.'

'One what?'

'One of those books.' She couldn't bring herself to ask for gay porn. 'I'm a fair woman,' she said in a dignified manner. 'As you rightly pointed out, it's wrong to judge something blind. Or unread, in this case. So give me one.' And she added, ominously: 'I'll tell you what I think later.'

Sara stared at her. When Caroline showed no sign of changing her mind, she moved cautiously over to the shelf of gay erotica and placed one of the books into a protective cover. Caroline nodded and paid without a word.

But once she was home, she didn't know what she should do with it.

There and then, in the heat of the moment, she may have agreed that it was unchristian to judge something without having read it first, but alone in the privacy of her home, she wasn't quite so sure.

The very thought that *she* had *one of those* books in her house made her break into a cold sweat.

She was drawn to it time and time again. First, to make sure the cover image wasn't visible through the protective wrapper. Then to put it beneath a pile of newspapers in the hallway, just to be on the safe side. Then to make sure that the title on the spine wasn't visible. Then to move it and hide it behind the embroidered picture on her nightstand, in case someone happened to come by and leaf through the newspapers. She shuddered at the thought.

Each time she gave in to the impulse to pick the book up, it grew stronger. A soft, tempting voice cajoled her: are you really going to judge it before you've read it? the voice reminded her. Then: how dangerous can one little chapter be, after a long and God-fearing life?

The book seemed to be staring at her. It had been a long time since something had managed to make her feel so uneasy. *No one* had managed to outstare her in over twenty years. Still, this little book was forcing her to avert her gaze and look away.

It was lying there in its sleeve, covered with calming, beautiful oaks. *Oak Tree Bookstore* was printed in the same warm yellow as the autumn leaves in the picture. But beneath it, the picture of two half-naked men embracing one another seemed to shine through like neon lights in the seedy area of a big town.

Filth! Filth! Filth! it seemed to be shouting to the world.

Surely no one would believe that she *wanted* to read it? Though it was certainly suspect to have it hidden in her bedroom. Carefully and deliberately hidden. Maybe she should leave it lying around, openly and demonstratively. Look what they're selling in the bookstore, she'd say indignantly to Jen if she came by.

She took two steps towards her bedroom before she paused. Good Lord, what was she thinking of? Having a book with two near-naked men lying in the hallway? And telling Jen about it? That would certainly give her something to talk about.

The book could stay where it was.

She slept uneasily beside the book. Each night, its power over her seemed to grow. The lack of sleep made her jumpy and unfocused, and she walked restlessly around the house in a way that was clearly improper for a woman of her age.

She decided to read a chapter, for the sake of research. She could have sworn the book was laughing at her when she finally picked it up.

'If other books are as shameless as you, it doesn't surprise me that people have been burning you on pyres for centuries,' she said as a rebuke, which seemed to make it fall silent. She smiled in satisfaction.

She steeled herself and opened the book. Fifteen years as a teacher, she reminded herself. Nothing scares me.

She started reading.

Sara Lindqvist
Kornvägen 7, 1 tr
136 38 Haninge
Sweden

Dear Sara,

Tom has never been much good at accepting help, or at admitting he might need any. I'm writing this with love, of course. Sometimes I think he's very lonely, but it's nothing he would admit to himself. Actually, I think he would argue that he doesn't need anyone at all. Or anything. If I told him that he needed oxygen, he would shake his head, smile, and tell me not to worry about him. 'I'll be OK,' he would say, and it's not at all impossible that he would believe he really was the only person on Earth who didn't need to breathe. There's a fine line between independence and stupidity, if you ask me.

When Andy fought with his father and decided to move to Denver, he spent the night at my house. I was a widow by that point, so I didn't need to explain anything to my husband. I never told anyone that he stayed with me that night, or that it was my money which paid for his bus ticket and put a roof over his head for the first couple of weeks. He went to Denver because he wanted to leave the whole state, not just Broken Wheel. I don't know if he ever forgave his father, but back then, I just hoped that the distance would make things easier.

I don't want you to think that Andy just took my money. He's as proud as Tom and Claire, it's just that his is a different kind of pride. I think he just needed to feel that there were people who cared whether he had a roof over his head or not, but a month or so after he left I got a parcel. In it was all of the money I'd lent him, plus a postcard of a barely dressed man. I didn't want the money back, but I was really grateful for the postcard. It showed that he could still laugh at life.

Best,

Amy

Dream Inflation

Now that the bookshop had been open for a little while, Sara was really starting to enjoy her days there, but it was a melancholy kind of enjoyment. She had started leaving the door ajar so that the scent of damp autumn air could mix with the smell of the books. For as long as she could remember, she had thought that autumn air went well with books, that the two both somehow belonged with blankets, comfortable armchairs and big cups of coffee or tea. This had never been clearer to her than right there, in her very own bookshop.

In Sara and Amy's bookshop. That was what was so sad about it. She was constantly coming across things she should have asked Amy about. They had exchanged letters for more than two years, but there was still so much she had forgotten to ask. What had she even written about?

'Do you believe in throwing books away?' she asked Amy now, putting the question to the silence. She tried to avoid talking to Amy whenever there were customers in the shop, but now, just before the market, the majority of people in Broken Wheel seemed to have better things to do than visit her.

She was busy preparing a new shelf. She was leaning towards calling it 'MEET THE AUTHORS' and was thinking about ordering in some more literary biographies. So far, there were three books on the shelf, but she thought she could also put books about books there. In fact, Helene Hanff was the reason she was now wondering what Amy had thought about throwing books away.

She had just put 84, *Charing Cross Road* on the shelf. It was probably one of the most charming books about books that had ever been written, even after *The Guernsey Literary and Potato Peel Pie Society* had come out. The outspoken American Helene Hanff's fantastic exchange of letters with an exceptionally British antiquarian was followed by the almost equally good *The Duchess of Bloomsbury Street*, which was all about Helene Hanff finally arriving in *her* England.

Miss Hanff couldn't understand people who didn't throw books away. For her, there was nothing less worthy than a bad or average book, but Sara didn't agree.

They were still *books*.

Sara sold them on or gave them away, but she couldn't throw them out. Not even when they were so bad that she wondered whether it was defensible to share them with innocent new readers. She wondered what Amy would have thought.

When it came to biographies of authors, Amy had owned one about Jane Austen, one about Charlotte Brontë, and a novel about the Brontë sisters' lives, *The Taste of Sorrow*. Fitting. Sara sighed. So far, her authors' shelf was very sparse.

'Do you think writing books makes you happier or unhappier?' she asked as she placed the Jane Austen biography on the shelf.

She hoped the authors had been happier. She had always hoped that Jane could have looked out over her surroundings and thought: 'I can create a better world than this', or 'You're much too unbearably boring, and perhaps I can't say anything about it without being impolite, but you are going to be absolutely wonderful in my next book. I need another ridiculous minister.' Still, Sara couldn't help but wonder what life must be like if you couldn't daydream about Mr Fitzwilliam Darcy (*how* had she decided on that name? One of literary history's most inexplicable mysteries), because you yourself had created him.

She had first read *Pride and Prejudice* when she was fourteen, and for a long time, it had almost ruined Jane Austen's other works for her. Other books in general, in actual fact, not to mention real men. It was such a perfectly formed world that it had been a disappointment to be forced to leave it. The best women ended up with the richest, most interesting men; the next best got the next richest, and so on. After that experience, Edward Ferrars was no longer rich enough, and also, Sara thought, even though she shouldn't have been judging anyone, he was a touch too feeble. *Mansfield Park* was certainly intoxicating and sharply written, but Sara had trouble forgiving Edmund Bertram for not falling for kind Fanny Price until much too late in the book, and then only in a vague, absent-minded way. She could enjoy them all now and thought that *Persuasion*, with its gentle melancholy, was almost as good as *Pride and Prejudice*, but it had needed years of work. She hadn't even had the good taste to be upset by *Sanditon*, Jane Austen's last, unfinished work. Secretly, though, she enjoyed both the first fifty pages – written by Jane herself – and the rest of the book, which was wildly and not particularly faithfully written by 'Another Lady'.

'Do you think Jane had stopped dreaming by that point?' she asked Amy.

Amy didn't answer, and Sara picked up the novel about the Brontë sisters. She had decided not to read it; thinking about them was much too depressing. Charlotte Brontë's great dream in life had been a house by the water, somewhere she could live with her brother and sisters, and perhaps continue writing. Ideally without also having to teach and run a school in the house, but that wasn't essential.

That was all, and yet as a dream it was still out of her reach, almost foolish to think of.

Sara thought that, nowadays, everyone seemed to be dreaming of absolutely everything. Travelling and loving and having a fantastic career and a happy family, all while being thin, beautiful, popular and in touch with your spiritual side.

'Amy,' she said, 'do you think our dreams are subject to inflation?'

'Yes,' a voice replied from the doorway. Sara jumped, turned round guiltily and saw Tom standing there with an amused look on his face.

She wondered whether he had heard her saying Amy's name. She decided to assume he hadn't. 'You're probably right. But does having dreams make us more or less happy?'

He shrugged. 'I don't think dreaming has ever made anyone happier.'

Sara agreed, but sometimes she wondered whether it didn't

make people more . . . alive. She didn't think Tom was someone who dreamt much especially, and that bothered her slightly. All the same, she had never had a single tangible dream. The other girls from the bookshop had all seemed to want to do things. Travel, if nothing else. Save up for holidays. Have children or meet someone or renovate the kitchen. *Real* things that they could fantasise and talk about at work. Sara had simply read.

But her time in Broken Wheel had made her think about what she had actually *done* in Sweden. Her evenings and free weekends were just hazy memories now, blending into one another. It frightened her, and she doubted she would be happy simply reading books and working in the future. But how, exactly, did you become someone who had dreams and goals? Sara couldn't help but think that she had somehow missed the moment when life was meant to begin. For a long time she had simply been drifting through it, reading, and while everyone around her had been teenaged, unhappy and foolish, this hadn't been a problem. But then suddenly everyone had grown up around her and she, she had done nothing but read.

Until now. She was still reading a lot, of course, but there were other things. People talked to her. Sometimes they even actively sought her out, and there had been a few occasions when she had actually decided to put down her book. She could read it later, she had thought, which in itself was a strange new feeling.

'Cup of coffee?' she asked. 'I just put a new pot on.' He nodded almost imperceptibly, as though he had been planning on saying no but had given in against his will.

She had brought a couple of real cups to the bookshop and she now poured a coffee for each of them, its aroma spreading through the room.

'Do you think Amy was a dreamer?'

Tom sat down in one of the armchairs and she settled down in the other, curling her legs up beneath her so that she could lean against the armrest and turn towards him.

'No,' he said, but then he hesitated. 'Actually, I don't know.'

Sara nodded. 'There was so much I never got a chance to ask her about,' she said.

He surprised her by saying: 'What about you? What's your dream?' He sounded almost ironic, but Sara thought she could also detect a serious undertone in his question.

'I don't have one,' she said quickly, taking a sip of her coffee so that she didn't have to say anything else.

'What are you going to do when you go home?'

She brushed the thought aside. *Home.*

'Start another bookstore?'

She shook her head. That was something she knew for certain. 'You need lots of things for that. A business plan, for starters.'

Tom looked around the shop, raising his eyebrows. 'I guess it might help.'

You definitely needed capital.

'Tom,' she said, 'do you think John has anything against this? The bookstore, I mean,' she added quickly, but what she really wanted to ask was: Do you think he has anything against *me*?

'Why would he?'

'Because of Amy, I mean. It's just that . . . he hasn't even been in here.'

'I don't think John cares about much any more.'

They were quiet for a moment after that, until Tom looked down into his empty coffee cup and said, almost to himself: 'I should probably get going.' But he was in no hurry to leave, and Sara didn't have anything against putting off reading a while longer.

She didn't know whether it was because he actually seemed to be enjoying just sitting next to her, or because she suddenly didn't want to spend another evening alone, cooking for herself, but something made her ask: 'Do you fancy coming for dinner tonight? At Amy's?'

She might not have been able to do anything else for him, but she could surely throw together a meal. He surprised her by answering: 'Sure. Sevenish? I've got a couple of things to do first.'

'OK,' she said, trying to control her panic. 'Seven sounds good.'

She had been planning to close early and do some shopping at John's, so that she would have plenty of time to get everything sorted, but she was delayed by Gertrude and May who had come by on one of their book-buying trips. They had started coming in after the reading campaign.

To begin with, it had been obvious that Gertrude was just coming along to mock May's choice of books. The first thing she had said to Sara was: 'Ha! Princes! Nothing but lies!' and then she had broken out into a fit of coughing that could just as easily have been laughter.

They came by a few times a week, when May picked up more books and Gertrude quizzed Sara on her literary taste.

'Do you believe in all that? Romance and all that rubbish?' Or: 'Why are they all so weirdly dressed? Would you sleep with a man with long hair and a silk shirt? *Lilac!* Silk! And it's not even buttoned up.'

Sara let May have her books free of charge, so long as she brought the others back. They had stopped by only the day before, when May had picked up five new Harlequin novels and Gertrude had even agreed to take something from the SEX, VIOLENCE AND WEAPONS shelf. 'No romance,' she had said threateningly, and Sara had given her *The Girl with the Dragon Tattoo*, just to be doubly sure there was no romantic love story even as a subplot.

Now, Gertrude was heading straight for the counter with quick, jerky movements. As she came closer, Sara could see that she had dark bags beneath her eyes and a desperate, haunted gaze.

'Quick!' she said, gripping the counter. 'The second part. I need the next book.' Then she seemed to come to her senses and reluctantly stood up straight before adding, more calmly and almost apologetically: 'Lay awake half the night reading. Even forgot to smoke.'

May looked as though nothing surprised her when it came to

Gertrude, but she still asked, nervously: 'You've got it, haven't you? Part two, I mean?' as though her peace of mind too depended on it. It probably did, Sara thought. An incomplete series could be catastrophic, even for those around you.

She smiled reassuringly at them. 'Of course,' she said. 'Do you think I'd sell the first part to you if I didn't have the rest?' She left the counter and went to fetch *The Girl Who Played with Fire* and *The Girl Who Kicked the Hornets' Nest*. In English, all of the titles began with *The Girl* . . . It might have made them sound a bit catchier, but Sara had always thought that *The Girl with the Dragon Tattoo* was a strange translation of the original Swedish title, *Men Who Hate Women*. She placed the two books on the counter in front of Gertrude. 'You might as well take both,' she said, as she went back behind the counter.

'*Two* more?' May asked with something like dread in her voice.

'Damn it,' said Gertrude. 'I'm not going to be able to sleep for days.' As soon as Gertrude had paid – she refused to hand back the first part of the trilogy in exchange – Sara closed up the shop. She still had no idea what she was going to cook, though it was already past five. She quickly turned out the lights, locked the door behind her and walked over to John's.

Not much had changed in the hardware store since her first visit. This time, she automatically picked up one of the old baskets from the doorway. There wasn't enough choice to make impro-vised shopping appealing, but she had never bothered to ask George to take her to any of the bigger shops on the other side of Hope. Now she was wondering what she could cook for dinner.

The last week she had been on a mission to try some real American food, but so far she hadn't been very successful. Her mac and cheese had been, well, disappointing. It had tasted exactly like Swedish pasta with cheese. She'd googled traditional American food, but as far as she could see, there were no tradi-tions to follow. No one seemed to want to cook American food the same way as anyone else.

She was doing her best not to keep glancing at John, or at least not so that he noticed. He was still distant every time she went in; not withdrawn exactly, just slightly . . . absent. Eventually, she decided upon an autumn-inspired meat stew, mostly because there were plenty of meat cuts and root vegetables in the shop. She paused at the limited selection of wine John stocked and picked a bottle of red. If nothing else, she could put it in the food.

When she paid, John went through all the necessary motions, but completely without feeling, without even looking at her. She held out the money, he gave her the change, and when she said 'thanks a lot', he looked at her in confusion, as though he no longer knew what he was meant to say.

'John,' she said spontaneously, 'I'm so sorry . . . about Amy, I mean. She meant a lot to me.'

But he simply looked at her in alarm and so she retreated to safer ground, picking up her bag of food and saying another feeble 'thanks' before fleeing.

Sara Lindqvist
Kornvägen 7, 1 tr
136 38 Haninge
Sweden

It's not possible!

We've been exchanging letters and books for months and I still haven't sent you *Dewey: The Small-Town Library Cat Who Touched The World* – probably the most charming book about Iowa ever written, and a source of constant state pride for me. It's got to mean something, living in a state which has had a library cat. I'm enclosing it now, anyway. I think it says something about how much meaning books can bring to a community on its knees – or, in this case, what a cat in a library can bring.

I've always thought that books have some kind of healing power and that they can, if nothing else, provide a distraction. Tom tells me he's seen 'For Sale' signs in Hope again. They used to be everywhere during the last crisis, both there and in Broken Wheel, but I suppose there isn't really anything left to sell here this time. How I hate those signs. During the crisis in the eighties, I developed a real rage toward them. They were always *there*. People being forced to sell their old homes, and then there was never anyone to buy; when they did manage to sell them, it didn't even cover their mortgage debt.

I think that towns in crisis need something to rally around, and in Spencer that was Dewey, the library cat. They found him in their book deposit box one icy January morning and named him after the Dewey classification system. They had a proper naming competition for him some time after that, but by that point people were already accustomed to Dewey. They often used to have competitions there, but they were never really very interesting. A competition with a prize might attract fifty entries, and if the prize was really expensive, like a TV, then they might get seventy. In the 'Give the cat a name' competition, there were 397 entries. Most of them wanted to keep the name Dewey, but they added 'Readmore Books' to make it worthy of him.

Dewey used to take naps in the box of library cards, in the box of return forms and in the box of tissues, on visitors' laps or in their briefcases. When people started turning up to use the library's computer to look for jobs which didn't exist, he sat on their knees.

I want to think that it helped.

Best,

Amy

Not a Date

It wasn't a date, of course.

Tom was just hoping Sara knew that too. If he was honest, he wasn't quite sure why he had said yes. He had been planning to go home, maybe have a beer, and drop the planks off later that evening, when Pete was back from work. It struck him that he didn't know whether Pete was working nights that week, so maybe it didn't matter when he dropped them off.

Tom headed over there right away to get it over and done with, and stacked the planks in a neat pile against one of the walls.

It was probably just as well if Pete wasn't in. He would have insisted on paying, but Tom had no intention of taking his money. Like always, it would end with Pete's wife giving him more food and home-made jelly than he could eat.

When Tom first got to know him, Pete had been a furniture maker. The exclusive kind. His business had been successful and he had often made use of Mike's for moving the furniture; he had a sweet wife and a house big enough to impress others in a town like Broken Wheel.

But he had been forced to close the business because of the recession, when people could no longer afford to spend their money on luxurious dressers, or didn't even have homes in which to put them. There were bigger towns out there, of course, and even more exclusive businesses which catered to richer customers who still had money. Tom had been round for long enough to know that no matter how deep a crisis was, there would always be people still earning money. Sometimes despite the crisis, sometimes because of it. He had also been round long enough to know that those still earning money would have no problem at all buying expensive, handmade furniture while the rest of the country could barely afford a good square meal a day.

But Pete's furniture hadn't been lavish enough for those luxurious companies or for the big towns, and so he had found work in two different superstores and was grateful for all the extra shifts he could get. It wasn't possible to live on six dollars an hour, however many hours you worked. The bank had taken the house and Pete and his wife had moved here, to a barely inhabitable cabin.

Three of the window frames were coming loose, the paint had long since flaked from the walls, and Tom was sure that it must leak when it rained, or at the very least during the worst of the autumn storms. The cabin itself consisted of a living room, small; a kitchen, even smaller; and a box room masquerading as a bedroom, in which you could barely fit a bed.

The planks were for fixing the porch. It was only a couple of yards long, but it acted as an extra room during the summer. Half of the existing planks were rotten, meaning it was only possible to enter the house if you knew where it was safe to stand. Maybe Tom could get them enough wood to turn it into a proper room.

He thought about leaving a note, but it was almost six and, date or not, he still needed to take a shower first.

He had almost made it back to the car when he heard the unmistakable sound of the inner door opening, followed by the sound of one of the planks creaking.

'Tom?' Pete's wife said, and he forced himself to smile before he turned around. She was wearing a pale blue cotton dress, thick socks and a knitted sweater, with one of Pete's jackets over the top. It must have been impossible to heat their cabin.

'Katie,' he said, waving awkwardly. 'I was just dropping off the planks.'

She glanced at the neat pile by the side of the house. 'Have you and Pete . . . straightened it all out?'

'We'll work it out later.' He prayed silently that she would take that to mean her husband would pay later and wouldn't force anything edible on him.

She looked hesitant. 'I don't know . . . he thought he'd be here when you came by.'

'I had to change my plans. I'll stop by later this week.'

'OK . . . But please, wait a minute.' She disappeared indoors and he fought the impulse to run. Just not the apple sauce, he thought. He already had a full shelf of it in his kitchen at home. He hadn't yet come up with anything he could cook which would go with it.

The cabin came with a small patch of land, and Pete's wife spent most of her time growing a kitchen garden that provided something to eat for as much of the year as possible. Whenever something was in season, she always managed to create new dishes with it, preserve some of it and give plenty of it away to neighbours who didn't have the time or space to grow their own.

Tom knew that Pete often took home food when its best-before date had passed, and when things were really bad, Katie would queue up for food stamps behind Pete's back. Somehow, they survived, and they never complained. Whenever Tom helped Pete or Katie, they would always offer him food, though he suspected that they themselves got by on one meal a day.

She came out again with a jar in her hand.

'Here,' she said. 'Some apple sauce.'

He nodded. 'Thanks a lot.' Then he smiled at her and, without hesitating, lied. 'I just finished the last of the previous batch,' and she smiled back, relieved to have managed to give him something.

When he finally made it home, it was almost half past six, but he still allowed himself a shower. As the hot water massaged his shoulders and back, he could feel the day's and life's tensions washing away. He took his time, closing his eyes and raising his face towards the water. It was his favourite moment of the day.

It wasn't a date, of course.

Sara was just hoping Tom didn't think that was what she had meant. Just a simple dinner between friends.

Not that it made things any easier, because she had about as much knowledge of how to host a dinner between friends as she did of going on a date.

When she had got home, she had unpacked all of the food onto the kitchen bench, taken out one of Amy's big iron saucepans and then stopped. Should she start with the food, so it would be ready when he arrived? Or was it more important that she had at least showered before he turned up?

She compromised, browning the pieces of meat with the onions before heating the stock and putting it all on the stove to simmer away while she got herself ready. The shower still wasn't anything more than lukewarm and the pipes were still giving out worrying sounds. She hoped that the boiler wouldn't give up. She still had some of her money left, but she would rather not spend it on a new boiler, and she had no idea about how to fix one. She smiled to herself as she imagined Tom's face if she asked him for help with it.

Though he would probably just shrug and then turn up after work to fix it.

She quickly washed her hair and stepped out of the shower before she had time to get cold. She wondered whether she should put something nicer on, but eventually just settled on a pair of jeans and a cotton blouse. She paused, contemplating what little make-up she had, and decided that a bit of mascara couldn't hurt.

Between friends, nothing else.

Down in the kitchen, the meat, onions and stock were simmering away nicely, and she moved on to the potatoes, carrots and thyme.

While it was all cooking, she rinsed two of the nicest plates in the cupboard – fine, cream-coloured porcelain with a thin ring of roses around the edge – and two wine glasses which seemed not to have been used for a long time.

She poured a glass for herself, mainly because it made her feel grown up and almost normal to be standing in the kitchen, waiting for a friend, with a stew cooking on the hob and a glass of wine next to it.

It was such a fine evening that she felt she had to take a quick walk in the garden. She still had to make the salad, but that could just as well wait until Tom arrived.

She pulled on the rubber boots which were always in the kitchen, went outside and left the kitchen door open behind her. The light from the window and the door illuminated the ground a few metres in front of her, but after that darkness began creeping into the grass.

It wasn't completely dark yet, but dark enough for the garden to seem cold and abandoned compared to the warmth of the house. Out of pure curiosity, she went over to the old potato patch and squatted down, digging a bit and pulling on a plant which gave her five small potatoes joined together by a web of thin, earthy stems.

She brushed the soil from them and carried them towards the house, but she didn't go straight in. She could smell cool, damp earth, so strongly that she could practically taste autumn with every breath she took. There was something so alive about the crisp air when you had been indoors all day.

In Sweden, she had never bothered growing anything. She had actually never even owned a potted plant. Now, though, she was thinking about tidying up the garden and restoring it to some of its former glory.

She had just started to shiver slightly when a jacketed figure appeared magically in her line of vision.

She held out the potatoes to show Tom how resourceful she was.

'I knocked,' he said, 'but when no one answered I just came in.'

She was glad they had met outside. She needed a moment or two to get used to having him around.

'I brought a bottle of wine,' he said. 'I left it in the kitchen.'

She glanced back at the kitchen and saw a bottle next to the one she had opened, exactly the same kind. She smiled.

'There's not much to choose from at John's. They're normally OK.'

When they stepped into the light again, she could see that his hair was still damp from the shower and she could smell his aftershave like a third presence in the kitchen.

He seemed to belong there. He poured himself a glass of wine and topped hers up before he realised that she was still standing in the doorway with the tiny potatoes in her cupped hands. He held out a dish and she tipped them into it.

'I hope that's not all we're having for dinner,' he said, putting the potatoes in the sink. She laughed and nodded at the stew.

'I wanted to make something American,' she admitted, taking the glass he was holding out to her. 'But I couldn't think of anything. A couple of days ago I realised that I've hardly eaten any American food at all, even though I've been here for weeks.'

He chuckled. 'How have you managed to stay alive if you've been refusing anything American?'

'You know what I mean. *Real* American food. The classics.'

She was in no rush to start preparing the salad. The stew was bubbling away. She sat down on one of the kitchen chairs and was struck by how cosy the kitchen was, worn yellow cupboard doors and all. Tom glanced at the salad ingredients on the chopping board but didn't bother starting to cut them up either. Instead, he took a sip of wine and looked at her.

'So what've you cooked so far?'

'Mac and cheese,' she said. 'But it just tasted of . . . well, pasta and cheese. Honestly, it was a bit of a disappointment.'

'You can't have made it right in that case.'

'I even put bacon in.'

'Bacon?' He shook his head. 'Blasphemy.'

'But . . . I found a recipe with bacon.' A couple of them, actually.

'I'm not sure that even counts as mac and cheese.'

'It's wrong?'

'Absolutely. I wouldn't tell anyone about the bacon if I were you. Un-American.'

'Bacon can't be un-American. You have it in everything.'

'There are probably as many different recipes for mac and cheese as there are mothers. My dad said that sausage was the only right way. But the real secret is the cheese. It's got to be Cheddar.'

'Mmm,' said Sara. She was sceptical. It sounded like a pasta bake. Hardly very exotic. She moved over to the sink and scrubbed and peeled the extra potatoes and threw them into the stew.

'What else have you tried?'

'I thought about making corn dogs tonight,' she said, and laughed when he spluttered into his wine.

'Corn dogs and mac and cheese,' he said. 'What an evening that would've been.'

'Except that I don't really know how to do it. Can you even make them at home?'

'Sure,' said Tom. 'If you wanted to. You can buy them frozen too, to heat up in the microwave, but I wouldn't recommend it.'

'Just as well, since I don't have one.'

He glanced around, as though he hadn't realised that before. 'Sloppy Joes,' she said. 'But I don't even know what they are.'

'Ah, an Iowa specialty. Created by Sloppy Joe in Sioux City.'

'I'll have to keep googling,' she said gloomily.

'I'll have to take you on a culinary excursion sometime,' he said, but she could see that he regretted it the moment he had said it. She smiled faintly and shook her head as though to reassure him that she wouldn't take him up on his offer.

Some of the relaxed atmosphere had disappeared. When he wasn't talking, Tom's face looked worn and tired. The lines around his eyes seemed deeper, and he looked paler than he had that morning. She suspected that this was what he looked like when he was on his own.

'Tom,' she said, 'do you ever relax?'

'I'm relaxed now,' he said in surprise.

'No, I mean . . . just not do anything. Just sleep in or read a good book in bed, or keep your pyjamas on all day?'

'I don't wear pyjamas,' he said, and for a moment she could think of nothing other than his naked body, warm and heavy with sleep on a sunny Saturday afternoon . . . She forced herself to think about the food and setting the table.

'And what would I do with a book, anyway?' His eyes shone in that devastating way that made her think of the way Amy had described him. Not quite a laugh, but nearly. 'Being forced to read one would hardly make me relax.'

'Coffee in bed, then,' she said, and wished she would stop talking about him being in bed. 'Watching TV on the sofa,' she said instead. 'You know . . . relaxed.'

He shrugged. 'Sometimes,' he said, but she strongly suspected it had been a long time.

He half turned away from her and started on the salad, and she went over to the hob to check the stew. A few more minutes, she decided. Tom assembled the salad and improvised a dressing, Sara set the table. It was big enough for four or five people, but small enough that it was fit for two.

While they ate, they made small talk about how their day had been, as though they were completely normal friends who just happened to be having dinner. Sara found that she wasn't even nervous. She told him about Gertrude and Stieg Larsson, and he talked about his friend Pete and the apple sauce. Just then, she noticed that there was a jar on the counter, next to the wine bottles. He raised an eyebrow. 'A gift.'

They helped one another with the dishes afterwards. She washed, he dried, in comfortable silence. The only sound was the occasional clinking of cutlery or the noise of a sudden gust of wind rustling the trees outside. It was in no way a magical evening, and she knew that it probably meant little to him. But for her . . . For her, it was an evening when she had joked and laughed, been relaxed with a man, an evening where she had somehow . . . *lived*.

Just lived.

It would have been unthinkable just a few months ago. She thought about what the girls in the bookshop would have said if they knew that she, *she*, had invited a handsome American to dinner.

Or if they knew she had stepped in as a bartender to help out an even more handsome American. If the bookshop at home had still been open, she would have sent them a postcard with Carl on the front.

Tom raised an eyebrow at her again, and she shook her head, smiling.

Then she turned to him with a half-washed plate in her hand. 'Were Amy and John ever . . . together?'

He looked straight at her. 'Are you asking whether they slept together?'

'No . . . Well, maybe.'

'Not as far as I know, but I never asked either of them.'

'But . . . were they, you know, in love?'

'Yeah.'

'From the very beginning?'

'I should think so.'

She couldn't help but feel disappointed in Amy. She started scrubbing the plate more forcefully than was strictly necessary, until he carefully took it from her, rinsed it and dried it off.

'When they first met, it wasn't exactly the right time for a black man to be chasing a white woman,' said Tom. 'I don't think John had any problems here, not like in Alabama, and Amy could be friends with him. But getting married . . . How could they even go on a date?'

'And then she got married?' she asked.

'Yeah.'

'But not to John?'

'No.'

'I hope she was unfaithful,' she said suddenly, making Tom laugh. He didn't argue. 'I know you can't always leave someone, but you can surely meet on the side. Just look at *The Horse Whisperer*. Sure, she couldn't exactly get divorced when her daughter had had her leg amputated and had only just recovered, but she could have gone there a couple of weeks a year just to sleep with him a bit?'

'Um, sure,' said Tom.

Sara shook her head. 'I mean, a couple of weeks with Robert Redford should be enough for anyone.'

'I'd rather not, myself,' he said.

'You know what I mean.'

The book was, of course, as bad as the film. It was a mystery to her how you could take one story and create two unhappy endings. At least in the book, they got together in the end, but on the other hand he was killed by wild horses. In the film, they had to make do with a platonic dance, but he survived. A typically American kind of moral, she thought.

She returned to the subject at hand. 'But why didn't they get married when her husband died?'

'Honestly, I don't think they thought it was necessary by then. They were already friends. I think they loved one another in a way that was bigger than just being married. Somehow John always seemed to know what she wanted, or at least that's what I always thought growing up. He might not always have been able to give it to her, but he always knew.'

She nodded.

'You know when you asked about whether Amy was a dreamer?'

'Yes.'

'I think she was, but Amy wasn't someone whose dreams ever came true. On the other hand, she was someone who was content with very little, and I don't know which is best. She never complained.'

When Tom was about to leave, Sara followed him out into the hallway, and for some reason they paused, Sara leaning against one wall with her arms folded, Tom facing the door and on his way out, but clearly in no hurry to do so.

'Tom,' she said, 'what are your dreams?'

'I don't have any,' he replied.

'Seriously.'

'I am being serious.'

She didn't feel she was in any position to push him, given her own measly ambitions. Or rather, her total lack of them.

Hesitantly, she said: 'Don't you ever get tired of it? Just working, I mean.'

'All the time.' The admission seemed to surprise him, but he didn't make any attempt to take it back or qualify it.

'But maybe it's worse if you do relax,' he said. 'The trick is to just keep working. It's when you stop and think too much that you run into problems.'

'Yeah,' she said. That was definitely true, but she couldn't agree that working was the key, not now that she had experienced something else.

Sara Lindqvist
Kornvägen 7, 1 tr
136 38 Haninge
Sweden

Dear Sara,

John's family never really fit in here in Broken Wheel. His mother was a formidable woman who brought her entire family with her. I remember she always appeared to move with the strength of a woman so used to surviving catastrophes that calmness bored her. She didn't seem to know what to do with that strength if it wasn't in constant demand. Aside from John, all of her children – another son and three daughters – had that very same strength. They lived and breathed political struggle, but once they found themselves here, in a sleepy little town which wasn't interesting enough even to keep up with current racial antagonisms, they seemed to be almost disappointed, and slightly disoriented too. Gradually they all moved on to Chicago. One of them became a judge, another a lawyer, one an author and one a doctor. It was that kind of family.

John, on the other hand, wandered around Broken Wheel as though all his dreams had suddenly, miraculously, come true; as though he couldn't quite believe his good luck. To him, the sleepiness was a kind of harmonious peace. The first time I saw him, he was sitting stock-still on a park bench. The leaves on the trees were moving more than he was, and it was an almost breathless day. When he saw me he seemed alarmed, as if life had already taught him, by the age of sixteen, that white people meant trouble, even when they came in the unlikely form of a scrawny fifteen-year-old with a faded cotton dress and thin, unruly hair that never seemed to want to stay in a braid. I think that must have been the moment I decided to be his friend, but it took years to convince him it was possible. Of course . . . at that time, he might have been right about white people. And there have definitely been moments in our friendship since when he has been the braver of us.

Best,

Amy

Broken Wheel Gets Ready for the Market

The town council divided itself into teams as it took charge of the planning of the market and dance. Jen was responsible for the marketing, Caroline for the market itself, and Andy for the party. The rest of Broken Wheel's inhabitants lay low, trying to sneak past whenever they saw any of those three in the street, and hoping it would all blow over. It was an utterly naive hope. Within the space of a week, the majority of them had been recruited.

George had nothing against helping out, even if he still hadn't quite managed to get anyone to tell him exactly what he was meant to be doing. He tried to put himself forward at the meetings, which now seemed to be taking place haphazardly, anywhere and at any time. He had just come across Jen and Andy sitting at the counter in Grace's, busy drawing up the general plans for the market. Caroline wasn't there.

'When should we have it?' Jen asked. 'We need time to organise everything and do some advertising.'

George wondered whether they would clear it all with Caroline later, or whether she had actually already decided when it should be and simply not told the others.

'In a month?' Andy suggested.

George cleared his throat. 'Won't Sara have gone home then?'

'Home!' said Jen. The thought didn't seem to have even crossed her mind.

'I think she's going at the end of October,' he said cautiously. He would rather not think about her leaving, and he definitely didn't want to be involved in any decision-making, but they couldn't have the market after Sara had gone home. It wasn't right. If it hadn't been for her, they wouldn't even be having one.

Jen and Andy looked at him. They'd need to have it soon. They put the question of the actual date to one side and spent the rest of the time talking about other things, before parting ways to continue the planning on their own.

On his way home George walked past Claire's apartment.

She lived in the same housing complex as he did. Small, impersonal apartments in an ugly single-storey building, with a shared streaky lawn outside, and communal, often overflowing bins. People had started dumping broken furniture, tyres, shoes, liquor bottles and other things they didn't need there. At that moment, there was a mattress, its yellow lining spread on the ground around it, and two mismatched shoes. George was so used to the rubbish that he barely paid any attention to it, but he couldn't help notice Claire.

She was leaning against the sink unit in her apartment, staring blankly ahead through the kitchen window. She was looking almost straight at him and yet it didn't seem like she had seen him at all. After a few seconds, she lowered her eyes and looked down at the sink with such a tired, resigned expression that he didn't feel like he could simply walk by.

He went up to her outer door, hesitated for a moment and then knocked.

She looked slightly better when she opened the door. She managed a weary smile, at least. As though she had put on the mask she usually wore, George thought, and this made him stop short. He was suddenly so nervous about what he was doing there. He couldn't imagine that someone like Claire might need help from someone like him, but now it was too late. She had already let him in to the hallway. She was forced to kick two pairs of shoes from the middle of the floor.

'Excuse the mess,' she said, pulling a face. 'God, I've turned into someone who apologises for mess.'

He didn't say anything, simply followed her into the kitchen where she brewed the coffee that they would drink standing up, George leaning against the fridge and her against the sink unit, possibly so she didn't have to look at the dishes. He hadn't been able to avoid noticing the dirty plates and glasses, and the particularly sad pots and pans covered in dried-on food.

She looked down at the floor between them. 'Aren't people's expectations funny? I've always gone against them. With Lacey, first of all.' He looked away, embarrassed, but she continued. 'Back then, when people still cared about teenage pregnancies. Then refusing to get married, and having a messy house, and then finally refusing to regret any of it. Honestly, I don't know what bothers people most. You'd think they would've worked out that they should just leave me in peace by now.'

He didn't quite know who 'they' were and wondered whether he was included.

She glanced up at the mountain of washing-up beside her. 'But when did I get so tired of it all? I just can't bring myself to start the dishes. And then I've got to go to work, if Lacey comes back with the car sometime soon, and it all just feels so hard. Isn't it funny? What the hell is life if it's not chores and working and making dinner, and then starting all over again?'

He had no answer to that. He took a sip of coffee instead.

'And now we're having a market,' she said. 'Things are definitely more lively since the tourist arrived.'

'Sara?' he said.

'I wonder what makes someone travel to a completely different continent. Would you do it?'

George shook his head. If he was honest, he couldn't even see himself crossing the state line.

'And for what? Broken Wheel!' She shook her head. 'Hardly the best place for a tourist. There's nothing to see. The only thing we've got plenty of is meaninglessness.'

'It's a nice town.'

She laughed. 'Broken Wheel. No jobs. No future. Guided tours every day at two.'

He smiled faintly. 'I don't really know if people are better off anywhere else.'

Claire seemed to be thinking that over. 'Oh, sure. The people aren't any better or worse, but I still can't understand why anyone would travel thousands of miles to come here.'

George didn't know either. 'She's here now, anyway,' he said, but it didn't seem to cheer Claire up.

'Isn't it ironic?' she said. 'She's had the bookstore for no time at all and it already looks more like a home than my apartment. I've lived here fifteen years. Fifteen years of ugly pale yellow wallpaper.'

He smiled. 'Mine's the same.'

'God, what I wouldn't give for a bit of colour. This isn't a home.'

'You're wrong,' he said. He was surprised by his protest but then lost his thread. Eventually, he said: 'Just look at that jacket and the shoes and the plates.'

Lacey's crazy jacket was lying on one of the armchairs in the living room. It was bright yellow and had some kind of feathers around the collar. There were a few plates on the living-room table. In the hallway, there were four different pairs of shoes in a loose pile. A family. That was more important than the colour on the walls.

'It's definitely messy enough to be a home,' she said with a shaky laugh. 'But tell me, when exactly am I supposed to get things done? And now Caroline has decided that I'm having a stand of home-made cakes.'

He looked away, troubled. 'I can't bake,' he said. 'Otherwise I could've helped you. I've got time, at least.'

'Jesus, George,' she said. 'I can't bake either. I'm going to have to buy those damned cakes.'

The bookshop had far fewer visitors when everyone was running around trying to organise things for the big day. The only person still stopping by was Tom. Sara imagined he was looking at her differently now, as though he had somehow accepted that she was there. He talked about people she had never heard of like they were old friends of the both of them, like she was part of the town.

He slumped down into one of the armchairs and for a moment they just sat there, together with the books, without feeling the need to speak.

She looked at him. 'You know,' she said, 'one day, I'm going to find a book for you.'

For once, he didn't even protest and she leaned back happily.

'I think I'm going to move to Hope,' he said.

She struggled to keep her voice neutral. 'Hope,' she said. It didn't sound at all natural. She cleared her throat. 'How . . . why's that?'

He shrugged. 'I've got a job there. Seems pointless staying here.'

Pointless. She swallowed. 'Would you really be able to move? Leave all this behind?'

She thought that he would answer dismissively, but he looked at her, smiled and shook his head.

'I don't know,' he admitted.

Jen walked past the bookstore and saw the two of them sitting there. She stopped Andy, who also happened to be passing by, and gestured towards the shop window with obvious satisfaction.

'Look,' she said. 'My plan's going well.' She continued, almost to herself. 'A bookstore, something to do . . . practically a dream come true for her, you've got to admit that, at least. And . . . her friendship with Tom, too. I wonder whether she will actually go home in October?'

It really did look idyllic, with the sun glittering on the window and Sara and Tom completely unaware that they were being watched. Andy was considerably more pessimistic.

'What'll they do when her visa runs out?' he asked. 'Have you thought of that? What's going to happen to her dream then?'

The Small Matter of a Visa

'Sara's visa is going to run out' was the first thing Jen said when the town council met. There was so much to take care of at that moment that they hadn't even bothered to meet in the cinema hall itself. Their meetings all took place standing, in the foyer. 'We've got to do something.'

'Oh?' There was a certain tone in Caroline's voice. She had grown tired of the plotting to do with Sara. Say what you liked about the girl, she was discreet at the very least. Caroline had been searching for signs that people knew about her . . . reading . . . all week, but as far as she could tell, Sara hadn't said a word.

'We've got to fix it so she can stay,' said Jen. 'We're *Americans*, for God's sake. If we can't invite our friend to live in our own country, what was the whole War of Independence about?'

'Does she want to stay?' Caroline asked. 'Has she even said a word about it?'

'Oh, there's said and said. But it's highly likely she'll want to stay, so we've got to be ready to help her.'

Caroline thought of how Tom and Sara had stood next to one another at the improvised opening party, relaxed and in silence, looking out over the mass of people. There were very few people who could stand together without talking. It worried her. And he had visited the bookstore. Perhaps there was more to Jen's crazy plan than she wanted to admit.

'Shouldn't we ask her?' she said.

'Maybe it's best we check it's *possible* for her to stay before we give her any ideas,' said Andy.

'Possible?! Of course it's possible. This is a free country, isn't it?'

Caroline didn't bother to reply, but she knew what she had to do.

After the meeting, she waited in the entrance for fifteen minutes, just to be sure that neither Jen nor Andy would come back. Then she headed for the bookstore, certain of her duty, but surprisingly undecided about how she would carry it out.

She sat down in one of the armchairs and motioned for Sara to take the seat next to her.

Amy should have been here to have this conversation, she thought wearily. Amy would have been able to wrap up the questions, take a kind and reassuring tone, and somehow get Sara to talk about her problems and her dreams.

As though talking could make a difference. She sat up straight and steeled herself for the conversation.

Just be diplomatic, Caroline. Put it nicely. She made a face.

'When does your visa run out, Sara?' she asked.

Sara stood up and turned away from the window, as though she could suddenly no longer bear to look at the street.

'At the end of November,' she said. 'But my plane ticket is for the thirtieth of October. From New York.'

Sara still had her back to Caroline, so she couldn't read her expression.

'And you're going to go home then?' she asked.

'I . . . yes. I guess I *could* try and change my ticket, just stay for a week or two more, but I don't think it's allowed . . .' Her voice trailed off, rather pathetically, Caroline thought.

Caroline nodded to herself and stood up.

'That's all I wanted to know,' she said.

She would have to take control of this, too. But at least she knew exactly who to call.

Broken Wheel, Iowa
March 28, 2011

Sara Lindqvist
Kornvägen 7, 1 tr
136 38 Haninge
Sweden

Dear Sara,

My husband never laughed. He wasn't a particularly happy man, but he wasn't always that way. His mother left his father when he was only thirteen, and when I look back at everything I think that must have left some kind of poison in him. One which worked so slowly that it was hard to tell exactly when it began. I do know that he laughed before that happened, and I know that he didn't laugh at all afterward. No happy laughter, anyway.

I think he took his mother's departure harder than his father did. At first, he was sad, but later he was angry. I think that's why he never found it easy making friends as an adult, which was a shame because I don't actually think he was a bad person. I've never been able to watch *The Bridges of Madison County* (it's set in Iowa, you know) without asking myself whether she didn't do the right thing, staying. But I've seen up close what happens to the families left behind. I've seen what happens with the women who stay, too. There are times when I beg Meryl Streep to turn that door handle and run out into the rain. Just run, I think.

Amy

Run-of-the-Mill Chick Lit
(Books 3: Life 1)

People always said that autumn was a dying season, but Sara didn't agree.

There was nothing so alive, nothing so constantly changing, as the autumn she was now experiencing in Broken Wheel. Every morning, she witnessed an explosion of leaves, wind and colour.

Summer was still refusing to loosen its grip, and there was still the occasional warm day, but the balance had shifted. The world around her was moving relentlessly towards winter and towards the end of her time in Broken Wheel.

When George came to pick her up, she stepped from beneath her blanket and headed slowly for the car. She responded to his attempts at small talk wearily and with one-word answers. Dark clouds were looming above the town and the wind was whipping at the trees, but not even that managed to make the bookshop feel warm and cosy. Instead, it felt small and claustrophobic and frighteningly meaningless.

She stood watching the leaves being ripped from the trees outside. It was as though winter took a step closer with each leaf that fell to the ground, as the branches turned bare and empty and her life in Broken Wheel whirled away with the wind.

Maybe it was just as well she would be going home, she thought. She had experienced Amy's town, toasted Miss Annie, met Andy and Claire and . . . well, everyone. And she had given them books. Perhaps her work here was done.

But it was strange, when it came to the people. However hard she tried to repay her debt to them, they always seemed to be finding new reasons for her to feel grateful. It was as though she was fighting a losing battle, trying to pay back the interest on her interest.

The conversation with Caroline had shaken her. She hoped that Caroline hadn't seen right through her. She had tried to conceal what a shock it had been, the realisation that she would have to go back to Sweden – and so soon at that.

Four weeks left before she had to return to Sweden. The image of Amy's comfortable house, the quiet charm of the bookshop, and the people around her – these all shone in comparison to the hazy outline of a flat in Haninge; another bookshop, if she was lucky. She couldn't really picture it, and that scared her.

When had she stopped thinking about Sweden? She tried to remind herself that her family was waiting for her there, but if she was really honest that wasn't a particularly effective argument.

She didn't think anyone would care when she returned to Sweden. She wouldn't even have anyone to talk to about everything that had happened here: the bookshop, her new friends, this sudden and unexpected feeling of belonging somewhere. Her parents didn't care, and wouldn't want to hear anything about it. Her sister probably wouldn't even have noticed she had been away if Sara hadn't sent her a postcard.

She walked around the bookshop while she tried to stop thinking about Sweden. There was nothing for her to do but she couldn't sit still.

Then her eyes landed on one of the books on the shelf in front of her. She laughed. At least she had found the perfect book for Grace. Strong women who built this country.

Not even Grace would be able to resist this book, she thought to herself as she pulled on her jacket and ran the few metres over the road in the wind to the diner.

She didn't have the energy to talk to Grace today so she simply threw the book down onto the counter with a triumphant smile and a 'strong women!', before running back out again.

It was still her bookshop. It *was*.

But the effect wasn't quite the same any more. She quickly grew restless again and realised she would have to force herself through the rest of the day.

Maybe she should close early, she thought.

At five, she was still in the bookshop, watching an approaching rain shower. It hit the far side of the street first and for a moment it was as though they were assessing one another, Sara and the approaching storm. The rain seemed to be hesitating to approach her.

Then it began. Small drops at first, like some kind of advance guard, before it closed in on her, pattering against the steamed-up window until Broken Wheel was nothing more than a blur outside her little world.

She waited half an hour for the rain to stop, but by then she could no longer bear the sight of the cosy bookshop, complete with rain lashing against the window. She grabbed Amy's raincoat, turned out all the lights and stood in darkness for a moment. Main Street was deserted.

Fitting, she thought. It was fitting.

She stepped out into the rain. It was lucky to have a rainstorm just when you needed one, she thought. She passed Grace's and saw her standing alone at the counter, drinking liquor as though the diner was still a bar. She had a glass and a bottle in front of her, and Sara could see the book she had given her leaning against the bottle. She could have sworn that Grace was actually laughing at it.

At any other time, such a sight would have cheered her up, but now she didn't even pause. She simply bowed her head and continued on her way out of town.

The cornfields surrounded her, following her as she went. The rain sounded different when it landed on the greenery of the fields, heavier and more mellow, almost like summer rain. Only the chill on her cheeks reminded her otherwise.

When she finally came to the road leading off to Amy's house, she kept on walking. She couldn't bear the silence and emptiness awaiting her there.

You don't belong here, she thought. It was stupid to think she did. Stupid, stupid, stupid. She raised her face to the rain in quiet obstinacy and kept on walking, the water and the cold finding their way into her legs.

Deep down, she knew she was heading to Tom's house. For some reason, despite the rain, she felt like she would be able to talk to him about this. He might be moving to Hope, she thought, but he must still care about the town. Surely he must? He must be able to understand how sad it would be to leave them all behind.

When she reached his house, she stopped. Suddenly, it felt intrusive to turn up like this. But she remembered how they had sat together in the bookshop, their conversation in Amy's hallway. About needing to keep working. Belonging somewhere.

She needed to talk about all this with someone. And at least Tom would keep their conversation to himself, she was sure of that.

She knocked on the door. The hallway was dark, but the light in the kitchen was on. No one answered.

Faced with the prospect of more rain and the walk home and the fact that the door, when she tentatively tried it, was unlocked, she decided that it was perfectly normal to go indoors for a while before she headed back.

She moved cautiously down the hallway. It led to an open-plan living room, with a kitchen and dining area at one end.

'Tom?' she said. Again, no one answered. She hung up her raincoat, kicked off her shoes and took a few more steps.

She looked around, her curiosity about Tom's home making her forget everything that had been on her mind.

Though perhaps home wasn't the right word. Everything was strangely impersonal, and very, very neat.

There wasn't a single bookcase, not even for a CD or DVD collection. As though he was deliberately attempting to avoid anything that might reveal something about him, or transform his house into a home. The furniture was neutral in colour and shape, and all of the surfaces were clean and free of dust.

There were no photographs, no dirty dishes or half-read books thrown down wherever he had happened to be reading them; no clutter of old pens, small change or receipts.

In the kitchen there were two plates on the drying rack and three empty beer bottles in a row on the counter.

But it was the windows which really dominated the room, making the boundary between the indoors and outdoors seem indistinct. The panes shook gently whenever a gust of wind blew against them. It made Sara feel surprisingly powerless against the weather, as though she were still outside. But there was also something comforting in it, having the night and the darkness so close.

Beyond the dark cornfields, she could see the lights from Broken Wheel through the rain. She could also see lights on in Amy's house. She must have forgotten to turn them out that morning.

She almost always did. It was less lonely coming home to a brightly lit house, as though Amy's house was waiting for her.

In Tom's house, Broken Wheel was constantly present, she thought. Surrounded by the timeless landscape, the corn, the clouds towering up above it, and the lonely barns out in the fields; everything which, long ago, had been part of life around here.

Eventually, she went back to the living area and slumped down onto the sofa. When the silence became too much, she stood up and turned on the radio in the kitchen. She went back to the sofa. She suddenly felt extremely tired, and very far away from home.

She did the only thing she could under the circumstances.

She fell asleep.

When she woke a few hours later, the restlessness had passed; sleep had made her body calm, warm and heavy. She stretched out until her foot nudged a leg.

A leg.

She sat up and looked around in confusion. Tom. She was at Tom's house. Under a blanket. He must have put it over her when he came home and found her asleep on his sofa.

Before he had fallen asleep on the sofa himself. She smiled. He was unbelievably handsome when he slept.

She reached out and touched his leg before she could stop herself, then she got up and leaned over him. There was a hint of stubble on his chin and cheeks, the lines around his eyes were less pronounced, and his expression was almost peaceful.

'Tom,' she said gently, her face close to his.

He moved and opened his eyes. If he was surprised to see her so close to him, he didn't say anything.

It all happened so incredibly slowly. So slowly it made her wonder whether the kisses in films were exaggerated at all, whether those long, drawn-out, hesitant moments before a kiss also existed in real life.

When she realised what she was doing, she backed up quickly. She sat on the sofa, trying to think of something to say.

It was useless. She tried smiling instead. Which was slightly easier.

'Sara,' said Tom. He was looking at her with an uncomfortable, penetrating gaze. 'I'm not interested in a holiday romance,' he said unnecessarily brutally. He continued, though he had already made himself absolutely clear and she was completely unable to say a thing. 'I've done it before. And long-distance relationships.'

Of course he had. She hadn't. She had never had a proper relationship at all. She had tried once, but it hadn't been a success.

She instinctively moved further away from him.

'If we fall for one another it'd be . . . irritating,' he said. 'And if we don't fall for one another then it'd be pointless.'

It was obvious that he wouldn't fall for her, she thought. Surely he didn't think she was so . . . unrealistic as to think that. But still. She couldn't help but feel a slight hint of righteous annoyance that he had described a fling with her as pointless and irritating.

She held her head high and said: 'Of course you're not going to fall for me.' Because she assumed things couldn't get any worse, she added: 'But I don't see why it would be pointless or irritating.'

He reached out and gently turned her face towards him. Slowly, almost unconsciously, he stroked her cheek, her jaw, her throat with his fingers. His touch was so light that she wasn't certain it had actually happened. Except for the fact that his hand was now resting against her collarbone and neck.

'Do you really think –' he said quietly, before breaking off.

'What?' she said. It came out more as a croak.

He pulled her towards him and without really knowing how or who had taken the initiative, she fell back on the sofa until she was lying with him heavy on top of her. She could feel his breathing in her body.

She reached out and touched the skin right above his waistband, while she still had the chance. 'Still' because she would be going back to Sweden sometime soon. But also because she knew that he didn't really want her, and so she needed to make the most of the time she had.

He recoiled slightly when she kissed him. It was almost imperceptible, but she could feel it in the way that his weight above her shifted. She tried to sit up, but then he kissed her back, slowly and gently at first, then more roughly. His body pressed down onto her again, his hand moving over her shoulder, jaw and hair in quick, intense movements.

The kiss died out and they lay there for a moment, looking at one another.

His breathing was short and heated. Almost as though they had actually had sex. The thought didn't help her own excitement levels in the slightest.

She closed her eyes and imagined all of the ways she wanted to touch him, how she wanted him to touch her. Take me, she wanted to beg him. She arched her back so that she was closer to his body. Her arms were around him, their legs were entwined so that she was pressed against his thighs. She moved her hips and felt an urgent, excruciating need that began somewhere deep inside and spread out until every part of her was, in some way, touching him.

She knew she wasn't any good at this whole sex business. She always felt so self-conscious and had somehow always known that she didn't have any . . . natural talent for it. But for once, her body seemed to know exactly what it wanted. For once it seemed to be quite certain. Maybe because she had never wanted anyone as much as she now wanted Tom.

For some reason, that thought made her sad. It was like the cruel joke of a bored God: creating that much longing only to leave it unsatisfied.

'Damn you, Sara,' said Tom, as though he had been thinking the very same thing. He didn't sound angry.

'Go to hell,' she replied in the same tone of voice.

'Do you really think,' he said, 'we could stop ourselves given the slightest chance?'

They didn't have sex. But still, when Sara left, she could remember the things they had done and the words they had said, the way his body had pressed against hers, and she sighed, half contented and half frustrated. Hands down, it had been the best sex she had never had.

She was sure he had actually said that he thought there was a risk he would fall for her – had implied that in some kind of alternative, parallel universe (one clearly governed by completely different laws of nature than this one) they might have had a chance. Plus, he had kissed her.

She realised that she didn't want to cry; she wanted to laugh and sing and tell the whole world about it. He had been attracted to her. She smiled. All her anxiety about eventually – in a few weeks, almost a month, plenty of time! – having to go home to Sweden vanished at the thought that she, here and now, was walking around analysing a man's feelings and actions, as though she were Bridget Jones for a day. As though she were the main character in a run-of-the-mill chick-lit novel.

She would see him again soon, at the dance. So long as she made it through the market first.

Tom watched as she left and told himself that he was a damned idiot.

Suddenly he hadn't been able to bear the thought of her going home to Sweden, leaving as though she had never even been in

Broken Wheel. It somehow felt as though he might then cease to exist, as though he and the rest of the town were nothing but a parenthesis in her life. A memory, an anecdote perhaps, told to people so far away that he couldn't even imagine them. *Sweden*. The timing and the holiday romance had been nothing more than excuses. Not exactly brilliant ones at that, but the only ones he could come up with at such short notice.

Pull yourself together, Tom, he thought, resting his forehead against the window in the living room, as though he could make the calmness and darkness outside sink into him by sheer will-power. As long as you just stay away from her for these last few weeks, he said to himself, then she'll forget all about you just as easily as she seems to have forgotten all of her Swedish friends. And boyfriends.

She hadn't said a single word about them. She might have left dozens of abandoned boyfriends in different corners of Sweden.

Not that it had anything to do with him. It was just that she would be going back to them, which, he quickly thought, couldn't happen soon enough.

He had absolutely no need for a woman whom he had nothing in common with, and who would rather spend more of her time with a book than with him. He had absolutely no intention of living up to any of her crazy romantic ideas of heroes losing arms, hands, their vision and their minds so that Sara could have her happy ending.

If he had learned anything in life, it was that there were no happy endings. Life simply went on.

So why had he kissed her? Or rather: why had he thrown himself onto her and practically molested her on the sofa?

He should have known better. He did know better. It was just the shock of coming home and finding her asleep on his sofa, how right it had all felt. As though all obligations and all responsibilities . . . they hadn't disappeared, exactly, but they felt so far away that, for a short time, he could imagine a life in which he might have a break from them. And then she had been there when he woke, near to him, and then he hadn't *thought* at all.

Because he was a damned idiot, plain and simple. That much was perfectly clear.

But it wasn't the end of the world, he reminded himself. The only thing he needed to do was demonstrate that he hadn't fallen for her, and that he had absolutely no intention of doing so.

He sighed. If only he could convince himself.

A little willpower and self-discipline, that was all he needed.

A Lawyer Gets Involved

'But you must understand,' the lawyer said, desperately gesturing to the group in his office. He had already explained it three times, but no one from the eccentric delegation seemed to be listening. They were polite and well behaved, and they didn't interrupt him, but it was clear that they just hadn't accepted what he was telling them. He could feel a headache coming on, and massaged his temples discreetly.

It had all seemed so simple when Caroline Rohde phoned. A question about visa regulations for a woman she had staying with her. He had assumed it would be a straightforward matter of extending a tourist visa, something he should have been able to get over and done with before lunch. He hadn't been at all prepared for five people turning up, each of them seemingly expecting him to conjure up a permanent residency visa just like that.

He should have known. Nothing was ever simple with Caroline damn Rohde. If it hadn't been for all the kindnesses she had shown his wife, he would have thrown her out by now. Of course, among those kindnesses was the small detail of Caroline talking his wife into taking him back after a certain indiscretion on his part.

The rest of the group was no better. A manic housewife, a nervous man in a jacket which didn't suit him, and two men he was starting to suspect were a couple. One of them was far too handsome. He had no time for handsome men. It wasn't natural, he thought grumpily.

'There must be something we can do so she can stay,' said Jen. 'What happened to all that talk about everyone being born free and having the right to find happiness?'

'It was more a . . . figure of speech,' he said wearily. 'That part of the constitution is slightly unfortunate. You must understand that it's always been more of a vision or a challenge than a description of reality. And besides, it doesn't apply at all to people who aren't American citizens.'

He rubbed his eyes. He didn't care whether Sara stayed or not. She was probably perfectly nice in her own way.

'The US has become something of a symbol, a dream – a country people have come to in order to, like the lady pointed out, create a better life and find happiness for themselves and those dear to them. But our immigration laws are tough. Sure, some things changed during the nineties, primarily to allow the immigration of people with certain specialist skills – scientists, engineers, doctors. Or people who were prepared to invest large amounts of money in American businesses. *Large* amounts,' he emphasised. 'But since then, the mood has hardened again, not least because of the anti-terrorism laws and the jobs situation. No one is really interested in letting foreigners take those few jobs we've got left.'

He shrugged in what might have been an apologetic gesture, but might well have been just a reminder that he wasn't personally responsible for the rules.

'So what are the circumstances under which people can stay?' Caroline asked.

'Asylum, of course, but only if you're fleeing war or persecution. And even that's not especially simple.'

'But if you've got a job?' Jen asked.

'It doesn't make much of a difference. It's a complicated process – plenty of paperwork and very expensive. Plus, the employer has to be able to prove she's got a specific competency that we're lacking here. Has she got any particular skills?'

'She's worked in a bookstore,' said Caroline. 'Very good at her job. Loves books.' There was something disapproving in her tone.

'But hardly something in short supply here,' he said.

'What about all those Latin Americans working in the meatpacking factories?' said the thin man in the terrible jacket. 'That's hardly a skill.'

'Some of them might have residency through their parents, or else they came here illegally and were then given amnesty. And you can't ignore the fact that many of them are simply here without visas.'

He looked them in the eye, one after the other. None hesitated in meeting his gaze. 'I must strongly advise your friend against staying here illegally. I've often wished there was more I could do to help those who are already here, but at least I can honestly warn others against heading down that road.'

They still didn't appear to be listening to him.

'Even just the chance of being arrested! We're talking about hefty fines, prosecution, maybe even a stretch in jail, both for her and whoever helped her. Plus, even if she could manage the fines and jail, which isn't at all certain, then she'd be deported immediately. After which it would be virtually impossible for her to come back at a later date.'

'Tom, though . . .' said Caroline.

'Tom?' he asked. The others looked just as surprised.

She smiled at them. 'He'll be broken-hearted.'

'Broken-hearted,' the housewife echoed.

'Who's Tom?'

'Her boyfriend,' the housewife said. 'It took them forever to get together, but we knew from the very beginning that they'd like one another.'

The housewife suddenly seemed animated in a slightly worrying way. There was a manic look in her eyes, a smile which seemed to cover her entire face. 'From the very beginning,' she repeated.

'Young people are so slow nowadays,' Caroline added.

The housewife sat up straight. 'Yeah,' she said. 'They're so in love, Sara and Tom.'

That was something, at least. 'So you're saying she met someone here? An American citizen?'

'Tom's as American as they come,' said Caroline.

The other woman nodded enthusiastically. 'Very American,' she said. 'Like apple pie.'

'Did they know one another before she came here, when she applied for her visa? It's important. If they think she came here on a tourist visa with the intention of getting married and staying longer, she could still be refused residency.'

'No, they met here,' the housewife said, adding determinedly: 'Through me.'

'And she definitely has a visa? She's not here on a visa-waiver programme?'

'She has a visa.'

'In that case . . . Well. If this Tom would be broken-hearted enough to marry her, she should be allowed to stay. It's a relatively simple process. Providing, of course,' he added, 'that she doesn't stay after her current visa expires. Not one single day.'

'Not at all. So a marriage would help?'

'If they love one another enough,' he clarified.

'Of course,' said Caroline.

'And they have to be married,' he added. 'Being engaged or moving in together isn't enough.' He suddenly thought of something. 'Why isn't Tom here himself, asking these questions?'

'Young people today,' Caroline answered. 'Not organised at all, not like in our day, when –'

He held up his hands. 'Yes, yes, it's true.' He looked at his watch. Definitely time for lunch. 'If anything comes of all this, I can help you through the paperwork. She'll need to have a doctor's certificate too, plus fill in some forms.'

He stood up and held out his hand to signal that the meeting was over. All members of the delegation stood up politely, and Caroline shook his hand and thanked him for his time.

'Jane?' he said into the telephone as they squeezed out of his office. 'Take my calls. I'm going for lunch.'

'Tom?' George asked the moment they were clear of the lawyer's office.

Caroline shrugged. 'I had to come up with something.' She wasn't entirely happy with her improvisation skills either. Was it ever morally defensible to get married in order to be granted residency? She doubted it. It had been a passing idea, a way of keeping all doors open, but she had a feeling that Jen would see it as something they couldn't back away from.

'She has to get married,' said Jen. 'You heard the guy. It's the only way if she wants to stay.'

Andy and Carl looked at one another, amazed by how simple it was for heterosexual people to say those words. 'She has to get married,' they said to one another quietly.

'Don't mention any of this to her yet,' Caroline said in an attempt to minimise the damage.

'No, we'll let it be a nice surprise,' Jen agreed cheerily. 'And the same goes for Tom. Let's not say anything to him either.'

'Tom's the obvious choice,' said Andy. Carl seemed much more sceptical, but Andy continued nonetheless. 'He's the right age. He's single. He's straight.'

'Plus, she likes him,' said Jen.

'But does he have the slightest desire to marry her?' asked Caroline. 'And does she want to get married to him?'

'There's want and want,' said Jen. 'It'd just be on paper. He can surely sacrifice himself for the town. It's actually about time he did something for it.' He had never even subscribed to the newsletter, she reminded herself with indignation.

Tom it was. He wasn't there to defend himself, which everyone saw as a bonus. A surprise attack. That was the right approach.

'We'll propose at the dance,' said Andy. 'It'll be the party of the century.'

An Unexpected Offer

George couldn't bake. He did, however, have all the time in the world, and he knew how to clean.

No one ever locked their doors in Broken Wheel. That was just how things had always been. There was very little worth stealing, and even fewer people to do the stealing. He let himself in without giving it a second thought.

Where should he start?

There was vacuuming, scrubbing, dusting and dishes to be done. He decided to tackle the dishes first, since she had specifically mentioned them. As he sorted the things waiting to be washed on the counter and fetched plates from the living room, he found himself singing.

He did his job thoroughly and properly, using plenty of dishwashing liquid, inspecting each glass and plate for stubborn pieces of food, drying them and putting them neatly back in the right place. With satisfaction, he saw the dirty pile grow smaller with each glass he washed. The kitchen seemed to grow before his very eyes: it became bigger and airier and much more pleasant, and though he hadn't cleaned the windows, even the sun seemed to be shining more brightly. Cleaning the windows was a job that always needed doing.

It was nice being able to do something where you could so clearly see your progress. Not like at the slaughterhouse, where the piles of dead animals waiting to be cut up never grew any smaller however hard the men worked, and where the slush they rinsed away always came back, often before they were even finished.

Once he had done the dishes, he wiped down the counter and the other surfaces in the kitchen so that they were practically gleaming. As close as they would get to gleaming, anyway. He could see they were doing their best.

It was a nice kitchen, he thought. Friendly and unassuming.

He decided to take on the floor next. It needed sweeping and vacuuming. He hung up the bags and jackets in the hallway, and put all of the bits and pieces he found in the living room in a pile on the sofa so that he could wipe the table.

He hummed to himself while he vacuumed. It had been a long time since he last had anything useful to do, apart from helping out with the bookstore. He stretched. Sophie would have been proud if she could have seen him now.

'So you see,' he said to her, 'Dad's not out for the count yet.'

'Ah, Claire,' Grace said, as though it was entirely normal that she was there. Claire hadn't stopped by for several years; Grace assumed that she saw enough hamburgers at work.

She poured them both a coffee as Claire sat down in front of her. 'You know,' she said, 'I've always liked you.'

There was nothing suspicious in Grace's tone.

'Smart move, not marrying Graham,' she continued. 'Boring type.'

'How did you know it was him?'

Grace dismissed the question with a sweeping gesture, cigarette in hand.

'Process of elimination. There weren't that many candidates to begin with, and you quickly decided you didn't want to get married. If it had been Tom or one of the others, you would've at least considered it.'

'Tom and I, we've never . . .'

'Well, that was a waste, if you ask me. Anyway, it's good that you stood your ground. You've raised your daughter to be strong. That's a sign of class.' She blinked. 'Despite Graham. Though if we're honest, us Graces have also fallen for the wrong men in our time. Nothing wrong with that, of course. The trick is just not staying with them.'

'Isn't it funny that you can be together with men who are so wrong for you that afterward you feel like you've been "cured" of them?' said Claire. 'Like a cold. You get them, you get cured, you move on.'

'Like colds,' said Grace. 'I like it. Hits the nail on the head, doesn't it?'

Claire asked for another cup of coffee. 'I've got a really long shift left,' she said.

Grace had taken in Claire's work uniform – the short black skirt, gym shoes and a white piqué shirt – her weary posture and facial expression, and come to the conclusion that Claire had already been to work. 'Not more work, surely?' she said. Claire worked in two different hamburger joints, all the shifts she could.

'I've got to find somewhere to buy home-made cakes.'

'Sugar craving?' asked Grace, and Claire laughed.

'Caroline's ordered me to have a cake stand. Apparently it's not a real market without one.'

There was a certain whining tiredness in her voice, but if she had been expecting sympathy she would probably be disappointed.

Instead, Grace chuckled and shook her head. 'I wonder how many of those cakes are just passed back and forth between markets?'

'Not as often as jelly,' said Claire. She gave a weary smile and made a move to get up.

'Wait,' said Grace. 'I want to test something on you.'

'Mm?'

'I've always said you should avoid being drawn into things, and especially into other people's business.'

Claire seemed to have no idea what Grace was talking about, but she sat down again. 'Sounds smart,' she said.

'Yeah. It does, doesn't it? But my friend Idgie has opened my eyes.' Claire looked like she was wondering who the hell this Idgie was, but Grace hadn't seemed to notice. She continued. 'If you're tough and ballsy and, well, not as wimpish or idiotic as everyone else – shouldn't you offer people support? Don't you have a kind of moral obligation?'

'Maybe,' Claire said cautiously. 'Though I don't know whether I could. It's hard enough just going from job to job.'

'Idgie gave liquor and food to hobos, and when an elephant

needed to be won in a game of poker, well, she didn't hesitate to do that either. Makes you think, right?' Grace leaned against the counter and lit a cigarette.

'Sure,' said Claire. 'But an elephant . . . do you need an elephant?'

Grace gestured impatiently with her cigarette.

'I can sort out the cakes for you,' she said. 'Not many people know it, but I can actually bake. I've got an old family recipe for a fantastic rum-raisin cake. The secret is not using any rum.'

Claire blinked. 'The market's on Saturday,' she said.

'No problem.'

'I'll pay you.'

'No chance. Away with you now.'

It felt surprisingly good to see Claire's car approaching. George was sitting in his kitchen and he watched her park and climb out, still moving lethargically but not looking quite as resigned as the last time he'd seen her. She paused at her front door, resting her forehead against it as though it would be completely impossible to open it and face everything again.

He was happy that he had cleaned. He thought she would appreciate it. He spent a moment imagining her smiling face when she saw the clean floor, her relief when she saw the empty sink.

Then the first doubts crept in: would she think it was presumptuous of him? Just going into her apartment like that? Would she even realise that it had been him? Should he have left a note, apologised?

Finally, she unlocked the door, stepped inside and pulled it shut behind her.

It was a kind gesture, wasn't it, Sophie? he asked nervously. He couldn't see Claire any more. He had no idea how she had reacted.

She came over half an hour later, and she did not look happy. Her face was expressionless and her body tense, like she was fighting to keep control. He looked nervously at her and showed her into the kitchen, where she flopped into one of the chairs as though she couldn't keep herself upright any longer.

He wondered whether he should say something, explain himself, but in the end he simply put the coffee on and leaned back against the refrigerator in the same way he had done at her place. It felt better to stay standing.

'I came to thank you,' she said, not sounding even the slightest bit grateful. In actual fact, she almost sounded aggressive. Just then, he noticed that she had a bottle of wine with her. She followed his gaze down to the bottle of wine, as though she had only just realised that it might not be the best gift for a newly sober alcoholic, and to his horror she reacted by bursting into tears.

Now he really didn't know what to say.

She gave what might have been a brief laugh but could just have easily have been a hiccup.

'My God,' she said. 'Look at me. Sitting here crying about an empty sink like a complete idiot.'

'I . . .' he said, before falling silent. 'Do you want a glass of wine maybe?'

She laughed, a real laugh this time. Then she added hesitantly: 'Are you . . . ?'

'I'll have a cup of coffee. Don't worry, I can resist a bottle of red wine. It's never really been my thing anyway. Liquor, on the other hand.'

She smiled weakly.

'OK,' she said. 'Good.'

'I hope you weren't angry?' he said. 'I just wanted to help out.'

'Help out!' She looked around his apartment. It was an exact copy of hers, though the mirror image, and utterly clean and tidy.

He smiled. 'I've got nothing better to do.'

'Clearly not.'

'No,' he said quietly. He opened the bottle of wine in a quick, fluid movement which made her raise an eyebrow. 'Plenty of experience,' he said. 'Just because it wasn't my favourite doesn't mean I turned it down.' He poured her a glass and a cup of coffee for himself. 'Though I'm not completely calm,' he admitted. 'I don't really know if I should go to the dance. Since it'll be at the Square, I mean. Maybe it's best to avoid temptation.'

'How's it going with . . . everything?' she asked, looking uncomfortable.

'It's going well,' he said.

Claire nodded.

'It's down to Sophie,' he said.

'And Michelle?'

He smiled wearily. 'No, she doesn't mean much to me any more.'

'Don't worry about the dance,' said Claire. 'If you want, I can keep an eye on you. If I see you anywhere near a bottle, I'll hit you on the head with it.'

That reassured him, but he wanted to be sure they understood one another. 'You don't need to do it if it's a bottle of Coca-Cola,' he said.

Claire laughed so much at his attempt at a joke that he wasn't even slightly uneasy any longer. She *would* hit him on the head if he was about to fall off the wagon. *It'll be OK, Sophie*, he said to himself.

Claire drank the rest of her wine and got to her feet. Before she left, she paused in the hallway. She seemed more relaxed to him now. If her eyes were still slightly blank, at least they weren't full of tears.

'George,' she said over her shoulder, not really looking at him. 'Your cleaning?'

He nodded.

'It's the nicest thing anyone's ever done for me.'

Once she had gone, he stood in the kitchen looking at the half-full bottle of wine. He paused for only a moment before he put the cork back in and placed it on a shelf.

'You know, Sophie,' he said, 'I think I can actually promise you I'll never drink again.'

Grace and Idgie's Friendship is Put to the Test

When Caroline visited her niece the following day, she was impressed for a number of reasons. Not only was the apartment unusually clean and tidy (even to her critical eye), but Claire had also managed to bake an utterly fantastic rum-raisin cake.

Caroline graciously cut a small piece for herself and amiably asked for the recipe. She felt more well disposed to her niece than she had for years.

But Claire managed only to stutter a completely improbable description of the cake standing in front of them. So improbable that Caroline couldn't help but wonder whether Claire had been slightly . . . tipsy when she baked it.

One part of her said that if Claire had managed to produce *this* when she was drunk, it was all the more impressive.

Caroline! said the other.

Eventually, Claire admitted that she hadn't baked it herself after all.

'Did you *buy* it?' There was plenty more Caroline wanted to say on the subject, but she managed to hold it back. Instead, she asked: 'What're we going to do about the market, then? We've got to have a whole stand of home-made cakes. If you'd told me earlier you couldn't manage, I could've sorted it out somehow, but now –'

'We'll have the stand,' said Claire.

'But how? You can't buy enough cakes to fill a stand. How will you afford that?' She paused for thought. 'I suppose I'll have to pay for them,' she said reluctantly. The thought of being involved in selling shop-bought cakes at a market was worrying but not, she admitted to herself with a dry smile, as worrying as other things she had been buying lately. 'How much do you need?'

Claire didn't seem nearly as interested in accepting her help as Caroline had thought. It looked as though she was weighing something up.

'I didn't buy it,' she said.

Fifteen minutes later, Caroline marched into Grace's.

'I hear you've been helping my niece,' she said.

Grace leaned against the counter and said: 'I do what I can.' Then, suspiciously, she added: 'Helping?'

'With the baking.'

'She told you I could *bake*? Couldn't she just have told you I was the Antichrist instead?'

'Your rum-raisin cakes are fantastic.'

'It's not rum.'

'I don't want to know.'

Grace shrugged.

'I think you should have a stand at the market. In your own name.'

Grace took an involuntary step backwards and stared at her in shock. '"Grace's Hamburgers"?' she said with as much sarcasm as she could muster.

'I was thinking of something more along the lines of "Grace's Home-Made Cakes".'

Sara looked up in surprise as a dark shadow blocked the light. Grace was towering in the doorway with an agitated expression which made Sara feel thankful that at the least she didn't have a shotgun to hand. She was still wearing her work clothes and smelled strongly of frying, but she had taken off her apron. She gushed the entire story about the cakes, Claire and Caroline in three short, agitated sentences.

'It's an insult!' Grace continued. 'And it's your fault. You and that damn Idgie and all those hobos, making me soft.'

'Uh,' Sara said. 'Do you want to come in?'

Grace stormed into the bookshop and sat on one of the armchairs with jerky, furious movements. Sara hesitated over by the counter. The shop suddenly felt very small. Grace had the ability to take up the entire room wherever she happened to be.

'They want me to have a stand at the market.'

'And, uh, what do they want you to sell?'

She wasn't quite sure it was entirely acceptable to be selling home-distilled alcohol at a market where there would be children and teenagers.

'Home-made cakes,' Grace said in an ominous tone.

'But that sounds nice,' Sara replied, relieved.

'Nice! She's just doing it to provoke me. The point is that we Graces never let ourselves be drawn into this town's problems. We might create new ones, but us Graces having a stand of home-made cakes! As though we . . . as though we were collecting money for *the church*. And out in the open, too. Not even we're that shameless.' She paused, thinking. 'Well, maybe Mom.'

'Do you want some coffee?'

'It's one thing doing it anonymously. I'm not saying the Grace women have never stepped up to help before, though probably not for church collections. Aside from Mom, but she was who she was.'

'A fine woman,' said Sara, though she had, of course, never met her.

'What? Yeah, I guess so.' Grace sounded hesitant. 'Madeleine. Hmm, it didn't do any real harm.'

'So what're you going to do about the market?'

'Say no, of course.'

'What on earth made her ask you in the first place?'

'Claire squealed. I offered to make the cakes for her. Undercover, of course. What's wrong with the world these days?'

Sara's smile faltered. 'So that means Claire has to make the cakes now? If you've decided not to, I mean.'

'What? No, I don't know. I guess so.'

'How will she have the time?' Sara wondered. 'I thought she had two jobs or something?'

'She can't bake. She can buy the cakes instead.' Grace looked troubled. 'I've got no problem baking the cakes for her. I offered to do it. Yeah, it might've been a mistake getting involved in someone else's problems, but I stand by it. I just don't want anyone knowing about it.'

'But what's Claire going to do now that Caroline knows . . . ?'

Grace looked at her suspiciously. She was thinking. 'I don't know,' she admitted. She put her head in her hands. 'I guess I'll have to help out. It's the last time I offer to do anything for this town, if this is the thanks you get.'

'Recognition? Yeah, that *does* sound ungrateful of Caroline.'

'You're messing with me,' Grace said accusingly.

'Very possibly.' She smiled at Grace. 'You know that Idgie was saved by a minister? After she murdered a man and cut him up, grilled him and sold him in her diner?'

'Makes you think, doesn't it?' Grace said, seeming impressed despite herself. She sighed. 'That damn book.'

People and Principles

It would have amused Grace to know that at that very moment Caroline was wrestling with her conscience. She had barely had time to recover from her book-reading before something else was threatening her peace of mind.

As morning turned into afternoon, she hadn't been expecting any new assault on the peace. She had stopped by the church on one of her near-daily trips there, and made her way slowly through it. Picking up an abandoned Bible from the floor beneath a bench, removing a burnt-out candle, refreshing the flowers by the altar. She wondered whether the windows needed cleaning but was forced to admit to herself that it was probably just because she needed something to do.

It wasn't a particularly impressive church, but Caroline liked it. It looked more like a meeting room with its beige-white walls, ordinary windows and smooth wooden benches, a wide aisle running between the sections. There was room for a hundred or so people, but Caroline had never seen more than about twenty there, not on this side of the millennium at least.

So, what do You think about this Sara?

God didn't answer, and Caroline was secretly relieved. If she had heard a voice from above, she would have thought she was finally going crazy rather than it being any kind of divine revelation.

Besides, she was quite certain that if, against all odds, God did deign to talk to her, she wouldn't hear anything nice.

The God she had grown up with had never been out to win any popularity contests. If people thought that she, Caroline, was strict, they should have met her God.

She was also quite convinced that He didn't read her thoughts. After the gay erotica she hoped so, anyway. For some reason, she couldn't let go of the story of the lonely boy.

It had been almost platonic, she said in her defence, but the God she had grown up with wouldn't have been much more forgiving of that.

Just a lonely boy and a forbidden love in a small town. Barely a kiss before page 178 (Caroline would never admit, even to herself, that her instinctive impression had been: long-winded story).

God has more than enough to be getting on with without having to follow your every move, she said to herself, in something between an admonishment and a comfort. But still. She tried to keep her thoughts respectful, and definitely away from books. She tried to be careful to use capital letters, too. Just in case.

Though there was something about churches which made conversation with God so tempting. Regardless of whether He was listening or not. She shrugged. He wasn't answering now, at any rate.

Once she had done everything she could think of in the church and completed one extra, unnecessary loop around it just to fill in time, she went out through the back door and locked it behind her. She should go home and get something done – what, she didn't yet know, but there was always something. Instead, she walked around the church and paused at the park benches in the only little hint of park that Broken Wheel had.

The park consisted of young birch trees which kept watch over a small, uneven lawn. By the benches there were two tiny maple trees, their leaves glowing red. Those trees always reminded her of children, eager to throw themselves headlong into each of the seasons. The birches with their pale mustard colours seemed commonplace in comparison.

It was such a beautiful day that Caroline couldn't help but sit down on one of the benches. She was wrapped up warm against the chilly autumn air in a coat, scarf and gloves, and as she sat there she struggled to hide just how much she was enjoying the afternoon.

Shocking the town's inhabitants with uncharacteristic bouts of good humour was never a good idea, but it was difficult, it really was, to be serious on such a glorious autumn day.

It was the air that did it. There was something so purifying about autumn days, at least when you were sensible enough to be wearing plenty of clothes. Her breath formed small clouds in front of her whenever she exhaled, for the first time that year.

Maybe it was just because of the beautiful day, but her thoughts kept returning to the boy in the story, and she thought about his and the other man's romance with amused indulgence.

There was something about the story she couldn't let go of. Maybe it was the feeling of being constantly *observed*. As though everything they did – each glance, each slight, slight touch – was being analysed, categorised and judged. People were allowed to get drunk, do much worse things to one another, even give birth to child after child, without anyone really paying any attention. But for others . . . it seemed as though one single glance was enough for people to start talking.

After that summer when she was seventeen, there had actually been one man who had been interested in her. They hadn't seen one another often enough for her to fall in love, but he had followed her home a few times after church. Not like *that*. Walked her to her front door. Smiled at her, maybe, even though she hadn't smiled back. He hadn't even held her hand.

But it had been enough. People had talked and they had laughed, and she had put a stop to it all very quickly.

She wondered whether it was regret she felt now, or simply curiosity. A slight feeling of *imagine if* which had, somehow, crept into her along with the crisp autumn air.

She was so absorbed in her thoughts that she hadn't even noticed the man who had sat down next to her until he turned, smiled at her and said: 'I hope you don't mind me keeping you company here.'

Maybe it was her good mood shining through, but the man didn't seem the slightest bit hesitant or apologetic. He smiled a smile which was just as radiant as the day around them. Her own mouth turned up slightly and he nodded in agreement, as though she might as well have just come straight out with a laugh.

'I saw you from the road,' he said.

She raised an eyebrow but said nothing.

'I saw you in the bookstore a few days ago, too.'

Initially, that made her freeze while her mind was wondering whether she should fight or take flight. But from the way he was looking at her, there didn't seem to be even the slightest hint of ambiguity in what he had said. It was as though he thought she had simply been buying books.

Which was what you were doing, Caroline, she reminded herself.

Yeah, yeah, another part of her added unhelpfully.

In retrospect, she wondered whether the sunglasses had been such a good idea. They might seem suspect at the end of September.

'Nice day today,' she felt compelled to say, just to change the subject. To be on the safe side.

He nodded and continued calmly looking around. Every now and then, he clasped and unclasped his hands, slowly, probably without even being aware of it. He had nice hands. Long fingers. No gloves, but then he was young.

'It's a nice town,' he suddenly said.

She looked at him in surprise. In front of them, they could see the little road which led to Main Street. On both sides of it were low, nondescript, tired-looking buildings, the former shops occupying their ground floors standing empty. Main Street wasn't much more impressive. You could see a small stretch of it from the bench, bathed in cold sunshine. Part of the bookstore and one small corner of the hardware store, a tree in between them, and that was all.

But he sounded serious and honest. She agreed with him, now that she thought about it. Strange that she hadn't thought it more often. 'Yes,' she said after a moment. 'You're not from around here?'

'From Hope.'

'Ah,' Caroline replied.

He flashed one of his quick, open smiles. 'Exactly,' he said, turning to her and holding out his hand. His handshake was warm and firm through her gloves. 'Josh,' he said.

'Caroline.'

He was silent after that, but it wasn't an uncomfortable silence. Very few people had sense enough to appreciate silence, she thought, even if her treacherous thoughts were using it at that moment to go from one personal failing to another.

And besides, it was the kind of day that invited quiet reflection, something which, in her, almost always meant quiet soul-searching. She thought about Sara and what on earth had made her go along with that ridiculous plan.

Truthfully, she knew perfectly well why she had done it. It had been the look in Sara's eyes when she had asked her whether she was going home. Not confusion, exactly, just a desperate kind of bravery, as though she was determined not to let anyone see how much she wanted to stay. Caroline could respect that kind of self-denial. She had felt it herself at times, even though she had been better at concealing it.

Was this one of those occasions when her mother and the women around her would have pulled together to help Sara? Or would they have slipped away to gossip about her?

It was hard to know. She suspected that they wouldn't always have known what to do either.

She surprised herself by saying: 'You know, life would be so much simpler if it weren't for all the people.'

He laughed. 'Some of them are nice, though.'

'Maybe.' He must have heard the hesitation in her voice, because he laughed again.

'People are overrated,' she said. 'I'm sure I'd be able to deal with things much better if it weren't for them.'

'You'd still need to cope with yourself,' he said.

But she wasn't the problem. She had been in complete control of herself for decades. 'It's just a question of discipline,' she said dismissively.

Though the marriage proposal is your fault, Caroline, she reminded herself. You're the one set the whole thing in motion in the lawyer's office. She grimaced. As luck would have it, the man didn't notice. She had absolutely no intention of revealing her latest weakness to anyone, not even a stranger.

'Do you never doubt yourself?' he asked. It sounded as though the question was meant honestly, as though for some reason he cared about her reply. This was a new experience.

'Complete waste of time, doubting yourself. If you make the slightest mistake, someone else is sure to let you know about it.' She added, smiling: 'Someone like me, probably.'

He laughed. 'So until you tell me I've done something wrong, I shouldn't worry? Practical. My very own new moral compass. Does it just apply to the more ethical things or to other life choices as well?'

She glanced at him to check whether he was making fun of her, but he seemed relaxed, like he was just enjoying the day and the conversation. She laughed. A deep, genuine, completely unintentional laugh which slipped out before she had time to stop it.

'If I were you,' she said, 'I wouldn't put much faith in my opinion.'

He smiled again, more confident this time. 'It's too late to back out now. I trust you completely. The question is just whether I have to come and ask before I do anything, or whether it's OK to come by afterward? For absolution.'

'I wouldn't come to me for forgiveness either. I've never been much good at that.' People expected too much from forgiveness. Caroline believed in confession and regret, of course, and in being forgiven your sins perhaps, but people often seemed to simply hop straight over repentance and atonement and put all their hopes on the Church and on people turning the other cheek.

In her opinion, being mollycoddled by others did no one any favours.

He looked at her then, almost searchingly, as though he was weighing up what she had said. Then he shrugged. 'No one's good at forgiveness. Not in practice.'

For once, she didn't know what to say. It felt as though it had been years since she had last had an honest conversation with anyone. His words sounded much older than he was.

She shook her head to herself, and said: 'Who knows, maybe I'll make an exception for you. No deadly sins, though.'

'I'm not sure I even remember which they are.'

She was about to list them off when she saw his smile. She laughed and shook her head again, this time at him.

'Andy asked me to help out at the dance on Saturday,' he said.

She didn't reply, but it wasn't an awkward silence.

'Since they're expecting so many people.'

When she still didn't reply, he continued, more hesitantly: 'I sought them out myself. To . . . meet others.'

'That's nice,' she said. It was the only thing she could think of. He seemed so grateful for her response that she wished she had thought up something more meaningful. Then she thought of the boy in the book and wondered whether it perhaps wasn't *what* she said that was important.

She adjusted her scarf and her coat against the cold, but decided to sit for a while longer. She glanced at him. He wasn't the kind to gossip.

'Are you going?' he asked.

Caroline hesitated. She straightened up, but he misinterpreted the movement and got to his feet.

'It was nice to meet you,' he said hurriedly. He started walking away while she stayed where she was on the bench. Before he disappeared onto Main Street he turned back towards her but with the sun behind him, she could no longer see his face.

'I hope you come on Saturday,' he said. 'If you do, I promise to make you a good drink.'

She stared at him as he left, completely stripped of her ability to speak.

Would she go? The thought hadn't even occurred to her before, though it really should have done. That was when they were due to propose to Sara. Some of the responsibility for the whole wretched state of affairs was hers, it would be wrong to shy away from the consequences of their rash idea.

It would also be completely wrong to take part in what would, in all certainty, be an orgy of drunkenness and immorality. 'Immoral,' she said tentatively. She didn't seem to be able to muster her usual severity.

One thing was absolutely clear. She *wouldn't* be having anything to drink.

Broken Wheel, Iowa
April 14, 2011

Sara Lindqvist
Kornvägen 7, 1 tr
136 38 Haninge
Sweden

You know, Sara, sometimes I see you here in Broken Wheel, as though in a series of small, clearly illuminated snapshots. It might sound strange, but that's how it is when you get old people to talk about the past. It's so easy to become a part of it. Maybe it's because so much of it, the past that is, exists purely inside me. It's something of a relief that it's part of you now as well, but I wouldn't pay too much mind to it if I were you. It's dangerous, getting caught up in other people's memories. I hope you realize that I've never cared about growing old, but right now, I do slightly. It's not just that you have so much less future, but you also lose so much of your past, one death at a time. I can see it in the old people here, how their lives revolve around deaths and anniversaries. Spouses, friends, even children. 'My husband died nine years ago', 'it's seven years since my son died'.

I guess I'm lucky, all my youngsters are still here. But sometimes it feels as though everyone, the entire town, is stuck in a similar cycle, where everything that's ever going to be has already been. That's why it's a comfort for me to imagine you here. In my mind you're strangely linked to my entire life. You might be selling Bibles with Caroline, handing out books with Miss Annie, or just chit-chatting a bit with my John.

Best,

Amy

The Book of Books

How, *how* could she have let herself be talked into this?

Sara was standing in front of the mirror in her room, glumly looking at her reflection. The expression on her face was a mixture of sulky child and utterly depressed teenager.

She was sure that others before her had felt exactly the same way when they found themselves at a market or in a shopping centre, dressed as whatever ridiculous product they were selling. Wasn't that how actors supported themselves, at least judging by those films and TV programmes about people who wanted to act? Didn't they dress up as tomatoes and chickens – in TV commercials if they were lucky, in malls if they weren't?

The difference being, of course, that she didn't want to be an actress. And that they had been paid. And been dressed as something harmless. She was dressed as a book. And not just any old book. The Book of Books.

How had she ended up here?

Books really shouldn't be humiliated like this, like some kind of C-list celebrity. They should be dignified, magical portals to mystery, entertainment, love.

Jen had been enthusiastic. Since the market would be taking place on the street right outside it, the bookstore would be open as usual rather than having its own stand. Still, she had said, something needed to be done to make it extra festive.

'The Book of Books' was what she had called her idea, with well-earned pride. 'People can come up to you and ask about your books!'

They could do that even if she was dressed normally, Sara had pointed out. She had even been prepared to go as far as wearing a special T-shirt, but Jen hadn't been impressed.

'A T-shirt?! When I can make a completely brilliant costume for you? It doesn't even involve any extra work for you because

I'll do everything – not because I have so much spare time what with two kids and all the marketing that has to be done, but because I *care* about this town.'

'I care about the town,' Sara protested feebly.

Surely there had to be other ways of showing your affection than dressing up as a book?

Apparently there weren't, so now she was standing there, ready to make a fool of herself for love, like so many others before her.

The costume wasn't flattering.

Jen's vision had been one of thin, glossy fabric, with a special metal frame resting on her shoulders like the spine of a book, and pretty golden lettering like on an antique book. But October was well under way and it was cold, and so she had been forced to compromise with flannel, and even agreed to let Sara wear her jeans underneath.

She thought about how she had been looking forward to seeing Tom again, the first time since that evening on his sofa, and about how she had been planning to be completely relaxed and natural, but still looking better than normal somehow.

It was eleven now, and the market was starting at twelve. George would be coming to pick her up at any moment, and she looked like an oddly bookish scarecrow. There was no other way of describing it.

It was a beautiful day too, just to irritate her, with light, mild winds and a bit of sun. She could just imagine all the people seeing the sunshine and looking forward to a day out, while she herself glanced in the mirror and foresaw nothing but a day of public humiliation.

She rested her head against the mirror and closed her eyes. She would be meeting Tom dressed as a book.

Broken Wheel had never looked better. Banners and streamers had been strung across the street, together making up the colours of the American flag. Unfortunately, the street was so wide that they drooped slightly in the middle, but everyone agreed that they looked nice nevertheless. The market stalls were spread all along the street, and firmly fastened down against the Iowa wind, just to be on the safe side. They made the street feel just the right size for the day. Even the asphalt looked cosier.

Grace was selling her home-made cakes and looked only slightly troubled. She had hung a sign reading 'Warning: may cause headaches' which Caroline was busy trying to pull down. Grace's protests seemed relatively half-hearted, perhaps because she had never quite believed it would be allowed to stay up.

There was a stall selling various ornaments and incomplete, hand-painted dining sets. Another was selling embroidered cushions and colourful knitted sweaters, gloves and hats, ahead of the winter's biting winds.

The majority of Broken Wheel's inhabitants were already there. Sara tried to sneak into the bookshop and put off the humiliation for slightly longer, but she was stopped by Grace. She wished she had arrived in her normal clothes and then changed in the shop, but she had been worried there wouldn't be time. She had been forced to sit twisted in the car so that the shoulder piece would fit, and now she had to see everyone before she had had time to prepare herself.

'What are you wearing?' Grace asked, laughing heartily at Sara's explanation. Jen came to her defence and explained the idea, but it was of little comfort since Jen wasn't the one being forced to look like this.

She suspected it would be just as effective as a deterrent against men as it was crows. As luck would have it, Tom hadn't arrived yet. Maybe he had come down with something, she thought hopefully.

Eventually, cars began pulling up, people streaming out of them like an invading army. Families of restless children and expectant adults. Young people who lingered strategically at the edge of it all from the outset and then, as if pre-programmed, made their way straight from there to the broken park benches. Unattached adults in noisy groups; a few grandmothers and grandfathers, the men placing themselves near to things which could be eaten, the women inspecting the incomplete dinner sets in murmuring tones. Everyone from Broken Wheel was there, along with many people from Hope.

Once they had been told what she was meant to be, the majority didn't seem to think that the Book of Books was so strange. Sara came to the conclusion that they must be used to stuffed chickens and things like that. She tried to hide in the safety of the shop, but it didn't take long for the market to succeed in tempting her out.

'Come and stand with us a while,' said Grace. 'You'll keep the birds away.'

The street was teeming with people.

'Where have all these people come from?' Sara asked.

Grace shrugged. 'This is Iowa. It might be miles to the nearest neighbour but that doesn't mean that news doesn't spread.'

Sara scanned the crowd for Tom but couldn't see him anywhere. She relaxed. It was a nice day. So long as she didn't have to see Tom before she had taken off the costume, it might even be perfect.

Andy was there advertising the dance. No alcohol was being served at the market itself. ('We don't want to encourage immorality,' Caroline had said to Sara; 'We don't want people to be drunk before they get to the bar,' Andy had said. Considering the number of hip flasks Sara had seen so far, both were likely to be disappointed.)

'So,' he said, 'are you going to be wearing this . . . get-up to the dance tonight?'

'Of course she won't be,' said Claire. She was helping Grace on the cake stall.

'Why wouldn't she be wearing it?' a voice behind Sara asked. 'It looks so good on her. What're you meant to be, by the way?'

Tom squinted exaggeratedly at her and kissed Claire on the cheek.

'I'm a book,' Sara said gloomily.

He managed not to laugh.

'It could've been worse, I guess,' Sara said, though she didn't believe that one bit. She thought for a moment. 'They could've buried me in a pile of books . . . dressed me up in a giant plastic book . . . Queen of the Books maybe, on a throne made of books and with a tiara . . . stuck real books to me . . . forced me to go naked with just a couple of books to hide behind.'

She could have kept going with examples of bigger catastrophes, but Tom seemed to have stopped listening. She trailed off when she saw the look in his eyes.

As far as Caroline was concerned, the market was such a complete success that it restored whatever self-righteousness she might have lost with the gay erotica. She regarded the scene in front of her with well-deserved satisfaction. Even Grace, she noticed, was behaving herself.

Then the man from the park bench appeared next to her. She realised she was happy to see him again, which was entirely unexpected and potentially awkward.

'Fantastic day,' he said, and to her horror she realised she was smiling. *Get it together, Caroline*, she thought. For some reason, she saw a Buick in her mind's eye.

'We had good luck with the weather,' she said. A safe topic of conversation.

He was in no rush to move away from her. She told herself that it didn't mean anything. With time, he would realise that there were more interesting people in town, and start smiling behind her back instead of to her face. And that, Caroline told herself, standing up straight, couldn't happen soon enough.

'Have you decided if you're coming tonight?' he asked.

Marry Us!

'Things are really going to kick off now,' Andy said to no one in particular.

There was nothing left to do. Everything had been prepared. The Square was ready. It would be a dance they would all be talking about for a long time to come. Drinks would be served, music would be played, things would happen.

The bar had never looked better, his Carl was as handsome as ever, and their helper Josh seemed to be a fast learner. The dance would be his great triumph, his best project to date. And the proposal was important too, of course.

Jen and her husband were among the first to arrive. The man looked resigned but relaxed, wearing a beige jacket which had clearly been his wife's choice and was a size too small. Jen was dressed for the occasion in a subtle black dress made from thick, stiff material which made her look slightly square.

'So we're first then?' she asked. It wasn't quite true. A few people from out of town had already arrived and were sitting with their beers and whiskeys at the furthest table away. She leaned over the bar and whispered loudly to Andy: 'And the banner? Everything's done?'

He nodded. 'We're ready.'

Then Tom came in, closely followed by Claire. That put an end to all further discussion.

In contrast to the out-of-towners, the inhabitants of Broken Wheel gathered around the bar and remained standing there, slightly rigid and self-conscious, as people who rarely get dressed up together sometimes can be. Grace managed to break some of their self-consciousness by being completely untroubled by it. She had put on a clean, freshly ironed shirt, and was acting as though she was someone who ironed her shirts every day. She sat down on one of the empty stools by the bar and ordered a whiskey before she even bothered to greet the others.

'Isn't Sara here yet?' she asked. 'Say what you like about her, but that woman sure makes things happen.'

'You don't say,' Tom said drily.

Andy and Jen exchanged a brief glance.

'Tough woman, that Sara.' Grace shook her head and laughed as though at a funny joke. 'Not to mention Idgie. Offering drinks to hobos, huh, before lunch. And elephants and I don't know what else.'

She continued, oblivious to the confused looks from the others. 'The other woman becomes really tough too, when she finally starts fantasising about killing men. Towanda, right?'

They were still staring at her and she flung her arms wide. '*Fried Green Tomatoes!* A book about this country's strong women. She knows her books, that Sara. There probably hasn't been a tougher woman than Idgie Threadgoode. Maybe with the exception of my grandmother.' Then she added, in the name of fairness: 'Though even my grandmother had nothing to do with an elephant. As far as I know.'

That brought a vague memory to life for Andy. 'Wasn't that a movie?' he asked.

Grace shook her head. 'A movie. Well, I thank you. I guess not everyone can be as educated as Sara and I.'

For some reason Tom couldn't quite understand, all their conversations kept returning to Sara. As though they couldn't make it through one evening without talking about her.

Though there was something touching in the way that everyone seemed to be waiting for her. Each time the door opened, someone would glance over to it, and each time it was someone other than Sara, their eyes would flit back to the others.

She had been in town for a month and a half but they were acting as though she had always been there. As though she always would be. With her bookstore. Among people who, if they ever actually picked up a book, would rather hit someone else on the head with it than read.

He smiled in spite of himself.

He already found it difficult to imagine Main Street without the bookstore, but he told himself that was just habit. With time, she would move on and everything would go back to normal.

He took a swig of beer and forced himself to smile at Jen, who was talking away next to him. He didn't bother trying to work out what she was saying. Something about elephants.

The best thing would be if he could just avoid her until she went home. He knew it had been a mistake talking to her at the market, but how was he meant to avoid it when she turned up dressed as a book?

As long as she didn't mention her naked body again he should just be able to greet her briefly to show he had been raised properly and stay away from her the rest of the evening. He turned his back resolutely to the door, and continued to exchange meaningless chit-chat with Jen.

But when Sara finally arrived, he looked.

She looked more grown up, and surprisingly beautiful. She was wearing a simple, sleeveless dress with a square neckline that was cut low enough for a party but not so low as to be too much. It flared out slightly at the hips, and stopped just above her knees. The deep burnt-yellow colour made her hair seem darker, almost black, and even her eyes seemed bigger than he remembered. The cut of the dress emphasised her slim body, and when she moved, she seemed lithe and self-confident, and irritatingly sexy. The dimmed lighting caught the dress, making her bare arms and pale skin glow.

Just avoid her, he told himself, unable to tear his eyes away. She would be going back to Sweden soon, he thought. He counted in his head. Two weeks, max. Then everything would go back to normal.

The warmth and kindness of the people in Broken Wheel struck her the moment she entered the room. They smiled welcomingly at her, waving her over as though they had been waiting for her. As though they actually would have noticed if she hadn't turned up. It was a completely new experience.

Eventually, her gaze instinctively sought out Tom. When their eyes met, he looked away immediately. She could have sworn he actually grimaced. That told her more than she wanted to know. Her smile faltered, but she allowed herself to be dragged over to the bar by Jen and Grace, saying a faint hello to Josh on the other side of it. People were surrounding her, greeting her and laughing with her as though she had lived in the town for years.

Apart from Tom, who nodded coolly at her and then moved in the complete opposite direction, laughing at something Claire had said.

She forced herself not to look at him. Almost as if to taunt her, he was wearing a white shirt, frustratingly well ironed, which emphasised his broad shoulders and which hung against his flat stomach and down over his muscular thighs, barely hidden by his jeans . . . She looked away again.

She started thinking of that time on the sofa, but then snapped back to reality. She longed for a time when he would have forgotten the whole thing, so that he wouldn't have to avoid her any longer.

The music and dancing had begun in earnest. Most of the inhabitants of Broken Wheel were still around the bar, but beyond them was a crowd of people from the market, along with a large number of the cowboy-hat women from before. They hadn't bothered coming to the market, but they were certainly here now. Andy and Jen were constantly glancing at one another, but Sara had so much else on her mind that she noticed it only in passing.

Of course she wasn't in love with Tom.

She just wanted his friendship, as it had been. The friendship which had made him visit the bookshop every now and then, and laugh at her reading.

And so she consciously ignored the part of her – now relegated to somewhere in the region of her solar plexus – which was, yet again, constantly aware of exactly where he was in the room.

It was just a . . . kiss. These things happen. Even between friends. You find yourselves sitting on a sofa together, lose concentration, and then suddenly you're lying there with them on top of you.

An accident, Sara thought. Nothing they needed to take seriously. They would move past it, forget it had ever happened, or else laugh about it together. Ha ha, how crazy, to think that you ended up on top of me like that. And then they could be friends again.

Simple.

She wouldn't ever say a thing about that evening, she thought, and she hoped that Tom wouldn't either. Things would eventually go back to the way they had been.

And yet, only a few minutes later, she was the one who came dangerously close to bringing it up.

She had just left Grace to go and talk to George, and had relaxed so much that she didn't notice that Tom was, at that very moment, on his way over to Claire. They ended up together in an awkward quartet. Sara looked demonstratively at George, but not before she detected wry amusement in Tom's eyes.

It was just too much. She hadn't talked to him all evening. She hadn't even *seen* him for the past hour. And now she had cast one – one! – unconscious glance at him, just to make sure she didn't bump into him, and he had the nerve to smile at it, as though he thought she had deliberately gone over to be near to him.

Her eyes flashed. She turned towards him, ready to . . .

The music fell silent.

She suddenly found herself standing under a spotlight. A banner appeared from nowhere behind the bar. It covered the entire length of it.

On an old white sheet, in big, red, hand-painted letters, it said, utterly incomprehensibly: 'MARRY US!'

The Comfort of Candide

She was like a rabbit caught in the headlights.

Caroline involuntarily gripped her pink drink and she heard Andy attempting to explain their madcap idea. For a second, it seemed as though the whole thing would work. Sara smiled, uncertain and hesitant at first, but then increasingly dazzlingly. Her eyes glittered with something which genuinely looked like gratitude. She turned around so that she could include everyone in her smile.

There was a look of such pure, open joy in both her smile and her eyes that Caroline found herself blinking, disconcerted, barely able to smile back.

Andy and Jen were still talking in the background, but Caroline knew that no one was really listening to what they said, Sara's gaze was so strong. At least that was something, she managed to think before everything went wrong; the fact that they had been the cause of such a look, and such a smile, in another person.

It was true that Sara was happy. It was such a mad, strange idea that she couldn't help but laugh, and she was also moved. It was a way of showing that they liked her, she knew that, some kind of grand farewell gesture. Regardless of what happened next, the banner was a sign that she had belonged here.

Andy and Jen continued. 'Of course, towns can't get married per se,' said Jen, and Sara laughed. 'So we've decided to appoint a, well, a representative.'

'A representative,' Andy agreed approvingly. 'And we've decided to sacri— appoint Tom.'

'Strictly a marriage of convenience, of course,' said Jen, and Sara nodded. Of course. She cast a quick glance at Tom, full of the moment's humour and laughter, all thoughts of ignoring him temporarily forgotten in her need to share this crazy moment with someone. It was only then that she saw his face.

He seemed completely expressionless, aside from a stiff, forced smile. Two fierce red patches had flared up on his neck and were spreading slowly upwards over his cheeks. Since he was smiling, no one other than Caroline and Sara noticed the cool, almost angry look in his eyes. She swallowed.

Then the spotlight disappeared, the music came back on, and everyone gathered around her. She scanned the crowd for Tom to see whether she had merely imagined his expression, but people kept appearing next to her, cutting her off from him. She replied mechanically to whatever it was they were saying to her. When she finally caught sight of him again, he was over by the bar, where Carl poured him a whiskey. He drank it improperly quickly.

She told herself that she didn't care. This was her proposal. They liked her.

They liked her enough to have come up with this crazy idea of a marriage of convenience, and she was planning on enjoying it.

And so she laughed and smiled and made sure to hold her head high as she moved slowly through the room. People she barely knew and people she had never met were patting her on the back, and more than one woman wearing a cowboy hat pulled her into a bear hug.

'Does this mean the guy at the bar is free now?' one of them asked, but Sara didn't need to come up with an answer. Another woman who had pushed her way over to congratulate Sara had managed to hit her so hard on the back that she temporarily lost the ability to speak.

She ignored Tom's rigid figure by the bar.

Damn Tom.

When she couldn't avoid it any longer, she finally went over to him. 'What a mad plan,' she said pleasantly. That would surely make him relax a little, she thought.

He looked around, presumably to make sure that no one was listening. Carl was busy at the other end of the bar and the music was so loud that they couldn't hear what anyone near them was saying, but still he lowered his voice. 'I guess I should congratulate you. Or us, rather.'

His voice was so overtly disapproving that she couldn't fight the temptation to say: 'I see you're clearly the happiest man in town.'

There was still lightness in her voice but he didn't seem to appreciate it. 'Christ, Sara,' he said. 'What are you thinking?' He glanced about. 'We need to talk. I'm going to drive you home,' he said coldly. She realised he already had her jacket in his hand.

Around them, the party was in full swing and everyone else seemed to be in a fantastic mood. The majority of people were gathered in a big crowd in the middle of the room, some of them dancing. There was even a band playing on an improvised stage at the front; a guitar, a woman singing, a violin and some drums. Sara looked longingly at the dancing.

You hardly ever get the chance to dance, she thought, and it was still so early. He held out her jacket and she took it with a quiet sigh.

There would be other occasions, she told herself.

She paused.

There wouldn't be other occasions, no more dances or improvised proposals. She would be going back to Sweden and this evening would fade away, along with everything else she had experienced here. Tom was already halfway to the door. What did she have to lose?

'Don't you fancy a dance before we go?' she asked.

'Jesus,' he said, tearing open the door. He almost pushed her out.

'Guess not,' Sara muttered to herself. She took a last, sentimental glance at all the others. They were the first to leave. Even Caroline was still there.

She knew what was coming. There could only be one reason for him to have dragged her out of there in such a fashion.

Sure enough.

'What the hell do you think you're doing?' he exploded the moment they'd stepped outside. They were standing there in the huge parking lot, alone except for the dark and silent cars around them. Even when only faintly illuminated by the few working street lights, she could still make out the disapproving look on his face, and the tense posture of his body.

She smiled knowingly at how predictable he was, which may not have been especially diplomatic.

'I'm serious, Sara.'

He was still stupidly attractive. His white shirt was barely crinkled. He had rolled up the sleeves and hadn't bothered to put on his jacket.

'I don't know the exact rules, but if you get arrested you'll never be allowed back in the country, and you'll definitely be fined. It's a crime, for God's sake.'

She was hugging her jacket and shuddered in the cold evening. She would be getting back to Sweden in November. It was an awful month to return to, she thought.

'Are you even listening?'

'Crime – fines – terrible consequences,' she repeated obediently without looking at him.

'This isn't a joke.'

He was standing by the car, his keys ready in his hand, but still talking, as if he had to get it all out of his system. She tried desperately to keep her eyes directed at anything but his face.

'. . . about us,' she suddenly heard. She couldn't help but meet his eyes then. 'There is no "us", you know that. But does this have anything to do with what happened that night?'

She blushed. 'Of course it doesn't,' she said.

He looked hard at her, but she wasn't planning to say anything else.

'I meant what I said. It would never work.'

She nodded.

'You're not in love with me –' he started, and this time she interrupted him quickly.

'No,' she said. 'Of course I'm not.'

'And I'm not in love with you.'

She knew that too, of course.

'How long had you been planning on staying here?'

As long as I can, she thought.

'What had you been planning? Marry me, stay a couple of months 'til you got bored, send the divorce papers from Sweden?'

He seemed surprisingly angry. As though he was determined to make her see that she didn't belong here. It felt like an unnecessarily mean thing to do after something which had been nothing more than a kind gesture.

She smiled at the memory. The banner had been fantastic. She leaned against the car door, so that she could face the Square, where everyone was still enjoying themselves. *It's not as if I have anything to go back for*, she thought. It scared her more than she wanted to admit, the future. All alone again.

But she said nothing. She had no intention of revealing how little she had to go back to. Not now it was so clear he didn't want her to stay.

She shrugged. 'All is for the best in the best of all possible worlds,' she said quietly to herself. She had always found a certain comfort in the adventures of Candide. Regardless of what ended up happening to her, Candide had already suffered worse. Perhaps that wasn't quite the result Voltaire had been hoping for, but it worked.

Tom's eyes grew cold once more. 'For God's sake,' he said.

Excellently observed, dear philosopher, but let us take care of our garden, she thought.

He was moving around the car to open the door for her, as if he just assumed she would leave this party only to be further lectured by him. She took a step back and shook her head as resolutely as she could. She was going nowhere.

'Maybe it wasn't a joke,' she said. 'But it's not so damned serious, either. It was a kind gesture, that was all. The only thing you – or I – need to do is to tell them that we're not planning on getting married. We're obviously not going to get married. You can't seriously believe that I'd expect you to? No one can force you to marry someone.'

He turned away from her and got in the car, ready to leave her there, alone and angry – and strangely thrilled about refusing to go with him.

Before he drove away he leaned over the passenger seat, rolled down the window, and said: 'You don't know them like I do,' followed by a 'Jesus Christ' under his breath.

And then he was gone, and she was still there, just like that. She looked at the clock. Half past nine. The party was still in full swing.

Sweet Caroline

Things had begun to die down at the Square and Caroline started to relax for the first time that evening.

When she had arrived, she had almost been shocked by the number of people, the unbearable level of noise, and how impolite everyone was. She had pushed her way through the crowd, saying 'excuse me' and then '*excuse* me'.

She had been very close to just turning around and leaving.

Her, at a party, to meet a man. Deep down, she knew that was the real reason she was there. She wanted to see him again. But it had been such a long time since she had believed that you could be a strong, intelligent woman and still live a normal life. Until that summer evening in '84, she had even believed that there might be men out there who appreciated strength in a woman.

It was funny, she thought, as she was jostled this way and that, trying to work out whether it was worth fighting her way forward, that she couldn't remember the man's name, but could still remember exactly how her nylon stockings had felt against her skin, the smell of fire and exhaust fumes, and how wildly her heart had been pounding when she arrived. She had forgotten the sex itself but could still recall the taste of tobacco and liquor when he kissed her, and how heavy he had been on top of her.

Get it together, Caroline, she thought. She was here for Sara's sake. But at that moment, Josh caught sight of her and, before she had time to say anything, had made her a drink. A ludicrous pink drink which definitely wasn't alcohol-free.

She still didn't know whether she would have fled if he hadn't caught sight of her just then. Once she'd got the drink in her hand, she'd sort of just stood there, watching him handling the drink orders as if he'd spent half his life behind the bar. Despite the crowd, it had been surprisingly pleasant, until that whole proposal thing.

Now, though, the dancing had died down and people were

sitting in small groups, talking about subjects which interested them. They were leaning forward over the tables to make themselves heard, touching an arm or a hand to get someone's attention or to show a hint of friendliness. Three couples were still dancing slowly and comfortably, like old friends, and every now and then a couple went outside for some fresh air. Caroline nodded understandingly. She could definitely see the need for it by this point.

She couldn't help thinking about that look in Tom's eyes. Panic or anger, she wasn't sure, but there had been something there. She could have sworn she saw him leave with Sara, but then Sara was back, acting as if nothing had happened and everything was just fine. So maybe it was.

Andy, Carl and Josh were more relaxed now, idly cleaning up and tending to the last few guests. Sara was sitting by the bar being amused by some of Grace's stories. Grace was gesturing so wildly she seemed to be in danger of falling off her stool. Caroline even contemplated joining them, when she was saved by Josh bringing two beers over to her. He touched her arm lightly and pointed to an empty table with one of the bottles.

'Come on,' he said, guiding her over to it. He leaned back in the chair and closed his eyes. 'What a night,' he said.

'Are you tired?'

'A bit,' he admitted. 'But what a night.'

He sat up and leaned forward over the table. 'Thanks for coming,' he said, touching her hand in an almost unconscious movement. His fingers barely grazed her skin, but she felt a sudden flutter in her chest. She swallowed and strained not to pull her hand away in panic. Instead, she slowly clenched and unclenched her hands.

'It was nice,' she said uncertainly. But it was definitely nicer to be able just to sit down for a while, and talk in peace and quiet. She cautiously sipped her refreshingly cool beer. Not that she was going to drink the whole thing, of course.

For a while, they simply sat there quietly together, like they had done on the park bench, watching the handful of people still having a good time. One of them stumbled on the dance floor and had to be picked up by their partner; Caroline instinctively looked at Josh, and their eyes met in shared laughter. The guitarist and singer were still going, but the man behind the drums was leaning against the wall with a beer in his hand and the drumsticks resting on his lap. The woman with the violin had gone outside for some fresh air with a man from one of the farms nearby.

'Can I give you a ride home?'

She nodded, but neither of them made any move to leave. 'You were great this evening,' she said.

'I had fun. Did you like your drink?'

She nodded again. A white lie couldn't hurt, after all.

When they left, Andy and Carl were tidying up in earnest. They gestured for them to go home in response to Josh's raised eyebrow.

They didn't say a word during the car ride, which somehow seemed to take much longer than normal, and yet also seemed to be over in a flash. Josh surprised her by following her right up to the door.

She hesitated before she opened it. In a way, she didn't want the evening to be over yet. And he showed no sign of being in a hurry to get back to his car.

'Thanks for coming tonight,' he said, so quietly that she almost didn't hear him.

He leaned in towards her. She looked at him in confusion.

For a moment, she almost thought he was about to kiss her, he was so close. *Don't be stupid, Caroline*, she had time to think before he did that very thing. His lips gently touched hers and she froze.

She knew that she should go. Open the door and run. But she couldn't move.

He pulled away slightly and touched her cheek with a finger. She couldn't quite meet his eyes. 'Look at that,' he said. 'You aren't busy telling me I've done something wrong.'

Then he kissed her again.

Good Times Never Seemed so Good

You know what, Caroline, she said to herself, *I think you've completely lost your mind.*

She was sitting in her usual armchair in the living room with a cup of tea to calm her nerves. It wasn't working. The tea had long since gone cold. Outside, her beautiful garden was nothing but a dark shell. The flowers had wilted weeks ago and the leaves had already started to fall. Things weren't much better with her. She was a shadow of her former self: she could see her reflection in the window; pale, stony face, a hunted look in her eyes.

She had started her internal talking-to the moment she woke that morning. The previous evening hadn't been right. She should have known better than to encourage him. She was forty-four years old, for goodness' sake. A respectable Christian lady acting like a teenager in love. With a teenager. A gay teenager.

He must be at least twenty-five, she had told herself.

Is *that* your defence? Twenty-five!

Oh Lord.

Her morning had been spent sitting at the kitchen table, worrying about what people would say if they found out about Josh. They'll laugh at you if they ever do, she said repeatedly to herself until the world started spinning around her. And it was just this type of thing that people always did find out about.

That summer when she had still been young and stupid, she'd fallen for one of those handsome and adventurous men who took nothing seriously and was idolised because of it. He was two years older than her. Even in those days she'd somehow known that everyone her age saw her as too headstrong, too prim, too, well, too boring.

The man had smiled at her, told her a joke she'd barely under-stood – in hindsight, she was pretty sure the joke had been about her. But it had been enough to turn her head. She had known instinctively that he wouldn't be impressed by intelligence, but she had also thought that she had a choice, that she could just decide to be like everyone else instead of smart.

She had gone to a party and hidden her personality behind a new dress, some make-up, and a completely ridiculous hairstyle. She was shocked by how naive she had been. As though people would forgive intelligence just because she drank alcohol one evening, coughed her way through a cigarette and lost her virginity in the back of a Buick.

They'd returned to the party together but later that evening she'd seen him with his arm around someone else. When people saw the look on her face, the laughter started. The only thing that had happened when she tried to be normal was that she had willingly lowered her defences, happily abandoned her weapons, and been completely powerless against their laughter as a result. They'd move on to new gossip eventually, but it had been an awful summer until they did.

And here she was, again. Still stupid.

When she had heard a knock at the door just after lunch, she had known it was Josh. For a moment, she thought about not answering.

He had seemed irritatingly alert and rested, and not the least bit embarrassed. He had walked into her living room as though he belonged there. She could see him before her now: strong and self-confident and humiliatingly young and handsome. She sank deeper into the armchair, as though in an attempt to protect herself from the memory.

'Yesterday was nice,' he said simply.

Then she had been forced to explain that yesterday had been wrong in every possible sense. He hadn't protested, hadn't demanded any kind of explanation. He just shrugged and said: 'I just wanted to be sure you weren't hiding out here because you were afraid of seeing me.'

A mean thing to say, she thought to herself now. Of course she was hiding.

It was all Sara's fault. Before she arrived, something like this would never have happened.

She stood up and went into the kitchen to make a new cup of tea. She was much too old to be carrying on like this. She had behaved like one of those overly made-up older women who tried to flirt with young waiters; the kind of women who didn't understand that those same waiters then went home and laughed about them with their equally young girlfriends.

Or boyfriends.

It's not exactly like you have the right equipment for this, Caroline. Josh must just be having some kind of crisis about his sexuality. And now you've got yourself caught up in the middle of it. Josh belongs in Andy and Carl's world, not yours. And besides, let's be honest: the equipment you do have is old and worn out. It's beyond repair.

Not all of it, though.

Caroline!

(Well, it's true.)

Josh came back that evening.

'Why was it wrong?' he asked before he had even stepped into the hallway.

She turned around and went into the living room. The hall was much too narrow to be alone with him there. 'I don't want to talk about it,' she said.

He followed her. 'It was just a kiss. Plus, I like kissing you.'

She went pale. 'Oh Lord,' she mumbled to herself.

'I hardly think He had anything to do with it.'

He was right about that at least, she thought, but he managed to tease a slight smile out of her all the same.

'It wasn't right,' she repeated calmly, as though simply stating a fact. Which, she reminded herself, was exactly what she was doing.

'Does it have something to do with the Church? Some commandment about Christian ladies and bi-guys?'

She looked at him in surprise. Bi? Bee? The birds and bees? Did people still talk about that?

'It wouldn't surprise me,' she said. When it came down to it, the Church had rules about most things relating to the birds and the bees. 'But that's not why.'

'I could've sworn you enjoyed it too.'

She shuddered at the thought of being so transparent and was forced to turn away from him. 'I . . . it wasn't right.'

'Why?'

He was standing right next to the comfy old armchair she normally sat in, and she involuntarily took a step backwards. She didn't quite know where to look. He seemed absurd, standing there in her living room. Young and full of life, power and energy, surrounded by things which were old, unfashionable and feminine. She felt trapped between him and the embroidered pictures.

'You're young and I'm . . . not young,' she said. Not young? My goodness, Caroline. 'I'm old,' she corrected herself. 'Much too old for you. You should be with someone as young and beautiful as you . . .' She blushed fiercely when she realised what she had said. 'As young,' she said quickly, hoping he hadn't heard the rest.

'You're beautiful.' He didn't seem to be listening to her. 'I think you are. Does it really matter? And it was just a kiss, for God's sake.'

'Of course it was just a kiss. What else could it have been?'

He raised an eyebrow but thankfully said nothing.

'So it's about the age difference?' he asked.

'Amongst other things.'

'You think I'm too young?'

'I'm too old.'

He gestured irritatedly with his hand. 'Same thing,' he said.

She laughed. 'Hardly. Your problem will pass. Mine is going to get worse.'

He smiled at that. 'The age difference will be constant, at least.'

She stopped smiling at that thought.

'So what else?' he asked.

Her gaze shifted. 'Else?'

'You said age amongst other things. What else do you have against me?'

People didn't normally ask her what was wrong with them. She normally told them without being asked. So ironic, she thought, that now, when someone was asking, she was the problem.

'It's more about me,' she admitted.

'*It's not you, it's me*? Shit, Caroline, no one says that any more.'

She blushed. 'You don't need to swear at me,' she said. 'I've never claimed to know what it's in vogue to say.'

'It's not about what's in vogue, it's about clichés. Trite, meaningless clichés.'

'It's not trite for me,' she said. 'I've never actually said it to anyone before.'

He made a stifled groaning sound and laughed. 'OK,' he said. 'What's wrong with you then?'

She realised that now she was the problem, she had absolutely no desire to talk about it. That was ironic, too.

'I'm too old.'

'You've already said that,' he said brutally. She noticed that he wasn't arguing, which was logical since it was true. She felt strangely depressed.

'I'm not . . . pretty enough.'

She continued quickly, before he could not protest against that either. 'Worn out. This body has done too many miles.'

'And yet it's practically new. The previous owner only used it to go to church on Sundays.'

It was so depressingly true that she couldn't even bring herself to laugh. He said nothing, just stood there in the middle of her living room, refusing to leave her in peace.

'I don't have the right equipment,' she said desperately. She was thinking of the boy in the book. 'You should find a nice young man to settle down with.'

'Equipment, Caroline?'

She blushed again. She had lost control of the conversation; it wasn't going at all how she wanted.

'What a fantastic woman you are,' he added, almost to himself.

Not at all how she had planned.

'But it's true,' she said.

He raised an eyebrow, daring her to explain herself.

'I like both sexes,' he said. 'It's possible, you know. Who knows what's going to happen in the future? Maybe I'll settle down with a nice, polite young man, maybe not? Does it really make a difference to us now?'

'There is no "us",' she said quickly, just to make it clear.

He shrugged, but a dangerous look had appeared in his eyes. Something determined and defiant. It was pitch black outside now, so the living-room window looked more like a dark mirror. His tall, nonchalant body really was everywhere.

He took a step forward, put an arm around her waist and pulled her towards him. She gasped and was forced to admit to herself that it wasn't a horrified gasp. She was almost certain he was planning on kissing her, but still, he drew it out. Something – some kind of smile – flashed in his eyes. When her gaze shifted, one side of his mouth curled upwards. He was definitely laughing at her. It irritated her enough to make her meet his eye. And then he kissed her.

His lips were at once gentle and insistent. His body was firm and young and manly, and when she closed her eyes she had a vision of firm, naked men touching one another in the darkness.

She was surprised to find herself enjoying it. She felt deep, strange parts of her body stirring to life. She hadn't thought she was capable of enjoying it. She had always thought any capacity for that must have disappeared with age. Part of her was enthralled by it.

Another part of her was terrified.

She pulled away from him slightly and said: 'I'm churchwarden, for goodness' sake.'

He smiled at her. 'I'm bisexual, for goodness' sake.' But he let her go, the glint of laughter still in his eyes, and took a step back. He winked at her. 'I told you that you didn't have anything against it.'

She would never have admitted it to herself, but when he moved away from her, she felt something very close to disappointment.

'I'll be back on Tuesday,' he said. 'Make your mind up by then.'

She was close to asking him: make my mind up about what? But she strongly suspected that she didn't want to hear him say it out loud.

Caroline wasn't the only resident of Broken Wheel to be feeling somewhat shaken the day after the dance. Most affected was George, despite being the only one not to have drunk a thing.

As day broke, he was blissfully unaware that chaos and confusion were currently hurtling towards him at nearly a hundred miles an hour, along Interstate 80.

His evening had been calm and pleasant. He hadn't had a drop to drink. Most fantastic of all: he had given Claire a ride home and she had leaned over and kissed him on the cheek in thanks, like a genuine friend.

He got up, smiled to himself, drank coffee, and even had a shave, though he had already done it the day before; he glanced at the second *Bridget Jones* book and wondered what the day might have to offer.

He actually felt that way, like the day might have something to offer. It was a revolutionary feeling.

He sipped his coffee. He had felt like having cream and sugar today, and it had been an easy decision.

He wondered whether he should set off and give Sara a ride somewhere, but he suspected she preferred walking anyway. There were a few clouds in the sky but it wasn't raining, and if it did then he could always pick her up in the afternoon.

When the doorbell rang, he smiled to himself and wondered whether it was Claire. He opened the door with a friendly smile on his face.

He stared.

She looked much older than he remembered, and smaller. She barely came up to his chin, but still, in his mind, she had grown to almost mythical proportions. She was cute rather than beautiful, but she had a hard look in her eye. He remembered that.

'Hi, George,' she said.

'Michelle?'

'Nice to see you too.' The damp air had made her hair go frizzy, the way he knew she hated.

'Where's Sophie?'

'No idea. I dumped her at an ex's a couple of years ago.'

He went pale, scarcely taking in what she said.

'Don't be such an idiot, George. She's in the car.'

He looked over her shoulder, as though he had just found out what a car was. There was someone in the passenger seat, but he couldn't see her clearly.

She pushed past him into the hall but he hesitated in the doorway, torn between his longing to see Sophie and the thought that the meeting might be awkward.

'Well, go say hi, for God's sake,' Michelle said unsentimentally.

'What are you doing here?' he asked, gaining some time.

Michelle shrugged before heading towards the living room. When she reached it, she made a sudden halt and looked around her. 'I can't believe I'm back here,' she said.

George couldn't either.

'I swore I wouldn't, you know.'

He could believe that quite easily.

'And . . . how long are you planning to be here?' he asked.

'Not forever, if that's what you're worried about.'

He hadn't been. He glanced over to the car. Sophie was making her way round the back of it to grab their bags. She was as tall as Michelle, but much cuter. She was a teenager who hadn't quite grown used to her body yet, and she was completely lacking Michelle's obvious self-confidence. She was the most beautiful person he had ever seen.

He went out to help her with the bags. They had two. Both were worn-out and flowery, one considerably bigger than the other. 'Mom's,' she said. He didn't say a word. She was silent too, thankful to have someone helping her. She went into the house ahead of him, carrying the smaller of the bags and pausing in the hall.

Though he had been talking to her in his head all these years, he couldn't think of a thing to say. Of course, he hadn't always been sober while doing so, and he turned red when he thought about everything he had let her see, though obviously she hadn't actually seen a thing, which was a shame, but maybe just as well, since he hadn't always been sober . . . he got lost in his thoughts and couldn't come up with anything to do other than smile at her again.

'I'm Sophie,' she said, as though they had never met.

He felt a stab at his heart when she said that, though it was nothing he couldn't handle. He had an absurd desire to talk to Sophie about this.

'I'm George,' he said. 'Once upon a time you used to call me Dad.'

'Call him George,' Michelle shouted from the kitchen. He was glad he had tidied up the day before. The apartment was drab and impersonal, but at least it was clean. If he had known she would be coming, he would have done more. Repainted, maybe. Bought new furniture. Bought a new house.

Sophie smiled uncertainly at him and glanced towards the kitchen.

'George is fine too,' he said.

He realised he was still holding his book and put the bag down on the floor. He glanced around to see where he could put the book. Eventually, he put it down on the floor too.

'Is it good?' she asked. She had a lovely voice.

'What?' he said, and then, when he had straightened up again: 'Do you want to borrow it?'

'Maybe a bit later,' she suggested, smiling.

He nodded. She glanced into the kitchen again.

Of course she wanted to be with her mother. He had to remember that she didn't know him at all, that she might not want to. He needed to give her time to get used to him.

She doesn't even have to like me, I'm not asking for that, he said to God or the patron saint of forgotten parents or whoever it was you made promises to when you could no longer make them to your daughter in your head. As long as she knows she can trust me and come to me whenever she has any problems. He would tell her all this once she had time to get used to him, and show her he was completely normal and, well, *cool*? Or that he could be. For her sake, he would even stop being awkward and embarrassing.

At that moment, he planned on simply asking a calm, relaxed question about whether she wanted anything to eat or drink. Not forcing it on her, of course, just a friendly question.

'Can I do anything for you?' he asked. 'Do you need anything? A pop? Something to eat? A new car?'

She actually smiled at the offer of a car. He smiled back, relieved, and pretended it was a joke.

'I don't have a licence,' she said.

'Do you need money for lessons?' He could sell something. The sofa, maybe.

Her smile faltered slightly, and she glanced to the kitchen again.

'A pop would be good,' she finally said.

A Book for Everyone

Somehow, Sara made it through the day after the market.

She was glad she had been able to walk to the bookshop – she needed to get the irritation out of her system. The rest of the day had been spent behind the counter, watching the town's inhabitants laugh and joke as they pulled down stalls and tidied up the street.

Neither George nor Caroline had been there, but she had seen Tom's car pull up at one point. She really couldn't go out after that. Who knew when he might come by again.

And so she had stood there, silent and idle, tired of both Tom and herself.

She hadn't been at all sure that the next day would be any better, but when she got to the bookshop in the morning, a customer was already waiting outside.

A solitary, meagre little figure craning forward to look through the window. She could hardly have been much older than fifteen, Sara thought. She must have been waiting there in the drizzle for some time, because her hair was hanging down over her face in damp strands, but she smiled as Sara unlocked the door.

'Is it your bookstore?' she asked.

'Kind of.'

Sara hung her jacket up in the little cubbyhole and switched on all the lights. She gathered a few books to put out onto the shelves, but placed them in a pile on the counter instead and waited behind it so the girl could browse in peace. She was still standing in the doorway, looking around in fascination.

'I'm Sophie,' she said.

The name set a little bell ringing in Sara's head, but she didn't know why. She shrugged. It would come to her eventually.

'So you like books?' Sara asked.

Sophie nodded. A smart girl, Sara thought, and sweet. It was still raining outside, but the shop had become cosy the moment Sophie stepped into it. That was the effect a girl with straggly, damp hair could have.

'What're your favourites?' Sara asked. 'Do you have any?'

Sophie shook her head. She took a few steps into the shop and gazed at the shelves with a serious expression. 'Are all these books yours then?' she asked.

'Yeah . . . in a sense.' Sara paused for thought. 'Or the town's, really. Until someone comes and buys them.'

'Doesn't it feel sad to lose them?'

At that moment, Sara should perhaps have explained a few of the salient principles of market economics to her. That she wasn't really losing them, but exchanging them for money which she could then use to buy other things or else save in the bank or hide under her mattress, but doing so seemed unbelievably cynical and also completely unbelievable. Why would anyone prefer banknotes to books? A little bit of paper with a pathetic quote about God and a picture of a politician, over reams of paper with fantastic stories printed on them?

Sara suspected she had never really understood the principles of market economics herself.

So she took the question seriously, and thought about it. 'No, actually,' she said. 'I could never read every single book myself. If someone else takes them, then at least they'll be appreciated. And if you love a book, you want to share it with others.'

'What about the books nobody wants?'

'There's always a person for every book. And a book for every person.'

The girl flashed a smile and turned to one of the shelves at random. 'Even for me?' she asked.

'Sure.'

The girl seemed pleased with that answer, though didn't ask for any tips or any particular book. But she didn't seem to be in any hurry to leave.

'I haven't been here since I was a little girl,' she said. 'I hardly even remember it.'

'Really?' asked Sara.

'We left when I was really young but my mom's from around here. Mom always said she'd never return. It just made me more curious to see everything again.' She smiled. 'Things you're not allowed to do always seem more interesting, don't they? I've already walked through the entire town. Twice.'

Sara smiled. So had she, when she got here.

'Mom always said the only way she'd go back would be in a limo. And even then she would just speed right through town. Not even lower the windows. Just to see the look on all those–' She stopped abruptly.

'All those . . . ?'

'It's quite rude.'

'I gathered,' said Sara. 'She really didn't like Broken Wheel, did she?'

'Well, she called them inbred morons who had nothing better to do than go about judging what everyone else was doing and meddling in people's affairs.' She seemed embarrassed. 'I shouldn't be talking so much,' she said and added politely: 'It was nice to meet you.'

Sara smiled at her. 'Come back soon.'

Then she was alone again and could busy herself tidying up the shop.

Sara didn't mind the rather harsh words about the town. She probably would have enjoyed watching a black, shiny limo come cruising down Main Street without stopping. No, Sara was thinking about the first part of the conversation. It had set something in motion in her brain. There was a category missing. It was true that it was the town's bookshop, yes, but most of all, it was Amy's.

Before she got to work on the cleaning, she gathered all of the books she and Amy had exchanged, along with all the pearls of Amy's book collection, and placed them together on one shelf. Louisa May Alcott came first. It was fitting. She named it AMY'S SHELF. She thought it was enough.

How could an empty bookshop get so dirty? Sara wondered as she swept the floor so that it would be clean enough to mop.

She tried not to think about Tom too much as she worked, but she couldn't stop the irritation building up in her manic cleaning. He really was being ridiculous.

It wasn't as though she had fallen for him. That could have been annoying, she could understand that. Infatuation could be unrequited, along with love and sexual attraction – they all still demanded something of the recipient. Love was selfish. It was obviously hard work, having to put up with sentimental sighs, another person's exaggerated expectations, having to keep one's balance up on a pedestal which you yourself hadn't asked for.

But she wasn't in love with him, so that was all irrelevant. What she couldn't understand was why he didn't even want her as a friend, as an acquaintance. She would be perfectly happy if they saw one another once or twice a week, if only to sit in comfortable silence for a while. So long as she got to see him.

When she gave up sweeping, and started cleaning the floor properly, she could still hear the occasional crunch of gravel beneath her feet. She sighed and was almost grateful when Jen interrupted her cleaning.

She headed straight for the counter, and so Sara put down the mop and went over to stand behind it. 'What can I help you with?' she asked.

'Sign here.'

She looked down at the paper in front of her. *Form 1-130* it said in the top right-hand corner. *Petition for Alien Relative*. She couldn't help but smile at legislation which likened non-citizens to extraterrestrials.

'It's a tourist visa you have, right?'

Sara nodded. Jen pointed to a line at the bottom of the page. 'Sign here.' She had already filled in Tom's name. *Tom Harris.*

Sara hadn't even known that was his surname. She suspected that was a bad basis for a marriage. She looked up at Jen.

She was about to say something about it when the memory of Tom's anger flashed through her. His unreasonable behaviour, the unfair and simply annoying assumption that she was somehow in on the plan.

Let him worry about Jen, she thought, and then signed her name with a dramatic flourish.

'Wait,' she said as Jen was about to leave. Sara turned around and found the book she'd been keeping behind the counter.

The Complete Guide to Self-Publishing: Everything You Need to Know to Write, Publish, Promote and Sell Your Own Book by Marilyn Ross and Sue Collier.

'In case you ever want to turn that blog of yours into a book,' she said.

Jen was rendered completely speechless.

Not Something You Talk About

When Josh came round on Tuesday evening, Caroline hadn't reached any kind of decision.

She had actually refused to think about it. Part of her was trying to argue it was best that way. That it was so obvious she wasn't going to do anything she didn't even need to think about it.

Another part of her was perilously close to admitting that the reason she hadn't thought about it was because she didn't want to hear all the reasons why nothing would ever happen between them.

With him standing there outside her door, one of the strongest feelings she had was surprise that he was actually there. She had been sure that a few days' thought would be more than enough for him to realise how insane it was to be the least bit interested in her.

The next strongest feeling was a confused kind of joy at seeing him again. When he leaned forward to kiss her on the cheek, she didn't even wince.

He looked tired. A strand of hair was hanging down over his forehead, and there were lines around his eyes that hadn't been there before. As he sank down onto the sofa, he closed his eyes briefly, as though it was the first time that day he had been able to relax. She sat down next to him and fought the impulse to reach out and brush the hair from his forehead.

He smiled at her, an open, completely relaxed smile, as though he was glad to see her and as though they were . . . friends. She smiled back, intrigued. Very few people ever smiled at her like they were glad to see her, or even like they were completely relaxed in her company. Friendship was good.

'How're the wedding plans going?' he asked.

'The plans?' she said. She obviously hadn't been paying much attention to the town lately. A shameful neglect of her duties.

She shrugged. She didn't imagine anyone would actually be missing her.

Josh seemed to have abandoned the topic already. Now he was looking at her, smiling an entirely different smile. There was a questioning gaze in his eyes. Or an invitation.

'Caroline,' he said. She glanced at him cautiously. Oh hell. The glint in his eyes was back. 'Don't you think it's time you kissed me?'

She stared at him. *That's not something you talk about, for goodness' sake*, she thought. Which, she had to admit, was a long way from *that's not something you do*.

She stood up confusedly in order to physically escape the sudden tension between them. Josh stood up too. He seemed annoyingly calm.

But still, he made no attempt to touch her. He simply stood there, barely a foot away from her, waiting.

It was obvious that she was meant to make the next move. She almost wished he would just kiss her again so that she could avoid having to make the decision. She knew that the whole thing was wrong, but now that she actually had the chance to touch him, she couldn't really remember why she shouldn't.

Just once, she said to herself. I can touch him now, just a little interlude in my otherwise God-fearing life, and then I can go back to the church bazaar again.

She didn't quite believe herself. But she did believe she would never get another chance to touch him.

And so she simply reached out and did it. She could practically hear the blood rushing in her ears and swallowed nervously as her hand found his collarbone and moved down over his chest. She hesitated slightly at the first button on his shirt, and then undid them all, since they were hindering her.

Why shouldn't I do it? she thought defiantly. Then she looked around as though she were afraid that someone – God? her mother? – would answer.

I might never have another chance to touch anyone.

He was still standing still, but the look in his eyes had changed. The laughter in them had disappeared, and his gaze was deeper, darker. She realised that it was desire, and that made her feel more daring.

He noticed and put his arm around her waist, pulling her towards him. Even now that she had set it all in motion, it was clear that he was the one taking the initiative. He seemed older, more sure of himself. She enjoyed letting someone else take control and responded to his kiss with more feeling than reason.

'My God,' he said, and she was inclined to agree with him.

Living with Michelle and Sophie wasn't easy. George still didn't know how long they would be staying. From what he had managed to work out, there seemed to have been an argument of some kind with the latest man. He didn't think they would be staying especially long, but just hoped he would have enough time to get to know Sophie again. He tried not to think about what would happen afterwards. It wasn't easy.

Michelle kept mainly to his room (he had been relegated to the sofa). She had brought a computer with her, which surprised him. When they were married, she had never had much of an interest in technology, but now she spent the majority of her time in front of the thing.

One day he asked if she planned on going to see anyone while she was here, and she'd treated the suggestion with contempt. 'What? Going around making courtesy calls to the neighbours? Visiting Mom and Dad, perhaps? Some reunion that would be.'

He strongly suspected she'd married him partly to get away from them, and then left him when she realised she hadn't gotten far enough away.

He had no problem living with Michelle. In a way, he was still used to her. It was Sophie who was tricky.

He had to keep reminding himself that he couldn't have imaginary conversations with her. Once, when he'd thought he was alone, he had begun: 'Sophie . . .' and then heard a surprised 'Yeah?' from the hallway.

She was so sweet and kind. It was hard, having her back and being forced to act like a stranger. He was grateful, he really was, but he wished he could do more.

'I went to the bookstore today,' she said as they cooked together.

He was careful not to look at her and kept his eyes firmly on the chopping board. It was the first time she had voluntarily told him anything. Normally, she waited for him to speak first. They both seemed to enjoy being quiet together. He would sometimes ask her about school, her life and her friends, and she would always reply politely, but without enthusiasm. He didn't even know where they had been living. He assumed still in Iowa, but he wasn't sure. There was a man in the picture in any case, though that didn't surprise him.

'Did you meet Sara?' he asked.

'Yeah,' she said. 'She told me there are books for me out there.'

'I didn't know you liked reading.'

'I don't know if I do.' She smiled at him. 'But all the books . . . they were so pretty, George.'

He winced slightly at the George, but he was starting to get used to it now, he really was. He wouldn't say anything.

'She said the bookstore belonged to the whole town?'

He thought about it. 'I guess so. But the credit's all Sara's.'

'But does that mean some of the books are yours?'

He smiled. 'Maybe a few of them. I helped out when it was about to open.' He added, in the name of honesty: 'Mostly with the cleaning. And the driving, of course. Sara doesn't have a driver's licence.'

'So do you think she's right? That there's a book for me?'

'If Sara says so then it must be true.'

She smiled back at him. 'Thanks . . . Dad.'

Michelle appeared behind them. 'George,' she said automatically.

But Sophie simply grinned at him, almost conspiratorially, and waited until she was sure Michelle was out of earshot. Then she leaned in closer and said: 'Mom thinks people in this town secretly looked down on her.'

George gave this some thought. 'That might be true,' he said. 'But people aren't always right.'

'I know that,' Sophie said. 'We moved around a lot when I was growing up.' She hesitated. 'What I mean is . . . is it disloyal of me to feel that people here are actually *nice?*'

He smiled. 'I figure you've got the right to your own opinion, same as everyone else. But perhaps –'

'Better not tell Mom?' she finished.

'Might be best.'

'She thinks he'll come after her, you know.'

'Who?'

'Her boyfriend. Ronald Lukeman.'

'Do you like him?'

She shrugged. 'He's OK, I guess. He's the manager at a Taco John's.'

George didn't know what to say about that, so he just nodded, which seemed to do the trick, because Sophie continued in a whisper:

'I'm not so sure he will come. But perhaps that's disloyal too.'

Sara Lindqvist
Kornvägen 7, 1 tr
136 38 Haninge
Sweden

Dear Sara,

There are very few men in this world whom I'd like to look straight in the eye and tell: you should think more about yourself. Be selfish. Most men seem to know that without ever being told. But I would like to say it to Tom.

I'm sure I've mentioned my nephew. He has just been here, and I felt unreasonably cross with him. People with a strong sense of duty can be surprisingly irritating, don't you think? In my less charitable moments, I wonder if it's not a strange form of self-assertion: if I'm not here to save everyone, the world as we know it would come to an end. To be honest, though, I think it's more about habit. He's been taking care of people for so long that he probably just doesn't know how to quit.

I'm not saying that loyalty is a bad thing in a man. But you've got to know where to draw the line. Tom was loyal to his father, he's stayed on with Mike and his freight company through thick and thin, he's been here for me, and it wouldn't surprise me if he feels that this whole town is his responsibility. Sure, loyalty pays off sometimes. He has a nice job at Mike's, which he enjoys. He's still doing the odd repair job, but only for friends. It's just that there will always be someone you can't save.

Tom couldn't save the farm, and he couldn't save his father – my brother, Robert. Robert never made it into journalism. He went on with the farming, same as most people round here. Well, Tom tried, by God how he tried. He worked full-time at the farm, and part-time for Mike. He turned down a scholarship for Iowa State University's Agricultural Studies program. I don't think he cared about the farm, but he cared about his father, so he stayed. In the end they had to sell, of course. Most folks round here did. Tom managed to arrange a deal so that his father could stay in the house for the final few years of his life. They kept the farmhouse and the small yard and the drive. Everyone knew it wouldn't be for long. When his father died he went to hand over the keys to the new owners. They didn't need the farmhouse, they said. They would just level it all.

There was a lot of talk about the new house Tom built instead. This is a small town, everyone talks. Ironic, isn't it – so few people, so many opinions? Some thought that he was trying to be better than everyone else, what with the panoramic windows and all the open-planning. Others (Andy) thought it was his way of saying 'fuck you' to the world: You can keep those keys, see if I care. That kind of thing. Me, I always believed he just didn't want to risk getting too attached to a house ever again, not after what it did to Robert. So he made it practical, impersonal, telling himself that's what he wanted and setting up his defenses against having to care.

Do you know what the worst thing is about loyal people? Everyone is forever telling them to start focusing on themselves, but no one wants them to stop helping *them*. Not when it really comes down to it. Me, I find comfort in knowing that if anything were to happen to me, Tom would be there for my John.

So you see, Sara, I'm really no better than anyone else.

Best,

Amy

For the Good of the City

If George had been uncomfortable at the lawyer's office, it was nothing compared to how he felt now, sitting in Tom's living room witnessing how Jen was taking Tom on.

So far it was an equal battle. Jen had a certain dogged focus, not unlike a bulldog refusing to let go regardless of its chances. Tom met everything she said with a stoic, almost good-humoured perseverance which naturally annoyed the hell out of Jen.

'You *have* to marry her,' Jen said.

'I don't love Sara, she doesn't love me.'

'Well, and whose fault is that? If you had just damned well done something she would have been head over heels in love with you by now!'

Tom smiled blandly.

'Don't you care about this town?'

'As towns go, I've seen worse,' he countered.

'Well then?'

'Well what?'

'Tom, if you don't marry her, she'll have to leave. And she got me a book!'

This argument did not seem to impress Tom. As far as George could see, Tom hadn't been in the slightest bit worried when they'd turned up, him and Jen and Andy, with Jen so clearly on a mission. And if anything, after half an hour of Jen's most concerted persuasion, he was looking even more determinedly uninterested. Tom was sitting on the armchair; they were squeezed in on the sofa, so close together that Jen almost hit George several times when gesturing too heatedly.

George couldn't help but feel that Andy wasn't really pulling his weight. He had barely said a word, and when he spoke now it was if he was treating it all like a joke. 'Come on, Tom,' he said. 'What's two years of your life for the good of the town, eh?

It's not like you have someone better to marry, am I right?'

'Why should he have someone better?' Jen said. 'Our Sara is perfectly . . . well, she's perfectly nice!'

'Very nice,' Tom said pleasantly.

'For God's sake, Tom. It's not like we're asking you to love her.'

Which George thought was rather crude.

'Of course not,' said Andy. 'If straight people only married people they loved, heterosexuality as we know it would cease to exist.'

George was starting to feel slightly annoyed at all of them: Jen and her scheme, Andy who just laughed at the whole thing, and Tom, well, he sort of understood why Tom was being antsy, but he couldn't accept that Tom would rather win a childish argument against Jen than help Sara. No one seemed to be thinking of her in all of this.

'So what will it take?' Jen asked. 'Money? Is that what you're saying? I'm sure we can scrape something together.'

At least that got Tom's attention. 'Jesus, Jen,' he said, appalled. 'Just leave it, will you?'

Tom suddenly looked very tired. George could sympathise. But it didn't help anything.

George rose abruptly, bringing the conversation to a halt. He hadn't meant to make any sort of speech, he'd just wanted to get away before he heard anything he'd really mind. But when he stood up he saw them there, all unconcerned, still not getting the point, not even Jen. For her, the whole affair seemed to have become a matter of prestige; for Andy, a joke like everything else; and for Tom, well, probably nothing.

'It's *Sara*,' he said. 'Our Sara. I didn't really know Amy, but she was nice to me when . . . when Sophie was gone, and I know how much this town needed her. And I know Sara, and I know we need *her*.' He wasn't doing a good job of it, he could feel it. He'd never been good with words, but he had to make them see. 'She'll leave, and she'll be all alone back there, in Sweden. Her folks don't seem to care. And then we'll be all alone here, too. That I do know.'

It was silly, he knew, but he couldn't shake the feeling that everything that had happened had been down to Sara. Even Sophie suddenly coming back to him – things like that had become possible since Sara had arrived.

Jen seemed about to say something, but he ignored her. 'All right then,' he said. 'I'll marry her myself.'

Everyone stared at him.

'That's very kind of you,' said Jen.

'Yes, why not?' Andy said, nodding encouragingly.

'George . . .' said Tom. 'I just . . .' But he didn't seem to know what to say.

'Well, *someone* has to,' George said.

'Yes, but . . .' Jen seemed to be searching desperately for reasons against it, but eventually she said: 'Yes, well, precisely. Why not?'

George was uncomfortable with the whole thing, he readily admitted that. He was very sure that Sara would prefer to marry Tom. Who wouldn't? But at least she'd get to stay, and he could keep driving her.

'Look, George, I'll –' Tom said, but George interrupted him.

'She'll get to stay. She won't want to marry me, of course, but she can stay.'

'The lawyer!' Jen blurted out.

'What about him?' said Andy.

'We've already told him about Tom.'

'Quite a love triangle, this,' said Andy.

'We're back to square one,' Jen said, looking utterly defeated. George looked at Tom, who didn't say anything. George turned to leave. At least he'd tried.

'Fine,' Tom said. 'I'll do it then, George. I'll marry her.'

'Good,' said George.

And then he left.

The Smell of Books and Adventure

'Hi'.

Sophie was standing in the doorway, looking hesitantly at Sara. She had found her with her nose literally in a book. Sara looked up and slowly lowered it to the counter. She was busy unpacking a box of new books which had just arrived, and had obviously been putting them to her nose, breathing them in.

'Have you ever smelled a book?' Sara said, coming out from behind the counter.

Sophie shook her head. Sara held out a paperback. The latest Marian Keyes. The cover was all glittery pastel colours, warm blue and pink shades, with big, ornate letters. 'Open it,' she said.

Sophie opened the book carefully, as though she was afraid of damaging it.

'No, no,' Sara said, causing Sophie to look up in alarm. 'Open it properly.' She showed her. 'You need to be able to shove your nose into it.'

Sophie lifted the book to her face, still cautiously and carefully, and slowly breathed in through her nose. She smiled.

'Can you smell it? The scent of new books. Unread adventures. Friends you haven't met yet, hours of magical escapism awaiting you.'

Of course, Sara was aware that Sophie probably wouldn't have put it like that, but she was sure that she could feel it too. She pulled another book down from a shelf, a nice hardback full of photographs of oaks, with thick, glossy pages. The thick pages smelled completely different, of plastic and quality colour printing.

'And this one.'

A normal book this time, though still hardback, but with thinner paper and a slightly yellowed colour. They smelled it.

Sara smiled. Hardback and paperback books smelled different, but there were also differences between English and Swedish paperback editions. Classics, for example, had a smell all their own. Course books had their own unique aroma, and university set texts were different again from those used in schools. Interestingly, adult education books smelled just like school books: that familiar scent of classrooms, restlessness and stuffiness.

New books always had the strongest aroma. She assumed it just was the printing smells lingering behind, and that they somehow, logically, disappeared once a book had been opened, read and leafed through. That was what she thought on a purely intellectual level anyway, but she didn't quite believe it. She still believed that what she could smell were all the new adventures and reading experiences awaiting her.

Sophie seemed much more confident now. She put the book down and walked slowly along the row of shelves. Sara went back to unpacking. Maybe it was idiotic to be ordering new books when she had less than two weeks left, but it was the only way she could make it through her remaining time. Just going on as normal and pretending that nothing had changed. Eventually, she would be sitting on the plane home, and that would be that.

'What would you like to read about?' Sara asked.

Sophie shrugged. 'Don't know,' she said. She continued around the shop. She didn't seem to be reading the titles themselves, just looking at the books. Every now and then, she reached out and touched the spines as she walked, just like the way people in boats dip their fingers into the water swirling past.

She stayed almost half an hour. Before she left, she said: 'Dragons. I like dragons. I'm sure I'll find a book about them some day. Or with one dragon. It doesn't matter.'

Dragons, eh, Sara thought. 'Wait,' she said. 'How long are you going to be in town?'

Sophie shrugged. 'Don't know.'

'Where do you live normally?'

'Bloomfield.'

Sara passed a pad of paper over the counter and asked for the girl's address. She wrote it down without asking why Sara wanted it, and Sara said nothing. She was determined to find the perfect book for Sophie, preferably before she had to leave.

She was still thinking about dragons when Jen made her entrance.

'You're going to need a wedding dress.'

She must surely have spoken to Tom by now, Sara thought. And he must have said no? If he hadn't, then this was definitely the right occasion for her to.

She looked Jen straight in the eye, as determined as she could, and said: 'I –'

'You've got to go to Madame Higgins,' Jen interrupted. 'She's been selling wedding dresses in Broken Wheel forever.'

Sara had seen Madame Higgins's shop window. It hadn't been an encouraging sight.

Jen glanced down at the piece of paper she had in her hand. It seemed to be a list, because she sounded as though she was reading from it: 'Bachelor and bachelorette parties, for the pictures. Documentation. Suspicious people at the USCSI.' She had almost got the name of the authority right.

So unfair of them, Sara thought cynically. 'Jen,' she said, 'this is madness.'

'I'm not saying they have to be proper bachelor and bachelorette parties.' She laughed. 'Though it would be worth it just to see Caroline's face when the stripper turned up. Don't worry, I've thought of everything. We'll invite a few select friends to the dress fitting and add a bit of wine. Nice pictures, nothing to organise. Plus, you'll get a few style tips.'

'This wedding is madness,' Sara reiterated. 'It's illegal, for one thing. And Tom doesn't want to get married.'

'Tom!' Jen said dismissively. 'Don't you worry about Tom.' She looked Sara straight in the eye. 'Do you want to stay?' she asked.

That was one question Sara could answer 'Yes' to without a moment's thought.

Gavin Jones was a good bureaucrat. He knew many people saw that as something of a contradiction in terms, but laws were there for a reason. People voted for representatives, and then a majority of them decided that the laws were good. It would have been pointless to go through the whole process of elections and so on if there was no one to make sure the rules were introduced and adhered to. He was needed. He was paid to do a job, and so he did it. He was competent and smart, and he did it well.

Gavin was good at his job for three reasons. Firstly, he could instinctively tell when something wasn't right. Secondly, he took this feeling seriously and was prepared to work hard to investigate the circumstances. Finally, he picked up bits and pieces of information and he remembered them. A tourist who had been living in a neighbouring town for a long time, for example, without him having seen any visa application. Rumours about workers who couldn't speak English. Temporary residences which popped up.

Because he wanted to do a good job, he read the local papers, memorised things, followed up on side issues. His intuition probably depended on some stored, half-conscious information that he had picked up somewhere. On this particular occasion, there was nothing to immediately set any alarm bells ringing. He looked at the application form.

Broken Wheel . . . ? Had he even heard of that town? He didn't think so. He shrugged. If something didn't add up there, he would find out, sooner or later.

Nothing to Tell

'Are you ever going to tell your parents?'

She was lying naked in bed next to him. The lights were off, of course, but since it was the middle of the day the room was still light. She couldn't decide whether it felt sinful or liberating or just plain old indecent.

In actual fact, Caroline didn't know what she thought about any of it. Even her inner voice had fallen silent. She hadn't heard as much as a stern word for hours; it was as though all . . . this . . . was so unthinkable that her moral compass had been thrown off track. The sex she'd had before, that time all those years ago, had been an entirely insignificant experience, definitely not worth the bother or the sin. But *now*. She hadn't had any idea that sex could be like this. She had just had sex with *Josh*, for God's sake.

'About us?' Josh asked.

She stared at him, about to sit bolt upright in bed before she realised she wasn't wearing anything. She pulled the covers up to her chin and lay back against the pillows.

'No, of course not about *us*,' she said, shocked. She couldn't understand how he could even entertain the thought. Absolutely no one could find out about this. Not his parents (she was dangerously close to burying her head beneath the covers at the thought of *that* scene), and definitely not anyone from Broken Wheel. 'About you. About . . . liking men and women.'

He laughed and pulled her towards him so that her head was resting on his shoulder and neck rather than the pillow. Strangely enough, it was more comfortable.

'Doesn't seem so relevant right now,' he said.

She tried to work that out but failed. Eventually, she simply said: 'You know that there is no us, right?'

He didn't bother answering.

'You'll end up finding a nice young man and moving on. Or

a woman, if that's what you want. Your own age,' she explained.

Of course he would. It wouldn't be a problem for her. So long as no one found out about any of this, though perhaps she could cope with that, too.

Are you mad, Caroline? You wouldn't stand a chance if anyone found out. They would tear you to pieces.

It would be catastrophic for him, too. She was sure he had no idea how cruel and careless even the nicest people could be once they had found something to laugh about.

He didn't bother replying to that either. Just to be on the safe side, she added: 'No one can find out about us, Josh. They'd just . . . laugh at us.'

His finger grazed her shoulder. He drew slow, meaningless patterns on her skin. She relaxed, but couldn't help wondering whether he had understood.

'Since there is no us, there's nothing to tell,' he said.

She nodded into his shoulder. Exactly. It could just be nice, as long as it lasted.

A Conspiracy is Suspected

'Ha ha,' Gavin Jones's neighbour said. He was the kind of man who expressed his laughter in words rather than actually laughing. At that moment, he was leaning over the fence at the edge of Gavin's plot, showing no sign of leaving him in peace. 'Deported any Mexicans lately?' he asked.

Gavin sighed. A few moments earlier, he had been busy raking leaves on a quiet Friday evening, and now he was being subjected to this idiocy.

'That crackdown in Postville a few years back?' the neighbour continued. 'Hundreds of poor Mexicans who hadn't done a thing other than work their asses off for lower wages than lazy Americans are willing to take . . .'

Gavin hadn't liked Postville either. It was one of the reasons he had applied to one of the USCIS local offices and now spent his days investigating Europeans who may or may not have married American citizens. Paperwork, for the most part, but there was satisfaction in that, too.

'Doesn't it make you sick? Surely we should be able to just leave the poor souls alone?'

Just a month ago, his neighbour had been complaining about them not arresting the 'darkies' taking their jobs. Not the kind of jobs you would want, he had thought at the time. And now they were all poor souls. He shrugged. He simply couldn't win.

His sixth sense for lies impressed his colleagues, but sometimes they looked at him with something verging on contempt. As though they didn't have enough belief in their job to appreciate that someone might actually be good at it. Because he *was* good at it. And so he had slowly moved away from arresting illegal immigrants simply trying to make a living to sending down spoilt Europeans who didn't seem to think that the law applied to them, that it was their human right to be able to stay in the US as long as they wanted. In contrast to the Latin Americans, who didn't know that there *were* any human rights in this life and expected nothing more than hard, thankless work, being separated from their families, and terrible wages.

He still gained no satisfaction from the actual busts. He knew some of his colleagues thought that it was the part he liked, that he enjoyed watching people grow nervous and trip up in front of him. And he knew that there really were people who got off on that. But now, it wasn't so serious. The Europeans were given fines and sent home. It had been worse with the Mexicans. Some went to jail barely having understood what had happened to them, and if they were sent home it was a catastrophe.

'I might have a tip-off for you,' his neighbour said. Gavin forced himself to put the rake down and turn to him, in case being attentive would make the man finish speaking sooner.

'Wait here,' the neighbour said, walking away. He returned a minute or so later, with two printed sheets of paper. Gavin reluctantly took them. At the top, they said *Broken Wheel Newsletter*. He was looking at his neighbour with more interest now.

'A new bookstore in Broken Wheel,' said the neighbour.

Gavin read the articles. Sara. It could be a coincidence, of course. Or perhaps there were two Saras in town. The article didn't give a surname, but the Sara Lindqvist from the application awaiting completion on his desk had come to the US on a tourist visa (which hadn't yet expired) and apparently met and fallen in love with an American citizen.

You couldn't open a bookstore on a tourist visa, that much was clear. And if she had done so, then that made her whirlwind romance with the good Tom Harris appear in a whole new light.

'Is it OK if I keep hold of these?' he asked reluctantly, nodding towards the papers.

'Sure,' the neighbour said, gesturing widely and revealing more of his chest. It was October and the man still had a suntan, Gavin thought to himself with distaste. Three of the buttons on his shirt were undone beneath his jacket.

He sighed. Now he would just have to visit the bookstore and talk to this Sara. He saw his free Saturday disappear before his eyes.

The next afternoon, Gavin had no trouble recognising Sara from the picture in the newsletter. From where he was standing on the sidewalk outside the bookstore, he had a perfect view of her at work. Just then, she was busy recommending two books to a customer, and she was moving with the natural calm of someone clearly used to working in the shop.

He didn't go in right away. In cases like this, he preferred to have something solid to go on before he spoke to any suspects. That said, he didn't doubt that he would get to the truth.

The Sara Lindqvist from the application form had been in Iowa nearly two months. If she really had fallen so head over heels in love that she was now prepared to get married for reasons other than residency, then other people living in town would be aware of it. The place would be abuzz with their romance; they would have spent plenty of time together in excessive infatuation; they would, in all likelihood, already be living together. It would be impossible to have missed it.

Unless they had known one another from before. But people would probably be aware of that, too. He would have introduced her as his girlfriend or his friend from Sweden. It was just as illegal to enter the country on a tourist visa if you were planning to get married and stay.

The diner next door to him was relatively full, but the woman behind the counter was standing alone and idle. She had the bearing of someone who kept her eye on what was going on. A diner was second-best to a bar when it came to picking up gossip.

He went in and clambered up onto one of the bar stools. The woman began frying a hamburger he strongly suspected was for him. He could already feel waves of nausea washing over him as a result of the greasy smell. Just endure it, he thought. And find out as much as you can, as quickly as you can.

He had conducted countless interviews before, with impatient people who had been just like the woman behind the counter.

People wanted to talk, that was his experience. If you gave them the slightest encouragement, they would tell you all you wanted to know. The trick was to get them to talk and to drop all caution and then simply listen to whatever they had to say, asking a couple of questions along the way. Repeating their last sentence with a question mark at the end of it was often enough to keep the conversation flowing. Hardly brain surgery.

He grunted a thanks for the coffee which had appeared in front of him, raising the cup in a silent toast. 'I guess your family has been living in Broken Wheel a long time?' he began. A friendly question about family was normally enough to break the ice with anyone.

Grace's face lit up. 'Ah,' she said. 'Funny you should ask.' She held out her hand. 'Grace,' she said. 'Though I was actually christened Madeleine.'

Forty-five minutes later, Gavin was feeling exhausted. He hadn't found out a thing about Sara, but he now knew more about the shotgun being kept under the counter than he really wanted to. At one point, a sheriff had also been involved.

He hoped it had been an old anecdote, though she had said something about upgrading to a hunting rifle which sounded worryingly current. He had only made it out because the place, for whatever reason, was closing early. And when he did come out, the bookstore was also dark and empty.

Just for Sex

'Are you sure you're going to get married in a dress?'

They were crammed into Madame Higgins's crazy boutique. Sara wasn't at all sure. She was wearing a fluffy white wedding dress, almost yellow with age and clearly made for some matronly Iowan woman with more . . . authority.

'You look fantastic,' Jen said.

'Do you know why women get married in white?' Andy asked. No one bothered to answer him. 'It's obvious. All household appliances are white.'

Sara laughed. Jen took a picture.

Madame Higgins's boutique was just big enough for them all, but they were forced to split into smaller groups in order to move among the various voluminous gowns. The view out onto Second Street was entirely blocked by three monstrous dresses made from a deep pink fabric.

Andy had placed a couple of bottles of wine and a row of plastic glasses on the counter. Now he was amusing anyone unlucky enough to be standing anywhere near him with selected stories from Sara's time among them. 'Her face when we proposed. Terrified or what?' He winked at Josh. 'But not as terrified as Tom's. Though he was the logical choice. For a while, I thought they'd try to convince me or Carl.' He elbowed Josh. 'Almost as crazy as picking you, eh?'

Josh gave him a nervous look. He was squashed in between Andy and Grace, a clothes hanger pressing into his back. Caroline was at the other end of the shop. She started every time he came close.

'I mean, Broken Wheel's pretty tolerant, but people aren't so crazy that they'd go along with that.'

'Why –' Josh began, but he was interrupted by Jen's rippling laugh. Sara noticed that Jen had given up trying to get Andy to take the beautiful situation seriously. She crept back to the changing room (a corner, with two scraps of material the only 'walls') and squeezed out of the utterly catastrophic dress. Well then. The main thing was that it was white. Not even USCSI could demand that she looked nice in the pictures.

'My God, no,' said Jen. 'I have to admit that I was thinking about Carl at first. At least he's handsome enough to convince anyone that Sara could have fallen for him in just a couple of weeks.'

'But no one would've believed that Josh had suddenly fallen in love with a woman.'

'I don't get why it's so inconceivable that I'd marry a woman,' Josh said, annoyed. 'There is such a thing as bisexuality, you know.'

Claire and George were standing slightly outside the group. He felt more relaxed than normal, almost self-confident in a simple – ironed – cotton shirt. The top button was undone and the edge of the bright white T-shirt he had on underneath contrasted starkly with his blue shirt. He leaned in to Claire and said, smiling: 'You might be wondering why I haven't stopped by lately.'

'No.'

He laughed. 'Of course, you must've seen her.'

'Yeah.'

'Sophie, I meant.'

'And Michelle.'

'Yeah . . . but Sophie is worth it. She's a great girl.' He added, generously: 'Like Lacey,' but got nothing in response. Claire was staring stubbornly ahead at Tom and Sara with a resolute expression on her face. George shrugged.

While the others were caught up in their own topics of conversation, Sara hung the awful dress back up and started mindlessly rifling through the other options.

She didn't know why she was doing it. Once again, she vowed

to talk to Jen about the entire mad plan and call the whole thing off. Then she glanced at Jen's manic smile and eager photographing and shuddered. Just not tonight.

She held up a dress to get a better look at it. It was a dress which didn't seem to have any illusions about love and marriage. Perfect for a fake wedding.

She sighed and hung it back up, but not quickly enough. When she turned around, Tom was standing next to her and she knew that he had seen her there, among the dresses. As though she was still planning on tricking him into marriage.

'Tom,' she said, placing a hand on his arm before he had time to say anything.

The look between them deepened when she touched him, and something in his eyes softened, as though he was seeing *her* for the first time. She thought about how little people normally expressed with their eyes, and about how much she liked him.

Strangely enough, the realisation wasn't all that shocking at first. She didn't even panic. She simply looked at him, unmoving, and her entire body relaxed in the absolute certainty that she loved him. A calm assertion, just like stating that the Earth was round: there it was, utterly clear, and there was nothing she could do about it. She was certain that this love would lead to problems in the long run, but at that moment, the realisation felt more like a kind of . . . peace.

And at the very least, it gave her the courage to say: 'Tom, you aren't going to have to do this.' Her hand was still resting on his arm. 'I told Jen the whole thing was mad.'

Tom laughed. 'And she listened to you respectfully and called the whole thing off, of course?'

'I'll talk to her again.'

'Sara, I signed the form.'

'But . . .' She blinked. 'Why?'

He shrugged. 'It's what Amy would've wanted.'

'It's not right,' she said.

He was only doing it because he had to, she thought.

'Why not?' he said, nodding towards the rack of dresses in front of them. 'You've found a dress.'

She pulled a face.

'And I know for a fact that Jen already spoke to the minister and booked us in for next Saturday.'

'We might as well go along with it – there's no stopping it now. You can always say no when the minister asks you.'

She was trying to cling to some kind of reality. You couldn't get married for a residency permit. You couldn't go to a foreign country and get married to someone you didn't even know. And you really couldn't force someone else to do it.

She stared at the clothes hangers and the old dresses, as though the tired-looking fabrics or the old-fashioned colours and cuts would keep her grounded.

But all she could see was a precipice.

It was funny, she thought, how often we stuck to the safe path in life, pulling on the blinkers and keeping our eyes to the ground, doing our best not to look at the fantastic view. Without seeing the heights we had reached, the opportunities actually awaiting us out there; without realising we should just jump and fly, at least for a moment.

She had kept well behind the safety barrier her entire life, but now she was standing there, at the edge of the precipice for the very first time, fumbling blindly at the realisation that there were other ways to live, at how intense and rich life could be.

She reacted to the view the same way she would have reacted if she had been standing before an actual precipice. She felt dizzy, had a strong urge to jump, regardless of the consequences; she could imagine how it would feel just to fall, she *wanted* to do it, but felt an equally strong pull back to safety.

You love him, she thought, but she didn't know whether that was an argument for jumping or backing up.

'Come on, Sara,' Tom said, as though he could read her thoughts. She really hoped that he couldn't. 'You want to stay, don't you?'

'Yes,' she said simply. She looked at him. 'It's just that I like everyone here so much. And it's the first time in my life I've ever felt like I belong somewhere.' She fell silent. Then she asked: 'Are you still moving to Hope?' She couldn't help it.

'I would never have moved,' he said, 'but I'm starting a job there in a few weeks. It's actually OK.' He shrugged. 'If we get married, you're not going to have to move with me to Hope,' he said, smiling wryly. 'But maybe it's best if you move in with me for a while,' he continued. 'We need to know more about one another. Whether you eat birdseed for breakfast, for example.'

'Birdseed?' she asked. She was lost.

'From a movie,' he said. 'Gérard Depardieu and Andie MacDowell?'

'Oh,' she said. 'I haven't seen many movies. I –'

'Prefer books,' he finished. This time, he was smiling as he said it.

'So,' said Jen, 'do you really think Josh is in love with Sara?'

'Why should he be?' Andy asked.

'All that talk about being bisexual. I thought it was a bit suspicious.' She filled her plastic glass. 'He was very animated on the subject.'

'Has he even been to the bookstore?' Grace wondered.

'No . . .' Jen said hesitantly. 'Not lately.' She raised the bottle of wine for Grace and Andy, who held out their glasses.

'Exactly,' said Andy.

'But there's a woman involved somewhere,' Jen persisted. 'Though maybe not someone in Broken Wheel. The only woman I've seen him with is Caroline.'

Grace and Andy stared at her. 'Jesus, Jen,' Andy said, adding musingly: 'They were drinking beer together after the dance. And they did leave together.'

'Beer?' said Jen. 'Caroline?'

The three of them automatically looked over to Josh and Caroline. Josh had just placed a hand on Caroline's arm and was laughing at something she had said. She moved her arm away immediately, but it wasn't the touch that bothered them. But laughing at something Caroline had said? Something had to be going on.

'Maybe he's been drinking . . .' said Grace.

'So, you see,' said Jen. Andy wasn't protesting any longer. A worryingly determined look had appeared in his eyes.

The next time Josh passed, Andy grabbed hold of his arm and said: 'Jen's come up with some interesting theories.'

Josh looked at him calmly. 'Oh?'

'Really funny, actually. She thinks you and Caroline are together.'

Josh said nothing.

'A crazy accusation,' Andy continued. 'Caroline, of all people.'

'Mm-hmm.'

'I knew it wasn't true. All due respect to bisexuality, and to older women as well, but no one could get close to her without getting frostbite. Or without taking a sudden vow of chastity.' He laughed at his own joke, but added in the name of fairness: 'No, no, I'm assuming that *some* people could have sex with her. She's well preserved, at least. But you? With *Caroline*?'

'Of course there's nothing going on between me and Caroline,' Josh said tonelessly.

Andy patted him on the arm. 'Sure, sure,' he said, adding hopefully: 'And you're sure that she isn't into you? Lots of older women suddenly fall for younger men. I see it happening all the time.'

Josh laughed, but it was completely lacking in humour. 'I can promise you Caroline isn't the least bit interested in me,' he said.

'No?' Andy sounded disappointed.

'No,' said Josh. 'She's just using me for sex.'

Sara Lindqvist
Kornvägen 7, 1 tr
136 38 Haninge
Sweden

Sara!

I've only got one piece of writing paper left so I'll reply to your latest letter in more detail once John has brought me some more, but I just had to write you right away to say that I had Tom taking books down from my bookcases for me all morning. You were right! They smell completely different. What a thing to discover in the autumn of my years! I probably wouldn't manage a blindfold test just yet, but you can bet I'll be practicing. I've already ordered three different kinds of paperback, a photography book and a hardcover novel to see how they smell 'fresh'.

I must admit, Tom didn't really understand what I was up to. I said it was a tip from 'my good friend Sara, in Sweden', and that certainly shut him up. At my age, it's something very special to have new friends to shout about.

Not that Tom actually said anything. He's much too polite for that. He just looks at you *in that way*, as though he's laughing with or at you, but likes you enough to go along with it. Tom may take things a bit too seriously at times, but at least he also has a twinkle in his eyes. Maybe you can be happy without it, but my personal advice is this: never marry a man who doesn't have laughter in his eyes.

It's not advice I followed myself. In my defense, I'll say that I was young back then, and didn't know what I was looking for. Not even John's eyes ever laugh at me, but they do smile often, so I think it mostly depends on the circumstances.

If you ever come here, I hope you'll like John. He is without doubt the most extraordinary person I've ever met. As I'm writing this, he's sitting in his usual armchair next to my bed (did I mention that I've got a stupid little complaint which keeps me in bed sometimes? It doesn't matter). I'm almost certain he knows I'm writing about him and that he probably wants to protest – he knows I only write positive things, and thinks I exaggerate – but still, he's sitting there smelling a paperback. It's one of the things which gives me the most satisfaction, when I look back on my life: that I was able to experience such a friendship, know such a man, and had enough sense to appreciate him.

So there you have it. My paper is full, and just as I was becoming unbearably sentimental. One last thought, though – won't you come visit?

Best,

Amy

PS This isn't just the confused, passing fancy of some old woman. If ever you feel like visiting a small town or even just taking a vacation somewhere peaceful, then I hope you know you'd be very welcome here. I can show you Jimmie Coogan Street and we could talk about books and, well, spend time together. And you wouldn't be completely at my mercy. We would take care of you, all of us, and keep you entertained as best we could. Think about it.

Mrs Hurst
(Books 4: Life 0)

It tasted like a mix of extremely sweet pancakes and sausage which, when Sara thought about it, was probably exactly what it was.

Tom had made corn dogs for her, and while she ate them as a starter, he chopped onions and fried mince for the Sloppy Joes. She was sitting there desperately trying to fight back tears. He had made *corn dogs* for her! Completely genuine American food.

He had done some shopping after dropping her off at Amy's, where she packed up everything she would need for her stay at his house. When he picked her up again, he had refused to say what they would be having for dinner.

Corn dogs turned out to consist of a batter made from egg, lots of sugar (it seemed to feature in the majority of American recipes, she thought, having also watched Tom add a healthy amount to the minced meat) and cornmeal, which the sausage was then rolled in. You fried the sausage as best you could in a deep frying pan with plenty of hot oil. The batter normally seeped out, so they became flatter and more rectangular than the uniformly round versions you saw in the picture on the recipe, but Sara felt it was more genuine that way. The sausage tasted boiled, and sweeter than normal. She helped herself to another.

Neither of them had mentioned Caroline, but Sara couldn't help thinking about her. There had been something so . . . vulnerable in her eyes.

Everyone in the clothes shop had heard what Josh had said and turned instinctively towards her, but Caroline had simply raised her chin slightly and looked at them with her normal, self-confident, slightly icy look. Then she had nodded to Madame Higgins and left, without looking back.

Her face might have been slightly paler, Sara thought, the lines more pronounced, but that had been all. Not a word. Not a glance.

A dignified exit.

Everyone had known it was only a joke, but Sara was disappointed in Josh. It hadn't been a funny one.

Andy had enjoyed it, of course, but Sara had felt only sympathy, even though Caroline had handled the situation well, and even though she wouldn't have wanted it.

Tom turned around from the bench and took a swig of beer. His posture emphasised his stomach and shoulder muscles, and the kitchen suddenly felt much smaller.

'The trick with Sloppy Joes is the consistency,' he said. 'You've got to be able to take a bite without the whole thing falling apart, even though it also has to be a bit messy. The secret is to keep splitting the mince as it cooks.'

'So Sloppy Joes are just mince in hamburger buns?' she asked.

'Yup.'

'No vegetables?'

'There's ketchup in the meat, if that counts?'

She laughed and took a sip of her beer, and as Tom turned around again to finely chop a green pepper, an onion and some garlic, she thought about how life could be. Working in the bookshop, coming home every evening to make dinner with someone who poked fun at her and her books, a kind of magical world of . . . everyday life and friendship. Was that really too much to ask?

'You know the meat's done when you can take a big lump on the spatula without it all falling apart,' Tom continued. He demonstrated by lifting some up, only for it to immediately fall off at the sides. 'A while yet, then.'

She smiled, but reminded herself not to get distracted. It was precisely because the evening had been so nice that she knew she had to bring up something which had been bothering her since their conversation in the dress shop. Perhaps because she needed to remind herself, perhaps to show him she was under no illusions.

'Tom,' she said, 'we don't have to keep living with one another afterwards. You can go on as normal. There won't be any . . . feelings in any of this.' She had meant to say it firmly, calmly, but it came out more like a question.

The smile in Tom's eyes disappeared. He turned towards the sink again.

'Of course,' he said. 'No feelings.'

'I can stay at Amy's. Or sleep on the sofa.'

She should have stopped talking a long time ago. Sleep on the sofa? What an idiotic thing to say. The image of the cosy life she had imagined disappeared and was replaced by one of a constant stream of Tom's lovers passing through his house during the two years they had to be married for her to be granted permission to work, while she tried to make herself invisible in the living room.

Get it together, Sara. You'll be able to stay.

Not being with Tom was a relatively small price to pay to finally belong somewhere.

'You can keep seeing other people,' she said because she had to.

Tom didn't even bother to reply. She assumed it had been obvious to him from the start.

They would be sleeping in the same bed.

She had repeated her idiotic offer of sleeping on the sofa but, as he had pointed out, it was definitely a stupid idea. Unless they slept in the same bed, how would he know if she snored, for example? Surely that would be one of the immigration department's first questions? Sara had protested, but he had simply answered that it wasn't something you knew about yourself.

She wouldn't have had anything against sleeping next to him if she had thought for a moment that it was simply a plan on his part to get her into bed.

But it wasn't. He had made that clear depressingly quickly, and now they were lying as far apart from one another as they could.

They had undressed in darkness, but the light of the moon

was filtering in through the curtains and she managed to catch a glimpse of his bare skin and naked chest before he lay down. That hadn't helped her peace of mind.

She sighed quietly.

His sheets smelled strange, fresh and manly. She could hear him breathing next to her and felt an overwhelming desire to reach out and touch him. To stop herself, she clasped her hands to her chest and lay there looking up at the unfamiliar ceiling.

He wasn't interested in her, but, she reminded herself, that was hardly a catastrophe. Or news to her. Sometimes, feelings simply weren't reciprocated. She hadn't expected anything else, really.

The same was true in books. She knew that Tom thought she preferred them because they were happier than life, but even within their pages, people were dumped and broke up and lost those they cared about. And in life just as in books, people eventually moved on to new loves. There was no difference between books and life there: both involved happy and unhappy love stories.

Still. Lying there rigidly on her back, staring up at the ceiling and listening to the soft, regular sound of his breathing, she felt more lonely than she ever had before in Broken Wheel.

Of course, with books, you could have greater confidence that it would all end well. You worked through the disappointments and the complications, always conscious, deep down, that Elizabeth would get her Mr Darcy in the end. With life, you couldn't have the same faith. But sooner or later, she reminded herself, surely someone you could imagine was your Mr Darcy would turn up.

Though that was assuming you were one of the main characters.

She almost sat up in bed at that startling realisation. Tom stirred next to her, and she forced herself to relax again, but her mind was still thoroughly worked up.

Help me, she thought, don't let me be one of the minor characters.

She could live with not having found her Mr Darcy yet. In

actual fact she had never expected she would. Once upon a time, she hadn't wanted to be anything other than a minor character. Being the protagonist, that would have been too much to ask, much better to be given the occasional appearance and the kind of character trait that could be described in a couple of sentences whenever she happened to encounter the real heroine. But now . . . The thought that Tom had been meant to meet someone else all along filled her with sheer horror. Her thoughts naturally drifted to Claire, but she tried to forget the idea.

Imagine if she, Sara, was *Caroline Bingley* rather than Lizzy Bennet.

Or Mrs Hurst.

Broken Wheel, Iowa
May 22, 2011

Sara Lindqvist
Kornvägen 7, 1 tr
136 38 Haninge
Sweden

Dear Sara,

Naturally I'm happy to hear you've been saving money, not least if your work situation is so uncertain (though then you would have more time to stay with us?), but money doesn't come into this. It was meant as an invitation between old friends – since our books have met, don't you think it's time we did too? – but I can't let you pay for it. I'm afraid you're going to have to let me decide this time.

Just the thought of you having to pay to be bored to death by an old woman! Honestly, life isn't a competition for paying your way.

Live a little. Read a little. Stay as long as you like, completely free, but come soon.

With warm regards,

Amy

Amy Harris Gets Involved, through a Representative

Maybe it's not the end of the world, Sara thought. People have got married before. Even to completely ordinary people.

Outside the car windows, the corn marched past. The harvest had already begun in some of the fields, which cropped up at regular intervals like bare, flattened strips in an otherwise billowing landscape of corn.

Tom seemed shamelessly alert and rested next to her in the car, and as though to confuse her, the day was warm and clear.

If she was going to stay, she thought, she would need to find a way to support herself. She still had some money saved, but it wouldn't last forever, and she wasn't planning on letting Tom pay for her.

More customers had started coming to the bookshop. Nowadays, barely a day went by without her selling something, but you couldn't live on three paperbacks a day.

If she was going to stay, she would have to polish up her sales strategy.

She smiled to herself and glanced at Tom. It was a dizzying thought. Having time, being able to continue her work with the bookshop. When he noticed that she was looking at him, he flashed her a smile before turning his attention back to the road. They missed another car by the narrowest of margins.

Maybe she could launch a website for the bookshop? It was something she had considered before, back in Sweden. A combination of a book blog and online shop, with a personal feel to it. Interviews with local authors, every book ever written about Iowa or by someone from the state. An online version of those small, independent bookshops that had once existed. She wondered how far people were actually willing to travel for a charming little bookshop. A long way, she suspected, if it sold books by people they knew. You should never underestimate the marketing power of enthusiastic amateurs. With a Cedar County shelf, and maybe even a virtual shelf for all the other counties in Iowa.

You're only kidding yourself, she thought perversely. Part of her seemed determined to be in a bad mood. Probably the part that hadn't slept all night and was tired and had a headache.

Even the sight of Tom smiling at her didn't cheer her up.

'Why did you dislike me the first time we met?' she asked before she could stop herself.

She instantly regretted it. *Don't answer*, she wanted to say. *Let's just go on pretending.*

'Dislike you?' he said.

'When you gave me a ride to the Square?' Great, he probably didn't even remember it.

He pulled up outside the bookstore, turned off the engine, and looked at her.

'I didn't dislike you,' he said.

'It sure seemed like it.'

He raked his fingers through his hair. 'I was just tired. It was the week after Amy died. I just didn't want to bother with anything right then.'

'What made you change your mind?'

'About you? I told you, I didn't dislike you.'

'About bothering. You're definitely bothered now.'

He laughed. 'Always the romantic.' He seemed to sense that she was serious, because he added: 'They can be very persuasive.'

'They?'

'Jen and Andy were the leaders, but funnily enough, George was the most effective.'

Sara blinked. 'George convinced you to marry me?'

'Like I said, he was pretty effective.' He smiled. Sara didn't. 'Besides, it didn't feel like the first time we'd met.'

'What?'

'When I picked you up. It didn't feel like the first time. Amy talked about you constantly.'

She smiled then, but sadly.

'And then there you were, all of a sudden, as if you'd stepped out of one of her books. You even had one in your pocket. And don't pretend you wouldn't rather have read it than talk to me.'

So he did remember. 'Well, you weren't very nice. Then, I mean.'

He looked at her until she had to look away. 'I'm sorry,' he said.

She shook her head. 'It's OK. You were tired, and grieving, and besides, you didn't know me.'

'I knew you made Amy happy. And maybe I couldn't deal with it. With you suddenly being there, when she wasn't. She really wanted to meet you. It seemed sort of a shame at the time that I was the one who got to. She called you her "friend from Sweden".'

Sara swallowed. She had no idea what to say. In the end, she just sat there until Tom leaned over her and opened the door.

'Go sell some books now,' he said, and somehow she managed a smile.

So he'd been talked into marrying her. Was that really such a big deal? She wanted to stay, and he was prepared to offer her a way to do so. If he'd been dead against the idea, surely he would have been able to say no to George?

Grace was leaning against the door and nodded to Sara as she passed by. 'Coffee?' she shouted, and Sara was grateful for the interruption. She wanted a break from her own thoughts.

Grace poured a cup for each of them and leaned against the counter. 'I just don't understand why you want to stay.'

Why shouldn't I? Sara thought. Grace herself clearly had no plans to move away. Why should she get to belong there if Sara couldn't, just because there had been some kind of mistake at birth and she had ended up in Haninge instead?

'Have I ever told you about the time they started a petition against my grandmother? "Amazing Grace is the Devil in

Disguise", that was what they called it.' She looked expectantly at Sara, who was playing with her cup of coffee. 'Like the Elvis song! Can you imagine. An Elvis fan in Broken Wheel. Whoever came up with it must've had a lot of fun with that. The church women didn't realise it was a quote. This was during the years when Elvis was still provocative.'

'Yeah, but I see you haven't left town.'

'They might force me out yet,' Grace said dramatically before adding, more prosaically: 'Home-made cakes!'

'Come on,' said Sara. 'Neither you nor your grandmother really seem to have had any problems being accepted here.'

'What a horrible thing to say!'

'They like you,' Sara said. 'They want you here. And you like them, even though you pretend you don't belong here. Even your grandmother stayed. I'd bet she liked the town too.'

Grace looked as though Sara had hit her. 'Like!' she said. She continued, desperately: 'It's not just my grandmother. Us Graces have always been outcasts. We sold liquor! We fought! It's –'

'– practically a family tradition,' Sara finished for her. But she didn't want to be unfair, so she added: 'Maybe it's not only your fault. The times have changed. I guess it must be harder, being an outcast today.'

'Tell me about it,' Grace said sourly. 'Nothing is shocking any more. Being drunk, immoral, violent . . . it's all Hollywood's fault.'

'That, and the fact that you're selling hamburgers nowadays.'

Caroline let him in the second time he came over. He had already been round later That Evening (she could still hardly think of it without shuddering), but she hadn't been able to bring herself to talk to him.

'I know I made a fool of myself,' he said, running his hand uncertainly through his hair.

'Yes,' she nodded. She wasn't angry with him, really. She couldn't muster enough energy for that.

'I said you weren't in love with me.'

'You said we had *sex*.'

'I *know*.' He forgot to sound remorseful. 'But they were provoking me,' he said angrily. 'Maybe it's actually a good thing?' he tried. 'The strong, older woman with a young man in tow –' He broke off at the look she was giving him. 'Maybe not.'

'Maybe not,' Caroline agreed. She hadn't left the house all day. She was seriously considering never leaving it again, but she noticed that he hadn't quite understood and felt that she should at least try to explain. She just wished that he had kept quiet so they could have carried on for a while longer, but it had been inevitable that it would come out eventually.

'As a single, older woman . . .' she began.

He looked interested. As though her thoughts meant something to him. They wouldn't for much longer.

'As a single, older woman, the only thing you can be sure of, even if you do nothing at all, is that you'll be ridiculed. People will laugh at you. That's what they do. And normally I don't care, because it's the choice I made. Do you understand?'

He clearly didn't.

'People might not exactly like me, but I get things done. They laugh at me, I nag them, and in some way you might say that I've chosen what I'll let them laugh at. Everything goes smoothly. But now . . . the balance has shifted. They'll be laughing at me for other things. Do you understand that from now on I'm never going to be just Caroline?'

'Who else would you be?'

She didn't quite know how to explain it. 'Our former relations . . .' she started. 'From now on, it's going to be part of who I *am*. I'll be Caroline-who-throws-herself-at-young-men or Caroline-did-you-know-she-has-affairs-with-young-men? You, I guess, will probably still just be Josh. And they'll be right. They'll laugh at it and I won't be able to say a thing. When they laughed at me for being determined or for nagging, I could defend myself. And I was still just Caroline.'

'But why do we have to sneak about? Sara and Tom have been

open about it, getting married in front of the whole town, proposing collectively?'

'Firstly, because Sara and Tom aren't together, and they're also the same age.' She added, more quietly: 'And because the world isn't fair.' She tried reasoning with him. 'Though it's not right that you should have to hide it. I'm not going to go over to your house, storm in to your parents and start telling them about your boyfriends, am I?'

'I haven't got any boyfriends, for God's sake.'

She didn't bother to reply. They were still standing in the hallway; she wasn't planning on inviting him any further in, but it meant that he was standing very close to her.

'I'm sorry,' he said in an abrupt, angry tone which, again, didn't sound the least bit sorry. 'Isn't there anything I can do to fix this?'

She wished that the world was better or that she hadn't needed to be the person who showed him what it was really like. She leaned back with one shoulder against the wall, slowly touching it with her hand. 'This isn't something you can fix, Josh,' she said. 'In a while, when they realise we're not together, maybe I'll get to be Caroline-the-poor-lonely-woman-who-thought-a-young-man-would-want-to-be-with-her, or Caroline-you-know-she-got-dumped-by-a-younger-man. Maybe they'll leave me in peace eventually.'

'When they see we're not together?'

'I'm not planning on seeing you any more,' she said as kindly as she could, even though she knew that he wouldn't care for much longer.

Josh went pale. His face went a worrying shade of white, and for a moment something almost ferocious appeared in his eyes. She took a step back, not because she was worried he would hurt her, but because she was worried he would touch her again and that she would like it.

But when he finally spoke, his voice was cold, almost expressionless with barely veiled anger. 'Leave me if you want, Caroline, but don't pretend it's because of what people are saying. You might be Caroline-who's-just-been-dumped right now – hardly a fair title, is it? – but you've never just been Caroline. Before I came along, you were poor-lonely-Caroline or Caroline-the-walking-Church-cliché.'

She stared at him. 'Goodbye, Josh,' she said, no longer friendly, pushing past him to tear the door open. She gestured towards the street with her head, and he backed out.

'*Caroline*. I didn't mean it . . .'

But she had already closed the door.

It was when she was just about to change the piles of books by the armchairs that Sara's eyes fell on *Eragon*. She smiled to herself, suddenly inspired. A book for a girl who liked dragons. She put it under the counter to give to her next time she came by.

'I guess you already know, but Amy and I were good friends.'

Sara looked up. John was standing in the doorway. The sun was behind him, so it was hard to see his expression, but his voice was slow and tired, his shoulders drooping. The time since Amy's death hadn't been kind to him.

She nodded.

'You never met her, but she was a fantastic woman.'

'I know,' she said. She thought about Tom's word in the car and added, without really looking at him: 'Would she have liked me, do you think?'

'She liked you.'

'And . . . the bookstore?'

A flicker of a smile passed over his face. 'The bookstore too.' He looked at her gravely. 'But she wouldn't have wanted you to marry without love.'

Sara involuntarily clutched the books in front of her. 'Of course,' she said. She didn't think John realised how completely unnecessary his warning was. She had been in love with both Tom and the town for a long time now. She found the courage to say: 'I know how much you meant to her. Much more than her husband. You were her Robert Kincaid, standing out in the rain.'

He continued as though he hadn't heard her: 'And she wouldn't have wanted Tom to do it.'

She wondered whether he thought she had tricked Tom into all this, whether he thought she was just using him.

Her anger made it easier to meet his gaze, and made her say: 'Amy did it.' She couldn't stop herself from adding: 'Why didn't the two of you just get married? How could Amy be so . . . *weak*? Why didn't she dare defy any of those prejudices?'

She couldn't understand it. Amy had taken care of Andy and been pleased to receive a postcard of a half-naked man. It was incomprehensible.

'She knew what it was like to marry without love,' John replied, an admission of sorts, and one he seemed to have made very reluctantly. Sara found a certain comfort in that. *So what*, she wanted to say. *Amy did it.* Though even as she thought it, she knew that wasn't a good argument. Amy wouldn't have wanted her nephew to be subjected to the same thing that she herself had gone through and which, Sara was sure, she had regretted.

'She wouldn't have wanted Tom to do it,' John repeated.

She sighed. No, she wouldn't have. It wasn't enough for one person in the marriage to love the other.

On his way out, he paused and turned around. She didn't dare look up from the counter, her eyes fixed on the pile of books in front of her.

'It wasn't Amy who was too weak to get married,' he said. 'It was me.'

The Darkness Catches Up with George

George came home from the improvised dress-fitting party to his own personal hell. It appeared in the unlikely form of a blue Suburban and a Taco John's manager named Ronald.

The car was parked in George's space, and beside it were two flowery bags, packed and waiting.

His first thought was: so, he did come after her. He was actually happy for her, that's how stupid he really was, he would think later. Just an old fool. Again.

The Taco John's manager came out of George's apartment as if he owned it, although to be fair he didn't seem that obnoxious. He smiled a lot, and greeted George with too much ease.

'Ronald Lukeman,' he said. 'I'm sure Michelle's mentioned me.'

'Yes,' George said.

'Women, eh?' and George said 'yes' again, because he couldn't think what else to say.

Michelle came out next, dressed in tight jeans, hair all done up and freshly made up. She had too much eyeshadow on for Broken Wheel, but she looked better than she had since coming back. She also looked ever so slightly foolish, standing there next to Ronald, but pleased, too.

And then Sophie came. She had her jacket on and was holding a pair of gloves in one hand.

'You're . . . you're leaving?' George said, and Michelle went from pleased to exasperated in two seconds.

'Get it together, George,' she said.

'But . . .'

He couldn't think what to say. Michelle just swept by him, leaving the oversweet smell of her perfume in her wake. Ronald stuck out his hand, and George shook it absent-mindedly.

'Sophie,' he said, looking intently over Ronald's shoulder.

She stopped when she reached him. 'He did come after her,' she said, echoing George's thoughts. She was smiling, like she was glad she'd been wrong.

George swallowed. 'So,' he said. 'You're . . .' He cleared his throat. 'You're really leaving, then?'

'Seems like it.'

'Sophie!' Michelle called.

George turned and looked at them: Michelle and Ronald standing there beside the car, the bags already inside it . . . he tried desperately to think of something, anything, to say, and in the end he couldn't.

Sophie gave him a small hug, he blinked, and then they were gone. She was gone. Again.

When he went inside, the pale yellow apartment was empty of any sign they'd ever been there except for two short notes on the kitchen table.

'*George, we're taking off,*' said one of them.

'*Thanks for letting us stay,*' said the other.

And he realised two things, standing there by the refrigerator, the notes still in his hand. She hadn't left an address, and the darkness had caught up with him again.

Losing her was even more difficult this time around.

Perhaps it was because everything had been so much more uncertain the first time. It all came gradually back then; all the problems, the arguments, the packing of bags. The leaving. He hadn't allowed himself to think that it might be forever. Sophie would be back, he had thought, long after people started giving him pitying looks.

When he had finally been forced to admit that she wouldn't be coming back, he had already started drinking and it had helped. Drowned out the worst of his sorrows when he finally gave up all hope.

He had forgotten how much it had hurt. But even so, he couldn't remember it having been as bad as it felt now.

He knew without a shadow of a doubt that no father could

be expected to lose his daughter twice. That realisation gave him a perverse kind of comfort. He had managed to cope with losing her once. He had no intention of doing so again.

Strangely enough, his thoughts didn't turn immediately to alcohol.

For the whole of the first day after Broken Wheel had gone dress shopping and Sophie had disappeared, he sat at the kitchen table thinking about how something as simple and automatic as breathing could suddenly feel so hard. He saw the darkness opening up once again and did nothing to protect himself from it.

But finally, his eyes moved from the notes on the kitchen table to Claire's open bottle of wine.

He wondered whether he should empty it.

Thinking about it didn't prick his conscience, despite the fact that he had promised Sophie never to drink again. It hadn't even been the real Sophie, he knew that now, just a voice in his head. Not even a voice, she had never answered him, and he couldn't talk to her any more. The real Sophie had taken the Sophie in his head with her when she left.

He couldn't muster enough energy to get up and reach for the bottle. Even sitting up felt like a struggle. He staggered off to bed and lay down, still dressed, without even taking a book with him.

Maybe he would drink it later, once he felt a bit better.

He spent the whole of the second day in bed.

He hadn't given up, he thought. Giving up implied that he had been trying at first. You had to give *something* up. Like before, when he had initially protested and lied to himself and then ultimately, during a long period of drinking, given up his illusions one by one. This time, though, there was nothing left to give up. He had simply accepted that he had lost her.

No denial. No anger either. That was something else he had experienced that first time, though it hadn't changed a thing.

Of course, if you looked at it from a different angle, then he supposed you could argue that what he was giving up now was the attempt at pretending he was capable of living a normal life without her. Maybe it was life itself he had given up, but he truly felt as though it wasn't something he had any choice over. It was more like life had given up on him.

Otherwise, it wouldn't have sent Sophie back to him only to take her away again. For a moment, he teetered on the verge of thinking the thought: *if only she hadn't come back to me*. But he shied away from it. A week with the real Sophie was worth the loss of the Sophie in his head. Even a much shorter time would have been enough. A day, an hour, a minute, even a brief glimpse of her.

Not that he would have recognised her if life had given him only a brief glimpse, of course. That thought put him into a real cold sweat; small, delicate pearls of water gathering on his forehead. To have seen her and not recognised her, that would have been awful.

So. He hadn't given up. He just didn't care enough to do anything.

The ceiling needed repainting. There were huge cracks in the white paint which, in places, had turned yellowish brown with dirt and age.

He traced the cracks with his eyes and took a certain comfort from them. They gave him something concrete and real to cling to and think about.

Paint. Repaint. Cleaning. Cover the furniture.

He turned his head. The curtains were drawn. Maybe he should have opened them before he went to bed so that he had more to see and think about.

Change the curtains. Sew new ones. He couldn't sew, of course. Besides, he had no intention of moving from bed.

Someone knocked at the door, but he couldn't bring himself to get up and answer it. That would just be the beginning. He would have had to talk. Listen. Exchange words.

Unthinkable.

He suspected it was Claire. That was OK. Claire would

understand, she had a Sophie of her own. He felt a short, unexpected pang of conscience at the thought it might be Sara. She might not understand, and she might need a ride somewhere.

Broken Wheel Drowns its Sorrows

By half four, Sara had given up all hope for the day. Before she left, her eyes fell on the piece of paper with the girl's address written on it, and she suddenly realised that she didn't know whether Sophie was still staying with George. She wrote a nice note and decided she would post the book if she had already gone back home. If Sophie liked it, she would send the two following books later. Though, she thought glumly, she probably wouldn't do that after all. Because, by then, she wouldn't be in Broken Wheel any more.

She didn't bother waiting to see whether George or Tom came to pick her up. She would walk home, either to Amy's or to Tom's, depending on where she ended up, and maybe she would come up with something on the way. A depressing thought. The only thing she managed to come up with was that she couldn't stay. Amy had said so. There was just one day left until the wedding.

Josh passed by Grace's after yet another of his trips to Caroline's front door.

'God, I need a drink,' he said, sitting down at the counter.

Grace tried a joke. 'Ha ha,' she said. 'Has Caroline dumped you?'

Josh didn't laugh. Grace had the feeling her jokes often hit a nerve nowadays. She was struck by something in his expression.

'Tell me it's not true,' she said.

'Not any more.'

'Caroline hitting on small boys!' Grace said to herself. 'No offence,' she added quickly. 'On younger men, anyway.' She smiled wryly and said, comfortingly: 'Don't worry, no one'll believe she was the one who ended it. Or if they do, then they'll know that you would've dumped her sooner or later anyway.' She added, enthused: 'You know, this has made my day. Caroline, who's always been so damn proper.'

'Tough,' said Josh. Grace looked at him questioningly. 'Not proper. Tough.'

'Sure, sure.' Grace was fair. 'Tough too. But annoying. Who would've thought it? She'll never be able to boss people about now.'

That didn't seem to cheer Josh up.

'It would've been better if you'd kept it up a bit longer, so she really had time to make a fool of herself over you.'

'Caroline would never have made a fool of herself.'

'Oh yeah? Older women always make fools of themselves when they fall for younger men. Law of nature. Same thing with older men falling for younger women.'

He rested his head in his hands and made a half-stifled noise which sounded like a pained grunt. 'I need a drink,' he said again.

'That I can help you with.'

When he left Grace's, he seemed to be in an even worse mood than when he'd arrived, but at least he had an entire bottle of home-distilled liquor with him. She saw him pause just outside the door, before he shrugged exaggeratedly and set off in the direction of Hope. He was holding the bottle in one hand and just before he started walking, he took a swig from it. Even from where she was standing behind the counter, she could see the grimace on his face. Good liquor was wasted on some people. Grace was left alone with a faint feeling of unease. She could just imagine Sara's kind smile. Friendly, but slightly reproachful.

'Damn you, Sara,' she said to no one in particular. 'She deserved it. She would've said the same thing about me. It was just a joke.'

Since when did she have a conscience, exactly? It wasn't as though she was a part of this hole of a town.

George had made it to the kitchen table, but only because his body was kicking up too much of a fuss to stay lying down.

He stared at the red wine. He could drink it. Or go for a walk. Or keep sitting there.

If he was going to drink it, he would need to buy more liquor. That much he knew: half a bottle of wine wouldn't be enough, not nearly enough. Grace had always refused to sell him liquor, Andy too. In the good old days, it hadn't been a problem. Back then, he had still had contacts who could help him out. He could ask Claire, of course, but he suspected she didn't have much alcohol at home.

He could even walk to Hope. He could keep on walking forever.

On the way to Hope, George came across Josh, who waved a bottle in the air when he caught sight of him. He seemed to have already started on it, but he wasn't drunk yet. 'Can I tempt you with a glass?'

'Sure,' George eventually said without much enthusiasm.

Josh shrugged and handed him the bottle. 'Women,' he said.

They kept walking. Neither of them much cared where they ended up. Josh took another swig and handed the bottle back to George, who drank without grimacing in the slightest.

'The darkness is back,' George said.

'I should've stuck to men,' Josh said. 'Though if I'm honest I didn't have much luck there either.'

George raised the bottle. 'To Sophie,' he said. He drank and handed the bottle back.

'To Caroline,' Josh said, raising the bottle again. There was a defiant look in his eye, but George didn't even notice that he had spoken.

'I want Caroline,' Josh explained.

'She's not coming back this time,' George said.

When Tom got to the bookstore to drive Sara home, she had already left. He was just on the way back to his car when John waved him over from the hardware store.

'I talked to Sara,' he said. 'About the wedding. Couldn't let them sacrifice you.'

'I agreed to do it,' he said.

'Amy wouldn't have liked it.'

'What did Sara say?'

'She agreed, of course.' John nodded. 'I think she realised that it's not right for her to stay here. There's nothing to stay for.'

Tom went quickly back to his car, annoyed at Sara for having said something that he himself had been thinking. Why the hell couldn't she just make up her mind? One minute she was talking about wanting to stay, looking so sad (that he couldn't help but want to make her feel better). Like a damn puppy, with those big eyes of hers. The next minute, she was talking about there being nothing to stay for.

She wasn't at his house either. Clearly the charade was over. He went through the living room to the kitchen. The sight of Sara's books almost made him smile.

He took a glass and a bottle of whiskey out onto the porch. There was a natural calmness out there; the sound of the birds and the insects so familiar that they slipped softly through his consciousness without really registering. He noticed them only because of the faint sense of home and peace they created.

To the south of the house, he could see the few bright lights which made up Broken Wheel. The town itself, or what was left of it, was barely visible at night. He could see scattered lights from the apartments where Claire lived. Between them, the compact darkness of the cornfields.

The light from the houses reminded him that the town was still out there. The darkness created distance, told him that everything going on there could wait.

Maybe it was mad, thinking that she might actually want to be married to him. Especially now that the whole town seemed to love her. Sometimes, when he looked at the way everyone somehow lit up in her presence, he couldn't help but think of Amy.

It was as though the town needed a centre, something to gather around, and Sara had filled the void Amy had left behind, with Amy's shop and her books and her almost universal kindness.

He thought of Sara and the bookstore and the market and of

a street which seemed alive once more, which suddenly seemed to be almost constantly bathed in sunlight, and he thought of a town which in a few short weeks had been transformed from black and white to Technicolor.

Broken Wheel – now in colour! Coming soon to a movie theatre near you. Aside from the fact that the cinema had closed down long ago, of course. And that Sara would be going back to Sweden, the bookstore would be closing, the people who had gathered around it would scatter again, and Main Street would return to its former . . . tranquillity.

He had a strong suspicion that the contrast would be too much for them. That it would be the death blow to a town which, in some strange way, he loved; that the quiet, calm everyday would no longer be enough after Sara and her books.

What did it matter, anyway? He didn't need books and markets and dance evenings at the Square, nor big, expressive eyes . . . his treacherous mind lingered on that moment on the sofa, the look in those irritating eyes just before he kissed her, the feeling of her body pressed against his, warm and inviting.

You're a damn idiot, Tom.

Caroline was sitting in the kitchen with a cold cup of tea, trying to ignore the clear signs of depression. Caroline didn't get depressed. Her spirits were never low. She definitely didn't feel passive or apathetic or sit staring blankly ahead of her.

Perhaps she should have been furious instead, she thought. Break something, scream, throw things. She took a sip of her cold tea and couldn't bring herself to make a new one.

It was already night, it must have been nearly one. Two, even. A few hours earlier, she had been standing motionless in the middle of the hallway; just as passive, just as silent, just as completely incapable of doing anything.

He had knocked on the door with more force than sense and waited almost an hour outside her house, maybe in revenge, to really give the neighbours something to talk about; maybe because he really did want to see her again.

'Come on, Caroline,' he had said to her door. 'Is that really the worst you can be? Caroline the-beautiful-woman-who-breaks-young-hearts?'

But she had simply stood there. She hadn't even touched the door, though she somehow knew that his hand must have been pressed against the other side of it.

That in itself was no revolutionary realisation. *Everyone* who talked to a closed door eventually put their hand on it. If she actually had gone over to the door, she was convinced that she would have been touching the exact same spot as he was. That was simply how things were.

She had no intention of touching him in reality. If she *almost* touched him from behind the safety of a closed door, she might as well have actually opened the door, and then she might as well have actually touched him.

Or kissed him.

But she had taken a step towards the door when he said her name. Certain things simply couldn't be helped. He wouldn't miss her, but she couldn't quite bring herself to think that that was a good thing.

It was stupid, really, that it all felt so . . . sad.

Broken Wheel has a Headache

On the day of the wedding, William was getting ready to openly, albeit under the cover of early morning, defy Caroline's words about how undignified it was for a minister to tend to his own garden.

He was planning on pottering about in the garden without a single thought for his clerical duties. It was essentially true that there wasn't much to be done in the garden in the middle of October, but there were bushes and there was earth, and a real enthusiast could easily make do with that.

He set about his work with suitable reverence in the face of the greatness of God. It smelled of cool earth and near-rotten leaves, and the remains of a slowly dispersing early-morning mist. He imagined he could smell its damp scent, but it might have been nothing other than the dew-covered grass.

It was a glorious day.

And there would be a wedding! Not many got married in Broken Wheel these days. Fewer than those who came to church services, even. He would have preferred the opposite. Weddings were actually more important to a town than ordinary services. And, he thought, they were days when people found it easiest to get close to God, days where they were reminded of what God was really about.

He was just going through his sermon in his head when he spotted a lone foot sticking out from beneath a bush.

For a moment, he was worried he would have to round off the wedding with a funeral, but then he heard a faint, pained sound. The foot twitched slightly.

He leaned forward and said, uncertainly, to the bush: 'Excuse me?'

He wondered what was required in a situation like this.

'Is everything OK, my child?' He tried to sound calm and

fatherly, but sounded mostly foolish. The next time, he addressed the bush as 'my friend' instead.

The foot was twitching more now, until eventually it pulled back beneath the bush and a tall, thin and clearly worse-for-wear figure crawled out from beneath its branches.

'Good morning, Father,' Josh said.

William grimaced. He wondered whether to correct him and point out that he wasn't Catholic, but then he looked at the young man standing in front of him and decided the theological discussion could wait. He was clearly shaken after an evening of . . . debauchery, William thought. There was something resigned in his eyes, which might of course have been a result of the usual rapid punishment dealt out by that particular vice, but seemed to have a deeper root.

William nodded to himself. 'Coffee?' he suggested, walking back towards his little house next to the church without waiting for an answer. He heard Josh getting to his feet behind him.

'Hardly the season for sleeping outdoors,' he said as the water was boiling. He took down the coffee and the sugar. Josh declined any cream, which was just as well because he didn't have any.

'Sorry for intruding,' said Josh.

'Not at all. I was just going to potter about in the garden while I went through my sermon for today.' He smiled, delighted. 'A wedding! Here in Broken Wheel!'

'Are you looking forward to it?'

'Of course I am. Weddings are fantastic events.'

'I would have thought . . . all things considered? The background . . .'

William simply looked blankly at him. 'So,' he said eventually, 'what can I do for you?'

'I hadn't exactly been planning this visit,' said Josh.

'Of course,' said William. 'And does this have anything to do with . . . disappointments in love?' He had, of course, heard all about the evening at Madame Higgins's. No one seemed to have taken it seriously, but he hadn't seen Caroline for a few days now.

Josh didn't answer.

'Giving up is never a good idea,' said William. 'And in this particular case, if you'll excuse me saying so, it seems rather hasty.'

Josh laughed drily. 'In this particular case, I think I should've given up a long time ago.' William looked so sorrowfully at him that Josh pulled a face and said: 'Sorry.'

'And have you talked to . . . her about it?'

'It was more a case of her talking to me.'

'Yes,' he agreed. 'Caroline is a . . . formidable woman.'

Josh didn't seem surprised that he knew about it. He simply said: 'But a bit too focused on what others think of her.'

William sipped his coffee while he tried to work out how he should answer. He turned the coffee cup absent-mindedly in his hands. 'Yes,' he said hesitantly. 'But the world can be so cruel to women who never marry. Even now, you know.'

Josh pulled another face, an apologetic, slightly self-reproaching grimace. 'Don't worry, I'm not judging her for it. Sometimes I think she's actually right.'

He didn't say anything else after that. He simply drank his coffee, thanked the minister politely and left. But William imagined he had seen a new determinedness in his walk.

William had forgotten all about his gardening amid the unfamiliar feeling of euphoria which had suddenly materialised at the thought of being needed.

Maybe he had been born simply to take care of those who stayed behind.

George woke on the edge of a field, just outside Broken Wheel. Someone was kicking his feet. He could smell liquor and damp grass, and wasn't at all happy to discover that it was Claire standing there somewhere above his feet. She shouldn't have to see me like this, he thought, and would have lain back down on the grass again if Claire hadn't leaned over him and said:

'For God's sake, George.'

He blinked.

'Get up,' she said firmly. 'Sara's getting married today. Now's not the right time to fall to pieces.'

He managed to drag himself up into a sitting position. She looked like some kind of goddess of revenge, he thought, though in a nice way, of course. Proper boots, jeans, a thick padded jacket, and flame-red hair, as though nothing could defeat her. It was hard to imagine she was the same person who had cried over a few clean dishes in his kitchen.

But he couldn't do anything for her now. She and Sara would have to cope without him. Maybe she needed an explanation. 'Sophie left me,' he said.

'And?' The shock almost got him back on his feet again. She grabbed his elbows and helped him up. 'Sara's getting married today,' she repeated.

He shook his head, trying to clear his thoughts. The only thing that happened was he realised that his head hurt. 'Sophie,' he said again.

'Sure, sure,' said Claire. 'Gone. Your bitch of an ex-wife has taken off again.'

He tried to get her to see the important part. 'With Sophie.'

'Of course with Sophie. And you've been drinking.'

She helped him to her car. He slumped into the front seat beside her without really knowing what he was doing. His clothes were cold and damp, but it felt good. Something practical to focus on. Maybe he would develop a really serious case of lung inflammation and never have to leave his bed again.

Claire looked at him with something that might have been sympathy. It was the first time that morning she had shown anything like warmth. Still, her voice was hard and determined. He leaned towards it like a drowning man to a lifebuoy, as though the sound of her voice would somehow keep him upright until he was home.

'I know it seems tough,' she said. 'We're gonna find her for you, but now's not the right time to get bogged down in it.'

He blinked. 'Find her?'

He wouldn't make the mistake of believing her. Accepting his fate. That was the only way to get through this.

'Jesus, this is the twenty-first century. We know what she

looks like. It's got to be possible to find her. They're probably still living in Iowa, and the state's not that big. She's probably on Facebook, too.' He didn't even know what Facebook was. She seemed to know he wasn't convinced, because she continued: 'We'll find her regardless of whether she is or not. We'll talk to Sara about it. She'll be able to work it out. There's probably a book about this – *Private Investigation for Dummies* or something like that.'

Maybe Sara *could* work this out. There didn't seem to be anything she couldn't do.

'Or we'll just hire a real PI. A whiskey-drinking, chain-smoking detective.'

He smiled weakly.

'She's almost grown up, George. Things are different now. She might well come and find you herself.'

He shook his head.

'And anyways, you should've come to me for the liquor.'

'Didn't think you'd have enough,' he said.

She drove him home, followed him in and waited until she saw he was going into the bathroom to shower ahead of the wedding. 'I'll be back in an hour,' she said through the bathroom door, something between a threat and a promise.

He smiled again as he took off his clothes, but even more feebly now that she couldn't see him.

He should save his energy for something better, he thought.

Josh wasn't upset any more.

Enough now, he thought to himself as he walked away from the minister's house. Sure, the sex had been amazing, but there were other people to pick up. Go to Des Moines or Denver, ask Andy and Carl for help. Get over it.

He hadn't really thought she would open the door, but he still felt a pang of disappointment when he realised she wasn't even prepared to say goodbye to him face-to-face.

He rested his hand on the door and said: 'Don't worry,' despite the fact that the door seemed completely indifferent, and not the least bit anxious. 'I didn't come here to bother you. I'm going to Denver after the wedding. I just wanted to say goodbye.'

He waited a moment longer. The door didn't answer.

'Goodbye, Caroline,' he said.

Broken Wheel, Iowa
July 17, 2011

Sara Lindqvist
Kornvägen 7, 1 tr
136 38 Haninge
Sweden

Dear Sara,

I know you think it seems impossible to pay me back in books when you can only take 20kg of luggage on the plane, but I already have all the books and money I need. If you really *have to* do it, then I won't accept anything more than $300. That's my absolute maximum, and only under the condition that we do something fun together with it. If nothing else, we can eat plenty of dinners at Andy and Carl's.

Write back and let me know when you're coming, and we'll meet you.

Best,

Amy

If Anyone Knows of Any Reason . . .

She was wearing the plain dress from Madame Higgins's shop. There was something sad about the ordinary material and the straight, simple cut, and the way it barely reached her knees. It wasn't a happy dress, that much was clear, but it was at least mercifully free of frills and lace.

George had dropped her off at the church, and she had changed in the little room at the back. There was still half an hour until the ceremony, and the inhabitants of Broken Wheel had already started to arrive. She glanced through a crack in the door but didn't go and see them. Instead, she snuck out by the back door.

She felt slightly ridiculous, creeping along Broken Wheel's main street in a wedding dress, a meagre bouquet of pink roses in her hand. She needn't have worried though – there wasn't a person in sight. The entire street was abandoned; the hardware store was in darkness, Amazing Grace was closed and her own shop as deserted as a shop filled with books could be.

As she unlocked the door and crept in, she still glanced about. She didn't want anyone to spot her and come over. This was something she needed to do alone.

She didn't quite know why she had to do it at this particular moment. Maybe she was simply trying to distract herself. She had almost managed to convince herself that she would tell them all she couldn't marry Tom, but she couldn't make her treacherous brain focus on the problem of *how* she was going to do it.

She didn't bother switching on the lights. She looked at the titles on the bookshelves and the counter, and everything else which, for a short while longer, was still hers. She stood for a moment, blinking away the tears which were obstinately trying to obscure her view.

Then she closed her eyes, as though she was trying to etch it all into her memory; the dry air, the smell of books and old armchairs, the light flooding through the shop window and dancing behind her eyelids.

She opened her eyes. She didn't have time for this. There were things that needed to be done.

She put the bouquet down on the counter and took out the marker pen and the last few sheets of cardboard. The card was slightly worse for wear now, but she found two pieces which didn't have any bent corners. She put them to one side and started moving books.

She wrote a new sign: AMY AND SARA'S BOOKS. Not all their books, obviously, just the ones that meant most to them. It felt fitting that it started with Louisa May Alcott. Their friendship, immortalised.

Until the bookshop closed and the books were moved back to the house, that was.

At least they would remember her, in the same way they all still remembered Amy, even when they weren't talking about her. A faint presence, yet another fate bound up in the bricks and the asphalt, still lingering in the abandoned buildings.

And perhaps there would be a miracle of some kind, something which meant she could stay. Perhaps Tom would convince her again, perhaps Jen would force her to get married, perhaps . . . she was struggling to gain control over herself again. She knew what she had to do. Somehow, she would be strong enough to make it through.

There was one last category. She started moving books again, in high piles which she leaned against her chest and steadied with her chin. She wrote the new heading on the best card, fetched a rickety chair from the little cubbyhole and balanced unsteadily on it while she hung it up, as high as she could, in direct line of sight from the window and the doorway.

Sara clung onto the new category as though the shiny new sign was the only thing keeping her going. The best books gathered in one place, the biggest section in the bookshop; everything which made books better than life.

HAPPY ENDINGS WHEN YOU NEED THEM.

When she made it back into the church again, the whole of Broken Wheel was gathered there. John was sitting on one of the pews at the back, looking serious. Sara forced herself to think of Amy, of the price Tom would have to pay if she didn't say no to them all.

As she passed John, she leaned over his shoulder and quietly said: 'Don't worry, I'm not going to marry him.'

She was probably saying it as much for her own sake as for John's, but it didn't seem to make him feel much better, and she didn't even bother trying to smile. Instead, she walked slowly down the aisle.

When Tom eventually arrived, he looked just as serious as Sara, and his face was equally pale. He walked straight over to her without greeting anyone. He gave her hand a feather-light squeeze when he got to the front.

She wondered whether she would have been happier if she hadn't suddenly wanted things, if she hadn't felt like she belonged there. That was how people normally felt in books.

I wish I had never met you.

I wish I had never laid eyes on you.

If only I had never come here.

But she couldn't feel that way. Not even now.

The minister started talking in front of them, but Sara barely registered what he was saying. Would she have been happier? Or would the taste of wanting to belong somewhere make her happier later, once she was back in Sweden and reconciled with her loss? Maybe it had raised her ambitions, shown her alternatives which she could search for afresh, in another small town somewhere, perhaps in some other country. She knew there were countries which allowed you to stay and to work. They just weren't countries she had any desire to visit.

She should interrupt William now. But it was his sermon and

it was all going so well for him, and he looked so happy. She couldn't do it. He didn't even seem to notice when Caroline snuck in and sat down at the very back, or that Josh froze when he saw her. William was talking so confidently that he even managed to ignore Grace stumbling into the church, not particularly quietly – completely drunk, in fact – with a hunting rifle under her arm, presumably to celebrate in style afterwards. Sara turned her attention back to the minister. He seemed to have come to the end now.

He fell silent and glanced around expectantly, and for a moment, Broken Wheel managed to tear itself away and break out into spontaneous applause. William smiled and turned to Tom and Sara.

She really should say it now. But she didn't quite know whether her voice would manage it. There was an awful dry taste in her mouth. Her cheeks were burning so much they almost hurt. She felt like crying but her heart was pounding so hard in her chest that she didn't think she could.

My God, I can't speak in front of people, she thought.

For a moment, she forgot that she knew everyone there, that they were her friends, and all she could think of was how terrible she had always been at giving presentations in school.

Happily, she was saved by a discreet cough from the very back of the church.

Everyone turned around, looking in surprise at the little man who had crept silently in and was now clearing his throat to get their attention. 'I'm looking for Sara Lindqvist and Tom Harris.'

Tom took a half-step forward.

'You have, as I understand it, submitted an application for permanent residency on the grounds of the marriage I'm about to witness?'

'Yes.'

'Have you already married?'

Tom smiled ironically. 'We were kind of in the middle of it when you arrived.'

'Aha. I've got a little objection, you see.'

William stared at him. 'But I haven't got to that bit yet!'

'I'm afraid it can't wait,' the man said.

Everyone had begun whispering quietly at this unexpected development, aside from Grace, who had long ago lost the ability to talk quietly. 'Who the hell is he to have objections?' she demanded of Claire, who smiled feebly at her and shook her head.

'I'd recommend you reconsider this whole thing.'

'But why?' said William.

'Even if they get married, it's far from certain that we'll grant residency. As things stand, I must say it's doubtful that we'll do so.'

'He's going to take our Sara from us!' Grace said angrily.

Claire hushed her and patted her arm, as though she were an agitated horse or, in this case, a drunk horse armed with a hunting rifle.

'But how are they meant to be able to live together then?' William asked.

'I've got to say that from my point of view, this looks most like an attempt to gain a residency permit under false pretences, which is, I have to tell you, a crime.'

'But that's not at all why they're getting married,' William protested.

People were fidgeting in their seats. Sara smiled faintly.

'Even without the bookstore and the question marks around *that*, I'd probably be forced to recommend a rejection.'

Grace stood up. 'We Graces have never let any damn regulations decide what we can or can't do,' she said. Somewhat unsteadily, she aimed the rifle at Gavin Jones, who still seemed completely unfazed. 'Towanda!'

'Grace!' Claire said pleadingly as Andy, somewhat less helpfully, reminded her that the safety catch was still on. She lowered the weapon and looked hesitantly at them. Claire and George breathed a sigh of relief. Andy laughed.

Gavin Jones took the opportunity to call the police.

Objections

Gavin Jones glanced up from his notes. The policeman had gracefully agreed to accompany him to USCIS office in Hope. He'd also agreed to let Gavin do this his way, and deal with the gun as they went along.

Since the window was mirrored on one side, the people sitting in the waiting room couldn't see him. He had no idea why whoever built the room had opted for such extravagances but, at that moment, it meant he had plenty of time to observe them. The case should have been a simple one, but the sheer volume of potential madmen filled his orderly mind with dread. He already had a strong suspicion that when it came to Broken Wheel, nothing was ever simple.

Sara Lindqvist and Tom Harris were sitting slightly away from the others, squeezed into a corner, silent and dogged. The woman was thin and plain and wearing a dull white dress. She hadn't made the effort to look good. In his experience, women who were getting married spent a fortune on lace and frills and devoted hours to their hair and make-up. Sara Lindqvist hadn't even bothered to apply lipstick.

The man, on the other hand, was suspiciously handsome. If Gavin had been harbouring any doubts before he went to the church, they had vanished completely now.

He could think of only one reason a man like Tom Harris would want to marry a woman like Sara.

Money had changed hands, he thought resolutely.

'What should we start with?' the policeman beside him asked. 'The weapon? The minister? The wedding dress?' He seemed to think it was funny.

Gavin looked out through the window one last time.

Sara Lindqvist. Swedish citizen and suspected criminal.

Had it been worth it? he wondered to himself.

* * *

They got the least interesting of them over and done with first. Two men – a couple, the policeman noted merrily and Gavin disinterestedly – came in to be interviewed together. At the last moment, a woman who looked like some sort of manic housewife made her way into the interviewing room with them, demanding to be heard first.

'Please explain to me what's going on here,' she said, sounding like a mother asking a child to explain a broken vase.

Gavin gestured for her to sit down, and she reluctantly did so, clutching her small bag and staring at him like he was the naughty child. 'I demand to know what's going on,' she said. 'This is a free country!'

'Within reason,' the policeman said.

Gavin turned to the couple. 'Tell me about this wedding.'

'Sara and Tom,' one of them said. His eyes were shining. 'A perfect couple. We knew that long before they even realised it themselves.'

'And organised it for them?' Gavin's voice was dry.

'Sure,' the same man said. He didn't seem the least bit remorseful. 'Who knows what they would've come up with otherwise.'

'And the bookstore?'

'Which bookstore?'

'How many are there in Broken Wheel?' It was the policeman who had spoken, and Gavin looked at him sternly.

'What about it, I meant.'

'Sara runs it?'

The man paused for thought. 'Well, she's there sometimes. But she doesn't get paid, if that's what you were thinking, and she doesn't own it. Strictly speaking, I guess the town council does.' He laughed. 'Or Amy Harris.'

Gavin noted down the name.

'I don't see what all of this has got to do with Sara's wedding!' the woman complained. No one paid any attention to her.

'And the weapon?' the policeman asked. Gavin sent another displeased look in his direction.

'A misunderstanding.' The man smiled.

Gavin didn't bother putting any more questions to the two men. He could have sworn that one of them had winked at him.

'Don't think I'll forget about this,' the housewife said over her shoulder as the policeman escorted her out rather forcibly. 'Because I won't!'

Gavin had higher hopes for the next interview. The woman from the diner, the one with the hunting rifle.

'A good woman, Sara,' the woman said.

Gavin Jones looked down at the form in front of him. Grace. No surname had been given.

'Tom and Sara found one another straight away when she got to Broken Wheel,' she said. 'They've been practically inseparable ever since.'

Gavin made no attempt to write down what she said.

'And the weapon?' the policeman asked. Gavin glared at him.

'The weapon?' said Grace. 'A misunderstanding, that's all. A way of celebrating. Like the Fourth of July.'

'Mm-hmm,' the policeman said, smiling. Gavin wasn't amused.

'In my family, we take celebrations seriously,' Grace said. 'It reminds me of the time my grandmother's mother –'

'Thank you,' Gavin said quickly. 'If we could talk about Tom and Sara?'

'Damn predictable, that's what Tom and Sara were,' she said. 'Certain couples just have it too easy. Not like us, who've had to fight for it.'

'You?'

Gavin didn't even bother to glare at the policeman this time.

'Believe me, the Grace women have had to fight. Men just have no sense of anything romantic. Insist on wanting to get married and *have* you, rather than just hanging out with a bit of moonshine and some semi-automatic weapons. Or revolvers. Knives. We're interested in most things. Even a frying pan once, before we switched to the hunting rifle. Say what you want about knives and frying pans, but they're not much use against a revolver at twenty yards. Though nowadays,' she added as an afterthought, 'I've got a Marlin 336.'

'Thanks very much,' Gavin blurted out. 'Leave your contact details. You can go home for now.'

The policeman raised an eyebrow but said nothing.

Caroline was sitting alone at the edge of the waiting room, trying not to look at Josh.

The only other people left were the minister, Sara and Tom, and none of them seemed interested in what she was doing. The minister looked confused and unhappy; Sara and Tom were simply sitting in calm silence next to one another. They said nothing, which was probably just as well. What could they say? What could any of them say now?

When the policeman came to get her, Caroline glanced instinctively towards Josh. He moved away from the wall and came over to her. They had to go through a door and down a short corridor parallel to the waiting room; he let her go first and the scent of his aftershave put a knot in her stomach as she passed.

She paused despite herself and he gently placed a hand on her back and took hold of her arm.

'I've changed my mind,' he said, almost imperceptibly, as he guided her on.

He had already told her that he no longer wanted to be with her. That he was planning on going to Denver or wherever else he might end up. It had made her sad, it really had, especially since she had just decided that people might as well laugh at her. But she wasn't surprised.

What she couldn't understand was why he had insisted on following her into the interview room to explain it all again. Maybe she had annoyed him so much with her brief refusal that he simply wanted to emphasise how much he had changed his mind.

She smiled to herself. It wasn't completely impossible, she thought, and she liked him all the more for it. Why should he simply lie down and let her get away?

If she had been as tough when it came to relationships as she was with other things, she wouldn't have let him get away either.

The policeman opened the door to the office. The little grey man from the wedding was sitting at the desk. The policeman positioned himself slightly behind him and gazed nonchalantly out of the window rather than looking at them.

Impolite, Caroline thought without feeling.

Josh didn't seem to care in the slightest where he was or what was going on around him. He sat down in one of the chairs, but only because she had done the same, and immediately turned towards her. He was about to say something when the bureaucrat in the ill-fitting suit took control. She was so thankful that she smiled at him.

'Tell us about this . . . wedding,' he said. The suspicion in his voice was just strong enough to encourage them to tell the truth, without being so overt as to put them on the defensive.

'What do you want to know?' Caroline asked. 'They met when Sara came here to visit Amy.'

The bureaucrat looked down at his papers. 'Would that be a certain Amy Harris?'

'She's dead,' Caroline said calmly, which made the policeman turn from the window and look at her out of curiosity.

'What a town,' he said admiringly. The bureaucrat frowned at him.

'Well, it wasn't unexpected. Impractical, I guess you could say.'

'Very,' the policeman agreed.

'She still stayed in the house, though. It was what Amy would've wanted.'

'And worked in her bookstore?'

'Helped out.'

'And this marriage, would that also have been what Amy wanted?'

'I think she probably would've liked it, but since they hadn't even met when she died, she probably had no opinion on it whatsoever.'

'But the bookstore, she wanted Sara to have it?'

'The store isn't Sara's. The books were Amy's, for the most part. I guess you can say that we, the town council – a group of people who help the town, you see, completely informal nowadays – own it.'

'Not much of a town,' the policeman said.

Caroline didn't make the mistake of turning towards him. Josh was there somewhere, between her and the policeman, and so she kept her eyes fixed on the bureaucrat, to avoid having to look at Josh. He said nothing, but Caroline thought she could sense how tense he was. Maybe she was just imagining it, but she had no intention of looking at him to make sure.

'Was Sara working in it?'

'She definitely didn't get paid, if that's what you're wondering. She sat there reading sometimes, and she borrowed books from it. I don't think anyone really works there. We all helped out. There were never many customers, anyway. But it's a nice little store, in every sense.'

The bureaucrat made no comment, nor did he note anything down, despite the paper and pen lying on the desk in front of him. Caroline wasn't at all shaken by his nonchalance.

'And so we come to the little matter of their marriage . . .'

'I think that's a matter you'd be better off speaking to them about.'

'We will do,' said the bureaucrat.

He seemed to be about to ask something else, when the policeman suddenly looked up and fixed Josh and Caroline with a penetrating stare.

'Tell me you two aren't together too,' he said.

'We're just friends,' Caroline said.

'Like hell!'

She turned towards Josh. She couldn't help it. It was unlike him to be so fierce. Her hands were shaking.

'We're friends, aren't we . . . ?' she said uncertainly.

'I told you I'd changed my mind, didn't I?' he said.

That he had changed his mind about being with her, yes. Not that they weren't friends. Or rather, it was obvious that she had known they wouldn't be friends afterwards. But she had never thought he would come right out and say it.

He looked at her. She averted her gaze and blinked quickly. She forced herself to swallow and say 'Of course', as calmly as she could, but her voice sounded feeble and unhappy. She forced herself to nod as well, just to be on the safe side. 'Maybe it's for the best,' she said.

'I'm not going to go to Denver and leave you in peace just to make life easier for you,' he said. 'Isn't that the point of attraction? That it makes life *more interesting*?'

Caroline smiled faintly, despite herself. 'Definitely more interesting,' she agreed.

He glared at her. He was extremely attractive when he was angry.

'It *should* be hard work and complicated and wrong and strange. Let people laugh. It just means we're living more interesting lives than they are.'

Caroline tried to get her head around this latest development but failed. She said nothing.

'There are two types of people in the world, Caroline: those who take the lead and live, and those who follow, laughing at them. However much you pretend to be boring and sad, you're not. You're just going to have to learn to be a bit tougher than the rest of them. The only really weak thing I've seen you do was end things with me.' Something determined had appeared in his eyes. 'And I'm not planning to let you do it. I refuse. Give me one good reason why we shouldn't carry on like we were? It's not like we were planning on getting married or anything, for God's sake.'

'Maybe,' Caroline said cautiously.

He stopped short.

'Maybe?' he said. 'Not no?'

'Yes.' She smiled. 'Not no.'

The bureaucrat coughed in an attempt to regain their attention. The policeman seemed half fascinated, half doubtful.

'So we're going to carry on as before?' Josh said. 'You'll continue to see me?'

'Well, it *was* fun,' Caroline said.

'What *is* it with this town?' the policeman muttered to himself.

Josh looked at him. 'The sex was great, you see.'

Caroline smiled her most bland and polite smile at the policeman. 'So important, don't you think?'

The policeman had been about to drink some coffee, and

actually spluttered over Caroline's next sentence: 'I came to it late in life, you know. Lots of catching up to do.'

Caroline saw it as a form of victory, although one small part of her still prayed that he wouldn't tell anyone about it. Beside her, Josh shook with silent laughter.

The bureaucrat tried desperately to retake the lead.

'About Sara,' he said.

Both Josh and Caroline seemed surprised to discover he was still in the room. Caroline couldn't help but smile at Josh, and their eyes shone in silent, amused agreement.

'Sara and Tom. A lovely couple,' Caroline said. 'They go very well together. They're the same age, for a start, and . . . hmm . . . well, neither of them was with anyone else when they met. Tom had been single a long time. You've got to understand we all thought it was very . . . fitting that they got together.'

The bureaucrat rubbed his temples.

'Fantastic woman, Sara,' said Josh. 'She helped me get a job here.'

'And the armed threat?' the policeman asked.

'A misunderstanding,' Josh said.

'Oh yes,' Caroline agreed. 'A way of celebrating, you know? That wom— Grace has always been quite *inspired* in her celebrations.'

'If we could go back to Tom and Sara,' Gavin said firmly. 'They seem to have found one another amazingly quickly.'

'Very fitting.'

'Did they know one another before she came to the US?'

'No, not at all. I don't think she knew anyone here.'

Bored, the policeman turned towards the window once the couple had left.

'D'you think they know we can see them?' he asked.

'Probably,' said Gavin. He didn't look up from his notes. The next interview had to be right.

'So they're really just together to get residency?' The policeman continued to look out through the window into the waiting room.

'Presumably,' Gavin replied.

'I don't like it,' the policeman stated. 'People shouldn't get hitched if they don't really love each other. Enough problems are caused by unhappy marriages as it is.'

Gavin made no comment.

'Would it make a difference if they actually *were* together?'

Gavin thought about it. 'I don't actually know,' he said eventually.

The policeman looked at him. 'Do you realise we still don't have any concrete evidence that anyone has been trying to dupe us? I reckon we might have a genuine case of love on our hands.'

Gavin had indeed realised the lack of evidence so far, but he wasn't as sure about the love match. 'Just bring them in,' he said.

It was all so surreal.

Sara was sitting there, staring at a wall of faded wallpaper. There was a water cooler in one corner, and she could hear country music coming from a radio in the background.

So this is how it's all going to end, she thought.

The reception itself was in darkness. She could make out four desks through the Plexiglas, and little holes for passing passports and other documents through, all empty and unused on a Saturday afternoon.

It was quite strange, really, such a big operation just to make sure she wouldn't end up with him.

'Tom . . .' she said. She didn't know what she was going to say next, but she felt like she should say *something*. It was all her fault. She held out her hands in a gesture of helplessness.

He shook his head.

'We should talk,' she said, though she didn't sound particularly convincing. Doing so was always difficult when you yourself didn't even believe what you were saying.

'I don't think we can fix this by talking, Sara,' he said.

A new song had started. She raised an eyebrow. 'Want to dance then?' she joked desperately. Something had to be done to ease the tension.

He stood up and held out a hand, in an absurd gesture of gallantry, and after a moment's thought she got to her feet too. Why not?

He took her hand in his, put his other arm around her waist. She closed her eyes and leaned in to him.

His white shirt was surprisingly soft beneath her hand. Something within her began to flicker.

And then his hand started moving down her back.

To begin with, she wasn't sure she had actually felt it, whether his hand really was moving. She touched his shoulder and there it was. A definite movement. A harder grip around her waist. She touched the soft hair on his neck and could feel his jeans against her legs, his belt against her stomach, and the warm darkness which embraced them the moment she closed her eyes. Their bodies drew closer until, finally, one of his legs moved between hers and she was pressed up against his thigh.

In a remote corner of her mind, she knew this unexpected closeness would make the distance afterwards even harder, but there was nothing she could do about it.

She knew that reality was waiting somewhere out there, beyond their only dance together, but so far, miraculously, no one had come to collect them. For the first time, she wondered whether it would feel better or worse if he loved her too.

She didn't know, but one thing was certain: this was much too intense for a relaxed dance between friends, and she felt how the muscles in his arm tensed as his grip on her back tightened, just between her waist and her shoulder blades. She clung on to him, or perhaps they were clinging on to one another. Her head was resting against his shoulder, his cheek against her hair, and nothing else existed other than the music and their bodies.

The song was coming to an end. Her body noticed it before she did, how the song reached a kind of high point and then began the journey back down to the end. How the chorus was repeated one last time, with slightly more emphasis, signalling that the best was over and it was time for all this to end.

Her body reacted by pressing ever closer to him. Somehow, unconsciously, it seemed to be trying to memorise the feeling of his thighs and stomach and shoulders and jaw, the little lock of hair behind one of his ears, the scent of aftershave and his soft shirt, eyes closed as he danced. It seemed as though he could feel it too, because his grip grew tighter and he pulled her in to him until she could no longer breathe but also no longer needed to.

There was something so tragically simple about a dance ending. A hand leaving a shoulder, a waist; two hands unclasping and letting go of one another. Just like that.

Tom cleared his throat. She looked at him, in confusion. He took her hand in an almost absent-minded gesture. Then he raised it up to his lips which gently brushed the inside of her wrist.

'Who wants to go first?' the policeman asked.

Sara was much too confused to make any decisions, so Tom squeezed her hand gently and then left her dazed and alone in the confusing waiting room of a confusing authority.

Confused. She was confused. She sank down into the nearest chair.

The policeman moved away from the wall and leaned against the edge of the desk.

'So you were the sacrificial lamb?' he asked.

Tom said nothing.

Gavin took over. 'Whose idea was it, this mad plan?'

'Mad?'

'Getting married so she could stay.'

'Ah, *that* madness.' He looked at them. 'It was completely my idea.'

Gavin leaned forwards. 'So there was a plan? For residency?'

'The others must've told you.'

'They . . . told us a lot of interesting things, yes.'

Tom flashed a quick, weak smile. 'I can imagine. Anyway, it was my idea. Sara didn't want to. I convinced her. If anyone gets into trouble over this, it should be me.'

'It's a serious crime, of course,' said Gavin. 'But a confession always helps.'

'And Sara?'

'She'll obviously be sent home.' He shrugged. 'If you confess, I can arrange it so there aren't any fines.' As a warning, he added:

'Or any jail time. But she'll have real trouble being granted a visa at any point in the near future.'

Tom nodded.

'Or ever.'

'So you don't love her?' the policeman asked.

This time, Gavin Jones didn't attempt to stop him.

Tom looked at him in surprise. 'Of course I love her. I *wanted* to marry her.'

'And her?'

'I guess she just wanted to stay.'

The policeman seemed moved. Gavin did not.

The memory of being close to Tom faded fast in the tired office surroundings.

She could no longer remember exactly how his aftershave smelled, and in just a much-too-short period of time, she wouldn't remember his arm around her waist either. Her body was forgetting the feeling of his.

One day, she wouldn't even be able to remember the colour of his eyes, or how they looked when he smiled, and she experienced a moment of blind panic sitting there on the edge of an uncomfortable office chair. She closed her eyes and then forced them open again.

The grey man from the wedding was sitting behind the desk. He had taken off his jacket and was wearing the kind of cheap shirt which almost immediately develops sweat patches. He didn't seem to care though, and was looking at Sara curiously.

The policeman hadn't said a word when he came to get her, nor during the short walk to the office. Once they were there, he had sat down at the desk and started staring at her. His greyish-green uniform seemed remarkably formal in comparison to his youth, and Sara thought he seemed almost disapproving.

She didn't know where Tom was. She wondered how long this kind of decision usually took. Surely they wouldn't send her home before she had time to say goodbye, she thought desperately. Though on the other hand, what was there to say?

'So,' Gavin said. 'Tell us about this marriage plot.'

'It was my idea,' Sara said.

Neither of them believed her. She wasn't good at lying.

'Tom was practically forced into it.' Strangely enough, that sounded like the truth. She averted her gaze. 'None of the others knew a thing.'

The policeman laughed at that. 'Are you trying to tell us that none of the people we've spoken to today managed to work out the truth?'

'It was my idea,' she said stubbornly. But she looked so worried. It was her eyes which betrayed her; she was looking at them almost pleadingly. 'They're not going to get into trouble over this, are they . . . ?'

The policeman shook his head before Gavin had time to say anything, and Sara smiled, relieved.

'Thanks so much,' she said. It sounded as though she meant it.

'You won't be allowed to stay, though,' Gavin said.

Her smile faded.

'So you just wanted to get married for residency?' the policeman clarified.

'I . . .' She looked away again. 'Yes,' she said. 'To be able to stay.'

'To work?'

She laughed. 'Hardly.'

'So how had you been planning on supporting yourself? Or was Tom Harris going to be volunteered for that job, too?' The policeman seemed to have taken the whole thing personally.

She blushed. 'No, I . . . I've got some money. And no one lets me pay here. You know how it is, I guess? They help one another. Grace treats everyone to coffee, Andy gives them beer and John lets people borrow tools rather than buying them, if anything needs fixing. Tom helps with all the actual fixing. They're friends. I'll have money left when I go home,' she said.

'So you don't love him?' the policeman insisted.

She looked at him in surprise.

'Of course I love him. I love them all, but especially him. I shouldn't have done this, I know that. I *tried* to call it off, for his sake. He should find some nice woman he actually wants to marry, not be forced to live with me just because I . . . just because I couldn't bear the thought of leaving him.'

'What is it with this town?' the policeman said to himself once again. He turned back to her. 'So that means you weren't exactly getting married for residency?'

She looked embarrassed. 'I told everyone it was for residency,' she added sorrowfully, more to herself than the two men. 'I wanted to stay so much. I . . . I knew Tom didn't love me, but I went along with it anyway.'

Even Gavin was tense. He didn't like this part, whatever the others thought. He would rather have spent his time investigating, leave the questioning to others.

'Go home,' he said eventually.

She shuddered, but seemed to be fighting to hide it. 'Home?' she said, and then, more quietly: 'To Sweden, yes?'

'To Broken Wheel, I meant.' Gavin was annoyed by his failure to be clear. 'For now,' he added ominously. 'We'll be in touch.'

Sara got silently to her feet and left with the calm dignity of someone long since defeated.

Broken Wheel's Next Foreign Correspondent

When she stepped out of the office, she had to stop and squint in the bright sunlight. It was as though she was seeing everything in a series of film stills, as though everything had been cut up into small pieces and frozen in the moment for her to take in. She saw the car park, the empty spaces, the white lines marking them out, and the shadow of the lone parked car. The sun on its dusty bonnet. The buildings on the other side of the road, white and newly painted, with such a well-tended lawn in front of them that the whole thing looked like some kind of backdrop.

And then Tom, just the outline of his body, as though that was the only way she could take him in. Against the light, someone who didn't know him might have thought that his posture seemed almost relaxed. But he was unnaturally still, Sara thought, as though the only way to keep everything together was to avoid moving an inch.

The images flickered before her eyes, becoming a confusing mix of past and present, future and fantasy: a dove perched so unmovingly on a street light that it became a part of it; Amy in her youth, sitting next to John on a park bench; Amy surrounded by her books, though Sara didn't know if she was in her bedroom or the bookshop; the bookshop, the way it looked in the mornings, cool and dark; the rocking chair outside Amy's house, the two pairs of rubber boots; empty shelves; and then Tom. George, nervous and confused and chuckling at a book; Miss Annie, nothing but a vague, almost ghostlike outline; and then Tom again. Dozing in the armchair, his face unfeasibly relaxed compared to the real Tom's, who was standing there waiting for her to pull herself together enough to go over and talk to him.

She would just go over and do it. No complaints, no reproaches to an unfair world, no tears. Above all, no tears. She could give him that, at least. She wouldn't be just a problem that he hadn't managed to solve. With a bit of luck, one day, she might even be a funny anecdote to make him smile. That crazy woman and her reading. Do you remember her? From Sweden. Or was it Switzerland?

This wasn't a good train of thought. She had to blink several times before she went over to him. As she walked down the steps and over the wide pavement into the car park, she was desperately trying to work out what she was going to say when she got there. She couldn't come up with anything worth saying.

When he saw her coming, he pulled his hands from his pockets and made a helpless, silent gesture. He held his arms out to her and she took the final step into them as though it was a completely natural thing to do. She breathed in the smell of him, familiar again, and was relieved that she still remembered it after all.

She tried a laugh, but it came out more like a sniff. He hugged her more tightly.

'It'll all work out,' he said, presumably because he couldn't think of anything else to say. 'You can come back again.'

She wouldn't be allowed to do that.

He seemed to know that too. 'We'll come and visit you,' he said instead. 'I'll bring everyone. George can drive, Jen can make the newsletter into a travel guide, and Caroline can organise a collection.'

She laughed and he breathed a sigh of relief. A small, treasonous tear rolled down her cheek, and she tried to turn away from him. He touched her chin gently and wiped the tear away with his thumb.

'This whole mess is my fault,' he said.

'I shouldn't have let it get this far,' she said.

'Do you think,' he said hesitantly, 'if we'd thrown ourselves into a relationship right from the beginning . . . would it have been any different? They wouldn't be able to say we were getting married for a residency permit, at least.'

'I hardly think you would've proposed to me after just a couple of weeks,' said Sara. 'I'm not very good at any of this, at relationships. Definitely not good enough to make someone want to marry me so soon. The others would've still had to take charge.'

She looked at him uncertainly.

'Would you have wanted something to happen at the start?' she asked.

'I think I've loved you since the first time you explained that you preferred books to me.' He paused for thought. 'Or maybe it was when you offered to do the dishes for beer.'

'It was a reasonable offer!' she protested, and then he kissed her, as though to prove his point.

Neither Gavin nor the policeman saw the kiss, and it's entirely possible that it wouldn't have changed a thing if they had.

But one lone man was still standing outside the building and he saw the whole thing. The kiss had definitely changed something in him.

Grace bumped into John as soon as he got back to Broken Wheel. Something in his confused appearance made her pause. She even forgot to immediately light a new cigarette.

'I don't know what Amy would've wanted any more,' he said. He seemed to be talking as much to himself as to Grace. 'She wanted Sara to come, obviously. I've always known that, long before she dared to say the thought out loud to herself. But *now*? What does she want now?'

Faced with what threatened to be a long speech, Grace felt prompted to light a new cigarette. Her only words were: 'Right now, she doesn't want anything,' but John didn't seem to hear.

'I didn't believe any of it before, but now I'm wondering whether she somehow, unconsciously, in some strange way, knew that we needed Sara as much as she did. And that Sara needed us. But that's not at all the same as forcing Robert's son into a loveless marriage. She would never accept *that*. But *is* it loveless? That's what I'm wondering.'

'Jesus, man, people die. You must've been alive for long enough to have worked that out. If you ask me, you think too much.

Also, it's not so hard to work out. She would've wanted Sara to stay, of course she would. And she would've made sure that bureaucrat wished he had never come to town.'

John still didn't seem entirely convinced. Grace shrugged. 'You'll have to ring Caroline.'

A Conspiracy is Admitted

Gavin Jones was used to being visited by people in varying degrees of excitability. And when it came to Broken Wheel, there was very little which could surprise him.

But Caroline Rohde seemed worryingly calm for an agitated citizen. He couldn't help but think of her younger lover, and was annoyed with himself when he blushed. She, on the other hand, seemed completely unperturbed.

He showed her into one of the meeting rooms. His own office was nothing more than a booth comprised of thin, short walls, and when it came to this particular case, there was plenty he had no desire to discuss with his colleagues. He sat down at the table and, calmly and without being asked, she did the same opposite him.

'So, what can I help you with?'

His tone of voice suggested – he hoped – that he didn't think he could help her with anything.

But she simply smiled and said nothing.

'This case has caused me plenty of headaches, I have to say.' She didn't seem too impressed. 'The collective element . . . it's an interesting case.'

She took off her gloves, folded them up and placed them on her lap. 'You don't understand,' she said calmly. 'They love one another.'

Gavin smiled drily. 'So I understand, yes.'

'So . . . what's the problem then?'

'The law –' Gavin began, but she interrupted him.

'The law presumably allows American citizens to marry non-American citizens and then live with them because they happen to love them.'

'Yes,' Gavin admitted. 'But then there's also the small question of what seems to be a town conspiracy.'

Caroline shrugged. 'So arrest us then,' she said. 'Jen, Andy, Carl. Maybe even George.' She was counting on her fingers. 'Then there's Claire and Lacey, and Jen's husband too.'

'And you?' He realised that his glaring wasn't achieving a thing, and forced himself to unfurl his brow.

'And me too, of course.' Caroline looked thoughtful. 'Jen's kids were at the wedding as well, but are they not a bit too young? Probably,' she continued in her next breath. 'For jail, at least. Maybe a young offenders institution? The minister, William, he wasn't involved, I should point that out. You can let him off. But everyone else was definitely thinking they should get married purely for residency. We were all prepared to . . . what was it your colleague said?'

'He's not my colleague.'

'Sacrifice Tom – that was it. Not that we outright forced him to do it, but maybe you could charge us with having encouraged a crime?' She smiled. 'We were definitely encouraging, you see.'

'And Tom and Sara?' Gavin asked.

'*They* haven't committed a crime,' Caroline said kindly. 'They *wanted* to get married.'

'From the start?'

'Sure. They told me afterwards.' Caroline chuckled to herself. It was a surprisingly cheerful sound, but it didn't put him in a better mood. 'So they tricked us! We didn't know a thing about it. It's a shame they weren't more open.' It was obvious she was trying to hold back her laughter, but he could still detect it in her voice and in the irritating, understanding look on her face. 'So many people entering into a world of crime, all because they thought their feelings were a private matter. A tragedy.'

'The law,' Gavin said.

'Of course. There's nothing you can do. We've got to be prosecuted. Your hands are tied.'

'Tom and Sara confessed,' he said desperately. 'Everyone else denied it. Both Tom and Sara said they were responsible.'

Caroline seemed to hesitate, but then she said: 'I guess once they'd seen how many people *thought* they'd committed a crime, they couldn't really do anything but confess.'

'You don't seem especially worried,' Gavin said. The conversation hadn't gone at all as he had hoped. 'Considering you're one of the people who committed the crime.'

'The law . . .' she said. Gavin suspected she was actually enjoying this. 'I'm fully prepared to take my punishment. The others might be a bit trickier, but I'm sure *you* won't have any trouble proving things in court. Even if Grace and Jen and . . . well, even Andy might not be quite as cooperative as I've been . . . But the law must be allowed to run its course.' She stood up and pulled on her gloves. 'That much I do know,' she said. 'No one can be more concerned with lawfulness, order and control than I am. I'm sure we're in agreement *there*.'

With those kind words, she left, reassuring him that she would find her way out and patting him gently on the shoulder. All before he had time to come up with a single good answer.

He hated this town.

For a while, he considered arresting the lot of them. At the very least, the thought of arresting Caroline cheered him up. The thought of having to interview them in front of his colleagues and a possible courtroom made his smile falter, however. He could just imagine his colleagues' incredulity. The judge's desperation.

He needed someone he could talk to about all of this. You had to have been there to understand. He took his doubts back to his booth and picked up the phone.

'The town's full of love,' was all the policeman said.

Gavin laughed tiredly to himself.

'What're you going to do with all of this?' There was clear but unhelpful pity in the policeman's voice.

'I really don't know,' Gavin replied. He hesitated. 'If they do love each other . . . On the other hand, I'm pretty sure they set out to trick us right from the beginning, and that Caroline woman is just pulling my leg.'

'What did she say about the confessions?'

'Felt responsible, tried to take the blame, blah blah, you know the drill.'

'She might be right about that,' the policeman said. 'They did seem mightily determined to take the fall for each other. Quite romantic, when you think about it.'

'For God's sake, don't you start on me. And what about the whole conspiracy thing? They were all in on it, that woman said. I can believe *that* easily enough.'

The policeman was kind enough not to say a word about how much of a fool Gavin would make of himself if he actually started proceedings against an entire town. Instead, he asked: 'Do you want to do anything about the hunting rifle?'

Gavin sighed. The armed threat was the least of his problems. 'You heard the woman,' he said. 'Like the Fourth of July. Let it go.'

'Whatever you want,' said the policeman. 'There's not much I can do without a report anyway.'

'You can't always win,' said Gavin. He was starting to feel much more philosophical about the whole thing. Philosophical in the sense of being extremely tired of it all.

'Not against opponents like that, no,' the policeman said. 'There were more of them than you, after all.'

Broken Wheel, Iowa
August 5, 2011

Sara Lindqvist
Kornvägen 7, 1 tr
136 38 Haninge
Sweden

Dear Sara,

Jimmie Coogan! I'd completely forgotten I promised to tell you all about him. Oh my goodness. Jimmie Coogan. That's a real story. Jimmie was the first Coogan ever to own a suit, later the first who could read, the first to own his own house, the first to dye his hair, and the first ever to have a street named after him. When you get here, I'll tell you how it all happened. It can be our first trip together.

Taking the Greyhound to Hope is no problem. Hope's less than an hour away, so it's no problem to come meet you there. I should be able to come myself, but if I can't then someone else will. If you have even the slightest problem, just give me a call.

I'm looking forward to meeting you at the end of the month.

Best,

Amy

Epilogue: Happily Ever After
(Books 4: Life 4. Final score: a draw)

Life was full of happy endings.

As Sara stood there in church on her second wedding day, she thought to herself that real life still had a great deal in its favour after all. Not once during the minister's sermon did she long for a book, even though she had already heard his speech once before.

She wasn't wearing white.

Jen had protested, of course, but she had stood her ground. 'No one's going to fall for the whole white-dress thing,' she had explained firmly. 'It's the second time I'll be getting married in a month.'

'To the same person!' Jen had said, but Sara simply smiled and shook her head. She often found herself smiling nowadays, just like many of the others in Broken Wheel. She had compromised by wearing a white cowboy hat which Claire had lent her. Not that it seemed to have made Jen any happier. The opposite, if anything.

It was possible that Broken Wheel was listening more closely to the minister this time, but Sara doubted it. Caroline and Josh were there. Grace was there, along with her gun. Sara was almost certain she wouldn't fire it in church. She was also almost certain that Grace was sober this time.

John had started stopping by the bookshop and he had started talking about Amy. He would just turn up sometimes, sit down in one of the armchairs and start talking. His voice was always quiet and almost distant, and he never bothered to check whether she was listening. He simply talked, about things Amy had said or done or been. It made Sara feel as though Amy wasn't quite gone, and she hoped that John felt the same way. Now, he was sitting in the same seat as before, at the very back and slightly to the side of everyone else. It was impossible to tell for certain, but from his expression, Sara thought he was probably happy about the wedding.

There was still a certain sadness about George. Sara could see it in his eyes when he thought no one was looking. Not that he complained. He seemed almost surprised that he hadn't given up, but Sara wasn't. There was something so stoic about him; sometimes, she wondered whether he experienced catastrophes simply because he expected them. She smiled. George had Claire on his side now, and Sara didn't think the catastrophes stood a chance, not against Claire.

She glanced at Tom and realised that he was looking at her. He winked and she had to fight not to laugh. One day, she would find a book for him. There was no rush. She had the rest of her life to do it. She reached out and touched his hand, just because she could.

Broken Wheel really was on the way to becoming an extremely happy town.

A great deal of their happiness seemed to come from the knowledge that they had managed to deceive the authorities. Just like in the good old days, Grace had said, and Jen seemed inclined to agree. Jen's entire being suggested she had never really doubted it. When *she* organised things, her contented look said, there was no way that a trivial detail like the American immigration authorities could ruin her plans.

Naturally, there would be a wedding special in the newsletter. Caroline had been overheard asking innocently whether Jen would also be going on the honeymoon, immortalising it in print.

And Sara had changed her mind.

Reality really was just as good as books.

William was nearing the end of his sermon. She was still nervous at having to speak in front of everyone, but this time she wouldn't need to say much.

She was as ready as she would ever be, when the door behind them opened once again. Ah, Sara thought when she saw who it was. The only thing they had been missing.

A thin, ordinary girl with straggly brown hair and a dark blue padded jacket was standing in the doorway. 'Dad?' she said, as George half rose to his feet and said: 'Sophie!'

The girl took a couple of uncertain steps towards the bench he was sitting on and Claire moved calmly to the next space along. 'Sit down, sweetie,' she said, patting the empty space.

Sara smiled to herself and winked at Claire. They had sent an invitation to the wedding along with the second book from the *Eragon* series.

The world was simply full of happy endings, Sara thought, turning back to William. It would have been a waste not to make use of them.

She would marry her Tom.

She would marry Broken Wheel.

And they would all live happily ever after.